Sequel to The Undertaker's Wife

The Undertaker's Daughter

Val Case

A catalogue record for this book is available from the National Library of Australia

Cover: Oil on canvas by Val Case.

The author can be contacted by email: valeriecase393@yahoo.com.au

Also by the author: *The Undertaker's Wife*
                      Rediscovery

Book design: levelheading.com.au

As a musician applauds his listeners,
so does this author her readers ...

Acknowledgements

It may seem strange to acknowledge a pandemic but the statewide lockdown in 2020 provided the opportunity for me to focus on completing this novel.

Many readers of *The Undertaker's Wife* have asked for a sequel, but distractions intervened until the restrictions enabled the concentration and perseverance required to actually write it.

Two amazing local people have made a significant contribution to this book. I am deeply indebted to Christobel Comerford for her skilful refinement of the original manuscript, unfailing encouragement and belief in the story-line. Her judgment in offering suggestions for change is infallible.

Bernie Schultz is no ordinary editor. His scrupulous attention to detail in proofreading, wise suggestions for improvement and oversight of the finished product are beyond parallel. I could never thank him enough, and I recommend him highly for his professionalism.

The story so far ...

(Synopsis of THE UNDERTAKER'S WIFE, the prequel to this novel)

Who would have thought that going to a funeral in a nearby country town could be a life-changing event? Grace Miller, seventeen, convalescent from a severe bout of scarlet fever, certainly did not. But there she meets Jack Shaw, the Beaufort undertaker's son, and they become secret penfriends. However, it is 1939, war has been declared, and Australia joins the allies.

Despite her parents' initial reluctance and her older sister Lillian's scorn, Jack and Grace become engaged. He enlists in the Army, and, in common with wives and sweethearts all over the world, Grace endures years of separation and anxiety.

Though he is injured, Jack survives the war. The young lovers are reunited at Heidelberg Military Hospital and make optimistic plans for their future as the nation rejoices at the end of the war. But there is a cloud on Grace's horizon.

She learns from Jack's father, Jim, that his wife Hilda has been mentally ill for many years, often spending months at a time in treatment at the Ballarat Mental Hospital. Further information about her from other sources is worrying. Initially, Grace is well-intentioned towards her new mother-in-law, but Hilda is resistant. She protests at their wedding, destroys some of the young woman's property while they are honeymooning, and erupts in a fit of bad temper when told of Grace's pregnancy. As a temporary solution, the young couple moves in with Mary, their next-door neighbour.

Jack applies for a soldier settlers block, a venture that would give them a future on the land and, for Grace, an escape from Hilda's animosity.

While on their long-planned post-war visit to Scotland, Grace's parents are killed in a car accident. She is devastated by the loss. Only the thought of their first baby keeps her going.

During her hospital stay after the birth of their son, Brian, she is advised of the sale of her former home in Ballarat. She and her sister Lillian share a substantial inheritance from the estate. If their application is successful, Grace and Jack plan to use their share to build a home on their block of farmland.

Hilda's condition deteriorates, but she refuses to see the doctor and refuses to take her medication. She makes a surprise demand to see the baby. Jim has a desperate hope that she might be more accepting of little Brian if she actually saw him. Grace anxiously follows her father-in-law next door just in time to see Hilda grab a flatiron from the stove and attempt to strike the baby with it. Grace's scream alerts Jim who manages to deflect Hilda's arm. Enraged, she smashes the iron on to Jim's temple. He falls to the floor, unconscious.

Hilda is taken into custody and sent to the secure unit of the mental hospital. Jim regains consciousness in hospital but has suffered a stroke that results in paralysis down one side of his body and affects his speech.

Jack and Grace are forced to change their plans. Jack takes over the funeral parlour business and relinquishes his dream of becoming a farmer on his own block of land. When a letter arrives advising him of his favourable assessment for a soldier settlement block and offering an interview, he destroys it.

Jim recovers slowly but remains wheelchair bound. Recognising the debt they owe him – 'he saved our baby's life' – they decide to use Grace's inheritance to modify the family home to accommodate his future needs.

So, Grace's destiny now is to be the undertaker's wife.

Other characters who feature in *The Undertaker's Wife* are Alan (Jack's older brother) who is rejected by his mother (Hilda) and has been brought up in Melbourne by his aunt, Verna (Hilda's sister), a caring and responsible woman, very different from her older sister.

Also part of the story are Bridie and Phil Taylor who farm a property overlooking Lake Goldsmith not far from Beaufort. Their older son Joe suffered a tractor accident when he was young and has a problem with his mobility. Jack used to ride his bike out to the farm to help when needed. Their younger son Danny has what is now known as Down's Syndrome. Bridie, Irish by birth, is a good friend to Grace, the young newlywed, and had warned her about her mother-in-law's tendency to violence.

Chapter 1

It was a recurring image for Grace, kept coming back into her mind, not scarily, but persistently. Her father-in-law's face frozen in shock, eyes open wider than normal, mouth as well. Eyes open, but Jim was dead. She'd seen death often enough down at the funeral parlour. It didn't worry her unduly. 'Left us' or 'gone to God' were the words family members would often use at the viewing.

On that fateful day, she'd been weeding in the garden with her back to the ramp at the front of the house. The ramp had been built so Jim could manoeuvre his wheelchair with his left hand out the front door and on to the landing for a breath of fresh air and sometimes a whiff of the perfume of the daphne bushes transplanted from her childhood home in Ballarat, which had thrived despite the predictions of gardening experts.

On the whole, it had worked well. For over two years they had cared for him at home, with a nurse from the local hospital coming twice a day to help him with his daily needs. Jack assisted too when he was around. Together they managed, making Jim Shaw's well-being the most important part of their daily lives. Well, not quite the most. During this time little Brian had grown from baby to a lively two-year-old toddler, delighting them all.

Dr Santorini said that a clot in Jim's leg had come loose, travelling up to and through the heart, eventually blocking the blood supply to his lungs. No one could have done anything to prevent it. Grace remembered the loud crash of the wheelchair, out of control down the ramp, coming to a stop half-upturned, with its occupant dead. *Eyes and mouth open ...*

Everybody grieved. Jim had been such a respected member of the community; the undertaker for so many years until the stroke that curtailed his working life, leaving his son Jack to take over the funeral business. It had all looked so promising until that dreadful day when his mentally ill mother had attempted to kill the young baby with a flat iron. In diverting the strike, the blow had landed on Jim's left temple, resulting in the stroke.

The funeral was one of the largest in the community with the arrangements being handled by a Ballarat firm. People came from near and far. Grace was sorry her sister Lillian couldn't make the trip from Beulah in the Mallee, though her husband Barry came.

'Sorry about our timing, Grace. We hadn't planned to have another child – four would have been quite enough. But little Wendy came along, and I guess in time she'll be a playmate for Dawnie.'

Grace had smiled. She often wondered how her little niece coped with three brothers, one being her twin.

It was good to see Barry again. She noted how solid he looked these days, more serious. Perhaps it was because his own father had died suddenly only three years ago, leaving him with full responsibility for the farm, his young family and his mother. It had been good to see the quiet support he gave Jack before the funeral.

Grace would never forget Verna Jensen's response when told over the phone of Jim's death. The younger sister of Jack's mother, Verna had been an important part of their lives. She'd taken on the care of Alan, Jack's older brother, when their mother rejected him as a child. Her close relationship with Jim was always valued. It was no surprise to hear her words, 'It's like the end of the world for me, Grace. We've cared for each other for so many years, through so many troubles ...' She had paused. 'I won't come to the funeral. But you know I'll be there in spirit.'

She added that Alan would come up and back the same day, as his wife Deirdre was due to give birth any time now. And so it had turned out. Even as the earth was being shovelled on to the coffin, Francis Johannes Shaw was born after a difficult labour. A big baby, he was slow to respond to the increasingly urgent resuscitation efforts of the delivery ward staff. Then, only three weeks after Jim's funeral, Alan rang with the sad news that Verna had passed away in her sleep.

'I'll miss her,' he said, his voice trembling. 'She was like a mother to me.'

With this further loss to cope with, it was only natural that Jack sought comfort and solace in his wife's arms. During this time Grace conceived her second child. She explored in her mind her own sorrow after news of her parents' death in Scotland and how her first pregnancy seemed to somehow lessen the bleakness. *Maybe this is God's plan*, she thought. *One person dies, another life begins.*

Jack had not acknowledged the news of her pregnancy in the same way he had done when they were expecting Brian. He took the information without displaying any particular reaction at all. Grace was nonplussed. She made her way to the vicarage to seek advice from Elizabeth Langthorne who had been so supportive in the past.

'I just don't understand why he hasn't responded to the good news,' Grace said. The older woman thought for a minute before replying.

'Maybe Jack just isn't ready to think of anything else but his father. We know Jim's dead, and Jack knows that too, of course. But they were so close, he must feel his dad's presence still. Or I should say – his absence. All those memories ...'

'You're right. It's only been two and a half months. And then Verna going so soon after. I know it can take an awfully long time for the painful loss of a person to become less of a preoccupation, if that's the right expression.'

Elizabeth smiled. 'It's as good as any. Give him time, my dear. We all have our own ways of dealing with these things.'

She carefully got up from the chair, a wry smile on her face. 'I'm getting so slow these days.'

Grace was overcome with remorse. She was one of the very few people who knew about Elizabeth's medical condition and her burial plans.

'I'm so sorry – here I am burdening you with my silly worries when you – you've got so much ahead of you.'

'Well, I'm still around, as you can see, and there wasn't any certainty about that. So I get by, one day at a time, thanks to the painkillers Dr Santorini's given me. And, young lady, your concerns are not silly, not at all. I appreciate you sharing them with me and I'll pray for both of you.'

She moved towards the door. 'Please don't think I'm hurrying you off, but the Ladies Auxiliary is meeting here at two o'clock and I have to arrange the chairs.'

Grace considered Elizabeth's comments. *I should be more understanding,* she told herself. When Jack had been told he was going to be a father for the first time things were so different. He'd just come back from the war in New Guinea, had recovered from injury in the Repatriation Hospital, and not long after that they were married. The only fly in the ointment was the presence of his mother. Grace had been told of Hilda's long-term mental illness and had resolved to try to break down the resentment and jealousy the woman had shown her. But to no avail.

That dreadful day when Hilda had tried to kill their baby was one Grace would never forget, nor her father-in-law's brave intervention which resulted in the injury to his left temple. She shuddered. It was a horrific scenario. A tragedy averted, but at such great cost to Jim.

Hilda became a permanent patient at the Ballarat Mental Hospital and was under constant supervision. Jack made the yearly trip for the medical review of her progress, but there was never anything encouraging to report.

'She just looks like a – what's the word? – *zombie* – you know, eyes blank, no expression. I don't know if she even recognised me,' he said after his last visit.

On a happier note, Jack continued to engage with his young son with the same delight he had always shown. They even seemed to have their own language, Grace noted, listening to the babbling noises they both made in their rough-and-tumble play on the lounge room floor. Surely he would welcome another little one. One day a flash of inspiration triggered her suggestion.

'Jack, we could call the baby James, after your father. He could be Little Jim.'

Jack had smiled, then countered with, 'It could be a girl, don't forget.'

It *was* a girl, a tiny four-week premature bundle whose presence totally disrupted their lives. During her pregnancy, Grace had suffered high blood pressure and swollen ankles as well as untimely contractions. Dr Santorini was clearly worried and she was admitted to the local hospital for weeks at a time.

'I'm so sorry, darling. This puts a lot of pressure on you,' said Grace during one of Jack's visits.

Jack just shook his head. 'Not at all. People have been very helpful looking after Brian if I've had work to do, especially Mary.'

Grace smiled. Their kind-hearted elderly neighbour had proved to be a godsend many times in the past.

Jack continued. 'We're managing. The main thing is that you're all right.'

'And our baby,' said Grace.

Jack opened his mouth to reply but thought better of it, settling for a nod of agreement.

He had been speechless when Dr Santorini had explained that if it were a question of saving one or the other, the baby would take precedence. Jack had looked at the doctor's concerned face with total disbelief.

'Let's hope and pray it doesn't come to that,' he'd eventually replied.

It didn't, as things turned out. Grace's labour began suddenly during one of her spells in hospital. Dr Santorini came immediately.

'Your baby will be born prematurely and may require special treatment. We may be able to cope here with our humidicrib, it depends how big the baby is. Otherwise, we may have to transfer you both to the Base Hospital in Ballarat.'

Oh no, thought Grace. *I want to stay here. Please, God, make it possible.*

Her prayer was interrupted by the onset of regular contractions, and soon the delivery room was a hive of activity. She asked one of the nurses if Jack had been called, but the answer was lost when Grace heard the unforgettable high-pitched sound of a baby's first cry.

'You have a daughter, Grace. She looks fine, a little bit small but perfectly formed.'

Dr Santorini was holding up a wriggling, squealing doll of a baby and Grace could see he was relieved, even though his face was mostly covered.

Sister Ferguson took the infant and placed her on the scales. 'Four and a half pounds – that's pretty good for thirty-six weeks.'

Dr Santorini nodded in agreement. 'Now we'd better get that baby into the humidicrib. You can have a quick cuddle then it's into a nice warm bed for her.'

What will you bring into our lives, little girl? thought Grace as she gazed in wonder at the wet, rubbery-looking face of her new-born child, now wrapped in a warm, white bunny-rug. *And where's Jack?* She leaned back on the pillow, suddenly tired. *Thank you, God,* she prayed silently.

Dr Santorini was pleased that her blood pressure had dropped, but he detected an increased heart murmur.

'We'll keep an eye on you, my dear. Plenty of rest for the next few days.'

Grace was washed and her nightdress changed before she was moved to the maternity ward. She had settled into the fresh bed and was dozing when Jack came in.

'Grace – are you all right?' His voice was urgent.

'Oh Jack! I'm fine. Have you seen her?'

'They showed me a little thing in a sort of covered cot, looked like a skinned rabbit, what you could see of her. Couldn't see if she's got hair like Brian had 'cos they had a tiny little cap on her head.'

His head came down to rest next to hers, an arm went over her chest. It was an intimate gesture that heartened Grace. *We're going to be okay,* she said to herself.

'You're not too disappointed that Brian has a sister, not a brother?'

He shook his head. 'As long as you're all right. And our baby. That's all that matters.'

The name Miranda flashed into Grace's consciousness and wouldn't go away. She'd considered other favourites: Diana, Juliet, Virginia, all with some literary connection, but the name that seemed to fit best was Miranda. Jack didn't mind.

'Do you think it would be nice to have Mary as her second name?'

Again, he had no objection.

Grace had good memories of the next few weeks. She quickly mastered the technique of expressing breast milk. Baby Miranda thrived, gaining weight steadily and in less than a week was transferred from the humidicrib to a regular nursery cot. Grace was keen to breastfeed her daughter normally, and before long, a routine was established. Grace's anxiety melted away.

Chapter 2

Three sharp rings on the doorbell jolted Grace out of her daydream. She opened the front door to find two people there. One was very familiar, it was Mary Joliffe, her elderly neighbour, but the other, a middle-aged man, balding, of average height and build, was unknown to her. Mary spoke first.

'Grace, this is my nephew Bruce Gadd. Would you mind if we came in to explain some – some things to you?'

As she ushered them into the front room, Grace thought Mary looked worried. There was an awkward silence, finally broken by Bruce.

'Mary insisted I tell you what is going to happen. I understand you have been friends for many years.' He swallowed noticeably, before continuing. 'What we have decided to do, after a lot of discussion, is for Mary to sell up here and move into a nursing home with my mother.' He then shot a direct look at Mary to confirm the statement. She nodded, her expression uncharacteristically sad.

Grace gasped. She looked at Mary who nodded again.

'I'm sorry, Grace. This will come as a shock to you. It's something I'm finding hard to accept, too. The thing is, my sister Dorothy has not been well for a long time. She's nearly eighty-five and I'm not that far behind. Bruce says she's not managing at home anymore, and her doctor says she should be in care.' Grace nodded, understanding so far. 'Unfortunately, her house is quite run down and wouldn't fetch enough on the market to cover the cost of her being in a nursing home. Bruce has suggested that I sell up here and go down to Hawthorn to help Dorothy do likewise, and we both go into the nursing home.'

Grace looked from one to the other. She knew Mary well enough to know the situation was not one of her choosing. The nephew was looking uncomfortable, almost defensive.

'When it's family ...' he started to say.

'But you're family too,' Grace broke in. 'Couldn't your mother move in with you?'

Mary looked surprised at Grace's interjection. 'No, Grace, that wouldn't be possible. Bruce's partner wouldn't accept it.'

'Have you asked her?' said Grace, looking straight at Bruce.

After the briefest of pauses, he replied, 'My partner is not a woman.'

Ah, so *that's* the issue.

Mary, as usual, came to the rescue. 'Bruce has been honest with me, Grace. But there are things his mother wouldn't understand. Or approve of. We have decided this is the best thing to do, for all of us.'

'But I'm going to miss you,' Grace's voice had a tremor as the full realisation hit. 'You've been more than just a neighbour, Mary. You've been part of our family. You've been there when we needed you – always.'

The emotion in her voice was not lost on Bruce. He cleared his throat and stood up, obviously wanting to leave.

'Mary is happy for me to make all the arrangements ...'

He was interrupted by the sound of a young child calling 'Mummee' before a toddler burst into the room.

'This is Miranda, our daughter. She's two,' said Grace, scooping up the lively little girl.

'We'd better go.'

Bruce was clearly not interested in children, not even a pretty dark-haired cherub-like vision who was looking at him with curiosity in her green eyes. Mary followed him out after planting a kiss on the little girl's rosy cheek.

Grace lowered herself into a chair, her mind reeling. She just couldn't imagine life without Mary being close by. She'd been there for her and

Jack through the trials of the early days of their marriage when her mother-in-law became an increasingly threatening presence. Mary's house had welcomed various family members over the years. Brian had always called her 'Nanna Mary.' All this was to change, and Miranda would miss out on her love and kindness as she grew older.

A pang of resentment stirred in her. This nephew – Bruce – he'd never visited, even when Mary had been in hospital to have her gall-bladder operation a few years ago. Only now, when he had to take some responsibility for his mother, was he in contact with his aunt. And then only to persuade her to sell her home in Beaufort where she was so respected. Even the word 'persuade' seemed inadequate. Demand, more likely.

She kept an eye on the maroon-coloured car parked in the street outside Mary's house. It was still there when Jack came home from the funeral parlour. She couldn't wait to tell him.

'Jack,' she blurted out, 'we're going to lose Mary!' Seeing his blank startled look, she put him in the picture.

Jack sat down at the kitchen table. He sighed. 'It's just as well Dad's not around, he would have taken it badly. I mean, it's going to be awful for us, but it would have been worse for him.' He paused. 'Have you told Brian?'

'No, he's at kindergarten this morning. I've got to pick him up soon. Perhaps it'd be best to leave it until nearer the time she actually leaves.' Grace, silent for a moment, said, 'You know, Jack, we really should be thinking of her, not just ourselves. She has slowed up quite a bit over the last year or so. I've noticed her using her walking-stick more lately. In some ways it might be better for her to be somewhere where care's available.'

'Hmm,' was Jack's only response. What else was there to say?

Grace was grateful that looking after her children and the house kept her occupied over the next few weeks. Once or twice she noticed unfamiliar vehicles and gentlemen in suits coming and going next door. Mary had come to their back door a few times, but not as often as in the past. She looked even smaller than ever and clearly ill-at-ease.

'I don't know how I'll get on without you, Grace,' she said, on the day the big FOR SALE sign went up in the front garden. 'I don't want to be here for the auction. I want you and Jack to take whatever you want from the house. The furniture's staying, I'm not taking any. We don't need any where we're going. Dorothy and I will be sharing a room.' Grace said nothing. She could tell all this was going to be so hard, so big a change of lifestyle for her much-loved neighbour. 'Dorothy's house is going up for auction next week. Bruce thinks we'll get more for them if they're both furnished.'

Grace's arms went around Mary's shoulders in a warm hug. 'When are you actually going?' she asked.

'I don't want to be here for the auction. I just have to leave it to Bruce. He's decided to get Dorothy settled in Eventide Lodge on Tuesday now that they've been assured that the money will be forthcoming. I'll go down by train a few days later, probably next Friday.'

What could Grace say? It was all going to happen regardless of the pain this relocation would cause. Somehow Mary's spirit surged. She stepped back from the embrace and looked Grace straight in the eye.

'Now listen to me – you mustn't worry about anything. I'll be all right. In a way, it's taken my future out of my hands. I'm eighty-two, you know. And it's been hard the last few years, losing so many of my friends, Jim of course, and not long ago, Elizabeth.' Grace sighed. She, too, missed her dear friend. 'Perhaps it's the right time for me to go into care. One of the outcomes of not having children.' There was a wry smile and a sigh. 'The important thing is for you to keep going the way you are, with two lovely little ones and such a splendid husband.'

Grace laughed out loud at that description of Jack. She recognised that Mary was trying to lighten the moment.

'Well, at least have tea with us the night before you go. And Jack will take you to the station on Friday. And if he can't, I will, now I've got my licence.' They both smiled.

An auction in a country town always creates interest. A crowd of some twenty onlookers, mostly men, gathered in the front garden of Mary Jolliffe's house in Speke street, Beaufort, at one o'clock on the last Saturday of October. Some were there out of curiosity, no doubt, but there could be potential buyers too.

No, I don't want to be part of this, thought Grace. I'll take the children out for the afternoon. Brian was curious about the gathering crowd but was persuaded to walk down to the funeral parlour with them to see if Jack could close the business for the afternoon, or failing that, let Grace take the car.

'Maybe Dad could take us for a drive if he's finished work. Or I could. We could go out to Taylors.'

'Great!' Brian responded immediately, and his little sister echoed his response.

Grace smiled. The children loved going out to the farm at Lake Goldsmith where their father had worked part-time just after he finished school. And the Taylors, all five of them now, enjoyed their visits. Phillip and Irish-born Bridie had two sons, Joe and Danny, who both had difficulties. They'd also welcomed Declan, a young Irishman, into their family. They'd sponsored him to come to Australia to replace Jack when Jim's stroke had forced him to take over the funeral business.

A quick phone call established that they would be home and only too glad to have a visit. Even better, Jack was able to come too.

Bridie's big smile welcomed them into the farmhouse. She scooped the children into a warm hug then went over to the kerosene refrigerator, taking out a shallow tray from the small freezer compartment. 'Now who'd be wantin' an ice-cream, I wonder?'

'Meee!' yelled the children in unison.

'Another thing I've learned to make out here. You don't 'ave much call for it in Ireland.' She smiled at the youngsters' evident enjoyment as they spooned the delicious treat into their mouths, both sitting cross-legged on the floor. 'Would you like some too, Grace?'

'No thanks, Bridie. Maybe a cup of tea, later on? I hope you don't mind us landing on you like this. I just didn't want to be around when Mary's house is being sold.'

'Of course you don't, darlin'. Much better that you come out here and visit with us. An' I've got somethin' to show you.'

Her homely face creased in a wide smile. She reached up to the mantelpiece to bring down a letter. Grace noticed the overseas stamp on the envelope, and her heart skipped a beat. The childhood memory surfaced of letters coming to her Scottish-born mother at their home in Ballarat. And, poignantly, the more recent memory of mail coming from her parents on their ill-fated trip back to the United Kingdom at the end of 1946.

'From your family, Bridie?' she asked, forcing herself to focus on the present.

'No. Not my family, never hear from 'em. It's from Declan's folk – real nice people from County Kerry. See, here's a photo of the whole family. Well, not exactly all of 'em. They 'ad eight children, Declan's their third son. A couple of the older ones have married and moved away, an' two of the girls have gone into the convent. So of the three still at home, there's the two boys who work in their father's business an' the youngest who's a lass of twenty-two.'

Grace took the photo and studied it, Bridie watching her with a curious smile on her face.

'Notice anythin'?' she asked. 'Look at Antoinette, she's between her mum and dad.'

Suddenly Grace grasped what the older woman was trying to point out.

'She's got callipers on her legs!' she exclaimed.

'That's right. She got polio when she was just a wee mite, an' her life has been limited by that, just like our Joe's.' She paused briefly and, still smiling, continued her news. 'Declan told 'em about the accident Joe had when he was seventeen and sent 'em a photo of us all lookin' happy. The upshot is that Antionette an' Joe are goin' to be penfriends. What do you think of that?'

Grace's response was enthusiastic. 'That's how Jack and I got to really know each other. It's wonderful!'

'Thought you'd say that.' Bridie was positively beaming.

'I'm so pleased. And I can tell by your face you are too.'

The children had finished their ice-cream and were becoming restless. 'Where's Danny?' asked Brian.

With that, Bridie quickly left the room and returned with her second son. At fifteen he was a chunky lad. It was easy to see he had development issues with thick loose lips, eyes set close together, and an expression that made him look much younger than his real age.

'Here's Brian and Miranda to see you, Danny. Why don't you take 'em out to see the new chickens?'

A smile broke out on the boy's face. 'Chickies!' he said. Miranda confidently put her hand in his and the children followed him outside excitedly.

'It's good for the children to be able to come out here and see chooks and the other animals. I do appreciate it, Bridie.'

'It's good for Danny too, you know. Now, 'ow about that cup of tea?'

Sitting back in the large armchair with a cushion behind her back, Grace's eyes lit on a familiar publication.

'Oh, you get the *Weekly Times*,' she said. 'We used to get it right up until the time we had to give up the idea of becoming farmers. Can I have a look?'

'Of course you can, darlin'.'

The headlines stood out in bold type: 'Wool prices soar. Highest level since the War.'

'Hey, that's good news, Bridie. About the wool prices, I mean. You'll be shearing soon, won't you.'

'Aye. An' we'll be havin' a big one. Phil bought two hundred more crossbred wethers a couple of months ago when he got wind of the market trend. Anyway, I can hear the men at the gate now, they'll tell you all about it.'

On the way back to Beaufort, Jack spoke of the good prospects Phil and Joe had talked about. 'I'm so pleased for them, they've worked hard.' He turned to look at his wife. 'I guess Barry and Lil will be getting a bigger wool cheque this year, too.'

As the car turned into Speke Street, Grace saw the big red SOLD label covering most of the FOR SALE board in the front garden of the house next door to them. They looked at each other. Words were unnecessary.

This is a new experience for me, Grace acknowledged to herself as the next few weeks brought evidence of activity next door. *I've never had to deal with a new neighbour before.*

A rumour circulated around town that the property had been bought by the State Government as housing for staff of the new Langi Kal Kal prison out near Trawalla. Jack kept his ear to the ground, as did Grace when she went shopping. An article in the *Riponshire Advocate* confirmed the speculation: 'A superintendent had been appointed to oversee the project and would be occupying premises recently purchased in Speke Street. Governor Thomas Quinn and his wife were expected to move in very soon.'

Grace discreetly watched the comings and goings, not sure who were actually to be the occupants. Lights appeared in the windows and smoke emerged from the chimney. Someone had moved in.

Eventually, it became apparent that Mr Thomas Quinn was a middle-aged, straight-backed, military-looking man with a stern expression and greying hair. His wife was a shorter, slim, rather hesitant-looking woman who seemed to creep into the new house. She looked quite unsure.

I'll try to extend a hand of friendship to her when the time's right.

It started off badly. Brian was away at kindergarten. Miranda was used to going next door through the gate between the two houses to visit Mary who often let her pick flowers from her garden. Grace was busy inside when she heard a sharp knock on the front door along with the alarming sound of her daughter crying.

'I'll thank you to keep your child out of our property,' were the first words she heard from the angry neighbour whose hand was firmly gripping her daughter's shoulder.

'Mummee, Mummee,' cried Miranda, her face crumpled in distress.

Grace caught her up in her arms only to become aware of an uprooted flowering plant in her fist.

'I'm so sorry – Mr Quinn, isn't it? She's only two, she doesn't understand. I've been meaning to call on you, and meet your wife …'

'That is not necessary. We are not social people. Just keep your child, or children away.' His gaze had taken in Brian's bike leaning against the veranda post. 'Children need to learn to respect boundaries. And other people's property.'

With that, he strode down the path to the gate and into his front garden. Grace was seething. How rude and unfriendly. She soothed the little girl until her crying subsided.

'Him bad man. Him cross.'

'Let's go and pick up Brian now, Mirrie. Do you want to walk, or go in the pusher?'

'Walk, Mummy,' she replied, now recovered from her ordeal.

It was Brian who discovered that the gate in the dividing fence had been boarded up during Grace's short absence from the house.

'Well, if that's the way he wants it, that's the way it's got to be,' said Jack that evening. 'He's within his rights, you know.'

'It's his wife I feel sorry for. I'm going to wait until he's away at work and introduce myself to her. She may need some help settling in.'

Jack smiled to himself. The remark was typical of her, caring about people, especially those who needed support. 'Just don't ruffle any feathers if you can help it.'

Chapter 3

The next few years were comfortable ones for the Shaw family. Brian proved himself to be a talented footballer, much to his father's delight. At eight he was a younger version of Jack, dark-haired and friendly. Miranda, always a little livewire, continued to want to do everything her brother did, not always successfully. Her first attempts at riding a bike resulted in a number of tumbles and some painful skinned knees. But she was determined to keep trying, eventually mastering the two-wheeler.

Lillian rang at Christmas to suggest that they all make a visit up to Beulah in the January school holidays. The invitation created much excitement for the two young Shaws. The trip involved going up by the steam train, just the three of them, as Jack couldn't leave the business for more than a day. It was a chance to meet their cousins for the first time. They had already had dealings with Frankie, their cousin on their father's side. That was not a happy experience. Auntie Deirdre, Uncle Alan and six-year-old Frankie had visited for a weekend last year. It involved swapping beds, with Deirdre and Alan in Miranda's room, Frankie sharing Brian's, and Miranda sleeping out on the veranda. The visitor, though younger, was taller and larger than his cousin and was very bossy and loud. Brian hoped his country cousins would be more agreeable.

Lily and Grace sat on well-used cane chairs on the wide veranda looking out past the peppercorns and the dry sandy ground to the group of cousins, all so different from each other. An impromptu game of cricket was in progress accompanied by lots of shrieks and laughter.

Grace found it hard to believe that her two older nephews were almost on the brink of manhood. Peter was a sturdy sixteen-year-old, Hughie a year younger, while the twins were about to turn thirteen. The youngest, Wendy, was seven.

'What a mixture – four ginger-heads and three dark-haired!' There was a hint of amusement in Lily's voice.

'Have you stopped adding to your family now?' Grace asked.

'Sure have. I'll be forty in a couple of years. Even Edna confided that she's more than happy with the five grandchildren we've given her. She's got another six from the rest of the family.' Lillian wriggled her ample frame in the chair. 'What about you?

'Oh, I'm stopping at two. Doctor's orders. I was pretty sick with Miranda.' Lily nodded, remembering. 'I've had one of those coil things put in. Dr Santorini wasn't too keen, he's a Catholic, but he said another pregnancy could be a matter of life and death. And Jack was absolutely determined, too. So I have to be happy with what I've got, a pigeon pair, as they say.'

There was a sudden yelp from one of the children. Hughie came racing through the gate. 'Dawnie's been hit, Mum. She's crying.'

'I told you to use tennis balls – those cricket balls are too hard.' Lily was on her way to the little group huddled around the crying twelve-year-old who was clutching her left shoulder.

'You were supposed to catch it,' piped up Miranda.

'You're so smart, aren't you,' whined Dawn through her tears.

'Come on, it's not that bad. I'll put an iceblock on it, come with me. You lot can get back to your game.' Lillian's presence had the desired effect. It was Brian's turn to bowl at the kerosene can wicket, this time with a tennis ball Hughie had found. Peter was batting. His hit would have been a boundary on a regulation-sized ground. Grace smiled to see her daughter racing to get it first, even if the throw-in had to be relayed back to the bowler.

The sisters resumed their seats on the veranda. Lily poured two glasses of ice-water from the jug close at hand. 'I suppose his little girl is the apple of Jack's eye.'

Grace considered her reply. She wanted to be loyal to her husband but, then again, Lillian was one of the few people she could confide in. 'Not so much, to be honest. She's so different from Brian. He always does what he's told and really looks up to his dad. Miranda's favourite word is "Why?" which leads Jack to say "Because I said so." And on it goes. I'm the peacemaker.' She paused. 'There's another thing that's been happening over the last year or so.'

Lily leaned forward encouragingly. 'Go on,' she said, as Grace hesitated.

'Jack's been having – oh, I don't know what you'd call it – flashbacks, I suppose. Sort of nightmares. Sometimes he calls out in a desperate sort of way, "No!" I try to calm him, it usually doesn't work. He doesn't remember in the morning, but I think it's something to do with the war.'

'Gee, that's not good, Grace. Do the kids hear him?'

'Brian's a heavy sleeper, but one night Miranda came into our room and said "What's wrong with Daddy?" I took her back to her own bed saying it was just a bad dream, that's all.'

The sisters looked out to the yard to see that the children had abandoned their cricket match and had moved over to the pony paddock. Peter emerged from the stable with a handful of bridles.

'Looks like they're going bareback. I bet they'll want a swim in the dam next.'

The summer of 1956 had been long and hot. Grace was relieved to have a few cooler days, even a little rain, which was to be expected for April. Easter came and went. Miranda continued to go to Sunday School at the Anglican church, but Brian had opted out. None of his mates went any more.

'It's only for girls,' was his reply when questioned.

The feedback Grace received from the vicar, Nigel Langthorne, was that

Miranda was enthusiastic about hearing the Bible stories but tended to ask the aged parishioner in charge of the Sunday School too many 'whys'.

'Mrs Morgan often doesn't know what to say,' the tall, grey-haired clergyman explained.

This was not news to Grace, Miranda's teachers at the primary school had made similar complaints.

The front gate squeaked and footsteps sounded along the path. Only one set. Brian came inside, dropped his schoolbag on the floor and made for the fridge.

'Where's Miranda?'

'I don't know. She was probably kept in. Again.'

A glass of lemonade was quickly dispatched, and he went to his bedroom and closed the door.

Twenty minutes later, Grace heard the gate slam shut followed by fast footsteps coming into the house. Miranda stood there, her compact little body seeming to quiver with rage.

Grace's words, 'Where have you been?' were drowned by the child's explosive, 'It isn't fair!'

'Now come in and sit down, have a drink, then tell me what happened.'

Miranda accepted the glass of lemonade and drank thirstily.

'Well, what isn't fair?'

'It's not fair that I was punished when I was only trying to help. That horrible boy in grade three, Bobby Carston, well he was pinching his little sister who's in prep and making her cry. Well, I went up an' told him to stop or I'll pinch him. Then this little kid started yelling, "Don't pinch my brother!" and then Mr Fright came out.'

'Mr Fright, Mirrie?'

'I mean Wright – we all call him Fright 'cos that's what he's like. Then that horrible Bobby told him I was goin' to pinch him and Mr Fr … I mean, Wright, made me go back to the classroom and do all the tidying-up and kept me in. It's not fair.'

'It's your own fault for getting involved. I've told you that before.' The words came from Brian in the doorway.

'Ooh, you …' The rest was lost in a flood of tears.

Grace scooped the unhappy little girl into her arms and wiped away the tears.

Brian came to sit at the end of the table, an exercise book in his hand. He opened it and fished around in his pocket for a pencil. Both Grace, and Miranda, now comforted, watched him with curiosity.

'What I think is unfair is our family.'

Grace was surprised by this. 'What do you mean?'

'We're supposed to be drawing up our family tree an' everyone else has got grandparents to put on it, an' all I've got is one grandmother who's in the loony-bin.'

'Brian – that's not a very nice thing to say.'

'Well, it's true. Everyone knows it. All the other kids can do interviews with their grandpas and grandmas and write little stories about them. But I can't.'

He was right, of course.

Grace examined the simple chart Brian had drawn up with little boxes of names joined by ruled lines. Jack's parents were on the top left, hers on the right. The birth dates for Florence and Fred were different, but the date of their deaths the same. Such a tragedy. The car accident on a Scottish highland road, before Brian was born. At least her son could remember his grandfather, even though he was only a two-year-old when Jim died. Miranda was the one who really missed out. Grace made a determined attempt to change the mood.

'On the other hand, Brian, you've got a good number of cousins, probably more than some of your classmates. Let's see – you've got Frankie from Uncle Alan and Auntie Deirdre …'

Miranda's expression was scornful. 'I don't like Frankie.'

'Me neither,' said Brian, 'he's fat and clumsy, he can't play footy properly, and he's loud.'

Privately Grace agreed with all that. She'd told her children before how he wasn't quite right when he was born, but like all children, they assessed him as they found him.

'Then you've got five from Auntie Lily and Uncle Barry.'

'Why have they got five and there's only two of us and one of Frankie?' Miranda's question brought a smile to Grace's face. She decided to make the neutral response that she didn't know. Brian's homework was starting to look more detailed as he added the cousins, colouring in the boxes red and blue.

'Look – there are five boys and only three girls in our family tree. Why do boys get blue and girls red?' *Oh, Miranda,* thought Grace, *why does everything have to be a question?*

'It's just the custom, darling. Let's put your things away now, Daddy will be home soon.'

Jack had finally made an appointment to see the local doctor about his disturbed sleep. Earlier, after Grace had said firmly that he should talk to someone, he had reluctantly spoken to their minister. But that hadn't made any difference. Nigel Langthorne had listened and expressed sympathy. He'd spoken about all sin being forgiven through the Lord.

'But I don't feel guilt,' Jack had protested, 'I was just doing my job.'

'Perhaps you need to see the doctor and maybe get some tablets to help you sleep. I will pray for you, Jack.'

So the medical appointment was today. Only it wasn't with Dr Santorini. The much-respected GP had taken his family to Italy.

'We may even visit the Greek island that gave my family its name,' he'd said with a smile, 'and don't worry, I've got a good locum for the two months we're away.'

Grace eventually heard the crunch of steps on the gravel path and the front door opening. She hurried to meet her husband, her expression questioning. They moved into the front room and Grace closed the door.

'Nice bloke, a bit older than I expected, in his late fifties, I'd reckon.'

'Yes – what did he say?'

'He talked about what they used to call 'shell-shock' and some of the pretty barbaric treatments they used back then. He went on about repression of memories, and how when you're asleep you haven't got control over them surfacing.' He paused. Grace waited. 'He said I should think about what may be troubling me now that might make me more susceptible to bad memories.'

'Well, is there anything?'

Jack didn't answer straight away. He looked around the room then at his wife. His dear wife, his beloved, with whom he had shared so much. Time to tell her what was on his mind.

'It's Brian,' he said finally.

'Brian?' It was the last thing she expected to hear.

'He's ten and a half now. When I was his age I used to help Dad all the time. Used to spend more time at the funeral parlour than at home. Though, of course, Mum wasn't the sort of mother that you are. What I'm trying to say is that I don't think that Brian has the same interest as I had.'

'Have you talked to him about it?'

'No, I haven't. He's doing well at school. Did you see his mid-year report?'

'Certainly did. He did well in everything and brilliantly in maths. He got a perfect score.' *Wonder where he got that from.* The look on Jack's face cut her short. He was frowning. 'Are you thinking he might not want to follow you into the business?'

'That's exactly what I'm thinking.' He paused and continued, his voice sounding a little sad. 'If he doesn't, I'll have to look for another chap to train.'

Grace could see this was a major consideration for Jack. She remembered his 'Shaw and Son and Grandson' prediction years ago when Jim was still alive. They hadn't changed the lettering on the business stationery – it was still Shaw and Son, as it always had been.

'Jack, don't take it too hard if Brian doesn't want to follow the family tradition. Look at Lillian and Barry's kids. Peter always wanted to be a farmer like his dad, but Hughie's joining the Army.'

This was a surprise to Jack. 'When did you find that out?'

Usually, Grace told Jack everything. It seemed as though the last phone call from Lily had not been mentioned.

'I suppose I can tell you, now that it's all settled. It was an awkward time for them and could have been worse but …'

'What was?'

'Hugh got mixed up with some rough kids at high school. Apparently they did some damage to an old person's house and stole some stuff. Hugh was mixed up in it. They had to go to court and luckily the magistrate didn't sentence them to a youth training centre, you know, reform school. One of the teachers at the school had a session with Barry and Lillian and suggested Hughie look at a career where there would be some strong discipline as well as a future. So he's going to be an army cadet which could be a good choice for him.'

Jack was clearly surprised by the news. He remembered his own army experiences. But of course, it would be different being in the armed forces in peacetime.

'Thank you for telling me, Grace. I'll give Barry a ring and wish Hughie good luck.' Seeing the look on her face, he continued, 'I won't say anything about what happened before the decision was made.'

Relieved, Grace embraced her husband. 'I don't like keeping things from you. It was like when Elizabeth Langthorne confided in me about her choice of burial.'

Jack nodded. He'd only recently heard about the deception which preserved their minister's privacy in Beaufort for all those years. What a special person Grace was, so principled, so genuine.

For the first time in ages, he felt a smile coming, and on seeing it, Grace moved close to share a most satisfying kiss.

It was Brian who noticed the two men first. They were standing under the tree outside the Quinn property. Wearing overalls, they looked like labourers. As he and Miranda dismounted their bikes to go through their front gate, one of the men came over to him.

'Will yer tell us which house is Governor Quinn's?'

Something in the stranger's manner made Brian cautious. He glanced over to the other younger man who looked decidedly furtive.

'Governor Quinn? I think he might be further up the street.' He gestured vaguely to indicate the direction.

'But Brian …' Miranda's interjection was shrill.

'He's not talking to you, he's talking to me. You go inside. Now.' His voice was firm, almost rude.

Miranda thought better of disobeying him, but threw an aggrieved 'I'm goin' to tell on you,' over her shoulder as she dropped her bike and ran inside.

'It's his missus we want ter talk to.' This came in a low voice from the younger chap, to which the other said, 'Shut up, will yuh.'

Brian decided to confirm his earlier statement. 'I'm not sure, but I think it's one of the houses on the other side of the street, a block or two away.'

The two men conferred in low voices. Brian couldn't quite hear what was being said, but they obviously decided against the boy's directions and made off back towards town.

Grace's face had a 'please explain' expression.

Miranda, of course, had to blurt out, 'He told a lie, Mum!'

'Shh,' said Grace to her daughter. 'Would you like to tell me what happened, Brian?'

'I don't know, Mum, I just didn't like the look of them. And when one of them said they wanted to speak to Mrs Quinn, that didn't sound right to me …' His voice trailed off.

Grace nodded. She recognised in her son's judgement a maturity beyond his years.

'Who do you think they were?'

'I think they were prisoners, you know, on day release.' Realising his sister was puzzled, he explained to both of them. 'They're organised into work parties and go out into the community doing jobs under supervision. Me mate Bernie's father's a warden out there, he told me about it. They're supposed to be trusties, no risk to the public.'

'What else did he tell you?' asked Grace.

Brian paused, unsure about continuing. 'Well, I s'pose I can tell you.

He said Governor Quinn is really hated by the prisoners. He's very hard on them.'

'He told a lie, Mum – that's wrong,' insisted Miranda.

'It's all right, Miranda, I understand what Brian was thinking. There are times when … Let's wait until Dad comes home and see what he makes of it.'

Later that evening, Grace told Jack of the incident. 'Should we say anything? Or not?'

Jack didn't respond straight away. There was no obvious answer. 'Let's just leave it, for now anyway. It wouldn't be a good idea for Brian to have to be a witness. It could be …'

'Scary?' Grace interjected. Jack nodded.

'You'd better explain it to Miranda, you're better at these things than I am.'

Grace smiled. How many times had he said that to her …

The *Riponshire Advocate* ran an article a few months later announcing that Governor Quinn had been recalled to Pentridge Prison. In his place, an American custodial expert had been appointed who planned to live on the premises at Langi Kal Kal. The Beaufort residence, owned by the Department, would be used by sessional staff on a rotational basis.

'What does that all mean?' asked Grace.

'Who knows?' replied Jack. 'Probably means people will be coming and going at the gaol, using next-door for overnight or longer stays.'

That was how it turned out. There was little interaction with their neighbours, just an occasional 'good morning'.

The old days, when Mary was there like an extension of the family, seemed long gone. Things change all the time, and there wasn't anything anyone could do about it. On the other hand, there was plenty to be glad about. Grace unfailingly thanked God in her prayers for the love of her husband and family and the caring community in which she lived.

Chapter 4

The arrival of December '59, with the end of the school year looming, and Christmas soon following, buoyed the spirits of the Shaw children with the prospect of freedom and presents to come.

It didn't turn out that way.

On the last Tuesday before the end of term, Grace had news for them when they arrived home from school, together for once.

'Dad had a call from Uncle Alan. He's coming up here to stay for a week or two. So I'll put the camp bed up in Brian's room for you, Mirrie.'

'Why's he coming up, Mum?' asked Brian.

'Things aren't all that good at home, he said. He needs to get away for a while, so Dad agreed he could come up here. Just him, by the way.'

'Isn't he working?'

'I suppose he's taking some time off. I really don't know. But when it comes to family you feel you need to help. Anyway, he's coming tomorrow on the afternoon train.'

Brian and Miranda looked at each other but said nothing. Uncle Alan was their father's older brother. He always seemed a bit weak. Maybe that was because Aunt Deirdre was so strong. And noisy. And bossy.

Now eleven, a year younger than Brian, Frankie was large, restless and aggressive. He was too uncoordinated to play cricket properly, or even kick a football around. He would use his bulk to gain possession, even against the much-smaller Miranda, but didn't seem to know what to do with the ball. When his father tried to help with instructions from the sideline, Frankie would rudely ignore him. Their last visit was only a three-day weekend but had seemed much longer.

Aunt Deirdre kept telling them to 'be nice to Frankie because he can't help being the way he is.' Brian would mutter to Miranda, 'Let him be the way he is somewhere else.'

When they'd last visited, Frankie had shared Brian's room while his parents took over Miranda's who had to sleep on a couch in the sleep-out. That in itself didn't bother her – it was the reaction of some of the local kids who somehow found out and jeered, 'Miranda, Miranda – sleeps on the veranda!'

'Frankie isn't coming, I hope.'

'No, Mirrie, just Uncle Alan.'

Next day when the children arrived home, the visitor had already arrived. They could hear voices in the kitchen. Brian in particular was struck by the sight of his uncle who seemed smaller, somewhat shrunken even, and his face looked tired.

Miranda dutifully kissed him on the cheek then regarded him closely. 'Are you sick, Uncle Alan?'

He squirmed, trying to avoid her direct gaze. 'Uh, no, er – well, yes,' he stammered, before Grace came to his rescue.

'Your uncle needs some peace and quiet, so please go and do your homework in your room.'

'We haven't got any homework,' protested Brian. Grace opened the door into the hallway and firmly gestured them out. The expression on their mother's face forestalled any argument.

'Something's not right – I can tell,' said Brian.

'He looks so unhappy. I wish we could help,' said Miranda.

They could hear through the closed doors a low hum of conversation coming from the kitchen, with periods of silence. About an hour later, there was a knock on the front door.

'I'll go, Mum,' yelled Brian.

On the doorstep was the uniformed figure of the local policeman, quite new to the area since Tom Delaney moved on earlier in the year.

'Is Mr Alan Shaw there?' he asked.

Before Brian could reply, his mother came quickly to the door.

'Back to your room, Brian,' she ordered, before ushering Constable Enright into the living room and closing the door.

Grace spoke first. 'I know you need to talk to my brother-in-law, but could it wait until Jack gets home? He won't be long and Alan's not very well.'

The policeman looked unsure. Grace offered to ring Jack and ask him to come home early. Constable Enright was satisfied with that.

'Just ask them to come down to the station, the sooner the better,' he said before leaving.

Before long, Jack's rapid footsteps were heard. The children strained their ears to try and hear the muffled conversation.

'Dad's saying he'll go down with him – I can't hear what Uncle Alan's saying, his voice is so soft.' Brian paused, listening. 'They're going out now.'

There was a frown on Grace's face as she started preparing the evening meal.

'What's happening, Mum?' The children asked together.

'I'm not sure. Just that they want a statement from Uncle Alan. We'll just have to wait to hear anything more.'

And wait they did. It was nearly half past six before both men returned, this time in the police van. Jack went straight to Grace.

'The police need to escort Alan back to Melbourne to face charges. There was a phone call while we were at the station. What I heard was that they've upgraded the charge from serious bodily harm to grievous bodily harm. It doesn't look good, Grace. I asked Peter Enright if Alan could come back here and pick up his things before they go. He agreed to that.'

Alan had gone straight into his room and closed the door.

'How serious is it?' Grace's voice was full of concern.

'Serious enough. I'll tell you about it later when curious little people aren't around.'

The children looked at each other.

'Go on Dad – tell us what's happened,' urged Brian.

'Can we do something?' chimed in Miranda.

'No, you can't. This is grown-up stuff. You two just keep out of the way.' The sound of a car horn intruded. 'Peter said five minutes, I suppose that's up already. I'll just go and ask him to wait a few more minutes.'

He went out the front door. Grace went to the bedroom and knocked. 'Alan, can I come in?'

There was no answer. She rattled the doorknob before opening it. No one was inside the room. The window was wide open. Alan's kitbag was on the floor, but he had vanished.

'You'd better ask your father to come back here,' said Grace.

Brian raced out to the police car. 'Dad – Dad. He's gone!'

It seemed as though all Hell had broken loose. Constable Enright rushed straight into the house and through to the bedroom.

'I need to use your phone,' he said breathlessly. 'I'll have to get inst-instructions.'

When the connection was established it became clear to the listeners that HQ was taking it very seriously. 'No sir, I wasn't going to drive him down myself, I was going to charge him and lock him up for the night and book a divvy van for tomorrow … of course we'll do a thorough search, sir … I know that, sir … he didn't seem dangerous to me, sir … yes, sir. Thank you, sir.'

The young constable looked helplessly at Jack. In spite of her concern about her brother-in-law's situation, Grace could not help feeling sorry for Peter Enright.

'Usually, when people are needed, like for a fire or something, they ring the fire brigade bell,' Jack offered. 'I could ring Perce Laidlaw, he's the local captain. We'd have to go down to the fire station to meet up and get instructions.'

Within ten minutes, a group of men and boys had assembled, Jack and Brian among them. An air of curiosity prevailed – there was no sign of a fire, so what was going on?

The policeman stood on a chair someone had brought out from

the building. He began somewhat nervously by thanking everyone for responding. He explained that it was a case of a missing person – Jack Shaw's brother, Alan, had escaped from police custody and needed to be found. As far as was known he had no weapon, no money, and would be on foot.

One of the men suggested they put a vehicle on the highway just out of town in each direction in case the fugitive was trying to hitch-hike out of town.

'Do you have any suggestions, Jack?' Peter Enright asked.

'Not really. It's a good few years since he lived here. Should I go back home in case he turns up there again?' This was agreed.

As he made his way back to Speke Street with Brian, Jack felt very confused. How could Alan have got himself into such a mess? Part of him wanted to protect his troubled brother, but he also knew that the law must be upheld.

'Has he come back?' he asked Grace. She shook her head. Jack noticed she had been crying. He gave her a hug before going outside to look around in case Alan had crept back and was hiding. Both children also hugged their mother before asking their questions.

'Mummy, what if they can't find him?' wailed Miranda.

'I just want to know what he's done, why the police want him.' Brian's questions were legitimate, Grace knew. What should she say?

'Uncle Alan had a bad argument with Frankie and, well, he hit him and injured him. That's all I really know.'

Jack came rushing in through the back door.

'Grace,' he said urgently, 'the rope I use for towing, it was on a hook in the shed and now it's gone!' A look of alarm passed between them. 'I'm going to drive up to the pine plantation behind the school.'

'I'm coming too,' said Brian. 'I'll take my torch and my scout whistle.'

'Me, too,' said Miranda.

Before Grace could object, they were off on their bikes as dusk was gathering.

The pine plantation was a dark-green, almost black expanse close to the Catholic church. The children knew it well, as it was a great place to explore, play hidey and gather pine cones. They saw Jack's car parked on the side of the road, he was somewhere close by. In fact, they could hear him calling Alan's name. They went deeper into the plantation, watching the ground as they neared the edge of the dry creek bed. Branches stretched out over the gully, a good place to climb and swing, though the branches were rigid and didn't give that exciting swooping movement that other trees did.

Something made Miranda look up.

'Brian! Look. What's that?'

A dark shape was suspended from an overhanging branch only a few yards ahead. Brian instantly pushed his sister away behind him.

'Don't look.'

He pulled out his whistle and blew hard and long, then yelled, 'Dad, Dad. Over here!'

Within seconds, Jack appeared, took one look and ordered the children to go home and tell their mother what they'd seen. The whistle and torch were left with Jack. As they rode home in the semi-dark, they heard loud repeated blasts of the whistle. Several trucks and utes passed them heading up to the pine forest. The signal had been heard.

Brian, riding on ahead, turned to check on his sister. 'You all right?'

Miranda's teeth were chattering. It was all she could do to keep pedalling.

'I th-think so'

'Nearly home.'

Grace came running to the gate as they dismounted and brought their bikes in.

'I shouldn't have let you go. I was worried where you two were. Come inside, you look terrible.'

'Mummy – Mummy! I saw him!'

Grace's mouth opened soundlessly, she looked over to Brian.

'I couldn't stop her seeing him. It was awful, Mum. He was hanging from a branch over the creek.'

Miranda went straight to her mother and blurted out the terrible words. 'Mummy. His eyes were popping out!'

In an instant, the picture of her long-dead father-in-law's face came to Grace's mind. *I don't want this sort of image to torment my daughter,* she thought, her senses reeling.

From the cabinet drawer near at hand she rummaged and found a small black and white photograph.

'Look, darling, look – that's Uncle Alan, that's how I want you to remember him, not what you just saw.' Miranda took the photo, gazed at the half-smiling face captured in a happier time and nodded.

It seemed to Brian and Miranda that the house was suddenly full of people, even the minister had come. Though not a drinker himself, Jack always kept a bottle or two of brandy, as well as beer, for entertaining. All very much needed on that unforgettable evening in December. The presence of a senior policeman from Ballarat and his offsider added authority to the occasion, and Constable Enright gladly handed over the proceedings to his superior, including the task of notifying the Clifton Hill police that they should make a house call to inform Deirdre Shaw of her husband's death.

'Of course, she may be at the hospital – it's the Royal Children's, isn't it,' he'd said over the phone to Melbourne headquarters.

Grace found an opportunity to take the children into the kitchen, closing the door behind her. A long hard hug was needed first then to find the words to explain and reassure.

'This is a terrible, terrible thing that's happened,' she said 'I wish it hadn't, and I wish you hadn't seen – what you did. But we have to try to understand why Uncle Alan made his choice. In a way you could say he was brave because he would otherwise have spent a long time in gaol.'

'Why, Mum? What did he do that was so awful?' Brian blurted out.

'Yes, what?' echoed Miranda.

Deciding to be factual, Grace chose her words carefully. 'He would have been charged with grievous bodily harm, that is, assault with a weapon. And – and if Frankie had died – it would have been murder.'

The children gasped. Meek, timid Uncle Alan, who never stood up for himself. It sounded so unlike him. And Frankie was already bigger than his father, a real bully boy.

'I want you both to go to bed now, it's late. You must be tired. Things will seem a bit different in the morning. I hope so anyway.'

Brian recognised the despair in his mother's voice and turned to go.

'But, Mum,' Miranda protested.

'Come on, Sis, to bed now, Mum's tired out – can't you tell?' He physically propelled his sister out of the room just as his father came back into the kitchen.

'I managed to get everybody out,' he said. 'There's nothing more anyone can do now.' His voice had a tone of resignation and weariness. Grace put her arms around him. 'When you're ready, I'll get you to tell me what Alan actually said, I mean, what did he do, and why. He clammed up at the police station and said hardly anything.'

'Of course, darling.' Before she could say anything else there was a ring on the front doorbell. 'I'll go.'

Jack heard a brief exchange, and Grace's 'Thank you very much,' before she returned carrying a plate. 'Melva Jones has just brought us half an egg and bacon pie. She thought you might have missed out on tea.' Jack gave a grateful half smile and nodded. 'I'll just heat it up a bit first,' Grace continued.

After putting it in the oven she slipped out of the room saying, 'Just going to check on the kids.'

The photo of Alan was on the table. When Grace came back into the room Jack was gazing at it.

'It's so hard to believe … he's not here any more.'

Grace nodded. 'I'll dish this up for you, I ate with the children. I'll tell you everything Alan said to me while you're eating.'

'Good. I didn't think I was hungry, but that does smell nice.'

'He was a bit all-over-the-place when he first came in. So I made him a cup of tea and asked him to start at the beginning. So he said that yesterday he had a day off work and Deirdre had a medical appointment, so he was home alone with Frankie. This was quite unusual, I gather. The boy started taunting him, wanting to spar with him. You know Alan's not a fighter, he kept trying to fend him off. This made Frankie more determined, he began jeering at him, saying things like "You're not a real man, you're a poofter, you're weak." Alan put up with all this, just hoping Deirdre would come home soon. But Frankie kept on until he said, or rather, shouted, the unforgivable "You're just like your mother!" The one thing Alan couldn't tolerate. "Shut, up. Don't say that!" he yelled back. Sensing a response, the boy continued to goad him with "You're just the same as your loony mother! You are, you are!"

'Alan grabbed that long brass candlestick that had been Verna's and tried to hit him to make him stop. When Frankie was looking around for a weapon for himself, Alan landed a heavy blow to the back of his head and down he went. And stayed down. Suddenly appalled and panicking, Alan realised he had to get out, get away. He grabbed his kitbag, threw a few clothes in it and took about fifteen pounds from their savings jar. He got to the station, but the afternoon train had already left Spencer Street. So he went back to King Street and took a room overnight at the Peoples Palace. He rang us from there. He said he had a horrible night, kept thinking he heard noises and that they were coming for him, I didn't ask whether he meant the police or Deirdre. He didn't show any concern for Frankie. I think he was in a state of shock. It was all too much for him. Well, you saw him when he finally got here. Obviously, Deirdre called the police as well as the ambulance. They would have asked her where he was likely to have gone, and of course, she said here, to his brother's.'

Jack had finished eating. He was silent for a moment, still trying to take in Alan's story.

'Yes, I can imagine that would have been the worst thing to ever say to him – that he was like his mother. The thing is – he's the total opposite. Or … was. I wonder whether he had sudden doubts about himself when he became so violent. After all, he'd seen his mother in rages often enough in the past.'

They looked at each other. Grace whispered, 'Enough to make him end his life?'

That's something we will never know.

Next day. There's always a next day, regardless of the dramas that unfold the day before. Officialdom took over, which was a blessing. Alan's body was taken to the City Morgue in Melbourne. The Ballarat detectives, with the help of the local policeman, compiled a report for the coroner. In his interview, Jack reluctantly provided the information Grace had been given by his brother when the question arose of 'why?' The comment was made that if Frankie regained consciousness and was capable of giving evidence, it would be important to know his version.

But nothing could change the outcome

Making contact with Deirdre proved to be difficult. There was no answer to the several phone calls they made to the house in Clifton Hill. Grace tried to get through at the Royal Children's Hospital, but the person on the switchboard would only say that Francis was in Intensive Care and in a critical condition. Presumably, Deirdre was with him day and night. Grace asked the Reverend Nigel Langthorne to offer prayers for Frankie.

'I'll pray for him, his mother and also for your family,' he promised.

'I want you to go to school and do all your normal things. Or try to,' said Grace

'What do we say if they ask what happened, about Uncle Alan, I mean?' Brian was clearly concerned about having the right answers. Grace looked at Brian.

'The facts are as they are. It'll all be in the papers. The thing is, you've lost your uncle, and of course you're sad. And you may not want to talk about it,' he said.

The children seemed satisfied with that.

'Oh, before you go,' their mother interjected, 'I rang Auntie Lillian last night and she's offered to have you both up for a few days before

Christmas. It might be a good idea, as Dad and I will probably have to go down to Melbourne for the, er, the funeral.'

Miranda was all smiles. 'Wow-ee!' she said. 'That'd be great, wouldn't it, Brian?'

Brian wasn't so sure. 'It's the speech night tomorrow night, I don't want to miss that. It'll be the last one for the Beaufort Higher Elementary School, what with the new high school opening next year. And I think I'm getting a prize for mathematical ability.' There, he'd said it. He had wanted it to be a surprise for his parents, but now they needed to know, so they'd understand why he wanted to be there. 'And I want to be a bit more help to you, Dad,' he added as a sweetener.

'Aww – does that mean I can't go?'

'I'll look into it, Mirrie,' said Grace decisively. 'Off you go now, both of you.'

A phone call to the stationmaster confirmed that there would be an adult couple travelling from Beaufort to Warracknabeal on the morning train.

'The Methodist minister and his wife have booked. They're nice people, and I'm sure they'd look after your daughter for you. And Beulah's only four stops further on.' He had paused, and added awkwardly, 'Sorry about what happened, nasty business.'

'Is Dad coming down to see me off?'

'He wanted to, but someone's died at the hospital and he's had to go there. But you'll be back before you know it, darling – it's only for five days.' Grace tried to make it sound like nothing much, but it was, after all, the first time they had been separated for more than just overnight. Staying with school friends didn't really count. She felt an unfamiliar lump in her throat.

'I'll be all right, Mum. I'm ten and a half, you know. And I'll do what Mr and Mrs Jamison say on the trip up.'

The return trip hadn't yet been sorted. May Jamison said they might be coming back on the Tuesday train, 'Eric has to get his Christmas sermon ready.'

Grace responded gratefully, 'That would work out well.'

The sound of the approaching steam engine focussed everybody's attention. Mr Jamison checked the carriage number and beckoned Miranda with her small suitcase to follow them inside. A quick kiss and a hug, and up she scrambled into the dimly-lit interior.

This is going to be a real adventure, thought Miranda.

Chapter 5

It seemed that from the moment she got out of the car and through the gate at the Mallee farm – vaguely remembered from the visit a few years ago – people were hovering around her. Her Auntie Lillian, Uncle Barry and three of her cousins were there. She'd been told on the drive from the station that Hughie was away at army cadet camp and Dawnie was staying with friends. They were all looking anxiously at her, asking her if she was all right, murmuring things like, 'You're being very brave', 'It must have been awful for you', and from Auntie Lillian, 'Any time you want to talk about it, love, that's okay, just let me know.'

Miranda felt a bit strange about her reception. The Jamisons had been kind during the trip, saying they'd listen if she wanted to talk. She'd just shaken her head, giving them a little smile of thanks, and concentrated on reading her book. What was there to talk about anyway? It happened, yes, and she'd rather try to forget about it.

But how to say this to her relatives? She decided to avoid their questioning with, 'I'm really tired – it was such a long trip.'

'Of course you must be. I saved some tea for you. Why don't you come and eat, then have an early night?' said Auntie Lillian. 'Wendy, take Miranda's suitcase to the spare room, will you.'

As her aunt bustled around getting the meal served, Miranda noticed the others moving away to their own interests. Except for Russell.

The gangly youth crept up to her and insisted on asking the question she dreaded.

'You saw him first, didn't you? What did he look like?'

Miranda gaped at the intense expression in the boy's face only inches from hers. For some inexplicable reason, she burst into tears. Instantly he was banished, and the comforting arms of her aunt went around her.

It all seemed a bit unreal the next day. Miranda woke to the piercing sound of a rooster crowing. It took her a few minutes to realise that she was nearly two hundred miles from home. The door opened slowly and Wendy came in with a morning greeting.

'Did you sleep all right?'

'I did. Hey, what time is it?'

'It's after nine. D'you want to get up and have some breakfast? Mum says it's goin' to be hot today. Dad's gotta go to Warracknabeal an' Mum says we can go too an' have a swim in the pool. I've got a spare pair of bathers if you didn't bring any.'

Miranda hadn't brought any, it hadn't crossed her mind. Anyway, swimming was not one of her favourite activities. The pool at Beaufort was a muddy brown all the time, and kids used to say there were snakes in it. Brian always laughed at her. He'd say, 'Keep kicking an' you'll scare them away,' before swimming off in a flurry of splashes.

'I don't mind watching if you want to swim,' she said.

Wendy didn't reply straight away. A sturdy girl, she was a lot bigger than her cousin, though only a year older. She picked up Miranda's shorts from the floor and commented, 'Gee, you're pretty small, aren't you. Don't you get much to eat?'

Miranda was hurt by the remark. 'Of course I do – I eat all the time. The thing is, I was born early, premature Mum says, and I haven't really caught up.' While saying this, she grabbed her shorts and selected underwear from her suitcase. Not sure whether to undress in front of her cousin, she paused. It became obvious that Wendy wasn't moving, so she quickly slipped off her nightie and put her day clothes on. Wendy watched her intently.

'I've got little titties coming, an' some hair down there,' she said, quite proudly it seemed to Miranda. Keen to change the subject, she asked

Wendy's opinion on which of the cotton blouses she'd brought. The older girl shrugged, indicating that it didn't matter, so Miranda put on her favourite pink and white checked one.

It was hot, certainly warmer than Beaufort, but Miranda didn't mind. At breakfast, Auntie Lillian suggested that they might like to go to a film matinee in Warracknabeal instead of the pool. This was greeted with robust approval.

'Do you go to the pictures, Miranda?'

Mouth full, she nodded.

'What do you like best?'

'I like the cowboy ones, mainly 'cos of the horses. Some of my friends like the mushy ones, you know, lots of kissing, but I don't.'

'I do – I like them all,' declared Wendy. 'Anyway we just have to take what's on – they only have one movie for the matinees.'

On the trip back to the farm after they'd enjoyed a typical Western movie with the obligatory boos, hisses and stamping of feet from the young audience, Uncle Barry asked Miranda what she thought of the place.

'It's bigger than Beaufort. But not as big as Ballarat.' Barry laughed. 'There were quite a lot of kids with dark skin and no shoes.'

'Don't you have Abos where you come from?' asked Russell from up front in the passenger seat.

Miranda was puzzled. There were one or two kids at school who were said to have had a touch of the tar-brush, which her mother had explained meant that one of the parents was Aboriginal. But they weren't as dark, or indeed, as carefree as the ones she'd seen today.

Luckily, Wendy changed the subject by asking her father, 'When's Ruby coming, Dad?'

He replied, 'Tomorrow, I think. That's why Mum didn't come today.'

'Who's Ruby?' whispered Miranda to her cousin.

'I'll explain when we get home. She'll sleep in Dawnie's room while she's away.'

That evening, it was Auntie Lillian who told her about the new guest.

'She's an old friend of mine from Ballarat. Lost her sight when she was quite young. But she's pretty independent. Barry will pick her up from the train and bring her here tomorrow, she's only staying a day here, then I'll drive her over to Birchip where she'll stay with her brother for Christmas.'

Miranda's attention had focussed on the second statement, 'Do you mean she's blind?'

'Course she is. Can't see anything. She uses a stick to feel what's in front of her.' Wendy's tone of voice sounded quite superior, making Miranda feel taken to task. She just nodded.

Since Russell and Wendy had school the next day, Lillian asked Miranda if she'd like to go along with Wendy.

'It's the last day of school,' her Auntie reminded her.

It was a difficult question. She would be missing the school break-up at Beaufort. Perhaps going to the Beulah one would be some sort of compensation. *Be brave*, said a little voice inside. Wendy was enthusiastic about introducing her cousin to her grade five classmates.

'Yes, Auntie Lillian. I'd like to go. After today, it's Christmas holidays – yippee!' Miranda smiled.

The eleven children in Wendy's grade were sitting cross-legged on the floor in a semicircle. The teacher asked each of them to give a short talk on what had been the highlight of the year. There was a variety of responses, several about holidays to different places, two had a new baby in their families. One girl had won a prize for riding her pony in a gymkhana. Three of the boys declared there were no highlights in their year. The teacher asked Miranda if she would like to join in. She looked across at Wendy whose face bore a concerned expression as though she was worried what her cousin might say.

An inspiration came to her. She asked if it could be something from three years ago. 'That's perfectly all right,' said the teacher.

So Miranda told the class of the excitement she experienced going to the Olympics, although it was a few years ago in 1956. The school had hired a bus to take them all to Ballarat for the rowing competition at Lake Wendouree. There was a gasp from the children and a few 'gees!'

'What I thought was most interesting was there were lots of groups of people watching and waving flags that weren't Australian.'

'That would have been very special,' said the teacher. 'When you start to do geography next year you'll learn more about the different countries of the world.' She paused. 'I'm afraid it would be too far for us up here in the Mallee to make such a trip. You were lucky to live so close to Ballarat.'

That afternoon, the two girls got off the school bus at the letter-box near the front gate, about a hundred yards from the homestead. Sitting on the veranda with her Auntie Lillian was an ordinary-looking woman about the same age as her aunt. The only clue to her blindness was the pair of very dark glasses she wore. Miranda was introduced to Miss Ruby Andrews, who turned her face to smile in her direction when Auntie Lillian made the introduction.

'It's lovely to meet you, dear,' said Ruby.

'Thank you,' Miranda responded.

'Are you staying here long, Miranda?'

'She's staying a few more days, Ruby,' replied Auntie Lillian. 'There's been a family upset. I'll tell you about it later.'

After tea, the two girls went into the sitting room to play Chinese checkers. There was a knock on the door and Ruby asked, 'Can I come in?'

'Of course you can,' said Wendy.

For some inexplicable reason, Miranda picked up a footstool and put it a few feet inside the door. The blind woman advanced tentatively and stumbled over it.

'Oh, sorry!' said Miranda, hastily removing the little stool.

'It's all right. I suppose you forgot. I should have had my stick anyway.'

That night in the bedroom they were sharing, Wendy confronted her cousin with the obvious question, 'Why did you do that?'

Miranda felt very uncomfortable but decided to be honest. 'I suppose it was a test. I wanted to know whether she could actually see it or not. I'm terribly sorry.'

'You were awful to do that. I should tell Mum, but ...'

Together they decided on a punishment.

Next day, after Ruby had left, Wendy found a dark-coloured cotton scarf. She covered Miranda's eyes with it and tied it firmly at the back before leading her to the door of the little sitting room. She was asked to wait before coming in.

Miranda knew an obstacle would be placed in her way. She carefully edged into the room while Wendy called out 'over here' from several different directions. In due course, she stumbled over the footstool and pulled off the blindfold.

'That was horrible. I felt so – so vulnerable. I'll never play that sort of trick again.'

Wendy wasn't exactly sure what 'vulnerable' meant, but she was convinced her oh-so-smart cousin had learned her lesson, and said so.

'So you won't tell your mum?'

Wendy, savouring her advantage, pursed her lips and shook her head. 'No, I won't.'

'Gee, thanks,' Miranda replied.

It was amazing how quickly the next few days passed. The Methodist minister had phoned the Wards to say that he and his wife would be on the platform at Warracknabeal on Tuesday, and Miranda should look out for them.

They were easy to find and welcomed her into their carriage. The return was a contrast to the earlier trip. Miranda, clearly relaxed from her short holiday, was talkative, and, as a result, the journey seemed to take much less time.

At the Beaufort station, Brian was the first person she saw. How handsome he looked, she realised, so tall, upright, dark-haired.

'G'day, Sis,' he said, 'how was it?'

'Okay. I mean, good. Oh, by the way – what happened to Frankie?'

'He died.'

Miranda's first reaction was a silent 'good', then the realisation hit her. It *wasn't* good. Horrible and all that he was, he didn't deserve to die at such a young age. Nor did Uncle Alan.

Having parked the car, Grace appeared and Miranda rushed into her mother's embrace.

'It's good to be back, Mum. Are you okay?'

'We are. We missed you, Mirrie.'

Brian put Miranda's little suitcase on the floor behind the driver's seat, along with the brown paper bag filled with oranges from the farm and some jars of jam Lil had packed for them.

'Oh dear, with all that was going on I didn't send them anything for Christmas,' said Grace, her voice mournful.

'They'll understand, Mum. Don't worry about it.'

Brian was right, of course. In Grace's phone calls to Beulah, both Lil and Barry had expressed their sympathy and concern and had assured her that Miranda had settled in well with no sign of homesickness, or anxiety about the events of the past few days. That was good news.

Miranda's eyes took in the unfamiliar sight of several sympathy cards on the mantelpiece. There was also a certificate stating that Brian Frederick Shaw had been awarded the prize for Best Achievement in Mathematics, Form 3, Beaufort Higher Elementary School.

'I'm getting it framed,' he announced.

Along with his classmates, Brian was thrilled to be part of the first student intake at the new High School to open in 1960. It was near the Beaufort Lake, next to the Showgrounds and the football oval. For Miranda's last year at the Primary School, the two of them set off on their bikes in different directions.

It was fun being in the top class, even though she was one of the shortest of the grade six girls. However, she was fast on her feet and good at both rounders and tunnel-ball. She was voted to be one of the class monitors, which was an honour, and she somehow managed to get fewer detentions than in the past.

One day in October she came home from school looking subdued.

'Guess what, Mum. Annie Saunders isn't going to go on to the High School next year.'

Grace pricked up her ears. Annie was one of Miranda's best friends. She came from a grazing property south of Beaufort, travelling to and from school on the bus which, since 1947, picked up students from the outlying areas.

'Why is that?'

'She's going to boarding school in Ballarat, and, we're not allowed to call her Annie any more – her name is Anne. It's posher.' She paused, and blurted out, 'Mum – could I go to Clarendon too? It sounds really *great* and Anne told me they have a terrific uniform, brown and beige.'

Grace thought for a moment before replying. She knew that Miranda was a good student, she might even be scholarship material. But it wouldn't just be the fees. Uniform and book expenses, extra lessons like tennis and music – it all cost money.

'I'll have a word with your father. But don't get your hopes up, dear. The Saunders own a big property, and with the wool prices so high, they can afford things that we can't.'

Brian had heard most of this, having quietly entered the kitchen.

'What do you want to go to a private school for? You'd just turn into a snob like they all are. You're only an undertaker's daughter, remember.' Miranda turned to challenge him, but he'd left as unobtrusively as he came in.

'There'll be other girls not going away, you'll still have friends.'

'The thing is, Mum, Annie's not very clever. I have to help her a lot, especially with maths.'

'I said I'd speak to your father. Let's leave it at that.'

I know what he'll say, Miranda thought. *He'll say if it was for Brian there might be some possibility, but what's the point of an expensive education for a girl?*

The subject didn't come up again, as it turned out. Something more exciting was about to happen. Jack brought the news a few weeks later.

'Well, you'll never guess what Joe's going to do. He rang me today to tell me.'

Nobody could guess, so Jack continued. 'He and Declan are going to Ireland in the New Year for six weeks. He'll be staying with the O'Dwyers, and Declan will show him around the countryside.' There was a collective gasp from around the table. 'Gosh!' came from Brian and Miranda. Jack continued. 'The thing is, with the wool cheque Phil got this year, they can afford the airfares. I don't know who's the more excited – Joe or Bridie.'

Grace knew, from her phone calls with Bridie, that the penfriendship between Joe and Antoinette was blossoming. She also knew Bridie was concerned for Declan who hadn't been home for ten years. 'His parents aren't getting any younger, y'know,' she'd said.

So the news Jack brought home was not entirely unexpected. No doubt the Taylors had subsidised the cost of the airfare for their much-valued farm worker while recognising the great opportunity for their own son.

'After the boys have gone, I'll make it my business to go out to the farm more often. Maybe you could come too, Brian. See if we can help Phil and Bridie in any way.

'Sure, Dad.'

Miranda almost blurted out, 'Me, too?' but thought better of it. She knew her dad would have said no, anyway.

Chapter 6

From a vantage point in the top paddock, the farmhouse could be seen about half a mile away to the east. To the south, Lake Goldsmith was dry. It was, after all, only a flat depression with no creeks or rivers running into it. In summer it often looked like the brown pastures that were so dried out that farmers had to hand feed their stock until the autumn rains brought fresh green grass. That could be four, or even six, weeks away. Joe and Declan would be back from Ireland by then.

Phil parked the ute on the side of the hill. He and Bridie were quickly surrounded by a bleating mass of hungry sheep. The binder twine was cut and large hunks of hay were thrown to the milling flock.

There was adequate water, thanks to the windmill which dragged it up through the bore from deep underground to the troughs, at least when the wind blew. As with the lake, the dam was dry. The sheep looked scrawny, having been shorn not long ago, their wrinkly skin exposed in the heat. Luckily the Taylors had cut a lot of hay in the spring, so there would be enough for daily feeding until autumn.

A painful niggle made Bridie straighten up and rub her lower back. She looked back towards the farmhouse.

What she saw made her cry out in shock, 'Phil! Look!'

A thin streak of smoke was curling up into the sky from one of the chimneys. Even as they looked, stunned, it became thicker and darker.

'Shit!' said Phil.

He jumped off the back of the ute and into the driver's seat. Their

Kelpie cross sheepdog, Lucky, barked in protest as Phil threw him out of the passenger seat to let his wife in.

Although they sped across the paddocks, only stopping for Bridie to open and close gates, the house was well and truly on fire by the time they reached the back gate.

Bridie screamed 'Danny – Danny's in there! Get the hose, Phil – turn it on hard. I'm goin' in.'

They were overwhelmed by the heat and an ominous roaring as tongues of flame licked the weatherboard walls.

'Danny – Danny!' shouted Bridie as she tried to open the back flywire door, its wooden frame already ablaze. She heard the dogs locked in the shed barking and yelping.

Blind panic forced her to shout louder, 'Danny, Danny!' her voice straining above the inferno. Phil had brought the garden hose at full blast trying to douse the flames at the back door so they could get in.

Above the commotion, he heard a truck coming up the drive at high speed and men's voices shouting. Within seconds, the heavy firefighting equipment on the back of the truck was put into action. Strong jets of water from the thick hose began to douse the flames inside.

Bridie grabbed a towel from the veranda, wet it, and put it over her head. Calling for Danny, she forced her way into the smoke-filled kitchen and through to the dining room. She found him huddled in a corner of the front room which was almost burnt out, the last tongues of flame being extinguished with water from the fire truck hose. He was cowering, his clothes smouldering, his face and hands black. To her horror, she knew his hair was on fire. She could smell it.

'Here, bring the hose here!' she shouted. The grimy volunteers turned the hose on the shivering victim. He was sobbing, gasping for air, his teeth chattering. He kept trying to say what might have been 'Sorry', but it came out as a meaningless mumble.

'Phil – he's here, he's alive. We've got to get him to the hospital.'

The phone line was down. Almost everything inside the house had been destroyed, it was now a tangled mess of charred and sodden debris.

Some of the roof had fallen in. Among the smudged faces of the men crowding around, Phil recognised his nearest neighbour.

'I'll race home and ring the doctor and the hospital to let them know we're on our way.'

'Thanks, Bill. I'll see if I can find a sheet to put around him. I know – the shearers' quarters.' Phil was out and back very quickly. 'We'll put him on the back seat of the Chev. You sit with him, Bridie.'

Many willing hands helped to wrap the shaking young man in the sheet and carry him to the car as gently as they could. Bridie was already in the back seat.

'You'll be all right, Son, yuh gotta be,' she murmured shakily. He continued to moan, his voice sounded like that of a wounded animal.

As he drove off, Phil saw more men in trucks, mostly from the rural fire brigade, all wanting to help in whatever way they could. Time for gratitude later, saving his son's life was the priority now.

Dr Santorini met them at the hospital entrance. The staff carefully removed the stricken young man from the car and on to a trolley. He seemed barely conscious, though a few moans escaped his swollen and blistered lips. His face was almost unrecognisable – red and puffy, his hair charred.

'I'll give him some pain relief straight away,' said the doctor, hoping he could find a small area on Danny's body to insert the needle. He drew back the covering sheet and was horrified at what he saw. He found an unburnt area on Danny's thigh and injected the morphia.

Before long, Danny's rapid breathing slowed and his moans subsided.

'I can't let you into the operating theatre, Bridie. It has to be a sterile area, the risk of infection is great. You and Phillip go to the waiting room. The kitchen staff will get you a cup of tea.'

Numb with shock, the Taylors were escorted to the small side room.

'I can't believe it, Phil. Oh, Holy Mother of God – we need Father O'Malley. I just pray he'll pull through.'

Phil said nothing. He knew what must have happened. It was late summer, and no fires were lit at that time of the year. But the Taylors had always kept one set in the front room with paper, kindling and logs in place. With the first chill of autumn, the warming fire would be ready to light.

Danny must have moved the heavy firescreen and lit the paper. He was always fascinated by fire, eagerly watching the small flame grow towards the smaller branches which crackled and spat before becoming red coals on the side of the bigger logs at the back. One of these must have been unstable and rolled out on to the hearth. Danny would have grabbed a paper or magazine to try to put it out without realising he should have doused the flames with water. Everything near the fireplace was flammable: the frilled chintz covers on the armchairs, even the vase on the little wooden table had a dried arrangement at this time of year. And with the front and back doors open, the fire would be fanned by gusts of wind blowing through.

Phil reached over to his wife to take her hand and then realised she had sustained burns too. 'Oh Bridie – you'll have to get this seen to.'

News of the fire spread quickly, creating shock and horror, and then, 'What can we do to help?' Grace Shaw was one of the first to make contact with the Taylors at the hospital. Apart from expressing support, she made a practical suggestion.

'Where are you going to stay? You can't live out there. The house is burnt down.'

Phil and Bridie looked helplessly at each other. Phil spoke first.

'I can. I mean, I can kip in the shearers quarters. I'll need to be there to keep an eye on everything.'

'Bridie, why don't you stay with us?' suggested Grace. 'You'll be close to the hospital, it wouldn't be any trouble to us at all. I'll switch the kids' beds around.'

Bridie tried to murmur her thanks, but the figure of Dr Santorini appeared at the door, his theatre gown looking less pristine than before.

'It's taken us quite a long time to clear the burnt area, I'd say it's at least forty per cent of his body, mostly the front of his body and upper legs. I've inserted a breathing tube, and I managed to get an intravenous drip into one of his veins so he will be rehydrated.'

Phil and Bridie both spoke together.

'Will he survive?' came from Phil.

'Is he awake? Is he in pain?' from Bridie.

'No, Mrs Taylor, we're keeping him asleep and pain free. And, Phil, time alone will tell.'

'Can I see him please'? Bridie's voice was urgent.

'Of course you can. They've moved him into a special room. But I have to warn you, you will be shocked by his appearance. His burnt areas are covered with bandages. Also, I have to ask you to wash your hands and put on a hospital gown before you go into the room. We can't run the risk of infection.'

Phil hesitated. He gestured to Bridie that she should stay, but he needed to go out to the farm as soon as possible.

'I know she wants to be with Danny, Phil,' said Grace as Bridie followed the doctor down the passage. 'I'll go home and make things ready for her to stay, and you, too, when you want to.'

Back home, Grace saw a note in Jack's handwriting on the kitchen table. 'Gone out to Phil's place.' That's exactly what she would have expected.

Miranda was home first. 'Mum – someone said the Taylor's house has burnt down! How could that happen?'

'It's true, Mirrie. We think Danny lit the fire while his parents were in the top paddock feeding sheep. When they got back it was well alight, and Danny's in hospital with bad burns.'

'Oh Mum, that's awful. Poor Danny. Will he be all right?'

Grace paused. 'We can only hope he is. It will take a long time.' She changed the subject. 'Mirrie, are you okay in the sleep-out so Bridie can have your room for a while?'

'Course, Mum.'

Just then Brian burst in. 'Mum, is it all right if I ride my bike out to Taylors and do what I can to help.'

'It's quite a way, Brian. And it's still hot.'

'That's okay. I'll have a drink now, and take something with me.'

That prompted Grace to pack some biscuits, cheese and fruit, along with a thermos of tea into the spare backpack. She also found a stack of aluminium cups in case nothing could be salvaged from the house. 'There, you can offer them some refreshments. And tell Uncle Phil to come back here for tea.'

It was almost dark when Jack and Brian got back. Phil had put Brian's bike in the back of the ute, but wanted to call in at the hospital to see his son and wife before coming on to Speke Street.

'I told him it would be cold meat and salad, so he could take his time,' said Jack.

Grace was anxious to hear what Jack had found at the Lake Goldsmith property. He confirmed that the house had been almost totally gutted, and very little would be salvageable.

'Phil was very quiet. He made sure the dogs in the barn were let out for a run, fed and watered. There was no sign of the house cat, but that wasn't unexpected. Cats are like that. But, Grace, it would break your heart. The old house is just a shell with a few walls standing, but more than half of the roof is down. The police were there when I arrived. They have to investigate, of course. It could have been arson, but everyone knows how it happened. Lots of people from the surrounding district were there, offering to help in some way, like feeding the stock for the next few weeks, coming in to milk the house cow, that sort of thing.' He paused and went on with a smile. 'Your refreshments went down really well. We made sure Phil had something, I think he'd forgotten about needing to eat.'

The crisis was reported on the radio and in the local papers. Danny Taylor's condition was stated as 'serious' at first, and later changed to 'stabilised'. Bridie kept her vigil at her son's side, her own hands bandaged. Father O'Malley came every day with prayers and a blessing for them both, and had gently suggested that some of his parishioners said they would have liked to have offered her accommodation. She replied that it was kind of them, but the Shaws had been their friends for many years, and she was grateful for their hospitality.

In the days that followed, the Shaws learned something of Phil's possible future plans. 'I was just about to tell you, Jack, to get your opinion really, then this – this thing happened.'

At the dining table, they waited expectantly for Phil to continue. He looked across at his wife, who nodded. Following his gaze, Grace realised with a pang that Bridie looked like an old woman. She'd been spending almost all her day at the bedside of her intellectually disabled son, leaving only when his dressings were being changed. He was in and out of consciousness, but couldn't really communicate. It was continuing to be a 'wait and see' situation.

'You see, these chaps from Dalgety's came out to talk to me about, well, over a month ago, just after Joe and Declan left. They said they represented an overseas company that was keen to buy up pastoral land in our area. The price they offered was – well, you'd never make that sort of profit in a million years'

'They wanted to buy your farm?' Grace's voice was incredulous.

'Yep. They weren't interested in the house, it was the land they wanted. They had a good look at all the fencing we'd done, the dams, the bores, the shearing shed, other sheds – all of that, and the machinery, of course.'

'What did you decide?'

'We couldn't, at the time, Jack. It was a lot of money, hard to get one's head around. Enough to finance a retirement far beyond our dreams.' He paused. 'The thing is – most fathers with sons want to hand it all over to them when the time comes. But it's different with us. As you know ...'

Miranda interrupted brightly, 'You could go on a long holiday, spend the money travelling the world and ...'

'Shush!' said her father. 'This is a big decision for them to make, they don't need our input. How do you see it, Bridie?'

She didn't answer straight away. Care lines were etched on her face, and sadness tinged her voice as she spoke. 'Me main concern has always bin me children. Now one's overseas an' the other's,' she gulped, 'struggling to stay alive.'

Grace asked for the latest news on Danny.

'I'll try an' tell you what Dr Santorini said this mornin'. I asked him to be really, really honest, not that he isn't, so he sat me down an' just looked at me with a serious face. So I asked if I should get Father O'Malley in, an' he nodded. I guessed what was on his mind an' so I said straight out, "he ain't gonnna make it, is he?" An' he said that, in spite of everythin', some infection had got in – that's one problem. The other is his chest. So I asked what about it, an' he told me he might be developing pneumonia. He would have breathed in a lot of smoke at the time, an' just lyin' there as he is, his lungs don't expand properly. He said it's a common problem with burns cases.' She paused, looking around at the solemn expressions around the table. 'He's giving him antibiotics of course, but ...'

No-one said anything. It was such a blow. Hopes had been cautiously raised earlier, as Danny's condition seemed to have improved slightly. But Bridie couldn't deny there had been an unappealing smell about him in the last few days. From the waiting room, she could hear the nurses' bright voices saying kind things to him, like 'We're going to get you better, aren't we, Danny?' and, 'Just a little pull on this dressing, and we'll put a nice clean one on for you.' It was obvious the burns had become infected.

'I wish you would stay here too, Phil. We could put up the stretcher bed for you,' said Grace.

'Thanks, but no. I'm better out at the farm. Turns out it was a good idea we got that bungalow for the shearers when we did. It's basic, but at least I'm on the spot.' He thought for a minute. 'And I know someone will come out and get me if Danny gets worse.'

Brian assured him that he would be out there instantly if that happened.

'I wanted to stay all the time, but they said one of the night staff takes it in turns to sit with him, an' it'd be better for me to get some sleep.' Bridie's voice sounded tired. 'It's Friday tomorrow, just a week before Good Friday. Father O'Malley'll be busier then. He's bin so good to me.' Her voice faded. Grace led her firmly to the bedroom.

Father O'Malley was indeed conscientious, visiting the hospital as often as he could. Furthermore, he was Irish-born and always keen to hear any news of Joe and Declan. 'Oh, I miss home, to be sure, but the Good Lord sees a place for me here,' he'd say, and Bridie would answer, 'And I'm very glad He did, Father.'

Friday was cool and overcast. The usually good-natured face of the priest was solemn as he met Bridie on the steps outside the hospital.

'Bridie, I have given our beloved child Absolution. He is in the hands of Our Lord.'

Bridie gasped. 'You mean – he's dying?'

The priest nodded. 'He will soon be with Our Father in Heaven.'

One of the nurses, gloved and gowned, opened the door of the isolation room. 'I'm glad you're here, Mrs Taylor. You had better let his father know that Danny won't be with us for much longer. Dr Santorini had to go to an emergency at Buangor, and he asked me to make sure that you both knew, and Father O'Malley, too.'

Bridie's eyes took in the sadly familiar shape of her young son's body swathed in white. The intravenous drip was in place, and an oxygen mask assisted his breathing. A younger nurse stood up as they came in, a damp face cloth in her hand.

'We're trying to keep him comfortable, poor darling. His temperature's very high, I've been putting cool face cloths on his forehead.'

Bridie thanked her and said that she would sit with him and continue to sponge her son's face. Her fingers touched his skin – it was frighteningly hot. She choked back a sob.

'Please could you ring Mrs Shaw and ask her if she could go out to our place and bring my husband in. Tell her – tell her it's urgent.'

The nurse left quickly to make the call.

Bridie lowered herself into the chair at the head of the bed. Danny's breathing was almost imperceptible. She fingered the rosary beads she had placed around his bandaged right hand. 'Holy Mary, Mother of God,' she prayed in a whisper. Long minutes passed.

A nurse came in, tying her hospital gown behind her, and adjusted the flow of a new intravenous bottle. Its constant dripping had completely mesmerised Bridie. On the other side of the bed, the nurse busied herself under the covers, checking Danny's catheter bag.

'Much there?'

Sister Ferguson shook her head. 'Very little, Mrs Taylor. His kidneys – they aren't working properly anymore.' With an apologetic little smile she left the room.

Bridie lost track of time, it seemed to stand still. Then she heard a sound outside, and Phil came in, an anxious and questioning expression on his face. One of the nurses helped him with the gown. It crossed Bridie's mind that these precautions were now probably unnecessary. She looked down at her own gauze-covered hands. Her second-degree burns were healing, but still hurt. She had refused any pain relief. 'It's nothin' to what Danny's goin' through,' she'd said.

Phil looked at the body of his son, inert and helpless.

'Is he …?'

'He's not goin' to last much longer, Phil. Come here and sit with me, we've got to see him out together.' Her voice choked.

So it was, an hour or so later, as staff quietly looked in and then withdrew, that Father O'Malley reappeared at the door. '*Dominus vobiscum*', he intoned. All eyes were on Danny. He gave an involuntary gurgle, and shortly after, his breathing stopped. The priest dipped his thumb in the little vial of holy oil he carried and made the Sign of the Cross on the bandaged face.

From Bridie came a long-forgotten wail, the keening of bereavement from her childhood memory. On and on it went, the eerie sound of inconsolable loss.

Phil stood mutely. A tear coursed down his weather-beaten face, followed by another and another …

After the funeral came Easter and school holidays. Miranda remembered her mother had almost promised to take her on a trip to Melbourne. Was it a good idea to mention it? Probably not.

Bridie stayed on with the Shaws, a saddened version of her former self.

'Ya' know Grace, some of the ladies from the Church hinted that I should 'ave stayed with them, not you, seein' how you're Proddies.'

Grace was a little taken aback. 'If you want to go somewhere else,' she murmured.

'Nonsense. You've bin such a good friend to us, you and Jack. We feel at home here.' She paused before continuing. 'But we have to make a decision soon. The insurance would just about cover the cost of rebuilding. But …'

'It would be hard,' said Grace sympathetically. She settled more comfortably in her chair. 'Have you heard anything more from Joe?'

'Oh, yes. Remember I told you after we sent the first telegram about the fire and Danny he sent one back askin' if he should come home. Then we sent the one tellin' him Danny had died, an' not to do anythin'. There was no point in draggin' 'im back.' Grace nodded. 'Well, Phil rang 'im from the post office yesterdee, 'ad ter work out what time they'd be up. Got Mr O'Dwyer an' he put Joe on straight away.' She let out a small laugh, the first one for ages Grace realised. 'They kept sayin' "three minutes, are you extendin'?" An' Phil had to say, "Yes" – lots of times, in fact. But it was worth it.'

'How did he handle the news about Danny?'

'Ohh, he was really upset. His only brother. An' also worried about us. But on the good side – he said he was very happy there with the O'Dwyers, an' that Antoinette was a true Irish colleen.' They laughed together.

Just then, Brian and Miranda burst into the kitchen.

'What time's lunch?' demanded her son.

It was school holidays of course. Grace had almost forgotten about them. Bridie slipped into Miranda's room which she temporarily occupied and came back with a ten shilling note in her hand.

'Do you think you could get yerselves some fish 'n' chips with this?' she asked.

'Oh, yes!' was their excited response.

'You shouldn't, Bridie,' Grace tried to protest.

'Rubbish. You've bin feedin' Phil an' me for over two weeks now.

Anyway, I want ter bring you up to date. A cup o' tea would be nice, though.'

Over the next half hour, Grace heard about how the men from Dalgety's had been in touch again. This time Phil was more receptive to the proposal. They inspected the property again on the Tuesday after Easter, and came up with a new offer. The house would have to be bulldozed, of course.

'They made a better offer, which includes all the stock at valuation, to use their words. It's an awful lot of money, Grace. Sometimes I think I'm dreamin'. Well, we talked about it, talked and cried a bit, I can tell you. The thing is, we're too old, and let's face it, too tired, to start all over again.'

Grace let the reality of Bridie's words sink in before continuing. 'So what are you going to do?'

Bridie poured herself another cup of tea.

'Phil's seein' the bank manager this afternoon. We've already put the money from the insurance into Joe's account. It looks as though we'll get a big payout from the land sale which will have to be invested. Mind you, the tax people will be rubbin' their hands. Then ...,' she paused, took a deep breath and went on, 'then, I may as well tell you – Phil an' I want to go to Ireland.' Her words came out more quickly. 'I want to see Joe. I want to know he's all right. I know he is, but it's not the same with a letter or phone call. Phil's a bit nervous about it, though. He's got to get 'imself a passport, an' so 'ave I, I suppose. Mine'd be well out of date by now.'

Grace was stunned. It brought back memories for her, memories of people going away – her parents back in 1945, Mary, a few years later, and now Bridie and Phil. A little bubble of emotion welled up in her which she tried desperately to smother.

'What – what wonderful news, Bridie.' Impulsively, she moved over to embrace the older woman. 'It's sort of,' she searched for an appropriate word, 'liberating.' Bridie nodded slowly, a little smile on her homely face.

After her guest had excused herself to have a lie-down, Grace sat thinking. Jack would see the sense of selling the property, Miranda would be thrilled to find that they'd actually followed her earlier unsolicited advice. Brian? He was down-to-earth and would probably agree with his father.

But, for Grace, it would be the end of yet another chapter in her life. Memories came flooding back. That first visit out to the farm all those years ago, the first time she'd seen a rabbit skinned, Bridie's kindness to her before Brian was born when she'd yearned for her mother, and her warning words about Hilda that alerted her to avoid a tragedy to their baby, but at enormous cost to his grandfather. She could never, ever forgive Hilda for that. 'I 'ope she rots in Hell for what she did,' were Bridie's decisive words at the time. An' don't you be a hypocrite an' go to 'er funeral.'

Grace didn't, and Jack didn't pressure her into going to the bleak cremation in Ballarat four years ago now.

Look to the future, things change, life goes on, she told herself.

Chapter 7

High school was exciting for Miranda, most of the time anyway. Occasionally, she got into trouble with a few of her classmates for being just too good at answering questions. 'You're such a know-all' or 'smartypants' were common jibes, especially from the boys. The first form teachers soon learned to direct their questions to the more reluctant students and ignore Miranda's constantly raised hand.

Miss Prentice, who taught English, decided one morning late in term three to select four of the more able students for some extra creative work, given they had all completed the assignment set out on the blackboard.

'Joyce, Miranda, Marie and Josephine – you can go to the table at the back and, as a group, write an essay of about a page and a half about ...,' she thought for a minute, 'about how news is disseminated in our society. And yes, you can look up the word disseminated in the dictionary.'

'Gee, Mum,' said Miranda that afternoon, 'it was fun. We had to look up the word. We found out that it meant 'spread around' and then we had to think of the different ways we get to know things. So we decided to each take a topic – Josie took radio, Marie wanted to do newspapers, that left Joyce to do mail, and I chose word of mouth!'

'How did it turn out?'

'We had a double period to do it in, we needed it. We each had two paragraphs to write and then read to the class. Mine got the best response 'cos I talked about gossip and how sometimes it can be true, and sometimes distorted, depending who's telling it. The whole class clapped at the end and Miss Prentice said some really complimentary things.'

Grace smiled indulgently at her daughter, thirteen now, and fast becoming more mature. She had wondered about how the so-called Facts of Life discussion should be raised. As it turned out, the need didn't eventuate. Miranda had come home from school one day in her first term at high school and announced that they'd had a 'Girls Only' session about periods, and the body changes that would be happening. A few gentle questions from Grace confirmed that her daughter was appropriately informed, and fully confident about the whole issue. It had been somewhat of a relief for Grace, whose own introduction to the subject was less satisfactory. Jack had dealt with Brian's information needs a couple of years ago, aided by some literature from the Father and Son Movement.

The other discussion regarding Brian's future career had also taken place, with Jack finally accepting his son's decision to apply to join the Commercial Banking Company of Sydney, Beaufort branch, when he left school. Both parents agreed that with his flair for figures, he would have good prospects there. All being well, he would finish school at the age of sixteen and a half at the end of the year, and start at the bank in 1963. Jack had already engaged a young man in his twenties to work for him and learn the skills involved in becoming an undertaker.

'So what do you think, Mum?'

Grace realised she'd gone into a daydream and missed her daughter's conversation.

'Sorry, I lost concentration for a bit. What were you saying?'

'Mu-um, I said I'm thinking it might be good to be a journalist, but I quite like the idea of being a teacher, too. Except I don't know if I'd be patient enough. Some of the kids are just so dumb.'

Grace smiled to herself. So many possible careers had been thought of and forgotten about: from missionary work among the aborigines (influenced no doubt by an inspiring address given by a guest speaker at church some months ago), being a vet (after visiting a farm near

Burrumbeet) and treading the boards as an actress (after shining in the main role at her primary school break-up concert).

'You know I always wanted to be a teacher, but being sick and missing so much school, and then the war … it was impossible,' Grace said. Miranda gave her a hug to express her understanding before going off to do her homework.

Grace reflected on what might be seen as her own lost opportunity, but resolutely reminded herself that she wouldn't want to change anything now. She went down to the funeral parlour twice a week to do the accounts. She was also available, when necessary, to comfort grieving relatives. 'You're a natural at it,' Jack had said, years ago. Grace didn't consider herself an expert – all she really did was listen and offer comforting words. Somehow, these seemed to be appropriate, and people were grateful.

She was becoming increasingly aware that she didn't have the same stamina as in her earlier years. She needed to pace herself and take a rest during the afternoon. Well, she was forty, and no longer as slim as she used to be. Not fat really, but plumpish, and having swollen ankles seemed to accentuate it. Lillian was the one who'd really gained weight after having all her children. But being taller, it somehow seemed acceptable.

Never one for letter-writing, Lillian instead phoned her sister about once a month. Grace welcomed news of the family – Peter getting engaged was exciting. 'Nice local girl, not a redhead,' Lillian had said with a laugh. Hugh ('He's not Hughie anymore') was enjoying army life, while Russell wanted to stay on the farm. His twin sister Dawnie was planning to do a hairdressing course in Horsham next year. Wendy was at High School, and Lillian was not sure what sort of future work would suit her. Edna, her mother-in-law was still living with them, though, at seventy, was a bit slower these days.

The inevitable question came, 'And has Miranda decided what she wants to do?' It was not possible to give an answer. Miranda was doing so well in all subjects that it made choosing a career difficult.

Her rather tiresome habit of asking 'Why?' all the time was dealt with in the early years by the purchase of Arthur Mee's *Children's Encyclopedia*. 'Look it up,' became the parental response. Birthday presents were also an easy choice – books, every time. The only problem was the need to discreetly check whether it had been borrowed from the library and already enjoyed.

She's so like I was at that age, thought Grace.

Miranda was also pretty good at sport and music, though Jack had not agreed to have her learn to play the piano. 'They're expensive to buy, the good ones anyway, and learning piano was just a fad in my day – some people I know have unused pianos in their spare rooms.' Grace had been a bit upset at his attitude, but, fortunately, Miranda didn't take offence. She might learn something that would be more portable, like the recorder or violin or flute, which didn't require such a big investment.

Jack started to take more interest than usual in politics, in particular the situation where war could have broken out due to the Russians stockpiling nuclear weapons on Cuba in 1962. Then, a year later, the American president, John F Kennedy was assassinated. Along with the rest of the Australian population, the news stunned the Shaw household. No one could imagine Prime Minister Robert Menzies, being attacked in such a way.

But it was only two years later that Mr Menzies introduced the so-called birthday ballot to call up 20-year-olds for service in Vietnam.

'Thank God Brian's only nineteen,' said Grace with deep feeling.

'Yes, but it's not only that – the Yanks are sending loads of troops over. It's going to be another bloody war, and how can you tell who the enemy is?' Jack's concern was shared by many, and in the capital cities, protests were underway.

'You realise Hugh will probably be sent over there, now he's in the Regular Army,' Jack said as more information filtered through.

'I would have considered enlisting if our country was at risk,' said Brian at tea one night as news of the deaths of Australian soldiers at the Battle of Long Tan in August 1966 was revealed.

'No way,' muttered Jack. Seeing it all on television brought back unsettling memories. 'Anyway, you're in a secure job, you're up for promotion, why would you want to abandon that?

Brian was silent. He'd already told his parents that the Beaufort manager had recommended him for further training in Melbourne, especially as decimal currency had come in and he was already competent in the new system. So, in a month he'd be a twenty-year-old living independently in the Big Smoke until the course was finished.

Jack turned his attention to his teenage daughter.

'Well, is this going to be your last year at school? You're seventeen? I left school at fourteen.'

Grace interjected before Miranda could reply. 'Things were different then, Jack. Mirrie's doing Leaving this year, she'll have Matric next year ...'

'And then what?' Jack asked abruptly.

Miranda shrugged and turned away. She understood the implication of her father's remark. Getting a job, earning a living was important. He'd mentioned often enough that some of her former classmates were now behind counters or in offices, either in Beaufort or further afield in Ballarat. How could she admit that her form teacher, Miss Bassett, strict, old-maidish, but enthusiastic and inspiring to the few who actually listened in her classes, had told her she should go on to university. 'It would be *unthinkable* not to do so, Miranda.'

Mum understood. She was always proud of Miranda's excellent results. Not so Dad. He'd say, 'She doesn't get it from me, that's for sure' when people commented on her prize-winning at speech nights. The problem was, she still didn't know what she would study if she did go to university. The main thing at the moment was to finish high school. She certainly didn't want to leave early.

With Brian due to leave home, it occurred to Miranda that she might offer to help her father in the business, like her brother had. He nodded and said he'd think about it. That was something, anyway.

In the school holidays, the opportunity arose. It was Grace's idea, really. She had cast a critical eye around the funeral parlour and decided a freshen-up was needed, in fact well overdue.

'Mirrie – how would you like to be a painter?'

'Oh, Mum, I'm not that good at art, you know that.'

'Not that sort of painting – I mean, do you think you'd like to redecorate the reception room, it's looking a bit tatty. I haven't mentioned it to your father yet, I thought I'd ask you first.'

'Hey, Mum, that's a great idea. Can I pick the colours?'

Grace laughed. 'I'll run it by your dad, but I'm sure he'll agree.'

He did. It was a good bridge-building exercise, with Jack doing the high ladder work, leaving Miranda most of the walls and the window frames. The colour chosen was a pale apricot, much warmer than the pale blue of the past.

It was good to have Dad's approval for a change.

At least he can see I'm not completely useless, she thought.

Chapter 8

Everything changed in early 1967. Miranda was one of the few students doing Matriculation at Beaufort High School and had chosen a wide range of subjects: English, French, biology, chemistry and British history. Every two weeks she had to travel to Ballarat High School for the chemistry lab work. Being the only girl in the class didn't concern her unduly, though it was a bit of a spur to at least do as well as, and perhaps even better than, the boys. Some of the girls at Beaufort High were clearly envious. 'Are there any spunky guys there?' she was often asked. She would always shake her head, laughing. 'Nuh – no different from the boys here.' Though she was especially conscious of one of the six-formers from Buninyong until she found out that he had a girlfriend. *Oh, well.*

It was a shame that Miss Bassett had moved to another high school. There was some mystery about that. Miranda overheard a conversation between her parents on the subject. From what she could gather, Miss Bassett had been over-friendly with one of the senior girls in the year just past, resulting in a whisper campaign focussed on the unfamiliar word 'lesbian'. On reflection, Miranda had been aware of the teacher's piercing dark eyes fixing on her at times. Perhaps it was just as well she hadn't been the object of Miss Bassett's attention out of school hours.

Over the past six years she'd kept in touch with her friend, Annie, now Anne, mainly through birthday and Christmas cards, though once or twice they met up accidentally.

Miranda was surprised to get a phone call from her during the Easter break. It appeared that Anne had invited another boarder friend from school to stay with her. Helen lived on an isolated sheep station in far western New South Wales and would otherwise have to stay at the school during the holiday.

'It's a bit boring out here, Miranda,' Anne had explained. 'Could we come and visit you? Especially if Brian's home,' she added with a giggle.

'Sorry, Brian's not here. He's gone on a scout camp over Easter, he's a leader. And he's doing further training in Melbourne these days. But do come over after lunch. Bring your bikes, if you want to, and we could go for a ride.'

Shortly after two o'clock, the Saunders' state-of-the-art ute pulled up in Speke Street. Anne's father lifted two bicycles from the back.

'I've got to go to Ararat to pick up some stock supplement, I'll be back here about four-thirty, okay?' He got back in and raised a cloud of dust from the side of the road as he took off.

Miranda came out quickly. A hug for Anne and a handshake with Helen. The girls sized each other up. Annie looked much the same, a bit plumper perhaps, while Helen was definitely what Jack would describe as 'one of the greyhound breed', tall and lean, with short straight brown hair. She had a nice smile, not at all snooty as Anne seemed to be at times.

'Would you like to come inside and say hello to my mum? Then we can decide what we want to do.'

'I'd like that,' said Helen. Anne said nothing but followed them into the house. Miranda noted the slight look of disdain as Anne looked around. *I bet she's thinking how shabby it looks.*

Helen had a different response. 'Gee, it looks just like ours,' she exclaimed. 'We've got a central passage with rooms running off each side, too.'

Grace heard them and came out of the kitchen, drying her hands on a tea towel.

'Well, isn't this a lovely surprise? So nice to see you again, Anne. And this is your friend.' She turned to Helen who put out her hand to be shaken. 'Now, would you all like something to eat? I've made some jelly cakes and there's a nut slice too.'

'Thank you, Mrs Shaw, but no. My father's coming back in about two hours, so if we're going for a bike ride, we'd better get going straight away.'

The first destination was an obvious one – out to the high school next to the sports ground and the Beaufort lake. They had a trial ride up Speke Street and back with Anne quite wobbly as she strove to control the bike.

'I'm really out of touch,' she said, 'I just need to get the hang of it again.'

Miranda looked across at the visitor. 'You seem to be okay, Helen – do you ride a lot at home?'

Helen laughed. 'It's more horseback riding, though the bike's handy to go and get the mail.' Noting their puzzled expressions, she continued, 'Our house is over a mile off the main road, though we don't get mail every day, of course.'

Eventually they set off, encountering very little traffic on the way. After an hour of cycling around, Miranda glanced at her watch. 'We'd better turn back now and decide where else we could go.'

Grace had their afternoon tea all set out. With delight, the girls enjoyed the little red jelly cakes and glasses of lemonade. 'Well what do you think of Beaufort so far, Helen?' she asked.

'It's really nice, Mrs Shaw. The lake is so pretty. Especially with the ducks.'

'Lake Wendouree's much more impressive,' Anne said, her tone dismissive.

'We're a much smaller town, Anne. Maybe Ballarat needs a bigger lake,' Grace's response was a mild reproof.

'Okay, let's put our heads together. Are you up for another half hour's ride?'

Helen nodded in agreement. Miranda turned to Anne. 'Do you want to, or are you a bit tired?'

'I'm all right. As long as it isn't too far.'

'How about we go down to the station, then we could go up Camp Hill behind it. It's not a great road, but it would be downhill all the way back. We don't really need to get off and look around like we did at the lake.' It would be a short, comfortable ride, one she'd done often.

All went well as they crossed the railway line and turned left, winding their way up the gentle incline around the back of the hill. Miranda was in the lead when she heard the sound of a truck changing gear and climbing behind them.

She turned and yelled to the other two, 'Off the road, truck coming.'

As it passed, she saw it was loaded with logs. The driver swerved to avoid a pothole and one of the logs rolled off. Right into Anne's path. Her front wheel made contact, buckled, and Anne came crashing off. Her head hit the ground with a sickening thud. Her scream sent chills up Miranda's spine.

Helen rushed up too. 'Are you all right, Anne? Can you get up?'

Anne's eyes were wide and terror-stricken. 'I – I can't. I can't move.'

Miranda knelt beside her friend's twisted body. 'Don't try to move, Anne. I'm going to get the doctor. Just tell me – are you in pain?' She put her hand gently on Anne's right arm and the leg lying in a distorted position.

'No. No – I can't feel anything.' There was panic in her voice.

Miranda straightened and looked into Helen's eyes. 'You stay here,' she said firmly. 'Don't try to move Anne in case there are broken bones. I'll be as quick as I can. Try and stay calm, both of you.'

Helen nodded, and kneeling beside her school-friend, gently stroked her hair.

Miranda got on her bike and set off quickly towards the hospital. To her relief, she saw Dr Santorini opening the door of his car parked outside.

'Doctor Santorini,' she yelled, pedalling fast to reach him.

He quickly grasped the gravity of the situation. 'I'll call for an ambulance and then go straight up there.'

'Doctor, Anne's father is due back any minute. Should I wait for him at home, or what?'

The doctor's concerned face softened as he recognised Miranda's desperation.

'You go home and tell him where we are. And let Constable Enright know.' He was already at the hospital door.

Torn between her need to be with her friend and the awful responsibility she faced, Miranda headed home on her bike. *Mum will know what to do.*

Bill Saunders' late-model ute was already slowing to a halt outside the house as she pedalled up Speke Street.

'Good timing, eh?' Bill called out.

Miranda reached the gate and, almost breathless, managed to say, 'I've just got to go inside.' As she opened the front door she yelled, 'Mum – Mum.'

Grace, startled by the frantic state of her daughter, said, 'What on earth's the matter?'

'I've – I've got to ring the police an', an' Mr Saunders is outside.'

Puzzled, Grace reached for the Teledex and read out the number to dial.

'Is Constable Enright there? Can you give him an urgent message to come to the road at the back of Camp Hill? There's been an accident.' She hung up the phone, shaking.

'Miranda – what's happened? Tell me.'

'Anne was knocked off her bike when a log came off a truck and – and she's injured. Dr Santorini's gone up there. Oh Mum, it's awful. And Mr Saunders is outside.'

Grace thought fast. 'I'll ring your father, tell him what's happened and get him to call Anne's mother.'

The call resulted in direct action. 'He's going to drive out and bring her in. We'll get a lift with Mr Saunders.'

It was incredible how everything had changed in a matter of a few seconds. What had been a leisurely Sunday afternoon bike ride had become a disaster.

When they reached the scene, the ambulance was already there. Anne was lying in the same twisted position. The two ambulance officers and the doctor were discussing the safest way of placing her in the vehicle.

Seeing Bill Saunders running towards his stricken daughter, Dr Santorini stepped forward to say that he must not move her in any way. Miranda and Grace also came closer. Miranda saw Helen being questioned by Constable Enright. He spotted Miranda and beckoned her over as well, but she wanted to see Anne first.

She asked one of the ambulance offices if she could speak to her.

'That's all right, Miss, only don't move her at all.'

There were sandbags on each side of Anne's head, immobilising it. Miranda knelt, and choking back a sob, said, 'Anne – I'm so sorry, so sorry this has happened.'

She had to lean close to hear the husky voice. 'I'm – scared.'

Miranda stood up and was confronted by a fierce glare from Anne's father.

'You have to take some responsibility for this,' he hissed.

Both Dr Santorini and Constable Enright overheard him. The doctor spoke up. 'It was an accident, Bill. Just terribly bad luck. You can't blame Miranda. We don't know whose truck it was. Helen saw it all, she's put us in the picture.'

He returned to supervise Anne's transfer to the stretcher, ensuring there was minimal movement involved. Everyone was silent as the delicate manoeuvre was carried out. Anne's face had a stricken, ghostly expression. She gasped as the lift took place, and in a little girl's voice said, 'I want my Mummy.'

'Shit!' said Bill Saunders. 'We have to tell Evelyn.'

Grace calmed him as she explained that Jack was going to drive out and bring her in. 'They should be here any minute,' she added.

The decision was made between Dr Santorini and the ambulance officers to bypass Ballarat and go straight to the Austin Hospital in Melbourne. The doctor spoke to Anne's father explaining that the Austin was the centre for spinal injury treatment in Victoria. Full realisation hit him.

'You mean – she might be paralysed? Never walk again?' His voice choked with disbelief. Miranda felt desperately sorry for him. Impulsively, she reached out to touch his arm. He shrank back in anger. 'Don't you touch me, you – you,' He struggled for words. 'It's all your fault.'

'Steady on, Bill.' The doctor's voice was firm. 'It was an accident, I repeat, an accident. Nobody's fault. You must not blame Miranda.' He paused, listening. 'There's a car coming, it might be your wife.'

It was. Jack drew to a halt, and the matronly figure of Evelyn Saunders emerged from the passenger seat of the car. She rushed to the open door of the ambulance and took in the sight of her daughter lying with sandbags on each side of her head.

'Mummy – Mummy, stay with me.' Anne's voice was a husky whisper.

The practical country woman overcame her shock to reassure her daughter, 'Of course I will.' Turning to the nearest ambulance officer, she asked, 'Is that all right?'

The officer nodded agreement, saying he would be there too. Dr Santorini took a small white pill from his bag and gave it to Anne with a mouthful of water from an aluminium cup with a spout, provided by one of the ambulance officers.

'I'll put in the notes that I've given her some phenobarbitone which will help keep her calm.'

Bill and Evelyn Saunders had a brief conversation and decided that Evelyn would accompany Anne in the ambulance and Bill would go back to the farm to stay by the phone. He would pick up their thirteen-year-old son Charles from a neighbouring property on the way.

Miranda became aware of Helen in the background looking very worried. Just then Evelyn emerged from the ambulance to go over to her young house guest, comforting arms went round the tall teenager. They both looked over at Miranda.

'When your dad came out to pick me up, I realised it was serious, and I could be away,' she gulped, 'for some time. All Helen's things are in your Dad's car, Miranda. It seemed the best thing to do.' Another hug and she was back in the ambulance which was now ready to move off.

Miranda would never forget the slow progress of the emergency vehicle as, under Constable Enright's guidance, it turned and left, hazard lights blinking. To her dismay, she realised it looked like a funeral procession. She firmly dismissed the image and, turning around, noticed that the policeman wanted to talk to her.

Constable Enright's voice was gentle. 'I just want to know if you could identify the truck – colour, make, number plate?' The last was unrealistically hopeful. No, it was a blur, grey, she thought, nothing else. In her mind's eye, she saw the log coming off the top of the load, falling in slow motion – then the horrific consequence.

'Well, let me know if you remember anything else,' he said. 'I'll take the bike she was riding down to the station. And the log, too, I reckon.'

Miranda went over to the bike that Helen had been riding now lying on the side of the road. 'It could just as easily have been me.' Helen said.

'Or me,' Miranda agreed. 'Look, let's walk back to my place with the bike. We need to get away from here, and the walk will do us good.'

Along the way, Miranda asked a few questions about Anne, and her friendship with Helen, and learned that her old school friend was 'middling popular', more interested in the boys at Ballarat College than in her schoolwork. As Miranda had done, she'd had to tutor Anne in some subjects. Helen herself had her heart set on becoming a physiotherapist.

'Anne's not my best friend, but she did offer to have me stay over Easter, which was real nice of her. There's about five girls from overseas or interstate staying in the boarding house. I could have stayed too, but …' Her voice trailed off.

Miranda smiled. 'I'd have done the same thing and taken a break from school.'

The evening meal was solemn. In spite of hoping and praying that Anne would be able to recover completely, the harsh reality was that it was unlikely.

'No-one will know for sure until they do the X-rays. It might be just swelling that would settle with rest and being immobilised. What do you think, Dad?'

Jack thought for a minute. 'All I can say is – we'll just have to wait and see.' He paused. 'I have seen and heard of people who suffer a spinal injury that can't be reversed, but who live a good life with their limitations.'

'A wheelchair? Having to be cared for all the time? No independence?' interjected Miranda.

'She'd hate that,' said Helen.

Grace and Jack looked at each other. The conversation was becoming morbid. The older woman took the initiative. 'Come, Helen, I'll show you your room for the next few days. Brian's away, so I've put you in his room. If you like you can call your family to tell them where you are.'

Later that evening Helen rang her parents. When she returned to the sitting room, it was obvious she had been crying. Both Grace and Miranda went to embrace her.

Jack had a practical suggestion.

'Although we are not really drinkers, I think warm milk with a dash of brandy, would help, just this once. We all need a good night's sleep.'

Who could argue with that?

For Miranda, going back to school was difficult. She kept a low profile, avoiding contact with almost everybody. Then there was the question of Helen who had an extra few days' holiday. After another phone call to her parents, she decided to go back to Clarendon. She asked Jack if he could take her there.

'Not a problem, Helen. Would tomorrow morning be all right?'

Miranda asked if she could go along as well and miss school for the day. Grace had some paperwork to attend to at the funeral parlour, so she didn't intend to make the trip. She smiled at her daughter.

'You just want to see what the boarding school's like, don't you, Miss Curiosity.'

Well, that was true enough. Also, although it would be a quick trip to drop Helen off and return home, she would have the rare opportunity of sitting in the front seat of the car, at least after Helen had been dropped off.

The trip to Ballarat next morning was uneventful. Jack knew the way to Webster Street and before long it was time to say goodbye to Helen who had become a friend through sharing a horrible circumstance.

Miranda was surprised at the shabby appearance of the old building that was the boarding school. Nestled among some tall trees and leafy shrubs, it did not look particularly posh, as she had imagined it. Quite ordinary, she decided. There was a dark board with gold printing which confirmed the identity of the building, but not much else.

'It doesn't look very modern,' she remarked to Helen as the three of them made their way up the steps to the front door.

'Oh, it's really old. But comfortable and homely. Look, thank you for letting me stay with you. We, we'll keep in touch, especially because of Anne.' Then a quick hug before Jack and Miranda left for home.

It was a silent trip back to Beaufort, except for one question Miranda wanted to ask her father.

'Dad – Mr Saunders said it was my fault. Do you think he was right?'

Jack took his time before framing an answer.

'When something bad happens, it's natural to try to find someone to blame. That's human nature. I hear it all the time in my work. And the answer is – no, in no way was it your fault, Miranda.'

Thanks, Dad, was her silent response.

By the time they got back to Beaufort, Grace was home and busying herself in the kitchen.

'Everything go all right?' she asked, pausing in her task of peeling potatoes. Seeing them nod, she continued, 'I rang Bill Saunders and I've invited him and young Charlie over to tea tonight. Is that okay with you?'

Jack said, 'Of course.'

Grace noticed a flicker of trepidation cloud Miranda's face. 'It'll be all right, Mirrie. He's got a lot of worry on his shoulders, it'll take a bit of getting used to.'

It was almost dark when Bill Saunders and Charlie arrived. The tantalising aroma of roast meat greeted them as they were welcomed into the Shaw house. Jack shook hands with the burly farmer and his shy son.

'Any news, Bill?' he asked.

'No, not really. Evelyn's down there with her, stays in the ward as long as she's allowed to. She rings me every night about half past eight.'

Grace heard this from the kitchen and called out, 'I'll have the meal ready in no time, Bill. You won't want to be late home.'

Charlie was a shy boy. *Poor kid*, thought Miranda. She turned to her mother and said, 'What if I show Charlie the footy posters in Brian's room?'

'Good idea. I'm sure Brian wouldn't mind.'

Before long they were called to the table. This time Charlie had a smile on his face. 'He's got some great stuff, Dad.'

When they were all seated, Grace had an inspiration. 'Before we start – we don't always say grace before meals, but I'd like to tonight. Does anyone mind?'

Charlie, sitting next to Miranda, whispered, 'What's grace?'

'It's thanking God for our food, and perhaps a bit more,' she replied.

'Oh,' said the boy, still mystified.

Encouraged by the nodding of heads around the table, Grace began.

'Heavenly Father, we thank you for the food before us and the welcome company of friends. We ask your blessing on Evelyn, Bill and Charles, and especially, Lord, on Anne. We pray for her healing and recovery. We ask this in Christ's name. Amen'

There was a noticeable sniff from Bill Saunders as he fumbled in his pocket for a handkerchief. *He's close to tears*, Miranda realised, *and embarrassed by it.*

Meanwhile, Charlie was tucking in. 'This is yum!' he said, his mouth half full.

'I suppose it's a bit hard on you and your dad with your mum away, and Anne so sick,' Grace spoke kindly to the young boy.

'I just want her to get better. An' I won't ever tease her again.'

Everybody smiled.

Miranda had been quiet during the meal, but plucked up enough courage to ask, 'Mr Saunders, do you think it would be all right if I visited Anne?'

Bill was caught off guard by the question and paused before answering. 'I don't know. I'll see what Evelyn thinks when she rings tonight.'

'Thank you,' said Miranda quietly. She left it at that.

At the front door as they were leaving, Bill Saunders leaned across to Grace who was holding the door open. 'Do you really think that – that praying helps?' he said in a low voice.

'It's always helped me,' was Grace's response.

Two days passed without any further news, then a phone call came during the day from Evelyn Saunders. Grace took the call. She heard that there was no change in Anne's condition and that she'd said she would like Miranda to visit. Evelyn asked to speak with Miranda if she was home.

'Yes?' Miranda said breathlessly. 'How is she, Mrs Saunders?'

'Much the same, there's nothing new to report I'm afraid. I wanted to speak to you, Miranda, because I'm coming home for a few days, so I won't be there if you come down to see her. I wanted to explain things to you if you plan the visit soon. She's in a ward of people who all have spinal injuries, some of them involving the neck, like Anne. The thing is, she can't move and there are these big tongs clamped each side of her head with a weight attached to stop any movement. They've got a mirror attached to the top of the bed, angled so that she can see you. Are you with me?'

'Yes, I think so. Is there anything else I should know?'

'Only that all the patients have turning teams to lift and change their position every couple of hours. They ask you to leave the ward for that, and some other procedures they do.'

'Thank you for telling me, I appreciate it.'

'That's all right, Miranda. I'm going to take Bill and Charlie down with me when I go back next week. The farm will have to do without them for a few days.'

Grace offered to make the journey to Melbourne as well, but Miranda was resolute 'It's something I have to do on my own, Mum.'

Several people gave advice on how to get there. Hearing the instructions reminded Grace of her first anxious visit to Jack in the

Repatriation Hospital all those years ago. She realised that the Austin was not far from the Repat.

It's amazing how things go in circles ...

Chapter 9

Getting off the train at Heidelberg Station, Miranda looked up to her left to the hospital buildings that occupied a steeply sloping site. Signposts indicated the Acute Spinal Unit, Ward 7. Nervously she made her way up the steep path, glad that she'd thought to wear flat-soled shoes. *Trepidation, that's what I'm feeling, trepidation*, she thought, as the main entrance came into view.

A nurse in a grey, fine-striped uniform and a stiff white apron directed her into the ward and to a bay dominated by several hospital beds. She noticed a chart attached to the bottom rail of each bed, and the subtle smell of antiseptic teased her nostrils.

'Here she is,' said the nurse moving to her left. Then to the patient lying inert, 'You've got a visitor, Anne.'

Miranda would never forget the first sight of her friend's motionless body, her head secured by what looked like large metal claws, her hair clipped close to her scalp.

'Oh Anne, Anne. How are you?' Even as the words came out, Miranda thought she should have rejected them. But what to say?

She looked into the angled mirror to see her friend's face looking weary. Her voice, when she recognised Miranda, was sad.

'Oh, it's you.' She paused. 'How am I? You want to know? Shithouse.'

'What have they told you?'

'All I know is – my neck is broken, and it hasn't healed yet. I have to have this weight on my head to keep it stable.' The words came out with an effort.

Miranda, close to tears, realised it was pointless to hold Anne's hand. She wouldn't feel it. 'Is there anything you want to talk about? Do you want to ask me anything?' she asked.

A flicker of interest changed Anne's expression. She almost smiled.

'I do want to ask you something, and I want you to be truthful – will you?'

'Of course. What is it?'

'Have you, you know, done it yet?'

'Done what?' Miranda replied.

'You know – with a boy.'

Miranda considered how to frame her reply. In some ways, it was a pity she didn't have any juicy details to pass on. At the same time it seemed to her such a *trivial* question considering the gravity of her friend's situation. She looked up into the suspended mirror to meet Anne's questioning eyes.

'No, I haven't done "it" as you put it, Anne. But I have had some pretty exciting kisses which made me, well, wonder ...'

'Anyone I know?'

'No, one of the boys at Ballarat High, actually.' She decided against elaborating on the incident. To admit that she'd heard later that he'd done it for a dare was, to say the least, disappointing. Well, what about you?'

'Oh, I nearly did, it got close.' Anne's voice had a new animation as she recounted her experience. 'We have these end-of-term dances with the Ballarat College boys, and this boy I fancied – Geoffrey was his name– had a dance with me, held me really tight an', an' I could feel him hard down there. You know what I mean?' Miranda nodded. 'He said let's go outside, an' we did. But then a teacher came out and saw us an' said to get back inside, you two, so we had to.'

'Well, you've got that memory ...' Miranda said quietly.

Anne's voice changed. 'That's all I've got. That's probably all I'll ever have.' She sounded bitter, and a little agitated. A nurse came over to the bed and asked if she was all right, glancing at Miranda as she did so. Reassured by Anne's response, she moved away but looked in their direction from time to time.

'You don't know that for sure, Anne. You've got to keep hopeful. We're praying for you, you know?'

Anne sniffed. She suddenly looked tired.

'Would you like me to go now? I don't want to wear out my welcome,' said Miranda with an attempt at humour.

'No, stay a bit longer. The turning team will be here soon, and you'll have to go then.'

There was a period of silence, then Miranda asked about the doctors and nursing staff. She was told that they were mostly pretty good, and often tried to keep her spirits up.

'The other day I had a visitor from Ward 17 – that's the rehab ward. It was a guy in his twenties, I suppose. He was in a wheelchair, sitting up very stiff, a quad. Told me he broke his neck diving into the Murray, hit a submerged log. Funny, a log caused my problem too.' She paused. 'He tried to cheer me up, said it wasn't the end of the world, though he thought it was at first.'

'It must have helped a bit to talk to someone who's been through what you're going through …'

'Yes, and no. I tell you what, I get so jealous when I see the others who are paras – they're the ones who have the use of their arms. They can wheel themselves around, lift themselves into chairs and all that. It isn't fair.'

'No,' said Miranda quietly, 'it isn't fair.' She looked around and noticed an array of cards on a bedside locker. 'You've had a few cards, I see. Did you get mine?'

'Yes, thanks. And a nice one from Helen. Sorry I can't reply,' she said ruefully. 'I think Mum gets more of a kick from them than I do.'

'Are you looking forward to seeing your dad and brother?' Anne sighed, 'I suppose so.' Another silence. Miranda searched her mind for another topic of conversation when she noticed the doors swing open and four white-clad solidly built orderlies stride into the ward. 'Is that the turning team?' she asked.

'Yep. You'd better go now. Thanks for coming.'

Miranda felt herself choking. 'I'll – I'll come again,' she promised.

Outside, Miranda felt shaky. Luckily there was a seat strategically placed near the entrance to the ward, probably for the comfort of visitors after the steep walk from the street level. Trying to control her emotions she looked around and watched several groups of nurses walking in different directions along the covered walkways. *Perhaps it's a change of shift*, she thought.

Her last words to Anne were, 'I'll come again.' But – how? It wouldn't be easy. Catching the train from Beaufort, even once a week, for only an hour or so wouldn't amount to much actual time spent with her. A possible solution, an inspiration, really, came to mind. It made her gasp.

What if – oh, God, it could be an answer. I should find out while I'm here – see if it's possible. The idea came to her as she let out an incredibly deep breath. This could be life changing. She looked at her watch. Yes, time was on her side.

Retracing her steps downhill, she stopped at the next signpost, and instead of proceeding to the exit, turned left in the direction of the School of Nursing.

Two hours later, energised and excited, she quickly made her way through the pedestrian underpass to the platform opposite the one where she had alighted earlier. She didn't have to wait long for the city-bound train, and before long she was back at Spencer Street Station to catch the train home.

The big question mind was – *what will Mum and Dad say?*

It was dark by the time Miranda arrived home. All the way on the train, she'd rehearsed how she could explain her decision to her parents. Grace opened the front door, having heard the opening and closing of the gate. Her face had a concerned expression as she hugged her daughter.

'Was it awful, darling? Did you manage all right?' Grace fully expected a downcast, even teary response. Instead, there was a sense of excitement and a wide smile. 'Well, come in and tell me all about it.' Still Miranda hadn't spoken. 'Are you hungry?'

'I am a bit. Is Dad home?'

Jack was sitting in the armchair by the fire reading the paper. He looked up. Miranda's intense expression prompted him to fold the paper and direct his attention to her.

'Well, how was Anne? You look as though you've got good news – is she improving?'

'Sit down, Mum. Yes, I have got some news. Anne, first. Yes, I saw her and spent over two hours with her. There isn't anything new to report I'm afraid,' she looked at her parents and continued. 'I have made a very important career choice today. I want to do nurse training at the Austin Hospital. It's something I feel I have to do.'

Miranda heard a sharp intake of air, her mother's gasp. She became aware of her father shifting in his seat. It seemed an eternity before he spoke.

'I would have thought you would have discussed it with us first.'

'Dad, while I was there, I took the opportunity to find out what's involved. I could do it – they've had a withdrawal from the next PTS, that's the preliminary training school. It's in May. All I have to do is have a medical and a copy of last year's school results and three references – I was thinking of the minister for one and ...'

Miranda's speech had become faster and faster with words pouring out, until Grace said, 'Stop!' sharply.

Jack took over. 'Miranda, you're way ahead of us, just slow down.'

'Sorry, Dad.' She pulled out a chair and opened her carry bag, spreading some papers on the table. There was an information sheet about the hospital and several forms which needed to be filled out.

Grace shook her head and deliberately moved the papers to the side of the table.

'First of all, you need to eat. I've saved some tea for you. So, calm down, Mirrie. We'll talk after you've finished.'

To her surprise, Miranda realised she was ravenous. She enthusiastically dispatched the shepherd's pie with tomato sauce and gratefully accepted a second helping. 'I didn't actually have any lunch,' she explained.

A cup of tea all round, and it was time to continue the discussion. Jack cleared his throat, Grace and Miranda looked at him expectantly.

'Well, you know my position. I believe in doing something useful in life, and nursing certainly comes into that category. The thing is – why would you need to go to Melbourne to train when there's the Base Hospital much closer?'

Before Miranda could reply, Grace spoke up.

'What I'm thinking, dear, is that you may be doing this for the wrong reasons.' Miranda bristled, but Grace continued. 'I don't want this to sound cruel, but it might be that you're motivated by a sense of guilt. About Anne, I mean.'

Miranda's heart sank. Trust Mum to come up with this question. The problem was she didn't know. The principal nurse tutor had gently suggested this to her as well, although she didn't know the details of the accident, only that Anne Saunders was a school friend of Miranda's. 'You wouldn't be spending all your time in the Spinal Unit,' she'd said with a little smile.

'No, Mum, it's not that. I don't feel guilty, I didn't cause the accident. But it was being there, seeing how important nurses are in the running of the hospital, it, well, it opened my eyes. I wasn't sure what I'd finish up doing as a career, but now I know. I'm really sure it's the right choice for me.'

There was no problem with the medical certificate, though Dr Santorini was a little uncertain at first. 'I've always heard such glowing reports about your schoolwork, Miranda. I had the impression you would be looking at some tertiary course, perhaps even ...' He stopped himself, but Miranda was certain he was going to say 'medicine'. 'Well, you've decided on nursing, and I am sure you will be a very good candidate. Now let's get on with this assessment. What do they want to know?'

The reference from the minister, Nigel Langthorne, was readily forthcoming. He stated that he had known Miranda Mary Shaw all her life and that she came from a highly respected family. He attested to her character and suitability to undertake nurse training and wished her well.

'I almost feel like declining if it would help make you change your mind,' said Tom Appleton, the school principal, when she approached him with her decision and asked for a written reference. 'Is it possible you might at least finish your matric first? Think about it, that qualification opens many doors if you decide to change direction in the future.'

'I'm sorry, Mr Appleton. I have thought about it. But, for me, the time is now, and I know I'm doing the right thing.' She paused, 'I want to thank you and everybody here. I'll – I'll miss you.'

Initially, the only really positive response came from Anne's parents. Evelyn Saunders, back at the farm, phoned the Shaws to ask how Miranda's visit had gone. Grace took the call, and in the course of the conversation, told her of Miranda's plan to join the staff at the Austin Hospital as a student nurse. Evelyn had gasped and became a little tearful. 'Oh, how wonderful of her! Those nurses are absolute angels. You must be very proud.'

Grace had tried to look at the situation from the Saunders' point of view and managed to say 'Yes, we are proud of her. And thank you for reminding us.'

Miranda had another ally in her brother. Brian said rather cryptically that he didn't want her to end up with better school results than he got, so he was all in favour of her leaving early. 'Seriously though, Sis, I'm glad you've decided, and if I get transferred to Melbourne for good, I'll come and see you occasionally.'

The mail brought confirmation of Miranda's acceptance as a student nurse to begin training in the second week of May at the Austin Hospital, Heidelberg. It stated that there was a probationary period of three months, she would be accommodated in the Lesley Jenner Nurses' Home and paid a fortnightly salary.

'Gee, that's not much,' Brian commented when he saw the amount offered.

'It goes up every year, and I'll be paid much more when I graduate as a nursing sister.'

'She's not doing it for the money, Brian.' Their mother's comment sealed the discussion.

With little over three weeks before the beginning of her nursing training, Miranda found the preparations for leaving home more than a little stressful. *What do I need to take with me, what can I pick up later when I come back for a visit,* she asked herself.

In the middle of it all was her eighteenth birthday.

'Could we all go to see *Doctor Zhivago* – it's on at the Regent in Ballarat?' Miranda suggested, 'And perhaps go to a cafe afterwards? I'd like to invite Helen Osborne, if that's all right, and one or two others from school.'

She looked at her mother for a response, but none was forthcoming. Grace looked wistful. 'What's the matter, Mum?'

'Oh, sorry, I was just remembering. Many years ago now, when it was my birthday, and I was so unhappy and worried because your father was away at war and I hadn't heard anything for months and ...' she paused and shook the memory off. 'My mum said I had to pull myself together and think of others. We ended up going to see *How Green was my Valley* which was a really good film. Yes, I think what you suggest would be great.'

Chapter 10

It was a time of transition for Miranda. Turning eighteen made her feel more like an adult. Leaving school, even though the timing wasn't ideal, she acknowledged, was also a milestone towards independence. But the most exciting aspect was the prospect of learning and practical training in her chosen profession.

The more she looked at the syllabus, the more it sparked her interest. Experience would be gained in medical, surgical, children's, theatre, emergency and outpatients as well as specialist units like spinal, TB, psychiatry, and infectious diseases There was a long list of topics relating to nursing training, including laying out of the dead. Miranda smiled at reading that last item – at least she would be in familiar territory there, having helped out several times in the funeral parlour.

Also at the forefront of her consciousness was the plight of her school friend. The weekly phone calls from Evelyn Saunders to the Shaws told of very little change in Anne's condition. 'We just have to be patient,' she'd said in the last call. 'It's so hard. But it will be lovely to see Miranda whenever she's able to visit the ward.'

Now, at least, people stopped offering their unsolicited advice about her career. She had firmly assured dissenters that her mind was made up, and she was eagerly looking forward to doing the training. The prospect of being a sister and wearing the starched white veil at the end of it was tantalising. 'The world will be your oyster,' someone had said. Yes, it was a profession always in demand.

The last words Miranda heard from her mother as she said goodbye on Beaufort station were, 'Don't forget you're coming back in three weeks.' Hauling her suitcase up the step of the carriage she'd smiled in agreement, 'I wouldn't miss Brian's twenty-first for quids!'

The first letter from Grace updated her on the preparations for the party. It was being held at the football club pavilion, with a local four-piece band providing the music and the CWA ladies in charge of the catering. Jack had agreed to be MC. Nearly fifty invitations had been sent out so far. Grace finished by asking Miranda if there was anyone to be included on her behalf.

Now, three weeks later, she was making the return journey. In a way, the timing was good, she thought. *The focus will be on someone else, not me.* Though she knew that people would ask how her training was going, and some would probably ask about Anne.

As the train laboriously made its way up the Rowsley Fault, Miranda tried to summarise her first three weeks as a student nurse. There was not a lot to tell. The anatomy and physiology lessons started with the human skeleton. The topic was familiar to Miranda, her interest and curiosity had led her to borrow some books from the Beaufort library when she was in the second form. She got full marks in the tests on that subject, and also in both the respiratory and gastrointestinal systems. There were detailed instructions on the practical side of nursing, which included a lot of cleaning, and, of course, bandaging. What about all the new words she had to learn! *It will all fall into place in time,* she told herself.

Brian met her at the door. 'G'day, Sis. Saved any lives yet?'

Miranda's smile was as much an acknowledgement of his greeting as a pleasing realisation that her brother was growing into a very good-looking young man.

'Where's Mum and Dad?'

'Dad's down at the parlour, some old bloke snuffed it yesterday. Mum's getting gum leaves to decorate the clubrooms, not many flowers around, she said.'

Miranda went to her old room to unpack. It was a weird feeling to be back, all those memories of childhood. *Funny, I've only been away three weeks, and I'm seeing it all differently*, she thought.

'Mum's back!' yelled Brian.

How reassuring it was to feel the familiar arms around her, and a kiss on the cheek. Grace said, 'It's lovely to see you, Mirrie. I'll just get lunch ready, and then you can tell us all about it.'

No one expected rain, but shortly after seven o'clock, down it came, making the parking of cars a scramble of headlights and umbrellas. The catering ladies had arrived early and were busy organising the food, while behind the bar, Mitch Simmons was checking supplies and glasses in preparation for the demand.

Miranda wondered if she would know everyone who was coming. Probably not. Some of the football team and Brian's bank staff colleagues would be new to her. She had not put forward any names herself, saying it was his special night and he should be the one to invite guests. She had chosen a full-skirted red dress with white polka dots and shoestring straps. At her mother's insistence, she added a dark-red woollen stole. In the dash to the entrance, she was glad to be able to pull it over her head and shoulders to avoid getting wet.

By ten o'clock the party was in full swing. The speeches had been made, some in traditional style, others, particularly from his peer group, were light-hearted and full of anecdotes. Brian's speech in reply was more or less a mix of styles and was well received. In it, Brian had jokingly referred to her as his 'spotty sister', explaining that it was only the dress, she hadn't brought any infectious disease from the hospital, 'as far as I know.'

The large golden cardboard key to the door was acknowledged and passed around for guests to sign. It took a while to reach Miranda, by which time it had at least thirty signatures. Some of them jogged her memory and she vowed to search them out during the evening.

She found herself being partnered by a succession of Brian's friends, all smartly dressed for the occasion. In the breaks between dances, she renewed contact with some of the girls from school, all looking very grown-up now.

One of the young women looking for her was Naomi Loader who confided that she was four days younger than Brian and that their mothers had been in the maternity ward together. Miranda asked her what she was doing these days, and when she'd said that she was in her final year of nursing at the Ballarat Base Hospital, Miranda's interest was sparked. Before she could ask any questions, a tall, blonde young man approached asking for a dance. Miranda didn't know him, but she liked his courteous request and cultured voice.

'Should I know you? I'm pretty sure we haven't met before,' she said, raising her voice above the music.

'No, we haven't met – yet. My name is Michael McPherson. I'm new to the district. My father purchased a property out past Stockyard Hill, and since I've finished school I've come home to be a proper farmer's son.'

Miranda was intrigued by his light-hearted introduction. 'So, how do you know my brother?'

'I joined the local football team, not that I'm very good mind you.'

Just at that moment, the music paused and Brian came over to them.

'Ah, I see you've met. I was going to introduce you. He's not a bad bloke for a boarding school boy'

Michael McPherson looked a bit embarrassed at this, his face flushed. The music started up again. 'Shall we finish this one?'

'Gladly,' she responded. Off they went into the swirling mix of couples. The bandleader took the microphone and announced that the next dance would be a progressive barn dance.

'Looks like it's goodbye for now,' said Michael as the couples parted, each dancer taking on a new partner.

Miranda kept looking out for the distinctive blonde-haired figure, but in the crush, he dropped out of sight. The noise level was thrillingly high with music, especially the drums, and voices were louder than usual.

Several young men were spending more time than was appropriate at the bar. Jack noticed this and asked the barman to restrict their consumption. Mitch Simmons agreed. 'They're too young to know how to drink sensibly,' he said.

Diverted from the bar, three of them made their way unsteadily towards the exit when one of them noticed Miranda. He lurched towards her, thrusting his face into hers saying 'How about a bit of you-know-what.'

He made a grab at her. Miranda stepped back, feeling threatened. She looked around helplessly. One of the older women nearby said, 'Leave her alone. Go home and sober up.' With relief, Miranda saw Brian appear, and just behind him, Michael McPherson.

'I'll handle him if you like. I did a bit of boxing at school,' said Michael

One of the inebriated youths heard him and quickly ushered his mates out the door.

'Good riddance,' said Brian. 'I'll tell Dad not to let them in if they decide to come back. I don't remember inviting any of that lot, must have come as friends-of-friends.'

'Or gate-crashers, more likely,' said Neville Whitlock, the football team's full-back.

'Are you all right, Sis?' Brian asked.

'Yes, yes, of course. I was hoping to have a chat with Naomi Loader – she's doing nursing at the Base.'

'I think you'll find she's gone home, or somewhere else. She's going out with Ricky Douglas. Pretty serious, I'm told.'

It was getting late. The hall had been booked until midnight, and already many had left. Brian stood at the door shaking hands with departing guests. One of the tasks Grace had set herself was to make a list of those who had brought presents and cards. Brian had referred to the list and was able to give a brief word of thanks. There would be a follow-up letter in the mail, Miranda knew.

She reflected for a moment on Anne Saunders, immobile in her hospital bed. *How she would have enjoyed this party.* Earlier in the night, an older couple, neighbours of the Shaws, had told her that the driver of the truck had been identified and would be charged.

'But that won't help her, will it,' the kind-faced woman had said, shaking her head.

Everyone slept in the next day, even Grace, who usually attended the nine o'clock service at St John's.

Smiling broadly, Brian declared himself be to be totally satisfied with his twenty-first birthday celebration.

'Hey, Sis, you seemed to make quite an impression on Michael. And for your information, he doesn't like it shortened to Mike or Mick.'

Miranda opened her mouth to retort, but Jack got in first.

'You shouldn't make too much of it, Brian. He was brought up to be a gentleman, expensively, no doubt. And,' he said with a firm tone, 'he's way out of our league.'

Miranda decided to tactfully change the subject. 'Any offers of a lift to the station? The train gets in about quarter past four.'

'I'll drive you down, dear.'

'Are you sure, Mum? You look a bit tired, and no wonder.'

'I'm fine. You're not to worry about me. Remember you've got a bandaging exam tomorrow.'

'Bandaging?' Brian's voice was a mixture of disbelief and, perhaps, derision.

The exam went well, and Miranda was sure she'd passed despite making a mistake with a hip bandage and having to start it again.

'I usually hate exams, but that was rather fun,' said one of the trainees.

'Having some off-duty nurses as models made it seem less serious. The next lot, the written stuff, will be harder, and there's prac ones to come.'

Only another three weeks to go until the results. Next, hopefully, the ward allocations, which would lead to nursing real patients, not the dummies in the classroom. They were all agreed on that.

Miranda had developed a routine of visiting Ward 7 in the evenings. She noticed the director of the spinal unit, Dr Cheshire, talking to some medical students outside the entrance and wondered if there had been a new admission. Always a sad situation if that were the case.

It looked as though Anne was sleeping, so Miranda sought out the senior nurse on duty. The staff were aware of her visits to her friend.

'Is Anne okay? I mean, should I wake her, or leave it until tomorrow?'

'She's much the same. She keeps asking for another X-ray, but Doctor Cheshire told her it would have to wait for another three weeks. Look, I'd wake her up. She doesn't get many visitors, only her mother, really, and she's already left for the day.'

As she drew up a chair beside the specially designed bed, Miranda mentally ran through the names of several people who had asked after Anne, and the little messages they wanted passed on. A noise in the ward woke Anne, and she saw Miranda sitting there.

'Oh, it's you.'

Miranda smiled. Anne's greeting never changed.

'I thought you'd like to hear about Brian's twenty-first, and hear some messages from people who know you.'

The next fifteen minutes were spent in conversation, with Anne asking questions about what the girls wore and who was going out with whom. The ward doors opened.

'Oh, shit. Time for the turning team. You'd better go.'

The idea of going out together to celebrate the end of the PTS exams appealed to all of the class, especially those who, like Miranda, didn't live in Melbourne. A Saturday matinee at a cinema in the city was chosen where the popular new film *The Sound of Music* was screening.

Miranda loved taking the train to the Flinders Street railway station. She always marvelled at the array of clocks above the entrance showing the different departure times from all the different platforms. Then, diagonally across the road stood the amazing St Paul's Cathedral, into which she had ventured a couple of times, feeling awed and comforted in a way she acknowledged but didn't fully understand.

There was much to see and to learn in the busy city centre. She giggled to herself remembering her surprise at finding coat hooks inside toilet doors.

'How considerate that you can hang up your coat when going to the loo,' she'd remarked. She was soon enlightened.

'It's not for your coat – it's for your handbag, silly. If you leave it on the floor anyone could hook it out from under the door and pinch your money while you've got your pants down and can't do anything about it.'

Oh, thought Miranda. *Do people do that? I'll always hang my bag up from now on.*

It was early evening when the group arrived back at the Heidelberg station. In a happy mood, they made their way to the Lesley Jenner Nurses Home.

'Look,' whispered one of the girls, 'There's Sister Gray, and that's Matron in civvies. Wonder what they want.'

'Can't be us, it's Saturday and we don't need a late pass for a matinee,' said the girl next to her.

As the group approached the entrance, Miranda had the impression that the two women were looking at her.

'Nurse Shaw, would you mind stepping into my office,' said the elderly Home Sister.

Oh, what have I done? Or has something awful happened at home?

The other students quickly disappeared as Miranda followed the two senior nurses into the plain little office where three chairs were arranged. Following Matron's gesture for her to sit, she did so. They followed suit. It seemed like an eternity before Matron Gillespie spoke. Her expression was serious, though her face softened as she spoke.

'You must be wondering why we've called you in. It is important, very important, but it's not about you, or your family.'

A sense of relief flowed through her. She felt her breath escape. What, then, was this all about?

Janet Gillespie was an ex-Army nurse, known for her insistence on doing things properly. Woe betide any student nurse caught with a brown bobby pin instead of a white one securing her starched cap. Normally dressed in a grey long-sleeved uniform with a long white veil on her head, today she wore a navy blue tailored suit.

By contrast, the Home Sister, Sister Lorna Gray, was in her usual white long-sleeved uniform and veil. Perhaps it was her weekend on duty. She was a kindly soul, nearing retirement age and presumably, like Matron, unmarried. Rumour had it that Matron's fiancé was killed in the war.

The two women glanced at each other, and with a small nod, the Head of Nursing started to speak.

'What I have to tell you is not only very sad but utterly shocking.'

There was a pause. Miranda waited. The suspense was hard to bear.

'I have to tell you, Miranda, that your friend, Anne Saunders, has died.'

Miranda gasped, her hand went involuntarily to her lips.

'I'll tell you what happened and why it is so shocking. Just let me explain things first, and you can ask any questions after. There are some things we need to ask you, too. Let me start with a day or so ago. Apparently, the staff reported that Anne seemed to be more depressed than usual, and the Charge Nurse asked whether the psychiatrist should be contacted. He agreed to visit Anne, and the appointment was made for next Monday. He left instructions for the medical officer on duty to start her on an antidepressant. Otherwise, according to the nursing notes, things seemed much as usual. It was mentioned that you visited her yesterday.'

Miranda nodded and the matron continued.

'The incident resulting in her death happened about two o'clock this afternoon. Her mother had visited during the morning and wasn't due back until tomorrow. When the turning team arrived for the routine change of her position, Dusan Kabolich was in charge of manipulating the head tongs. Just as he was about to release the weight and control her head manually, she demanded a drink of water. "Can't it wait until we've turned you?" Dusan asked her. She insisted that she wanted it now. So he brought the glass with the drinking straw to her lips and she took a large amount. He then released the weight and held each side of her head firmly, the usual procedure. As he secured her head, Anne suddenly spat the water into his face, causing him to momentarily loosen his grip to shake the water away. He yelled something. In that split second of losing control of Anne's head, the bony fragments of her unstable fracture severed the spinal cord in her neck. She died instantly. That was the sequence of events. I'll give you a minute to take it all in.'

Miranda's mouth was open, she shuddered, and a small groan escaped her lips. Anne. Instant death. She shook her head in disbelief.

Matron Gillespie continued. 'The most distressing thing is that she did it so deliberately. A quadriplegic patient with an unstable fracture of the neck has normally no way of ending his or her life, even if they wanted to, but she managed to do it.'

Miranda's thoughts were racing. Amid the turmoil of shock, disbelief and pain was a tiny sense of relief, and even admiration. Anne did not want to go on living, and had managed to find a way ...

'What about Dusan, the orderly, how is he?' she managed to ask.

'As you can imagine, he's in a bad way. He feels guilty and blames himself. Needless to say, no-one else does. He has been given indefinite leave and the hospital will support him in every way possible.'

'And Anne's mother and father – do they know? How are they?'

'Again, it's a hard thing to have to tell a parent that their child has passed away, it always is. Mrs Saunders came straight back to the hospital when we rang her and is being comforted by the chaplain. She wanted to be the one who told Anne's father.'

The Home Sister poured a glass of water for Miranda.

'Here, my dear, or could we get you a cup of tea?'

Miranda shook her head, feeling numb as the full story registered. Anne – dead. That was sad enough, but to have managed to take her own life ... it was awful.

After a few minutes of silence, both senior nurses got to their feet. Miranda did likewise. Matron spoke again.

'Miranda, you will, of course, be affected greatly by this sad experience. I'm going to suggest that you take two weeks off to go home to recover from the shock. But before that, there will be a thorough investigation of the circumstances surrounding the decision this young woman made. The hospital manager and legal team will want to interview you, as Anne's close friend, in the hope that you might possibly shed some light on her state of mind.' She paused, allowing Miranda to take in what had just been said before continuing.

'I know it's Saturday and normally you'd be off duty, but I'm asking you to come to the Board Room at seven-thirty this evening. You don't have to be in uniform.' She noticed Miranda's expression of alarm. 'You have nothing to fear. Just be honest when answering the questions. I will be there too.'

They left, and Miranda shakily made her way to her room on the third floor. In the corridor, she noticed other nurses speaking in hushed tones. So word had got around.

'Sorry to hear your friend has passed away,' said one of her classmates.

Miranda couldn't speak. She opened her door and fell onto her bed, wanting to cry, but too choked up to do so. According to her bedside clock, it was six-fifteen, it was already dark outside.

There was a tap on the door. Jan Barrington, one of her closest friends, came in carrying a tray with a pot of tea and some biscuits and cheese.

'Here, have this. You've got to eat something. You take sugar in your tea, don't you?' she asked, pouring out a cup.

'Thanks, Jan. I don't know what to do. Or say. My mind's in a whirl.'

Uncharacteristically silent, Jan watched as her friend drank the tea and ate a biscuit. Eventually, Miranda spoke.

'I have to be interviewed by the authorities at 7.30. They want to find out what was behind Anne's – Anne's suicide.'

'Do you want to talk it over with me?'

'That could be helpful. Thanks, Jan.'

It was, in fact, helpful, and Miranda felt a little more confident when she presented herself at the Board Room. She was shown to a seat at the large polished oval table. She was ready to answer the questions put to her by the hospital psychologist, Ian Rankin, who was in charge of the inquiry. The Director of the Spinal Unit was there, and the charge nurse of that unit, also Matron, and several whom she didn't know. All wore serious expressions.

Ian Rankin began by welcoming her and expressing the sympathy of all in the room. Everybody nodded, some murmured in assent.

'Miranda, I understand you were friends with Anne at school in Beaufort, then she went to boarding school in Ballarat, but you kept in touch with her during your secondary schooling – is that right?'

'Yes, well I didn't see her that often when she went away.'

'How would you describe Anne if someonebody asked you what she was like?'

A difficult question. Miranda knew she would have to be honest, but not brutally so. She decided to be general in her response.

'She is, I mean, was, pretty ordinary I suppose. Normal, that is. She liked having a good time and was interested in boys. More than in her schoolwork I guess.' Her voice trailed off.

'Would you say she was moody, I mean, did she have highs and lows?'

'Not really, not that I know of. Even when she got low marks in primary school, particularly in maths, it didn't seem to upset her at all.'

'Let's look at the last few weeks now. We all understand how having such a serious accident and the consequences of it would be very hard for anyone to cope with, let alone a seventeen-year-old girl. The psychiatrist had prescribed an antidepressant for her but we know that medication takes some weeks to be effective.' He paused. 'Did you notice any changes in Anne's mood recently?'

Miranda considered her last visits to Ward 7. Had there been any particular changes? She tried to remember what Anne had spoken about,

'There were a few things that made her feel down. One of them was the fact that the most recent X-ray showed no improvement, which meant no change in her management. Her head tongs and all that. Oh, I remember just three days ago, she'd had to say goodbye to someone she really liked and could talk to. Jimmy, his name was'

The Charge Nurse of Ward 7 spoke up. 'Yes, that's right. Jimmy Reinhardt is a young quadriplegic who'd completed his rehabilitation in Ward 17, and was ready to go out to our hostel in the community. He uses a modified wheelchair he could operate using his mouth. He used to visit Ward 7 a lot. We encouraged him because of his amazing attitude and progress. Come to think of it, he did spend a lot of time with Anne Saunders. Everyone was sorry to see him go, but glad for him, of course,'

The psychologist had been taking notes. He thanked the charge nurse and resumed interviewing Miranda. 'We've got two things here which would have had an impact on her mental state. Can you think of anything else she might have mentioned?'

Miranda swallowed, uncertain as to how to continue. There was something, but disclosing it might have consequences.

Ian Rankin's professional expertise was evident as he persisted with his questioning. 'You seem a bit uncertain, Nurse Shaw. Please tell us, even if you're reluctant to do so. Remember Anne is dead, and it is up to us to try to ascertain why.'

'Yesterday I visited in the evening as normal. She seemed a bit withdrawn, more than usual. I asked her what was the matter. She said she'd tell me, but I mustn't say anything to anyone in case it caused trouble.' She paused.

'Go on,' prompted the psychologist.

'There had been a new nurse on duty the night before. From an agency, apparently. She said to Anne she couldn't bear to have the injury Anne had, she'd rather die. When Anne told me this I said she mustn't take that to heart, it was probably someone who hadn't worked in a spinal injury ward before, didn't realise what she was saying, and that Anne should forget it, put it right out of her mind. She said – and I remember this clearly – "that's easier said than done."'

There were a few whispers among the group.

Miranda suddenly had a sense of foreboding.

'Should I have told the staff? Am I in some way responsible?'

The worry in her voice was evident. The charge nurse quickly responded.

'Miranda, you are not in any way responsible. In my many years of nursing these patients, I've lost count of how many have said they wished they were dead. It is totally understandable. I'm not pleased that a staff member on duty said what she did, and this will need to be investigated.

But you have shown yourself to be a conscientious friend to Anne. You could not have done anything more for her.'

For the first time since hearing of the tragedy, Miranda's eyes filled with tears and she started to sob, powerless to control her emotion. The interview was immediately brought to a close.

'Thank you so much for your contribution, Miranda. I know it's been a great shock to you, and I regret that we've had to ask these questions. But,' he said, turning to face the rest of the group, 'we have gained some insight about the state of Anne Saunders' mind. Three negative experiences in a short space of time. We can examine these more fully for the coroner's report. But I think you can be excused now Miranda, unless anyone has anything further to ask?'

Nobody responded to the invitation.

Her episode of tearfulness subsiding, Miranda wiped her eyes. She stood, and made her way to the door.

'Would you like me to accompany you to the Nurses Home?' Matron asked, her voice kind.

'Thank you, no. I – I'm all right.'

Chapter 11

The next few weeks were the most difficult Miranda had ever experienced. She found herself preoccupied with every aspect of her friend's accident and its consequences. Images, both real and imagined, plagued her. It wasn't as if she hadn't been around end-of-life situations before. This was different, she was inextricably involved, and nothing could change that. Grace, concerned, had suggested prayer, but that didn't seem to help. Even going to church and singing the familiar hymns didn't bring the consolation she craved.

Some publicity had ensued, from the *Age's* measured factual reporting to the *Sun's* more colourful account, along with a photograph of Anne. The front-page coverage in the notorious *Truth* stated that this untimely death raised more questions than provided answers. Dad had advised her not to read it. 'They always dig for dirt in their so-called newspaper. Wonder how they got hold of the information about the accident.'

Miranda endured the events following Anne's death with self-control which somehow kept her emotions hidden. Evelyn Saunders had apologised to Jack for her husband's decision to use a Ballarat undertaker for Anne's funeral. Secretly, Miranda had been relieved, though she went to the ceremony with her family. She managed to spend a few minutes with Helen Osborne who, along with Anne's classmates, was in the Clarendon school uniform. Afterwards, the talk was all about how tragic it was, what a waste of a young life, all predictable sentiments, but also opinions seemed to be divided about Anne's own part in it. 'A brave thing to do,' was countered by pious comments, such as it was never right to take one's own life, or even that it was a coward's way out.

It was too much for Miranda. After embracing each member of the Saunders family, she told her father that she would go and sit in the car until they were ready to go home. When she opened the car door, she saw a white envelope on the front seat. To her surprise, it was addressed to her.

Inside was a plain white card with the words, 'I am so sorry to hear of the loss of your friend, and I want you to know I am thinking of you. Sincerely, Michael (McPherson).'

How thoughtful of him. Her lips moved in an inaudible 'Thank You,' but her heart felt heavy. And she felt incredibly tired.

Her parents found her asleep on the back seat. Grace saw the card next to her, and, for the first time that day, she realised, there was a reason to smile.

The thought of going back to the Austin Hospital at the end of the two weeks of compassionate leave made her whole being recoil. It was hard to explain. As days passed, Mum had gently asked her if it was time to resume her training.

It wasn't. The image of the empty bed in Ward 7, even if there was, by now, a new occupant, filled her with dread. If she went back, it was inevitable she would be pointed out by hospital personnel.

Grace tried to be practical. 'If you don't feel ready yet, darling, maybe you should see Dr Santorini and get a medical certificate to cover your absence. That's the usual procedure, I believe.'

The kindly GP allocated a double appointment for her and gently probed her state of mind with questions about appetite, sleeping, feelings of guilt and sadness. Miranda had always found him easy to talk to and knew he was trustworthy. At the end of the twenty minutes, he made his summary of her situation, noting that she had been through a most difficult experience, both initially when the accident had happened, but also its tragic outcome. She was right to feel implicated and conscious of the probable reactions of her colleagues. He also noted that she'd done exceptionally well in her studies and that she still wanted to continue her career in nursing.

'You know, I think I've got a possible answer,' he said, his face animated. Miranda looked puzzled. She couldn't see any solution. 'Why don't you apply to transfer to the Ballarat Base Hospital? With the good results you've got already, I'm sure they'd be glad to have you, and I think the staff at the Austin would understand and agree.'

It was a brilliant suggestion. Miranda gasped. It was as if a lifeline had been thrown to her. Here was the solution. Why hadn't she thought of this herself? She felt so relieved she wanted to hug the middle-aged doctor, but restricted herself to a big smile.

'I can see you're in favour. It does seem like a good idea to me. However, these things may take some time. So I'll give you a medical certificate for four weeks, which will keep you on the staff down there. I'll put stress as the reason. Then it'll be up to you to make contact with Ballarat Base and take it from there.'

The following week, a letter arrived from the Austin Hospital, expressing concern about her state of health, and asking about her plans to continue her training. It also warmly congratulated her on her Preliminary Training School results in which she had achieved the highest marks of the group and was therefore dux. It ended with personal good wishes from the Principal Nurse Tutor.

'How are you going to reply?' Grace asked, then added, 'And congratulations, darling, on those excellent results.'

'Thanks, Mum. At least I've achieved dux of something, even if it's not Beaufort High School. But I can't say anything until I've had the appointment in Ballarat next Tuesday, can I?'

It all went through without a hitch. Miranda had to agree that her record at the Austin Hospital be made available to the personnel department at Ballarat Base Hospital, but it was clear that her transfer was approved. Her PTS results meant that she could start working in the wards after a period of orientation.

'We understand the reasons behind your request,' Matron Watson had said, 'and we welcome you to our nursing staff.'

Joining the staff of a new hospital provided just the diversion Miranda needed. She threw herself into the challenge of learning the layout of all the wards and departments, the names of senior staff members, including the honorary doctors, and most importantly, the geography of the Nurses Home, an imposing multi-storied pale brick building on the northern boundary.

She discovered there were several other student nurses from the Beaufort district at different stages of their training. A few had known Anne Saunders and expressed their sympathy. Miranda endured the attention but was relieved when the subject was exhausted. Life had to go on for all of them.

A new interest came in the form of Michael McPherson. She had replied to his note of sympathy with a brief letter of thanks and thought no more about it.

Going to the local football matches was not a habit of hers, but Brian had insisted that she come to a home game that coincided with one of her weekends off duty.

She decided that it was good fun, sitting on the bench, well rugged up against the late winter chill, watching the young and not-so-young men vie for the football with yelling from the supporters and whistles from the umpire. Many of the spectators parked their cars around the perimeter fence and honked their horns noisily whenever the home team scored a goal. Her eye was drawn to the tall, blonde, curly-haired Michael McPherson, and she joined in the enthusiastic applause when he kicked a goal. It was an important score and brought Beaufort to within five points of the Lexton team.

Brian played well, she noted, his long arms brought down several marks with the resultant kick sending the ball deep into the forward area.

'Wait there, Sis,' Brian yelled as the teams made their way to the change rooms.

Before long he'd emerged in his dark-blue tracksuit, his football gear stuffed in a carry bag. Close behind him came Michael McPherson, his face beaming.

'How nice to see you, Miranda,' he said.

Miranda responded with warm congratulations on his goal.

'Should've been more than one, but thanks.'

Brian chipped in, 'Hey, five behinds and a six-pointer, that's okay. You were a bit unlucky with the wind on some of those shots for goal. Anyway, we're still second on the ladder, and that's a good thing.'

Miranda was listening to her brother, but her eyes were on his centre half-forward. She couldn't help smiling, he looked so healthy, so attractive. He leaned in towards her with a questioning look on his face.

'I wonder if you'd like to come out to dinner with me tonight. They say the Golden Age does a good meal. If you're free, that is.'

Miranda felt her face flush. The invitation was a welcome surprise. 'Thank you, I'd love to, Michael.'

'Shall I pick you up about six, then?' It was more of a statement than a question.

Their first date was a real 'getting to know you' experience. Miranda found Michael easy to talk to, and he was prepared to open up about his life. She learned that his mother had died some years ago while he was at boarding school in Geelong. 'None of us knew she had a heart problem,' he said. He had an older sister, Phee, Phoebe really, who had been to a finishing school in Switzerland.

To Miranda's question, 'What's she doing now?' he replied that, as far as he knew, she was living it up in Melbourne and probably looking for a suitable husband. *Oh,* thought Miranda, *this is a very different lifestyle from mine.*

'But I'm not like that,' Michael went on, 'I just want to lift some of the weight off Dad's shoulders. He's been on his own for over ten years.' He paused for a moment before deciding to continue. 'He wanted to make sure I was ready to stay on the land before he bought Bournagulla. It's such a great property!' He looked at her, his face animated. 'You'll have to come out and see it one of these days.'

That prospect excited Miranda. She decided not to say anything about it to her family. If it did happen, there'd be something to tell them then. The night finished with a gentle kiss on her cheek, a little awkwardly delivered, due to their differing heights, but gratefully received.

Miranda's nursing training continued with ward changes, another series of lectures followed by a spell of night duty in the female medical ward. Night shift was different, yes, but after a few days, sleeping during the daytime and working through the night became routine.

Days off were a problem though: Go to bed after the seven o'clock handover, set the alarm for midday and get up without having lost the whole day. It took some getting used to, but in time it felt almost normal.

Miranda was happy to ring home every week, and to get regular phone calls from Michael, usually at seven o'clock in the evening, which suited them both. Her roster gave her Monday and Tuesday nights off, which allowed for an afternoon outing whenever Michael came down for the Ballarat sheep and cattle market on Tuesdays. The sight of his leather jacket and well-cut jeans inspired one of her friends to label his style 'squattocracy'. Miranda laughed, but recognised some envy in the comment – the local boys neither looked nor behaved like Michael McPherson.

Off duty, there were plenty of things to do. Shopping was always fun, visiting the library was also a pleasure, and on Saturday nights after the night duty stint was over, there was the dance at the Town Hall. Sometimes Michael was able to meet her there. How satisfying were the dances they shared, with the delightful embrace after the last dance before he drove her back to the Nurses Home. Miranda felt a thrill through her body when their lips met.

'You are wonderful,' she breathed.

'You, too,' he'd reply with a laugh.

The year marched on. First Professional Exams came and went. Miranda's results were excellent, not surprisingly, as she enjoyed the lectures and had no problem with the written work. She found herself growing in confidence in the wards as more responsibility came her way. It was gratifying that junior nurses would sometimes ask her advice or seek information about some of the medical terms they encountered. 'Bet you'll end up a tutor sister,' one said after Miranda had carefully explained why the pulse had to be checked before a certain patient was given her heart medication.

The different areas of interest in her second year were exciting. Outpatients, casualty, speciality units such as the TB chalet, infectious diseases and older children and, of course, the operating theatre, all provided different experiences. The two stripes on her cap identified Miranda as a second-year nurse.

One Monday afternoon, a call came from Michael. 'Dad and I are bringing a truckload of wethers down to the sales tomorrow. What sort of shift are you on? Any chance of coming out with us for afternoon tea?'

Us? That's new.

'Oh, I'm on earlies all week with Sunday off. Yes, that would be lovely.'

'Dad's been asking to meet you since your name has cropped up over our dinner table a few times.'

Miranda was lost for words. Did this mean that Mr McPherson, or Major McPherson, to give him his proper title, wanted to check her out?

'Are you still there? Look, I'll come to the Nurses Home about four, if that's all right. We'll probably go to Craigs, that's his usual haunt.'

Just as well Ward 5 was full and all the staff, including Miranda, were kept busy until handing over to the afternoon shift. She didn't have much time to think about the invitation, except to contemplate what to wear. Her options were limited, but the rollneck jumper and the skirt with the Shaw tartan her parents had given her for her eighteenth birthday seemed appropriate. Her dark-green blazer complemented the ensemble. *I hope I make a good impression on the Major. I want Michael to be proud of me.*

'Hey, Miranda, you look real swish,' commented one of her friends as she paraded in front of the mirror in the entrance hall. 'You look as though you're going to Craigs.'

'I am, actually.' It was impossible not to smile. Almost at the same time, Michael appeared outside the glass front door. She kept smiling and found an answering one on his lips.

Craigs Hotel has an important role in Ballarat's history. It is an imposing grey stone building with tower and flagpole and is set back half a block from Sturt Street. It epitomises elegance and class. Michael parked the Land Rover in a convenient spot across the road, close to the equally historic Her Majesty's Theatre. They entered the impressive foyer.

'I left Dad in the tea room. He's probably had his first cup already.'

There were only a few people here at this time of the day, and it was easy to see the older man sitting with his back to them at a corner table. The set of his head and the sparse grey curls on his head were impressive. As he turned to greet them, Miranda could easily see the family resemblance. He stood and offered his hand to Miranda.

'Dad, this is Miranda Shaw – Miranda, meet my father, Major Alexander McPherson.'

She shook his hand, saying, 'How do you do, Major.'

They sat and discussed what to order.

'Is tea all right with you, Miranda?' the older man asked. 'I ordered a large pot in advance.'

She nodded. A waitress wearing a white frilled apron came to fill the dainty china teacups for each of them, handling the large teapot with an ease that comes with experience.

'Did you order anything to eat, Dad? You said you were hungry.'

'I have to admit I've already had a serving of quite delicious sandwiches while you were picking up this young lady.' He turned to her, 'Would you like something? The cakes are really special here.'

Miranda nervously shook her head and murmured, 'No, thank you. Just tea will be fine.'

'So that's how you keep so trim,' he said with a little laugh.

'That, and running after sick people all day, that's about right isn't it?' said Michael.

Miranda smiled, feeling a little more relaxed. 'Has it been a good season for you so far?' she asked.

'Yes, my dear, and I'm more than happy with the way the market's going. It could turn out to be another good year.' He paused and sipped his tea. 'Now tell me something about yourself, Miranda. What brought you into the noble career of nursing?'

Miranda glanced at Michael – hadn't he told him about the circumstances? Reading her questioning look accurately, he shook his head.

'Oh, it's rather a long story – is that okay?'

'Indeed it is. Please start at the beginning.'

Miranda began by explaining how hard it had been to settle on a career when she was at school. She'd done well in all her main subjects and everybody expected her to go on to university. Major McPherson nodded as though he could understand that. Michael studied his fingernails – he'd heard it all before.

She told him about Anne's accident and how she realised that she could deal with it by becoming a student nurse. But the tragedy still felt unreal and was painful to recount.

Major McPherson saw her discomfort. 'You don't have to go on if it makes you upset.'

'No, I need to tell you the whole story. Though you might have seen it in the papers …'

Michael interrupted 'Dad was overseas at the time.'

Miranda continued, 'Anne's death and the inquiry that followed would have to be the worst time of my life.' She concluded, with a knowing glance across to Michael, 'Things have been much better for me in the last year.'

Alex McPherson nodded, giving the impression that he understood the part his son was playing in her story.

'You made a good impression on Dad,' said Michael on the way back to the hospital. 'Next, you'll have to meet my sister. But we won't hurry that.'

It almost sounded as though Michael was claiming her as his girlfriend. It was an exciting and reassuring thought, though she was apprehensive.

What would sophisticated Phoebe think of me? Some time passed before she found out.

Chapter 12

The year seemed to be progressing rapidly, with Christmas not far away. Miranda's annual holidays were on the horizon – three weeks in October – and after that, she'd be back as a third-year nurse.

She smiled to herself. She remembered last year's annual leave as being like a respite. She'd gone home to Beaufort and seemed to sleep for most of the first week. Mum had been amused as her daughter emerged at lunchtime, still in her pyjamas.

'Looks like you're catching up on a lot of lost shut-eye,' Grace had said.

After a few days, Miranda had found herself unwinding and getting back to normal. Except that normal wasn't quite like it was before she started nursing training.

'I can't help wondering how some of my patients are getting on,' she told her mother.

'Would you like to talk about it?' Grace had asked, adding with a smile, 'Nothing too gory, though'.

Miranda stretched out on the old sofa, her feet just reaching the further armrest. 'I'm wondering what happened to one old lady who had big varicose ulcers on her legs near the ankles. They were dressed and bandaged and should have healed up okay. One night I saw her undo the bandage and scratch at one of the ulcers with a fork, making it bleed. I told the nurse in charge and she said they suspected she was doing it to sabotage her recovery. So I asked her in the morning – I was on night duty – "are you looking forward to going home?" and she said no, she didn't want to go home, she wanted to stay in hospital. When I asked why, she said, "They are awful to me." I told the senior day sister at handover and she said, very curtly I might add, "Nurse Shaw, our aim is to get our patients ready for discharge. What happens to them after they leave hospital is none of our business." I was really worried about that, Mum.'

Grace was silent for a few minutes, gathering her thoughts so she could make a helpful response. This was the Miranda of old, wanting to right wrongs, challenging the system when it wasn't all it should be.

'I don't know what to say, Mirrie. I know there are people who harm themselves deliberately to try to highlight their situations, you could almost say that's the case when people drink too much alcohol, even when they know they shouldn't.' She'd paused. Miranda was listening. 'I guess the thing is – we can only do our best. I suppose what the charge sister was saying is that you are responsible for them when they are in your care, and I'm sure you do that well.'

'I try. But there are times like a week or so ago we had this young girl come in with bleeding and abdominal pain. She was so distressed. She went on to have a miscarriage, I was there, I saw it, no bigger than an apple. The poor girl was hysterical. She kept insisting that she didn't want her family to know. It was awful.'

'What happened?'

'The doctor in charge of the case said she was underage, and therefore the parents had to be contacted. I don't know any more, as I went off duty, and she wasn't there the next day. There was a lot of chatter about it among the nurses. No-one knew if she had a boyfriend or had been raped or what.'

Noticing her mother's concern, Miranda made a determined effort to change the subject.

'Hey it's not all doom and gloom, we have some really lovely success stories too. Over to you – tell me what's going on in Beaufort.'

They'd spent the next hour discussing local events, the improvements being made to the church, newcomers to the town and bits of local gossip.

Back copies of the *Riponshire Advocate* had been keenly scanned and commented on. The holiday had passed quickly, she remembered.

Now, almost a year later, it was time to plan her next leave. The holiday roster was staggered according to staffing needs. Only six of Miranda's colleagues were taking them at the same time. Two girls had planned a trip to Sydney, travelling by themselves, which was considered very adventurous. It seemed the others planned to visit relatives either in Melbourne or elsewhere in Victoria. On hearing this, Grace had suggested that Miranda might like to visit her aunt and family in Beulah, 'like you did years ago.' She said she'd think about it.

When Miranda told Michael that she was due for annual leave soon, his response delighted her.

'That's good, because Phee's coming home for a few weeks and I'd like you to come over and stay for a couple of days to meet her, and also to see Bournagulla.' Well, that was something to look forward to! Before she could say anything he went on, 'And Dad insisted that I ask you too, he said it was about time.'

The invitation was not a complete surprise to Miranda. Their relationship was becoming more established. Twice Michael had been a guest for dinner at the Shaws' when Miranda had been home on a weekend and Beaufort had a home game. It was Grace who had suggested that he come for the family meal rather than taking Miranda to the Golden Age as he had done in the past. Brian had been pleased as well and brought along his girlfriend of the moment. Interestingly, on each occasion, he produced a different young lady, but the Shaws, amused, took this in their stride.

Initially, Miranda had wondered whether their modest home would seem inferior to her guest. She needn't have worried. Grace's warm personality and excellent cooking made a favourable impression.

'You're so lucky, Brian, to have such a lovely and hospitable mother. It's not quite like this for me – our housekeeper does her best, but it's not the same.'

Even Jack, a little reserved at first, relaxed in Michael's presence and asked questions about the farming practices at Bournagulla. Nonetheless, after their guest's first visit, he said, 'I hope you're not getting your hopes up, my girl. He really is out of our league.' Miranda said nothing, she just flounced out of the room.

Now the time for a reciprocal visit had come. *At last,* she thought. With her suitcase packed, she felt as ready as she could be to navigate the next step.

It seemed to be about eight miles or so along the Stockyard Hill road before Michael turned into a long driveway with an avenue of poplar trees leading to the homestead. The Bournagulla homestead was an intriguing combination of bluestone and brick, a two-storied manor house, with sheds and outbuildings behind it, and a row of pine trees to the rear.

'Oh – it looks like something out of an English country magazine,' Miranda exclaimed.

'It does look impressive, I know,' Michael agreed. 'We found out the history of the place when Dad bought it. He's got all the old photos, you'll see them.' He braked to a halt. 'Doesn't look like Phee's home yet,' he said, looking around. 'She's got a snazzy little red MG.'

Michael retrieved her suitcase from the back seat of the car and she followed him up the three stone steps to the large front door. Before they reached it, the door opened to reveal Major McPherson with a welcoming smile. He shook Miranda's hand before stepping aside and beckoning her to enter.

The interior looked just as splendid as the outside. Miranda caught her breath in delight. 'It's – it's just amazing, so grand.'

The long vertical windows had heavy burgundy-coloured curtains draped to each side and the head-high wooden panelling gleamed richly in the spring sunlight. The walls above the timber trim were a deep green. The paintings, mirrors and furniture were in perfect taste.

'You're not the first to be overwhelmed, my dear. The decor is a tribute to the previous owner, bless him. We can't take credit for any of it.'

Michael took her by the hand and said, 'Come on, and I'll show you your room. Then we'll go into the kitchen for a cup of tea.'

The bedroom, with primrose yellow walls, was small but neatly furnished. It seemed to be one of three or four, judging by the closed doors on each side of the passage.

'The bathroom and lavatory are down the end,' Michael explained. *In our house we call it the toilet,* she thought, amused.

The kitchen was spacious and practical with an impressive slow-combustion stove. A large wooden table with ten chairs around it dominated the room.

'It looks as though it's for a really large family,' Miranda remarked.

Alex McPherson responded, 'At certain times of the year we have quite a few mouths to feed, like when we're shearing and harvesting. But most of the time it's just Mrs Hardwick, our housekeeper, her son Lance who works on the property, and us. She'll be back later to get our evening meal. There'll be four of us if Phee gets here in time, and we eat in the dining room when it's special.'

Michael busied himself with preparing the afternoon tea, expressing his delight at finding some ginger nut biscuits in one of the tins.

'Does your daughter visit often?' Miranda inquired of Major McPherson.

The two men exchanged a glance before the older one replied, 'Let's sit down to our tea and I'll try to explain the situation to you. It is a bit unusual I suppose. I gather Michael hasn't told you much about our family background?'

'Well, I know you were in the Army. Michael told me you were a career soldier who stayed on after the War with peacekeeping duties, and after that with the Department of Defence in Canberra, and retired with the rank of Major. He said that's why he had to go to boarding school at an early age, because you were serving overseas.'

'That's right,' Alex McPherson said, 'My late wife and I … To tell you the truth, my wife and I weren't getting on very well – for a variety of reasons. Phoebe lived with her in our Sydney home and went to a private school nearby as a day student. This meant I didn't get to know her as well as I would have liked to, I'm afraid.' He paused. 'It's all a bit complicated.'

For a moment, no-one spoke. Miranda wasn't sure if she was supposed to respond or not. She looked over at Michael who cleared his throat before speaking.

'Dad, Miranda doesn't need to know all our family ins-and-outs, not yet anyway.'

'Yes, of course,' his father replied. 'Well, why don't you show her around outside while it's still light. I'll get a fire going in the sitting room and open the double doors through to the dining-room to warm it up, too.'

Though it was early October, there was a slight chill in the evening air. The predictions had been for a late Spring, even so, some of the fruit trees were already in bloom. It was a clear afternoon with the sky still bright, though shadows were lengthening.

Michael was in his element, proudly showing Miranda around the buildings adjacent to the main house. A small milking shed, 'we only have two house cows, enough for what we need, over there's the fowl-house or chook-pen, depending on what you're used to,' he said with a smile.

Miranda nudged him in the ribs and said, 'Nope, we'd call it a chicken coop.'

They set out on the path back to the house after visiting the vegetable garden which looked so vividly green and promised abundant produce. All Miranda could say was, 'How amazing!'

'I did a crash course in horticulture after I left school, it's come in very handy. Oh – listen.' The dogs had started barking as a furious tooting of a car horn announced an arrival. 'That'll be Phee. Always likes to announce herself.'

As they made their way through the back door into the house, voices could be heard in the front. Michael stopped to listen and turned to Miranda.

'Sounds like Phee's brought someone with her.'

Following Michael into the entrance hall, Miranda saw two tall well-dressed young women talking to the Major.

'Oh, there you are,' he said looking in their direction, 'come in and meet Phee and her friend – Marcia, isn't it?'

'Yes, Daddy, this is Marcia Hudson-Brown,' said one of the young woman who, judging by her curly blonde hair and poised demeanour, was obviously Michael's sister. Miranda felt a stab of envy. How she would have loved to be taller and so stylish!

'Hello, darling,' Phee said, kissing Michael on each cheek, continental style. 'Sorry I've sprung this on you, but I thought you'd like to meet Marcia, a dear friend of mine. Her father's an investment banker.' She caught sight of Miranda who had stayed in the background. 'Oh, I didn't realise you had someone else here.'

'Miranda,' said Alex McPherson decisively, 'come over here and meet my daughter, Phee, and her friend Marcia.'

Miranda was acutely conscious of the head-to-toe scrutiny to which she was subjected. She stepped forward with an outstretched hand which was briefly taken before Phee turned to her brother.

'You'll find you have quite a lot in common with Marcia. She was actually at school in Singapore, in fact about the same time that you visited when Daddy was stationed there, remember?'

Michael, looking a little uncomfortable, finally found words to greet the visitor.

'How do you do, Marcia? It's always good to have a friend of Phee's visit us.'

To Miranda, Marcia Hudson-Brown looked like a fashion model. Dark hair cut in a bob with a heavy fringe, and an olive-green cashmere suit very like Phee's pale-blue outfit. She murmured something to Michael which sounded like 'lovely to be here', and sent a nod in Miranda's direction. A small smile hovered around her well-defined lips. It was obvious that she was impressed with the property and, turning to Phee, she confirmed it, 'This is sooo lovely, it would be a marvellous setting for a party.'

'You're absolutely right, darling. That's just what I have in mind.'

Miranda noticed the slightly alarmed look that passed between father and son. *I know whose side I'm on*, she thought.

Major McPherson assumed control, much as he would have done in his military days. He instructed Michael to take the two newcomers up to their bedrooms. Phee muttered something to her friend as they went upstairs. Miranda just managed to hear the words, 'You can move over when she goes.'

Troubled, she turned to her host. 'Perhaps I shouldn't stay.'

'Nonsense, my dear. You were invited, and you're Michael's friend, remember.' He gave her a genuinely reassuring smile to which she responded gratefully.

Over dinner, the conversation was dominated by Phee. She had assumed charge of the seating arrangements and made sure that Michael and Marcia were side by side. Her father was at the head of the table, Phee on his left and Miranda next to her.

As Mrs Hardwick served the soup, Major McPherson asked his daughter, 'What have you been doing with yourself lately? We don't hear much from you these days.'

Turning to her father to reply, Phee kept her back to Miranda for the rest of the meal. 'Oh, this and that. I know a lot of people, many of them live interstate, so I can spend the winter in North Queensland, which I did, and had a lovely week in Darwin. Magnetic Island was the best though.' She turned to Miranda. 'Ever been there?'

With a shake of her head, Miranda admitted, 'I haven't been out of Victoria, actually.'

'Really?' Phee's voice had a bored tone.

'Miranda's doing nursing training, you know,' Michael put in.

'Oh?' There was a little more interest. 'At the Alfred?'

Miranda's heart sank. It was not the first time she'd heard that the Alfred was the hospital chosen by elite nursing aspirants. She shook her head, but Phee had taken up the conversation with Marcia.

'Do you remember that Spencely girl who was in Zurich with us that time? Didn't like her much, a real little snob. Well, I heard she did nursing training at the Alfred, couldn't believe she'd lower herself to do that. But,' she leaned over towards her friend, 'it turns out her father is a specialist surgeon there, and she's managed to grab one of the up-and-coming young registrars, or whatever you call them, *quite a catch, I hear.*'

Marcia gave a little laugh. 'I wonder if we'll get invited to the wedding.'

Mrs Hardwick cleared the first course dishes away. Miranda half-stood to offer to help. Michael recognised her willingness but raised his hand in a 'stop' gesture. 'It's okay, Miranda, guests don't need to work.'

Soon the main dish of roast lamb and garden vegetables was brought in.

'That looks lovely, Sarah. Thank you for making it stretch.' Alex McPherson turned to the guests, 'She is a treasure. I feel so fortunate to have her and her son with us. What you're about to eat is all produced on our property, I'm proud to say.'

After the dessert of home-preserved plums and custard, the group moved into the sitting-room for coffee and a small glass of liqueur. This time, Michael sat on a two-seater lounge and gestured for Miranda to sit next to him.

'I thought we might go round the paddocks tomorrow, let you see the stock and the little creek that borders our neighbour,' he said to her quietly. 'I don't know what Phee has in mind,' he said a little more loudly in his sister's direction

'I don't think we're dressed for going outside. Anyway, I saw the place back in January.' She paused. 'Actually, I was hoping you'd take us to Ballarat – you've still got the Pontiac, haven't you, Dad?' Phee's voice was imperious. 'Marcia said she'd like to see Lake Wendouree and the Botanical Gardens, then maybe we could go to Craigs.'

'Oh, I don't want to put you out or anything,' Marcia said sweetly. 'It's so lovely just to be here and to meet you two,' she added, looking from Alex to Michael.

I'm being excluded again, thought Miranda.

It was an awkward moment. Wisely, Alex McPherson decided that any decisions would be made in the morning and maybe it was time for an early night. Phee and Marcia were first to go upstairs, their whispered dialogue not audible to the others.

Miranda had moved across the room to examine a large watercolour landscape painting. Michael came over to her.

'Hey,' he said,' I'm awfully sorry about what's happened. It isn't the way I planned it at all.'

His voice was apologetic, which touched Miranda. She managed a smile. 'It's all right, Michael. It is, honest. I'm just a bit overwhelmed, that's all.'

'Yes, Phee has that effect on people.'

'Does she always get what she wants?'

Michael looked away and took a moment to answer. 'It's rather complicated, too much to go into now. It's better not to ruffle feathers.' He turned and smiled at her. 'Don't worry, we'll be okay. How about a little kiss goodnight?'

That was a more agreeable ending to her first night at Bournagalla.

He still likes me.

Sleep did not come readily for Miranda, her mind kept focussing on the events of the day. There was a mystery about Phee's role in the family which both Michael and his father alluded to by suggesting that there would be some explanation later. It was funny now, looking back, that Michael had said so little about his sister. It was different for her and Brian, he had always been there when she was growing up. Obviously, Phee had not been told of her year-long relationship with Michael, and it was clear to Miranda that Marcia had been brought along with the express purpose of meeting him.

Miranda's suspicion was confirmed at the breakfast table. She had risen early so she could use the bathroom first, and after dressing, made her way down to the kitchen. The radio was on, playing music from 3BA Ballarat, and the Aga stove gave out pleasing warmth. Alex McPherson appeared at the back door.

'Oh, good morning, Miranda. Did you sleep well?'

'Thank you, yes. Am I the first up?'

'Michael's out helping Lance with the milking, he'll be in presently. In the meantime, make yourself a cup of tea if you'd like one. I don't know how long before the others will be down.'

'Can I help in any way, like setting the table?'

Alex smiled. Miranda couldn't help responding – he reminded her so much of Michael.

By nine o'clock breakfast was on the table. Phee and Marcia had appeared, both fashionably dressed, their make-up so artfully applied that Miranda could easily imagine they were ready for a photo shoot. By not wearing any herself, she realised she must look the very opposite of glamorous.

Michael came in carrying a milk pail. Miranda was glad to see he was wearing overalls and heavy boots.

'Fresh from old Betty,' he announced cheerfully. 'Anyone for cornflakes with warm milk?'

Both older girls shook their heads having served themselves boiled eggs and toast. Miranda took up Michael's offer, smiling gratefully at him as he poured the milk over the crisp golden cereal. She was aware of a whispered conversation between Phee and Marcia, hearing the words 'that's what they have out here' and 'I prefer *croissants* myself.'

Phee decided to focus on Miranda and questioned her about how she was given her name, which she declared was somewhat unusual for a country person, before launching into the predictable 'And what does your father do?'

Miranda's response that her father was an undertaker was clearly unexpected, both visitors gave a discreet splutter of surprise. Phee looked over at Michael, her eyebrows raised.

Unsure how to respond to their reaction, Miranda tried to explain. 'It's a family business, my grandfather started it up early in the 1920s.'

'Oh.' Definitely a non-committal reply.

After a pause, Alex McPherson discreetly changed the subject and addressed the group. 'Now, have you decided what you want to do today?'

'In a minute, Daddy. One of the reasons I wanted to bring Marcia with me is for her to meet you, Michael.' She looked directly at him. 'Both Marcia and I are involved in a social committee that's organising functions for the coming season. One of our specials is, of course, the

Melbourne Cup, we definitely want you for that. Anyway, coming up on the 25th of October is – you tell him, Marcia.'

Marcia Hudson-Brown had a dazzling smile which she directed at Michael. 'My pet project is a dinner-dance at Leonardo's, very exclusive, only a hundred and twenty max, crème de la crème if you get my meaning. I'd absolutely love' – she gave the word a special emphasis – 'you to be my partner for the night!'

Michael looked across to Miranda who was frowning.

'That date rings a bell – isn't there something …'

'Angela Hall's twenty-first birthday.' Miranda's tone was flat.

Phee made a plea on her friend's behalf. 'I'm sure you could excuse my brother *just* this once. After all, it's a very special occasion, and a very special favour I'm asking you.'

It was a moment of truth, almost as though swords were drawn. Miranda, after a moment of hesitation, made the only reply possible, 'It's up to Michael.'

To her consternation, it seemed that the decision was final, and the subject was abruptly changed. 'You asked about today's plans, Daddy. As I said last night, a trip to Ballarat would be really good fun.' She turned to look at Miranda. 'Though not for you, I suppose. Perhaps you could keep Dad company while we're out.'

This was the last straw for Miranda. How *dare* she dominate everybody like that. She was aware her cheeks were flaming as she stood up.

'Actually, I think I'd like Michael to take me home.' She turned to him. 'Would that be all right with you?' Her voice was formal and controlled.

Major McPherson attempted a truce. 'No, Miranda, don't feel you have to go. I was hoping you'd spend at least a few days with us. I would be honoured if you would, as my daughter puts it, keep me company today. I was looking forward to showing you the historical information about Bournagulla, all the old photographs and memorabilia.'

This gracious invitation appealed to Miranda, who was on the point of accepting, when Phee intervened, 'Oh, I'm sure Marcia would like to see all that, too. Why not wait until we get back from Ballarat?'

Miranda's response was immediate.

'Thank you, Major. But no, not this time, if you don't mind. I'd really like you to take me home, Michael. Please.'

The atmosphere was frosty on the trip back to Beaufort. Michael tried to apologise, but was unable to ease Miranda's humiliation. She had already decided that their relationship was not going to progress any further, and it was a handshake, not a kiss, that she proffered at the front gate when they reached Speke Street.

It was hard to turn her back on this very desirable young man who had become central to her dreams and fantasies. It wasn't his fault – she knew that, and she recalled her father's words, 'He's out of our league, don't get your hopes up.'

Her parents were not home, which was a good thing. How was she going to explain her early return? She went to her room and shut the door firmly behind her. Under her pillow was the treasured photograph she looked at every night, a snapshot of the pair of them in a laughing embrace.

She felt tears prickling the back of her eyes. But she was too angry to cry. To be honest, she wanted to smash something into the supercilious face of Michael's damned sister. A squishy chocolate sponge, for preference. The image made her smile, and with it, her courage returned.

She decided to downplay the short visit when her parents arrived home. Just explain that Michael's sister and her friend had arrived unexpectedly and Michael had to play host to them. More or less true, but the rudeness she experienced needn't be mentioned.

There was a letter for her on the kitchen table. She was delighted to find it was from Gina, one of her closest nursing friends, with, of all things, an invitation! What a godsend!

When Grace arrived home from her CWA meeting, she found her daughter in good spirits.

'Mum, Gina Ryan has invited me down to her family's holiday house in Torquay for a few days – isn't that great?'

If Grace suspected that anything was wrong, she had nothing much to go on. A phone call to Gina confirmed Miranda's acceptance, in fact, the suggestion that she travel to Ballarat the next day to go to Torquay with the Ryan family was enthusiastically accepted.

At the dinner table that night she replied briefly to their questions about Bournagulla, describing the property favourably, but said little about the guests. She was more animated talking about Gina, who was also on annual leave, saying how they had quite a lot in common, even looking quite alike.

Grace and Jack exchanged questioning glances but decided not to probe further.

Chapter 13

'If Michael rings, tell him I've gone to stay with friends for a few days. Don't know when I'll be back,' Miranda said as she left to catch the Ballarat train the next day.

Those few days down at the beach proved to be just the distraction Miranda needed. Gina was one of the few friends she felt she could trust, and over the next three days, she confided in her, and in the retelling of her aborted visit to Bournagulla, she was gratified by the support from her colleague.

'I can't believe anyone could be so rude! She's ghastly! Imagine her as a sister-in-law,' she exclaimed.

'Well she won't be mine, thank God. I love Michael, at least I think I do. But I'm never going to be made to feel ashamed of who I am ever again.'

'Good on you, Miranda. Remember there are other fish in the sea, as they say.'

The Ryan family's holiday house turned out to be little more than a shack. One wouldn't want to live in it permanently, but basic needs were met, even if the beds were no more than camp stretchers. Gina's parents, Maureen and Bill, were easygoing and hospitable.

'It's good you could come down with Gina, all her other friends had their own plans, and her brothers are interstate, so she would have just had us. Do make yourself at home.' Maureen had said.

That was easy to do. After buying fish and chips at the local shop, Gina and Miranda spent the first evening on a long walk along the front beach. It was sunset. The tide was out, exposing clumps of seaweed on the shiny wet sand.

'Doesn't it smell strange!' Miranda exclaimed. Gina smiled in agreement. As they strolled barefoot in the shallows, a group of four or five young men approached them and stopped to talk.

'Hi,' said one of them, 'you visiting for the weekend?'

On being told they were student nurses on holiday, some of the boys exchanged knowing glances and moved a little closer. 'So you'd be up for a good time, eh?'

Quick thinking saved the day. Gina said they were waiting for their boyfriends to join them. 'In fact, we should turn back in case they're at the car park now.'

With that, they set off quickly without looking back at the group who, luckily, decided not to follow them.

'That was smart, Gina. They look like locals on the make. Could have been awkward.'

Fine spring weather greeted them next day. The canvas stretcher wasn't especially comfortable, but to her surprise, Miranda had slept well. *Must be the sea air*, she thought.

Over breakfast, she offered to provide something for the evening meal for the four of them, to which Bill said he had planned to light the barbeque outside since the weather was fine. 'You could get some sausages, and a chop or two from the butchers if you like – we've got everything else.'

A slow walk along the street brought them to the bakery. The smell of freshly-baked bread teased their nostrils.

'Let's get some fresh rolls, they'll be great with the barbeque, I'll pay for them, that'll be my contribution if you're getting the meat,' Gina offered.

That settled, they headed back with their purchases and then decided on their afternoon's activity.

'You haven't been here before, have you?' To Miranda's shake of the head, due to a mouth full of sandwich, Gina continued, 'You've got to go to the back beach, that's the reason most people come here, young ones anyway, for the amazing surf. And, of course, Bells Beach – you've heard of that, surely.'

Miranda indicated that she'd probably heard of it, but was only prepared to watch. 'I know I would be hopeless at surfing.'

Gina laughed. 'I am definitely hopeless at it. My brothers are pretty good though, I like to watch them in action when they're here. Don't worry, we'll find it entertaining just sitting in the sand dunes and taking it all in.'

The scene was magical. Choosing a spot halfway up the dune, the girls arranged their beach towels so they could sit and survey the panorama below. Waves formed, regularly rising to a crescendo before crashing at the water's edge in a cascade of frothy bubbles. There were several wetsuited surfers in the middle distance, while the horizon was a straight line of dark-blue sea meeting the pale-blue sky. The crescent beach was of soft pale-gold sand rising to a splendid rocky bluff at the western end. Groups of people lazed on the sand, children dug holes and made sandcastles, a dog or two sniffed around.

'Perfect, isn't it?' exclaimed Gina.

'I'm just going to lie here and drink in the sun,' said Miranda, rolling her cotton skirt up, allowing her bare legs to be exposed. Before long, she was asleep, oblivious to the occasional squawk of a seagull.

Gina stretched out on her beach towel, too, but soon became restless. She got up and wandered down towards the Surf Club. One or two of the surfers lounging around inside looked vaguely familiar, and it was easy to strike up a friendly conversation.

After about twenty minutes, she decided to check on Miranda.

'Hey, where did you get to?'

'Just went down to the Surf Club, had a chat with a couple of blokes I'd met on our last trip here. Guess what – there's a dance on here tonight. They said they need more girls to make up the numbers. We should go.'

'We've got your Dad's barbeque, remember.'

'I know. We'll go after that, it won't start until after nine.'

Miranda agreed. *Why not.* It would be strange going to a dance without Michael, but maybe it was something she'd have to get used to.

Maureen Ryan invited Miranda to sit next to her on the bench seat, while Bill and Gina prepared the meat and salad for the barbeque. They worked so well as a team, it was obvious they'd done it many times before.

'Now tell me – how are you enjoying your training?' Mrs Ryan asked.

'I am. It's so interesting, so many different illnesses and conditions. And the patients – from all walks of life, really. I'm learning new things all the time.'

'Did Gina tell you I started nursing training? Just before the war.' She paused. Miranda asked whether she'd finished it. 'No,' Maureen replied, a tinge of regret in her voice. 'I got married. Had to. Gina's older brother was on the way.' She laughed. 'No choice in those days. I ended up with two boys, then Gina quite a few years later. No regrets, though it was tough during the war years with Bill away. Thank God he came back safe and sound, lots of his mates didn't.'

Miranda agreed, saying her parents had a similar experience, though they didn't get married until her dad was discharged from the army. That made Gina's brothers quite a bit older than Brian, she realised.

Maureen continued, 'Do you and Gina ever work together?

'We did once, last year, night duty on male surgical which had some orthopaedic patients. I remember one night I was concerned about a young man in traction who seemed to be having a fit.' She called out to Gina who came over. 'Remember Vinnie in Ortho, how I could hear the bed and the traction equipment shaking, and thought we should get the doctor on call?'

Gina laughed. 'I certainly do. I had to acquaint you with some facts of life, one of the advantages of having older brothers and thin walls.'

Maureen looked puzzled. Her daughter provided enlightenment. 'He was, well, wanking. Perfectly normal.'

The delicious odour of cooked chops, sausages and fried onions pervaded the air. Bill announced that everything was ready.

They enjoyed the feast in silence until Gina announced that she and Miranda were going to the surf club dance later on.

'Don't be too late home now. Your mother and I thought we'd drive over to Queenscliff tomorrow, that way you'll see Barwon Heads, and Ocean Grove too. You haven't been down this way before, have you?' Bill asked Miranda.

'No, I haven't. Though Dad was always promising us that one day we would, but it didn't ever happen. So I'm really grateful. Thank you.'

'I didn't bring any glamorous clothes, will this be okay?' Miranda asked Gina as they got ready for the outing. She was reassured that it would not be a fashion event, in fact the opposite.

Night had fallen by the time they left. They took a torch with them, as well as a light jacket, as evenings were cool. As they made their way towards the back beach, the music, mostly guitar and drums, got louder, and on reaching the crest of the sand dune, looking down, many shadowy figures of young people could be seen, both inside and outside the building.

Just as well there aren't any neighbours, thought Miranda, as they edged their way inside the heaving clubhouse. Noise, voices, coloured lights, drinks, people jostling and vague apologies, it was a riotous affront to the senses. Gina paid the entrance fee and cautiously advanced towards Miranda with two full glasses.

'I think it's a sort of punch,' she said. 'Think I'll stick to one in case it's stronger than it looks.'

Miranda's recollections of the evening were of chaotic crush, being asked to dance by different young men, some were just boys, and very little room to move on the crowded dance floor. There were several girls too, also looking very young. It was impossible to make conversation, the sound was too loud, mainly due to the enthusiasm of the drummer who seemed to fuel his vigour with cans of beer at every opportunity.

After an hour, though it seemed longer, Miranda needed some fresh air and made her way onto the balcony. Gina was there and invited her to join the little group leaning against the railings.

'Hey, you two look like sisters!' said one young man.

'We're not,' said Gina, 'This is my friend Miranda. I'll try and remember your names – Sam, Joe, Tony and, and …'

'Mitchell,' the person in question offered.

'We were just hearing about what's going on in San Francisco. Tony's just come back and he's rapt.'

Miranda looked at the unusually dressed, long-haired and barefoot young man who, to her surprise, had a flower tucked behind his ear.

'Yes, man, that's the place to be. Flower power, they call it, and the motto is, "make love not war," I can't wait to go back.' He pronounced 'can't' with a broad American accent.

'Interesting character, wasn't he,' remarked Gina on the way home.

'Hmm. Yes, I suppose he was. But what got me interested is the idea of going to another country, not as a tourist, but to work, and be part of the local scene. How did he get to go there, did he say?'

Gina shook her head saying it was too noisy to hear everything he said. 'It was all a bit of fun, wasn't it? Did it take your mind off Michael?'

'No, it felt strange to have someone different holding me and trying to keep upright in the crush. I kept wishing it was him. All the time.'

'How was last night for you?' asked Maureen as they travelled in the station wagon towards Barwon Heads on their Sunday excursion.

'Fun, yes, but noisy. There was a boy who'd been living in California, he was interesting. He's inspired us to travel overseas, hasn't he, Miranda?'

'Well, just make sure you finish your training first.'

Everybody smiled. It was the obvious condition before approval.

Back home in Beaufort, Miranda's first question was to ask if Michael had been in touch. He had, but not by phone. Instead, Grace handed her an unstamped letter. Michael had spoken to Brian at the bank and found out she was away. Next day he returned with the letter and asked Brian to give it to his sister, saying, 'The post takes ages.'

Miranda took it to her bedroom, feeling anxious, opened it. *Was it his way of saying goodbye?* She need not have worried.

> My dear Miranda,
>
> I want you to know how bad I feel about the way you were treated when you visited Bournagulla You are very important to

me, and I hoped our friendship would develop into something deeper. Please don't shut me out of your life.

With much love – Michael.

The gentle, caring words had the desired effect. She reread the note and whispered, 'of course I won't, Michael,' to the last sentence.

At the dinner table, Jack commented, 'You look better for your time away at the beach.'

'Yes, tell us about it, dear,' said Grace.

Miranda described Torquay with its two very different beaches, the Ryans' holiday house, which was anything but lavish, though comfortable and fun. She mentioned the surf club dance she and Gina went to, made even more interesting by the presence of Tony and the lifestyle he'd recently been part of.

'Sound like hippies to me,' snorted Brian. Miranda recognised the derisory tone. Brian would never be attracted to the flower power movement, she realised. *He's too conventional, like Dad.*

'The thing is – it's not Tony himself that intrigued me …'

'I should hope not,' interjected her father.

'It's the idea of going overseas, being part of a different community and culture, working there, all that.' She paused and continued, 'He sort of inspired me. Gina felt the same.'

Grace smiled. She found herself unknowingly echoing the same sentiment Mrs Ryan had expressed when the subject came up last weekend.

'Of course, I'm going to finish my training first,' Miranda said, in a decisive tone of voice. 'I'm really looking forward to third year. Hopefully, this time next year I'll be a nursing sister in a veil and blue uniform.'

Miranda noticed an airmail letter on the mantelpiece. 'Is that from Bridie?' she asked.

'It certainly is. Read it, it's all good.'

In a sort of 'touching base' letter, Bridie apologised for not being in touch since Christmas because they were so busy with things in rural

Ireland. Miranda knew about the happiness that Antoinette and Joe's wedding had brought both families eighteen months ago. Now she was learning that Bridie and Phil were to become grandparents!

Her first thought was, *Hey, Joe's the same age as Dad! But it's still good news.*

'Isn't that lovely,' Miranda exclaimed. 'I'm so pleased for them, after all they've been through. Looks like he's beaten you, Brian, to the noble calling of fatherhood.'

Everybody laughed.

Chapter 14

The three stripes on her starched white cap indicated seniority and more responsibility. Miranda was equal to the task.

Her first assignment was the intensive care ward with all the new experiences it offered. There were fewer patients here, each one requiring highly specialised treatment with detailed observations to be recorded. There were times of frantic activity when resuscitation was required, often successfully, but sometimes not, when even the most intensive efforts failed to save the patient's life.

Not all student nurses enjoyed working under such pressure, but for Miranda, the challenge was stimulating. When a patient, critically ill when admitted to the unit, recovered to the point of leaving the ICU and moving to a regular ward, all the staff involved shared a sense of satisfaction.

Michael presented himself to the Nurses Home reception some two weeks after Miranda had returned to work.

'Visitor for Nurse Shaw, Nurse Miranda Shaw, come to reception, please,' sounded over the loudspeaker in the Nurses Home.

Initially tentative, Miranda's reserve melted as she was drawn into his familiar warm embrace.

'Did you get my letter? I gave it to Brian to give to you.'

'Yes, yes – I got it. Thank you. I intended to reply, but I got rostered to a very busy area and just didn't get around to it. I'm sorry.'

Together they went off happily in the Land Rover to their favourite little coffee shop not far from Lake Wendouree, both smiling.

'I hope we can get back to the way things were,' Michael said, anticipation in his voice.

'Yes, so do I. But I've got a busy year ahead of me, as you know. We just have to take things slowly.' Michael looked troubled. Seeing his frown, Miranda smiled and reached over the table to take his hand. 'It's okay. You're very special to me too, you know.'

That seemed to reassure him.

Later, back at the Nurses Home, she tried to analyse what she had really meant. Things had turned out differently from the heady anticipation she had felt in the past. Elements of doubt had crept in, one being the experience of meeting his sister and the unexplained family issues and, more recently, the tiny spark of possibly working overseas when she graduated.

It's just as well I don't have to make any decisions yet, she thought. *Maybe just wait and see what happens.*

She apologised to Angela Hall for coming to her twenty-first birthday party alone.

'I thought you had a steady boyfriend,' said Angela.

'Sorry, he couldn't make it,' was all Miranda was prepared to say.

Thinking about it, she decided that she didn't really need to know what Michael did when she wasn't around. She wouldn't ask about the lavish elite dinner party, the Melbourne Cup, Marcia, or any other glamour girl he might meet.

I'm not jealous, she said to herself. *He's caring to me when we're together, and that's all I need to be happy.*

Christmas loomed. She was rostered on right through the holiday period, this time as senior nurse in the Children's Ward. The staff had decorated the infants' room and the older children's ward with crepe paper and tinsel. Only the very sick children were hospitalised at this time, the lucky ones were able to go home and be with their family for a while. The nurses did duty as Santa whenever parents left presents for their child to find at the end of their cot on Christmas morning.

Most student nurses loved working with children, though the necessity of injecting little bodies was always heartbreaking. Though the needles were fine gauge, the procedure still hurt, creating cries of anguish. 'I know it's hard for you, but it has to be done,' said the Charge Sister to student nurses who were distressed by having to be involved.

Pathology, pharmacology and psychiatry lectures continued much as before. Some were given by specialist doctors, with the quality of teaching varying according to the aptitude of the teacher. Medical and surgical textbooks could be consulted if the lecture had been vague. Miranda continued to absorb, to question and to attain high marks for her written work.

'You could be top of the state in the finals,' one of the tutor sisters predicted.

'I don't know about that, I just love learning,' Miranda replied.

Summer was, as usual, hot, especially in January. Michael explained to Miranda that he would not be able to leave the property very often because of the danger of fire.

'We've got a tank and hose on the back of the truck ready to go, like every other landowner. It's a worrying time.'

'I understand. Is your father all right? I mean, in the heat?'

'He's not too bad, but he's getting older, you know. He always asks after you. Wants you to visit again when you can.'

That did, in fact, soon happen and proved to be much more agreeable than the first occasion. Major McPherson took the opportunity to show Miranda the photographs and documents of the property of which he was so obviously proud. She was impressed and expressed her admiration for his collection, which pleased him.

Mrs Hardwick, the housekeeper, remembered her and welcomed her warmly.

'You're much nicer than those city girls,' Mrs Hardwick commented. Tactfully, she did not elaborate. Miranda wondered if Phee had brought other friends besides Marcia to visit. The question was unimportant, Miranda told herself. It didn't matter and was none of her business anyway.

Michael seemed even more drawn to her than previously. She was aware of his physical arousal when they embraced. It's entirely natural, she knew. And there was no doubt her body responded. *This is desire*, she thought, *about which so many love songs are written*. Their kissing was delicious, their breathing warm and intimately connected. Michael was always the one who broke away first. Miranda took that as evidence of his self-control and knew that he would never overstep his gentlemanly code of behaviour.

During one evening shift in late January in the male surgical ward, there was time to have a cup of tea in the nurses' station during visiting hours. All the work was up-to-date, leaving a rare time to chat. The sister on duty, Rachel Holden, had recently become engaged. Miranda admired the small but pretty diamond ring on Rachel's left fourth finger.

'I suppose you'll be resigning after you get married,' she commented.

'Oh, no, I want to keep on working. We're saving up to buy a house.'

'But – what if you get pregnant?' Miranda regretted the question as soon as she uttered it, but Rachel didn't seem to mind.

Looking around to ensure that they were alone in the office, she moved her chair close to Miranda and said in a whisper, 'I won't, not until we're ready.' Miranda's mouth opened as she was about to speak, but Rachel continued 'I'm on the Pill – have you heard of it? It's very new, but I have a very understanding doctor who agrees that women should choose when to have babies. So I'm safe, or should I say, *we're* safe.' She finished with a broad smile, which left Miranda in no doubt as to her meaning.

'Do you mean – it's a contraceptive?'

Rachel nodded, adding, 'Beats the old methods hands down. Only thing is, you always have to remember to take it. Uh-oh, someone wants to speak to us.'

A visitor had come to the window wanting some information.

Miranda's mind whirled. Maybe this could be a way to enjoy full intimacy with Michael without the worry of an unwanted consequence. She dismissed the idea of asking for a prescription from Dr Santorini. As a Catholic, he would not approve, especially as she was unmarried.

Later that evening, after the patients were settled for the night, she sought Rachel again.

'Rachel, I wonder if it would be possible for me to see your GP and maybe get the same script you were talking about. I'm,' she hesitated, 'I'm about to become engaged too, but don't tell anyone yet, nothing's finalised. But if I could start on it …' she broke off, a little embarrassed.

'Of course, Miranda. I'll put the information in an envelope and put it in your pigeonhole.'

It was amazing how simple it all turned out to be. Dr Joske was kind and understanding. After a few general health questions, he provided the script. There were some words of advice 'Don't forget to take it as stated on the packet, and if anyone finds out and asks you, you could always say it's to regulate your cycle, it is used for that, too.' There was a brief hesitation, then he added, 'Protection may not be absolute in the first month, so bear that in mind.'

A few weeks later, a late summer storm coincided with Miranda's days off, meaning she and Michael could spend some time together.

'Let's go somewhere and have a cuddle. Somewhere where we won't be disturbed. Would that be all right?'

Miranda happily agreed. Michael had suggested that she pack a picnic lunch and a thermos of tea. They decided on an eleven o'clock start.

'What about Black Hill Reserve?' he suggested, 'It's a great view from the top, and there shouldn't be anyone else much around, being a weekday and the kids back at school. The weather might put people off, too.'

The picnic spot had many pine trees and was deserted. Michael put down an old tartan rug in a little nook under some native shrubs that provided shelter from the warm drizzly rain.

'Come down here and let me hug you. We can eat later.'

Michael's invitation was irresistible. Their bodies locked in a strong urgent embrace. Through Michael's cotton shirt, Miranda could feel the firmness of his torso, so strong, so warm. Their lips met in a kiss that was more passionate than ever, lasting much longer. Eventually breaking the contact, Michael breathed words Miranda had often fantasised.

'I want you, Miranda, I want you so much.'

Embracing again, the pressure of his arousal left no doubt in Miranda's mind that he wanted to consummate their relationship.

Yes, yes! her excited body entreated. *But here?* She was having second thoughts. She remembered Anne's words, 'Have you done it yet? I nearly did, got close … That's probably all I'll ever have.'

The effect was instantaneous. She drew in a breath, and the tension in her limbs subsided.

Michael felt it. 'What's wrong?'

'I – I thought I heard someone coming.'

It was enough to change the situation. He half sat up, listening.

'I can't hear anyone. But it could have been, well, awkward. Perhaps we can just go for a walk up to the lookout, and then come back for our picnic, okay?'

'Sure. Sorry.'

He smiled and clasped her hand to help her up.

'You know, it reminds me of that great song in West Side Story.' He began to sing; 'There's a place for us, somewhere a place for us,' before losing track of the lyrics. Miranda couldn't help laughing. What an amazing person! Who else would quote a romantic song from a popular musical after being denied such an experience?

'Hold my hand and we're half-way there,' she sang, as they started off on the track.

Maybe we will have a somewhere, somehow, some day.

Summer finally cooled off to autumn, and the splendid displays of colourful dying leaves added charm to the streets of Ballarat, especially around the lake and the botanical gardens. Inevitably, the leaves fell, making a colourful carpet before being dispersed into gutters and drains.

It was also the start of a new football season. Brian had decided to stay on as assistant manager at the bank in Beaufort to be on hand for the intensive pre-season training. Although there had been opportunities to become manager of one or two smaller country branches of the Commercial Banking Company of Sydney, he chose to stay at Beaufort, foregoing a salary increase.

Both Jack and Grace were happy about his decision.

Michael attended most of the practice matches but usually didn't stay on. However, after the home game to start the season, he accepted an invitation to share an evening meal with Brian and his parents.

Two weeks later, Miranda and Michael met up on Tuesday after his trip to the Ballarat saleyards. Following a warm hug in greeting, it was off to their favourite little cafe for afternoon tea.

'Miranda, have you seen your mother lately?' was one of his first questions.

'I haven't been home for a while, actually. Why?'

'I had tea at your place on Saturday after the game, which we won, by the way.'

'Good. Go on – about Mum.'

'I thought she seemed a bit short of breath, more so than usual. Brian said he hadn't particularly noticed it, but often you don't see changes when you see a person every day.'

Miranda was silent. An uncomfortable feeling of guilt crept into her mind. Here she was, a senior student nurse looking after sick people, and she hadn't paid enough attention to her own family. She resolved to make amends by going home on her next days off.

'Thanks for telling me, Michael. I talk to her on the phone at least once a week but, of course, she never complains. Never would. How's your dad?'

Michael assured her that he was well. Phee was in New Zealand again, in the North Island this time, probably yachting.

'How on earth can she afford it,' Miranda blurted out, instantly regretting the question. *None of my business.*

'Oh, she has independent means, as they say, inheritances and the like. She doesn't have any idea of how normal people live and have to work.'

Miranda had three days off before starting night duty, after which there would be study blocks leading into Finals in August, so it was a good opportunity to make a trip to Beaufort.

She decided to enter the house quietly and hope to observe her mother without her knowing. Her heart skipped a beat as she noticed the stooped shoulders and slower movements. Of course, Mum would say, 'What's the hurry?' but her movements and general appearance revealed lower energy levels.

Grace crossed from one side of the kitchen to the other, opened and closed drawers and checked a saucepan on the stove. Miranda watched quietly until her mother turned and suddenly realised she was there.

With a start, she exclaimed, 'Oh, Mirrie. You gave me a fright … I didn't know you were coming home this weekend.' She paused, a look of alarm on her face. 'Is everything all right?'

'Mum,' cried Miranda, rushing to embrace her, 'of course it is. I Just got three days off and decided to surprise you with a visit. Now, are you okay?' Her voice became more serious. 'Tell me, please.'

Grace made her way to the nearest chair and sat down to face her daughter. She sighed.

'Funny you should ask that – I saw Dr Santorini two days ago and told him that I seem to be getting slower these days and often get out of breath.' She paused.

'And?' prompted Miranda.

'He did the usual examination and ended up saying my heart was not working so well. So he put me on a new heart tablet and a di-re-tic …'

'Diuretic,' murmured Miranda

'… to get rid of the fluid,' she pointed to her ankles, 'see – they get a bit puffy. Trouble is, with these tablets I'm going to the toilet all the time,' she laughed.

'That's the general idea, Mum. It gets rid of fluid build-up. Sounds like the right sort of treatment to me.'

'Mirrie, please don't say anything to Dad about this – this conversation. I don't want him to fuss over me, I really am all right, you know.' Grace's tentative smile touched Miranda's heart.

'Not if you don't want me to, Mum. But do keep your appointments with Dr Santorini, and let me know if he alters anything.'

Grace nodded and changed the subject. 'So you're still seeing Michael, I gather. We love having him here for tea after a footy game.'

Miranda assured her that their friendship was strong. She also asked about Brian.

'He's very popular with the young ladies, nothing new there. But he doesn't seem to be in any hurry to settle down with anyone. I suppose there's plenty of time for that. Even the photo Bridie sent us of Joe's little daughter didn't seem to raise even a spark of envy. Here, have a look – isn't she sweet!'

There were lots of things to do around the house in the next two days. Gardening was not Miranda's favourite chore, but under Grace's guidance, she managed to clear out a lot of debris, dead leaves and some resistant weeds. She was pleasantly tired and satisfied after a few hours' work. The scones and tea, followed by a well-earned snooze on the couch, were ample reward for her effort.

It occurred to Miranda that she had not discussed her intentions with her family. However, when she woke from her nap, the question came from her mother.

'What do you plan to do after you graduate?'

'After I become a fully-qualified nursing sister, assuming I pass Finals,' she said with a smile, 'hopefully, in just a few months, first of all, I'd like to work here at the local hospital for a while, mainly to save money, because, well, I probably haven't told you officially, I want to go to England to work for about six months.'

This last bit came out in a rush. Her mother looked very serious.

'But, Michael ...'

'Michael knows all about it. He understands. He's already been overseas a few times, and once to England. He knows I want to do this, I need to do this now, otherwise I might never get there.'

'Well, you do manage to spring surprises on us.' Grace became reflective. She leaned back in her chair and gazed out the window. 'You know I always wanted to visit the UK, Scotland in particular, since my mother came from there. But it was never possible …' She turned to face her daughter. 'You're going to have to tell us all about it, everything.' She finished with a smile that Miranda would always remember.

I'd be doing it for Mum, as well as myself.

Dad wasn't so encouraging when Miranda's plans became the subject of discussion after the evening meal.

'Why on earth would you want to do that?' he said. 'This country is crying out for nurses – you'll always get a job here.'

'And probably better-paid,' chipped in Brian.

As usual, Mum stepped in to say it was Miranda's decision, and it was perfectly all right for her to go overseas to work if she wanted to.

'Do you know where, yet?' she asked.

Miranda admitted that she hadn't got that far, she had to concentrate on passing her Finals first, and anyway, one of the tutor sisters was from England and could give her advice nearer the time.

Whatever was going on in the world around them was of marginal interest to the cohort of third-year student nurses preparing for final examinations. The wards were particularly busy, as winter had set in, with cases of serious chest infections, including pneumonia, markedly increasing.

Miranda was still in uniform when Michael called at the Nurses Home unannounced. He began by saying it was a short visit only, so no time for the customary visit to their cafe. Instead, they went into the visitors lounge and exchanged kisses. He held her at arm's length and asked Miranda if she was all right.

'Yes, of course I am. Why?'

He replied that she looked a bit peaky, then asked with a hint of sympathy in his voice, 'Is it that time of the month?'

The question was right out of the blue, he'd never asked such a thing before.

'It is, actually, but I am all right, honest.' He smiled and changed the subject.

'Miranda, I'd like you to be part of my birthday celebration in two week's time.'

His birthday? She'd completely forgotten about it. Searching her memory she came up with a date. 'The twenty-eighth, isn't it? Gosh, how exciting. Are you having a big party or something?'

'You'll see,' he said with a smile, 'it's not a special one in any way. I'll be twenty-four. Getting old.' They both laughed.

Michael had more news for her, which he prefaced by saying he would like to buy her a really fashionable dress, 'top drawer' as he put it. Miranda, surprised at this, found herself bristling and on the defensive.

'Why?' she blurted out.

'I'm about to tell you. My sister is going to announce her engagement to this New Zealander, the one whose yacht she's been sailing on, and it's to be at a private afternoon tea at the Windsor. In Melbourne,' he added, noting her startled look.

'When?'

'The last week in August, I believe. Probably on a Friday, with the weekend to be spent in extravagant celebration.'

'Oh – that's not going to work out for me, Michael. I have exams that week. Finals. I'm sure Phee won't notice if I'm not there.'

'She mightn't, but I will.' He sounded disappointed. 'Never mind. Let's concentrate on my event. I'd still like to buy you a special dress.'

'No, Michael. I wouldn't feel right about it.' She glanced at the watch pinned to the pocket of her white apron. 'Hey, it's getting late. Don't you have to pick your father up at four-thirty?'

A quick kiss and he was gone, leaving Miranda very confused.

One thing was becoming clear – Michael was surer about their relationship than she was. Hovering in the forefront of her mind was the prospect of going overseas to work. Any emotional commitment would have to come after that. It would be hard, she knew that, but her mind was made up.

Now, what will I get Michael for his birthday?

Her contemplation was interrupted by Gina who had come looking for her, lecture notes in hand.

'We've got that extra tute on infectious diseases, remember. Come on, we'll be late.'

The winter flu season had taken its toll on the staff as well as the general community, consequently, as the rosters became depleted, overtime was frequently available. Miranda was only too happy to put her name down for the extra hours – the money would go towards her airfare to Europe. She had managed to get an appointment with the deputy head nurse tutor, Sister Fotheringham who had trained at the Middlesex Hospital before migrating to Australia. The slim grey-haired nurse still had a crisp English accent. Her advice was to read through the copies of the *UK Nurses Journal* in the library, and also *Community Care* which, she said, often had unusual positions advertised.

'You could also register with one of the nursing agencies and, if you wanted to, you could do short-term assignments, even in different parts of the country. Anyway – good luck, I'd be happy to provide a reference for you.'

July 28th dawned overcast and cold. Michael had rung the day before to confirm that he would be picking her up at five o'clock.

'What should I wear?' Miranda asked.

'Something warm. And pack an overnight bag,' was his response.

Sounds like we're heading for Bournagulla, she thought.

Promptly at five, Michael drew up, in the Pontiac this time.

After a kiss and 'Happy, happy birthday,' he put her small suitcase in the boot and they made their way out of Ballarat. But not in the usual direction.

'Where, exactly, are we going?' asked Miranda.

'We're going to Daylesford.'

'Daylesford? Are you having a party there?'

'You and I are having a party, my love. A special date, just the two of us.'

Well. So that was it. Miranda smiled to herself. This was romantic. If she'd guessed right, very romantic. And special. She felt a thrill of anticipation at what was very likely to happen knowing that the possibility, no, certainty, had been there for some time now.

They travelled through the quaint town of Creswick and turned right on to the Daylesford road. Nearer their destination, the route was uphill through densely forested bush so dark and majestic that it commanded silence. At the top of the last climb, the streetscape of the historic central Victorian town came into view.

'I know where to go, I came up last week to check out the place we're staying at.' He stole a sideways glance at her. 'I booked under the name of Mr and Mrs McPherson. Hope you don't mind.'

Miranda was surprised, then with a little giggle, set his mind at rest. 'No, of course not. That makes it a real adventure. I'll never forget your twenty-fourth birthday.'

Their destination was a small cottage down a side street. A placard said it was a B&B with the delightful name of Honeysuckle Cottage. Sure enough, a profusion of the leafy vine cascaded over the front veranda. Michael took a small packet from his pocket. It contained a welcome card, a list of instructions and the key. He opened the front door and found the electricity box just inside.

'I only have to turn on the main switch.'

Together they explored the cottage, the single bedroom with an iron frame double bed, the cosy lounge, the cute little kitchen.

'It says here that breakfast is self-service,' Miranda remarked.

Sure enough, she found cereal, fruit, four eggs and a loaf of bread in a cupboard.

The fridge had started to hum gently. Inside, as well as butter and milk, there was a bottle of white wine.

Turning to face Michael, she fell into his outstretched arms for a prolonged hug which contained more than a hint of passion.

'Whew,' said Michael, disengaging, 'enough of that for the moment. We've got dinner booked at the best hotel in town.'

Miranda was glad she'd packed her long-sleeved burgundy woollen dress, the skirt was long enough to just cover the top of the long black boots that Michael had admired when she first wore them. The platform soles and stacked heels gave her an extra few inches in height.

Dinner was perfect. The candlelit table for two, the gracious host offering complimentary cocktails 'for the birthday boy', the exquisitely prepared meal and, finally, two tiny glasses of liqueur, he chose Drambuie, and for her, Benedictine – a very pleasant way to finish.

'I'm on cloud nine,' Miranda whispered as they drove back to Honeysuckle Cottage.

'Let's see if we can make it cloud ten,' Michael replied.

In the bedroom, they scouted around for matches to light the scented candle on the dressing table and found them in a little side drawer.

They slowly undressed, each demurely glancing at the other, as clothing was discarded to reveal bodies gleaming in the gentle flickering light.

'You're even more beautiful than I imagined,' murmured Michael. Miranda smiled shyly as his body revealed itself to her. 'This is new for you, my darling. I'll try to be gentle but I – I want you so much.'

The memory of what followed was a kaleidoscope of heat, passion and excitement. The overwhelming sensation of being joined together in an act of love was bliss, pure bliss.

As they recovered in a tangle of limbs and sweat, Miranda found herself whispering, 'Thank you, oh, thank you.' All sense of time evaporated. It felt so right to be entwined and seemingly floating down to earth.

Michael raised himself to a half-sitting position and looked intently into her face.

'Miranda,' he said, a serious tone in his voice, 'I want you to know that if, well, if you become pregnant, that's all right. We'll just get married earlier, that's all.'

For a moment Miranda didn't know how to respond. A tiny tremor ran down her spine. It was possibly time to be totally honest. Or not.

She hadn't told him she had been taking the contraceptive pill for several months. Some reservation stopped her in the past, and she recognised that now was definitely not the right time. A tiny suspicion surfaced that perhaps he wanted her to conceive on this, her first sexual encounter, remembering he had discovered that her last period was two weeks ago.

She murmured something banal into his chest with its carpet of fine ginger hair.

'Oh,' she said suddenly, 'I haven't given you your birthday present yet!'

'You just did!' he said with a laugh.

Michael was impressed with the leather pouch she had bought for him.

'Men don't usually have handbags, I know. But this one is designed for maps, for when you're travelling.'

'For when *we're* travelling, you mean,' he corrected her.

Chapter 15

She had crossed the Rubicon, Miranda decided. There was no going back. An amazing leap from innocence to awareness. When she had a chance to talk privately with Gina, her best friend, it was hard to find the right words.

Gina started it off with, 'I'm so happy for you, I knew it would happen one day. Are you okay about everything?' Miranda's beaming smile reassured her. 'Well – how do you feel?'

What could she say? It could be the most significant experience of her life so far. Or it could be acknowledged as something that happened, but life goes on, with much more ahead to look forward to. Or something in between.

'Did he wear a condom?' Gina asked, 'Hope that isn't too personal, but remember the old saying, "If you can't be good, be careful. If you can't be careful, remember the date!"'

They both giggled.

'I'd rather not go into details,' Miranda replied. Even with her best friend, some things were better kept private.

The run-up to the Final exams meant swotting, practice exams, and tension. Revision of drugs and dosages, symptoms of common ailments and their treatment were all part of the preparation. The senior tutor explained that the exam would assess their ability and accuracy in dealing with situations commonly presented in a hospital setting.

'They may throw in a short question on some rare diagnosis, like, say, Addison's Disease.' She smiled as some of the students exchanged blank looks. 'Look it up anyway,' she said encouragingly.

By the beginning of September, it was all over. On the whole, the exam was manageable. The main essay subjects were familiar, as in the last three years, they had often come across patients with these conditions and illnesses. Some of the shorter questions related to less familiar diagnoses which were a problem for some, but not for Miranda who tackled each of them enthusiastically.

It was a relief to go back to work after the last paper. The 'if only' recriminations were fully aired until, eventually, the futility of post-mortems was recognised, and it was decided to just wait until the results were published.

During the exam period, Miranda had completely forgotten about Phee's engagement party. She brought up the subject when she next met with Michael. He was restrained in his response, just muttering that it was all right, he supposed.

'Well, what's her fiancé like?' she persisted. The pause indicated that there were reservations.

'He's one of those very confident businessmen whose main interest seems to be the stock market. He oozes prosperity. Guess that's what attracted Phee. I don't have much in common with him.'

'And your father? Do you think he approves?'

'Dad doesn't say much. He was his usual polite self. Wished them well, of course. On the way home he said we'll just have to bide our time and see what happens.'

Michael seemed happy to drop the subject. Strong arms embraced her and all other thoughts were abandoned.

The weeks passed, and, finally, the results were published.

Most satisfying was that everyone passed. It would have been disappointing if any of the group had needed to resit the exam.

'Gee, Miranda, you did well,' Judy Welsh exclaimed as they studied the notice in the foyer. 'In the top five of the State!'

Nice to hear, yes. But not Top of the State. That honour went to a candidate from the Alfred.

A flush of disappointment came and quickly went. So what. She had everything ahead of her, in particular, Michael. And her overseas trip. Mum, Dad and Brian were pleased, and Michael gave her a sweet little congratulatory card.

Graduation was an occasion to remember forever. Caps were replaced by starched white organdie veils, and grey-striped uniforms by the new blue nursing sisters' dress. No aprons – how different! How professional they all looked!

Dr Odgers, the new Medical Director of the hospital, gave the address to the graduates. In his mid-thirties, he looked youngish and very smart, his receding hairline conferring an impression of authority. He spoke of the future of hospital management trends and the consequent impact on nursing practice, based on his recent study tour of the USA and Canada.

He told the assembly that there was a trend, especially in America, to use pre-packaged disposable dressing and procedure trays as well as other innovative practices. But the main thrust of his speech was to assure the graduating nurses that the standard of care provided by staff at the Ballarat Base Hospital, was equal to, and possibly, better than any he'd seen anywhere on his overseas tour.

This brought spontaneous applause from the audience.

He concluded by saying, 'The most important person in any hospital is the patient who is being treated – that is universally recognised, and we must never forget it. Now, to the newly qualified group of nursing sisters – congratulations on your achievement, and may your career be long and satisfying.'

After the speeches, Matron Watson called the new graduates in alphabetical order to receive a handshake and the hospital badge.

When it came to S, and Miranda Shaw was called, Matron announced that as well as topping the Base Hospital final results, she had come third in the State. Miranda's smile could not have been broader as she advanced to shake the Medical Superintendent's hand and receive her badge to enthusiastic applause. She could see her parents, Brian and Michael in the audience and gave a discreet wave.

'Well done, Sister Shaw,' said Brian afterwards. 'They should pay you extra for that.'

Chapter 16

One-thirty in the morning. It was quiet in the wards of Beaufort District Hospital. Miranda made herself a cup of tea, moving quietly so as not to disturb her co-worker, Jan Thompson, who clearly needed an extra hour of sleep. No wonder. She had three young children at home, only one of school-age, and a husband convalescing from a non-workplace accident who was, it seemed, just as needy as the youngsters. Funny how some lives pan out. Jan was about six years older than Miranda, yet she looked worn out. Working as a nursing aide at the local hospital didn't pay a lot, but the income was crucial to keep the family going.

'You're so lucky,' she had said to Miranda, 'you've got so much ahead of you. Not that I'm jealous, mind you. Oh, let's be honest, just a bit. And going overseas, I always wanted to do that.'

After the graduation ceremony, Matron had summoned Miranda to her office. She was offered employment as a junior staff sister with a three-monthly rotation. 'You have great potential, Sister Shaw. We'd very much like to keep you on our staff,' Matron said.

It was tempting, but not part of her plan. *I have to keep control of my life.*

She continued taking the Pill, at the same time being aware that Michael was showing some concern that she hadn't become pregnant, despite their regular sessions of intimacy.

'Do you think you might have a, well, a fertility problem?' he'd asked tentatively.

She tried to make fun of it saying she hoped not, as she knew barren cows were sent to the slaughter. 'But if you're worried maybe we'll look into it when I get back – I'm not going forever, you know.' Michael had no choice but to accept her reassurance on the subject.

Dr Santorini was glad to see her when she presented for an interview at the Beaufort hospital. A genial smile creased his face as he shook hands warmly. Miranda was surprised to note the markers of aging – greying hair and evidence of some weight gain. *I guess I've changed a bit, too,* she thought

It felt strange at first. She knew, or remembered, the family connections of many of the patients, though others were new to the district. The hospital was much smaller than the Base, of course, but adequate for the local community of about fifteen hundred people.

As a single-certificated sister, she didn't venture into the maternity ward unless she was asked to help with babies in the nursery when there was a staff shortage. Night duty suited her well. There was always another qualified sister for the maternity area, one who had her midwifery certificate, when she needed a second signature for giving a dangerous drug. This was rare, though, usually needed for anyone following surgery who had been prescribed pain relief. This had to be recorded and the remainder counted and confirmed by the two signatures.

Night duty followed a routine: sedatives administered as needed, regular observations, prescribed medications and general nursing care. There might be an admission, or a death, though this was rare. More commonly, the labour ward was the busy area – there was always the possibility of a birth in the early hours of the morning.

The working pace increased as six o'clock approached, until the handover to the morning staff. After that, escape to home, breakfast and a warm bed.

One evening at dinner, Brian asked Miranda what was wrong with Daryl Lyons' mother.

'I can't tell you that – it's confidential,' she replied. 'You'll have to ask Daryl himself if you really want to know.'

'Talking about confidentiality – has Michael said anything to you about changing banks?'

Miranda bristled. He hadn't, but he did let slip that there were some financial issues he and his father had to deal with. 'Even if he had, I couldn't tell you, that would be a breach of confidence as well. And you shouldn't be discussing bank business anyway.'

Jack nodded in agreement. Neither he nor his father before him had spoken about the funeral business outside the office, keeping work and home life separate.

Grace wisely introduced a change of subject.

'How long are you planning to stay at Beaufort Hospital, Mirrie?'

That was easy to answer. Things were moving along nicely. The postman had brought several letters from overseas in response to her enquiries. One was particularly interesting. It was from an agency that dealt with both hospital and community staff vacancies and contained a list of available positions. Among the more usual ward and department opportunities was one listed as a six-month pilot research project which required a trained nurse to do assessments and conduct interviews. The closing date for applications was the end of the week. A decision would be made after Christmas, with the starting date being the second week of January.

'You won't get an application in on time if that's what you want to do.'

'It's all right, Dad,' she said with a smile. 'I've already posted it. One of the benefits of doing night duty is you have free time when everything's quiet. I sent it off nearly three weeks ago, but I guess it'll take a while to get an answer. But have a look – there are lots of interesting possibilities apart from that one.' She showed them the pamphlets. 'To answer your question, Mum, I only agreed to stay for three months. Matron said that would be fine, but she hoped I'd work over Christmas. So I will finish up at the end of December and fly out in the first week of January, whether I get this particular job or not.'

There was silence. Until now it had seemed like a vague plan. Now there was more certainty about it. The Shaw's looked at each other questioningly.

'Do you realise you'll be away for your twenty-first birthday?' Brian's tone sounded like an accusation.

Mum stepped in with a final statement 'We'll just have to postpone it until she gets back.' She pushed her chair out and stood up. 'You two can do the dishes tonight, Dad and I have a television date.'

Brian and Miranda looked at each other and smiled. She was referring to the serial *Bellbird* which had become a favourite, especially among country viewers.

Michael had explained that he and his father were going to celebrate Christmas in Sydney, as arranged by Phee. *Typical,* thought Miranda.

'Dad said he'd like you to be with us, but I explained to him that you were on night duty.' Miranda nodded. 'But you'll be off over the New Year, right?'

'Yes, I'm finishing on the second last day of December.'

'That's good. You can come out to our place, Dad wants to see you before you go, and I'll give you your Christmas present then, okay?'

I hope he's not going to try to pin me down with a proposal and an engagement ring, Miranda thought. She hoped her smile did not betray the touch of anxiety she felt.

New Year's Eve was warm. Miranda was glad to be able to wear a summer dress and jacket, all too well aware that she'd packed her suitcase full of warm clothes for the northern winter.

'You'll freeze to death over there,' Sister Stuchberry had said, a prediction based on several years of working in England. She'd married a Beaufort widower later in life and did part-time at the hospital. They only met occasionally at handover, but Miranda managed to get a few bits of advice from her which she tucked away for future reference.

Major McPherson greeted her, 'Welcome, my dear. Thank you for seeing in the New Year with us. I've asked Mrs Hardwick to take a photo of us to mark the occasion. Now don't let me forget, will you.' Miranda smiled. She'd already planned to do just that with her family, 'We'll all look rather different when you come back. Older, I mean.' His smile had a rueful tinge to it.

Her deliberately vague question, 'Have things gone well for you this year?' was answered with a reassuring, 'Can't complain.' Miranda knew he was unlikely to divulge any information relating to personal matters, so her next question as to how Christmas had been for them in Sydney, was answered, predictably, with another platitude. He seemed to be more interested in her forthcoming trip to England.

'I'm guessing you haven't flown anywhere before, am I right?' She answered with a nod. 'I was thinking you might have liked to fly with us to Sydney, but Michael said you were on duty.'

'That's right. I had to work over Christmas. But thank you for thinking of me.' Privately she thought it would have been a step too far, both in the cost of the airfare, and the prospect of Phee's reaction to her presence.

Before dinner, father and son offered suggestions on must-see places and events she should attend, though Michael seemed a little subdued.

'I should have brought a notebook with me, I don't want to miss any of these.'

Michael helpfully provided a sheet of paper and a ballpoint pen.

Mrs Hardwick appeared at the door and gave Miranda a welcoming smile. She was happy to oblige with the camera and took several photos before returning to the kitchen.

Dinner was a memorable feast. 'The last for the year,' as Alex McPherson put it. 'A fine repast, as usual.'

'Are we going to see the New Year in?' Miranda asked.

'Certainly, we'll listen to the ABC on the radio and imagine the crowd gathering in Bourke Street at the GPO. It's a great tradition, waiting for the clock to strike midnight. Did you have something else in mind?'

Michael and Miranda looked at each other. Michael spoke.

'No, Dad – we'll happily listen with you. But we'd like to be together for the rest of the night.'

There, he'd said it. They both watched for his reaction. To their relief, he said, 'Of course you do. Take over the end bedroom and sleep in for as long as you like.'

'Thanks, Dad.'

With a contented look on his face, Michael settled back on the couch with Miranda close beside him, his arm around her shoulder. It was a time of blissful enjoyment Miranda would always remember.

If only I hadn't set my heart on going overseas, this could be all I'd ever want. But if I didn't go, I'd regret it, I know I would. I have to follow it through, and then – who knows?

'Ten–nine–eight–seven–six–five–four–three–two–one – Happy New Year!'

Hugs and kisses were exchanged and a glass of champagne to toast the New Year of 1970. A new decade, new hopes and dreams.

Soon after, Alex McPherson got to his feet, yawned and said, 'Good night, Miranda. Good night, Son.'

Michael stretched out on the couch and with arms open, said, 'Come here my little darling.'

Another delicious cuddle – oh, how warm and masculine he was!

'Oh – I nearly forgot!' He jumped up to grab a small square box from the mantelpiece. 'My Christmas present for you.'

Oh no, thought Miranda, *I had hoped he wouldn't*. Michael, observant as always, noted her look of dismay.

'This isn't what you think it is, I know now's not the right time. But I want you to remember me, so please accept it in that spirit.'

Miranda's apprehension melted away. She opened the little box and gasped at the dainty gold ring with its emerald stone.

'It's – it's beautiful,'

He took the ring out of the box and slipped it onto the third finger of her left hand. How pretty it looked, but, alas, far too loose.

'Perhaps I could wear it on my middle finger,' Miranda suggested. Sure enough, the fit was perfect.

'The green reminded me of your eyes, I just had to have it for you.

Sorry, I hadn't realised just how slender your fingers are ...' Michael was babbling. Miranda put a finger against his lips.

'Shhh. It's absolutely beautiful, I don't know how to thank you.'

'Let's just go to bed.'

Chapter 17

The days passed swiftly, as they always seem to do when a deadline is looming. Before Miranda knew it, she was airborne, and on her way to the other side of the world.

I hope I've got everything I need, she thought, while mentally revising the long list of items packed in her large suitcase and her carry-on bag. It helped her to relax.

The plane was about two-thirds full. Miranda's seat was on the aisle side of the middle block, the two next to her were vacant. After the evening meal had been served and cleared away, the hostess came to her with an extra blanket and suggested she could stretch out over the three seats. 'You might get some sleep if you're lucky. It's a long flight.' Privately, Miranda thought that was unlikely, she was too excited and apprehensive to sleep. But the steady hum of the engines and the dimming of the cabin lights created an environment that proved her wrong.

Heathrow. The enormous airport came gradually closer as the plane descended. She found an unoccupied window seat at the back of the plane and gazed at the suburbs stretching to the horizon on all sides, interspersed with patches of green, parks perhaps. An instruction to resume seats and fasten seatbelts prior to landing sent her scurrying back to her seat.

Already some things felt different. The air was crisp, the clothing people were wearing was predominately dark, and their facial expressions seemed serious. It was bitterly cold outside – she'd been warned. It was not raining at the moment, but the sky was leaden.

After navigating Customs and Immigration and baggage retrieval, Miranda pushed her little trolley with her suitcase and carry-on luggage, following the signs to the Underground station.

She sent a silent 'thank you' to the travel agent in Ballarat who had been more than helpful, not only with the tickets, passport and visas, but had also made a booking at a youth hostel for her first week in London. The hostel, chosen at random, was in Holland Park. *Gosh, what a picturesque area!* The instructions had been explicit enough for her to make her way through the park with its bare-branched trees to the impressive building with the prominent YHA sign. She saw that classic image of upper-class London – at least two large-wheeled perambulators pushed by nannies.

The woman at the reception desk was dark-skinned and generously built. She greeted Miranda with a wide smile and what was clearly a West Indian accent, 'Hello, love. Did you have a good trip over?'

'I suppose I did. I feel a bit – dazed, just now. Everything is so different.'

The older woman smiled understandingly. 'It could be jet lag. Did you get to have a stop-over on the way?'

Miranda was confused by her accent at first, then realised what was meant. 'The plane landed at Singapore for three quarters of an hour, I just got off with everyone else and back on again. I was really tired.'

Another wide smile, then back to business.

Taking a key from a large wooden board behind her and a list of house rules, she handed them to Miranda and directed her to her room.

'It's cheaper if you share a room, but you'd probably be glad to be on your own for a start.'

The room was small, dominated by a single bed, and felt incredibly hot. The old-fashioned hot water radiator was the source of the heat. *I'll turn that down, or open the window*, she thought. Neither was possible, but taking off her heavy coat and cardigan, gave instant relief. She had been told about double-glazing but had not realised that it meant she could not open the windows

Miranda lay on the bed and stretched. Should she have a sleep? Before the plane landed the announcement of local time, Greenwich Mean Time, advised passengers to adjust their watches. It was now four-thirty in the afternoon, but didn't feel like it.

She forced herself to stay awake. She read the hostel handout she'd been given at reception and noted the mealtimes. She resolved to record everything in a diary and had bought a supply of airmail letters at the post office at Heathrow and promised herself to write to her family, and Michael, at least once a week.

Michael! She twisted the little ring on her left middle finger. She hadn't really thought of him since their hasty kiss at Tullamarine Airport. Already Australia seemed so far away. Resolutely, she turned her thoughts to the here and now.

The diary confirmed her first appointment with an agency for nursing work, and later in the week another for the job which had appealed to her when she'd first read about it. It was based at St Georges Hospital at Hyde Park Corner and involved research into strokes. It was connected with the Refugee Council and had been described as a collaborative venture.

In order to find her way around the city she had to get her bearings. An A-Z street directory had been her first purchase at the airport bookstall, and it proved fascinating. So many roads, streets, underground railway stations, bus routes – it would take a lifetime to get to know them all!

The first interview didn't go as well as she had hoped.

'We don't seem to have anything for anyone without experience. You've just finished your training, is that right?' Miranda had nodded. 'At the moment, all we have on our books is a part-time position in an aged care ward in Essex.'

The agent noted her disappointed look. 'I have to say they specify recently-qualified, that is, first year out, so it would be minimum wage.'

Miranda said she'd keep in touch, but left the agency deflated. So much for their glowing advertisement. *Never mind*, she said to herself, *something will come up*.

She was more tentative about the next interview. However, her reservations were swept aside when she met the panel. The interview was held in what seemed to be a small classroom, with a table at the front. Two men and a woman were sitting at the table when Miranda was shown in by the receptionist. As she entered, one of the men stood and approached her with a welcoming smile. He introduced himself as Ralph Romenski. He shook her hand and warmly welcomed her to the interview. He turned and introduced the others – Theresa Polkinghorne and Sam Loft – who also welcomed her.

Miranda took a seat at the table, opposite the panel. Ralph made a little small talk, asking her about her trip, how she was finding London, and whether she would like a cup of tea. *Sizing me up*, she thought.

Ralph then became formal and began the interview.

'Many Hungarians fled to England at the time of the uprising in 1956. They were granted refugee status and settled in inner London, with smaller cohorts outside the city. The Refugee Council is involved in monitoring their adaptation to the British way of life, their use of services, that is, health, welfare, education, and other social issues.'

He stopped and gestured to the other man to continue. Sam, the project manager, took up the information-sharing role.

'We were approached by a research fellow from St Georges Hospital. He has an interest in hypertension and stroke incidence in a migrant population. It's part of his post-doctoral thesis, for which he obtained a six-month grant. What we have been asked to look for is someone with a medical background who would be able to develop a trust relationship with this group, who would be mainly older, predominately male, living in a study area relatively easy to access. Specifically, it would involve an initial wide-ranging questionnaire, and practical procedures – taking blood pressure measurements, urine tests and blood samples.'

He noted her silent, 'Oh.'

'You would need to undertake a short course for that last requirement.' Miranda smiled in relief. 'There would also be scope for recording personal observations which may be of use in the future management of refugee groups. Anyway, how does all that sound so far?'

Miranda was unable to mask her enthusiasm. 'It sounds like such a worthwhile project. I've often thought that migrants, especially refugees, suffer disadvantages – because their culture is different, language differences make access to services, especially health services, difficult, and just mixing in society must be so hard. I'd love to be part of a team that's making an effort to overcome some of these problems.'

The two men exchanged glances, and to Miranda's relief, seemed to appreciate her response. Both made a notation on the assessment paper in front of them. Ralph nodded to Theresa that she should have her say.

'It's good to meet you, Miranda. I'm responsible for the day-to-day running of the research groups. We have conducted similar studies in the past with various immigrant groups, ranging from those from the Caribbean some years ago, to the more recent Polish asylum seekers after the Warsaw situation you may have heard about. Anyway, what we would require from the successful applicant is a good, non-judgmental attitude to people, accuracy in recording and a positive approach.' She paused and consulted her notes. 'Your academic results are impressive, Miranda. Do you think the position we've advertised would be enough of a challenge for you?'

It was a pertinent question. Miranda examined her motives before replying. 'I would be honoured to be connected with this project. I am familiar with the medical management of strokes, but not so much with the ongoing care of stroke patients in the community. This study has a humanitarian focus which is what first attracted me to the advertisement.'

They seemed to be responsive to her answer.

Heads together, the trio whispered something. Sam Loft looked up to meet Miranda's gaze.

'Would you mind waiting in reception, please Miranda? Myra will get you a cup of tea.'

She accepted the mug of tea from the receptionist and waited nervously.

Before long, the door opened and Theresa Polkinghorne poked her head out. 'Would you mind coming in, Miranda?'

Ralph Romenski spoke. 'We would like to offer you this position.

As it is for a fixed term, there will be no need for a probation period, but we will have a review after two weeks to see how things are going.' Miranda's smile conveyed her delight. 'May I say congratulations and welcome to the team. Theresa will fill you in on the details.'

The two men shook her hand before leaving.

Miranda breathed a sigh of relief. Across the table, Theresa Polkinghorne's homely face – *she must be at least fifty*, Miranda thought – wore a genuine smile. She, too, appeared to relax.

'I'm really pleased to have you onboard, Miranda. Without breaching confidentiality, let me say you were the outstanding applicant. As Ralph said, this is a fixed-term grant. However, the results may lead to further opportunities for you in the future. Anyway, let's get down to the nitty-gritty. I'll arrange an appointment for you to meet Dr Adam Gillies. He's the researcher at St Georges. We've done work with him before, though not quite like this one. He's easy to get on with. If you call me tomorrow, I'll let you know where and when to meet with him.'

An hour later, a very happy Miranda emerged with a folder containing her contract, literature about the employing agency's policies, and extracts of published research findings. As well, she had information about opening a bank account and finding long-term accommodation. The salary didn't appear very generous, but, she realised, it was in pounds sterling and needed some mental arithmetic to convert it to Australian dollars. She was to start in a week.

Back at the hostel, she realised she was hungry, ravenous in fact.

The cafeteria was still open and, although choice was limited, a generous serve of mashed potato, sausages and cabbage was very satisfying.

The next thing to do was to put pen to aerogram paper and send letters off with the latest exciting news, as well as her impressions of London so far. To Michael's, she added a special personal note, 'missing you!!' Her general tone was exuberant. *Gosh, how many exclamation marks I'm using! They'll probably think I'm high.* She giggled. *Perhaps I am.*

Chapter 18

Next day, she rang the agency from the payphone in the hostel to find out when she was to meet the supervisor, Dr Gillies. Theresa told her to go to the main desk at St Georges Hospital at one o'clock in two days' time. Good. That gave her time to work out how to get there by public transport. There were plenty of people around to ask for advice. There were also several others from overseas, who mistakenly asked her for help, probably because she spoke English.

It had started to rain, light at first, but then more heavily; the umbrella was regularly in use. She decided to buy a pair of sturdy waterproof boots for the home visits she would be making. 'They'll be good in the snow, too,' the salesman had told her. *Snow? Oh, boy!*

St George's Hospital was a massive four-storey building with four classical columns set above the front entrance. It was right on the edge of Hyde Park. A plaque set in the wall told her it was established in 1733 and that it was built as the country home of Viscount Lanesborough. It had been redeveloped and extended and used for casualties during the Second World War. Taking a deep breath, she made her way up the stairs to meet her new employer.

Theresa Polkinghorne was right – Dr Gillies was easy to talk to. Miranda's first impression was of a shortish young man with a pleasant manner and twinkling eyes behind his thick glasses. He launched into a preamble about the areas of research he had undertaken, some involved comparative studies of different ethnic groups, focussing mainly on high blood pressure, one of the main causes of stroke.

'This is to be a prospective study, that is, only new patients will be accepted onto our list. The prerequisites include being born in Hungary and registered with a GP surgery in a specific demographic area. This time we've selected a compact area in South London, actually it's near where this hospital is to be transferred to in the near future, near Tooting Bec.' He noted her amused look and smiled. 'You'll soon get used to these strange names.'

'We have some strange names where I come from, too,' Miranda replied.

'We use the World Health Organisation definition of stroke as being any cerebral incident resulting in disability lasting more than one hour.'

On the cluttered worktable at which they sat was a navy blue satchel. Adam reached over and opened it, pulling out an information pack, a thick pad, quarto-sized, and a clipboard.

'This is your recording material,' he said. 'It has two major sections – the section on the left is for recording the data, the right-hand side is for your subjective comments. The information pack will give you some suggestions of open-ended questions you could ask, such as regarding mood changes, interpersonal stuff, the sort of things psychologists dream up.'

Miranda managed to control the inevitable smile. How typical of research scientists who dealt with factual matters to make that comment.

'You'll notice,' he went on,' that there are three sheets to be carbon-copied so you'll need to use the board underneath each time you enter data. The white one comes to me each week, as does the yellow one which doesn't record clinical information – I periodically send them to the Refugee Council for their epidemiological studies. The bottom one, the pink, stays in the pack as a record. Okay with that?'

Miranda nodded, making a note to herself that she would have to write firmly to make sure there was a legible copy through three pages.

'The registration sheet for each patient is self-explanatory. Your job is to complete the assessment, record blood pressure and take a specimen of blood. By the way, I've taken the liberty of putting your name down for the next half-day training session.' He waited for her response which was a grateful smile.

The next step was to arrange for her official name-tag. She followed him along several corridors to the lift and up to the Personnel Department.

'Are you by any chance a midwife too?' he asked as they rode in the lift.

'No, I'm not. Just a general trained nurse, at this stage.'

'Oh, that's okay. It's just that my wife is having our first baby in four months. Any clues you could give me would be most welcome.'

'Congratulations. I'm sure she'll get all the advice she needs, you too.'

They reached the Personnel Department where Adam planned to leave her. 'Can you find your way out? If in doubt, just ask. Anything more you need to know before I go?'

A sudden panic gripped her. 'There is, it's really important – how will I be able to communicate if there's a language problem? I don't speak Hungarian!'

He laughed. 'Good point. There is a section in the material about communication. You're right, it can sometimes be difficult. We can provide an interpreter, or at least a family member who speaks English. As well, we have a list of simple questions in both English and the foreign language, so you just have to point to the question and response. So far we have managed to get clinical information fairly readily, just play it by ear.' He glanced at his watch. 'I've got to go, see you Monday at nine.'

With a cheerful smile he was off. Reassured, Miranda stepped inside to continue her registration as a research assistant at St George's Hospital, London.

Back at the youth hostel, she was surprised to find an airmail letter from her mother. *She wouldn't have received mine yet, she must have sent it as soon as I left,* she thought. It was a lovely warm message from her family, written by Mum, of course.

The next thing she had to do was find accommodation for at least six months. The Saturday newspapers had columns of rental opportunities – she used her A-Z guide to determine what suburbs were in the South London area and circled likely possibilities. N/S, S/D, female only were prominent among the advertisements she selected. That would be all right, she was a non-smoker and a social drinker. Not all of them specified the rental, that would be probably discussed over the phone.

Some of the vacancies were already unavailable by the time she started her telephone marathon, but one appealed to her, both in its locality and also the friendly-sounding voice of the woman who answered her call. Particularly pleasing was the comment that she loved Australians.

By the end of the day she had two keys on a ring, one for the front door which opened right onto the street, the other gave her access to what was called a 'bedsit' on the first floor and looked out onto the street, which was a bonus. The furniture was basic, a single bed, wardrobe and small table, on which were the necessities – cup and saucer, plates, cutlery. She had been shown where the bathroom and toilet were down the hall, and on the ground floor, the communal kitchen with a small dining room.

This will be just fine, she thought. *Walking distance to work, bus stop down the road*. There was much to explore. But first, she had to move her belongings in, and after that, she would need to advise people of her change of address.

She met some of the other tenants briefly, but names did not register. Plenty of time to get to know them.

Monday arrived, a day so full of information that, at five-thirty, she arrived home exhausted. To cap it all off, there was an airmail letter for her on the hall stand, redirected from the hostel. It was from Michael. Miranda's heart skipped a beat as she read his news, not that there was much to tell. 'I have a feeling this might be the way things go,' he'd written. 'You'll be doing and seeing so much that is new and interesting, while my life is just the same, though even less fulfilling, now you're so far away.'

Ouch, that registered. But not enough to change anything.

So far, she had kept up her diary writing as she'd promised. Not a day had been missed. Wisely she had chosen a large-sized one with a day to a page. Even writing small, the pages were filled with details of her exciting new life. The question was, how to convey the feel of this great city, the amazing underground railway, how *old* some of the buildings are, the Thames, so quiet and brooding.

In her letters home, she decided not to say much about her work until she had become more established. The first week was about getting to know the patients and recording their details. Miranda was grateful that Adam Gillies could accompany her on the first few home visits and could supervise her data collection. It was all very different from her previous experience, of course, but taking blood pressures and recording a medical history were routine and familiar, and after completing the course during her first week, she had no difficulty in managing blood collections, either.

The two-week review of her progress was a mere formality, but it was good to see Theresa again. The older woman leaned close and grasped Miranda's hands, her face beaming.

'I knew you'd land on your feet! Congratulations, Miranda, you've really started well.'

'Thank you, Theresa. I'm so grateful for the opportunity, it's amazing.'

She leaned back, smiling. It didn't last. A more serious expression came over Miranda's face and she sighed,

'Is there something troubling you? Do feel free to talk about it, that's if you want to.'

Miranda didn't immediately respond – should she take this very kind woman into her confidence? Her personal relationships had not come up in the initial interview, which was fine. They were not relevant. But she was conscious that she had no-one to share personal concerns, not like before when her friends were around. She decided to broach the subject.

'To tell the truth, Theresa, my only concern is about my boyfriend back home. He is expecting that we'll get married, though we're not officially engaged. He wasn't very happy that I came over here, but he said he realised I wanted to spread my wings before settling down. His letters, I've had two so far, are about how much he's missing me.' She paused.

'And you're not missing him in quite the same way?'

'That's right, I'm not. He'll just have to be patient. But I do feel a bit guilty, that's all.'

At Therese's invitation to, 'tell me about him', Miranda found herself telling the whole story, from their first meeting at her brother's 21st birthday party to their New Year's Eve tryst at his property.

'He sounds like a delightful young man, Miranda. I hope you do end up together.' Therese paused. 'The love of my life was killed in a plane crash just before we were due to get married.'

Miranda uttered a sympathetic, 'Oh.'

'It's all right, that was a long time ago. Anyway, we'll keep in touch, won't we?'

Miranda left with Theresa Polkinghorne's phone number on a slip of paper in her purse. It gave her a sense of security, even if she never actually needed to use it.

Michael's third letter two weeks later was short and cryptic. He said things were a bit worrying at home due to Phee making financial demands on their father. She realised it must be very serious for him to have made this disclosure. Her first response was to condemn his sister, but it was clearly a complicated family issue. There wasn't anything she could do to help except to offer reassurances in her next letter, along with snippets about her work, and a couple of weekend trips out of London.

Her letters to Beaufort were more straightforward, and the replies were always encouraging and supportive. All was well, according to Mum's last letter. They'd had some rain and autumn was on its way.

Chapter 19

At the monthly meeting of the Refugee Council in mid-March, to which all staff were invited, Ralph Romenski referred to a talk on the subject of advocacy to be given by a prominent sociology lecturer at London University on the following Thursday. He recommended that as many as possible attend, as it would enhance their understanding of the issue. Miranda's hand went up, along with four others. They would meet at the venue after work for the six o'clock lecture.

Later, Miranda would identify this event as being a turning point in her life.

The audience was small in number, she estimated about twenty-five. With her colleagues, she took a seat in the second row of the lecture room. Miranda didn't know what to expect, but she knew the subject matter would be relevant to her current work. She hadn't heard of the speaker, Adrian Banks, but that was hardly surprising.

As six o'clock showed on the large wall clock, two men approached the lectern at the centre of the stage.

'Good evening, thank you all for coming along,' the shorter of the two said in his well-modulated English voice. 'My name is Harvey McBride, I am the coordinator of the Sociology Department, and I am proud to present Dr Adrian Banks, our senior lecturer, who will, I'm sure, enlighten you with his talk tonight.'

He surveyed the small audience which applauded politely.

Dr Banks adjusted the microphone to suit his height, a smile on his handsome face.

'You think I'm going to talk about advocacy, don't you. Well, I'm not, not immediately anyway. The theme I want to focus on tonight is Human Rights.'

Miranda was transfixed as he starting speaking, not only by the undeniable value of his words but by the man himself. Tall and well built, he had a large head with a mass of shaggy greying curls which looked uncombed. His eyes were exceptionally luminous, his expression animated. The discourse on human rights explored several aspects: privacy, education, healthcare, accommodation and gender issues. The topic resonated with Miranda who found herself saying silently, *'Yes, yes!'*

Adrian Banks paused, walked around the front of the stage, surveyed the audience and returned to the podium.

'I'm sure you agree with what I just said.' Nods all around. 'Well, it's all easy to say. But harder to do, the reason being that people are not all equal. We know that. So there needs to be a strategy to redress the imbalance. What do you think is the main thing that people impacted by this imbalance need?'

He looked around the group. A couple of hands went up, including Miranda's. The first responses were 'money', 'opportunity', 'recognition'. He shook his head, clearly not satisfied, and noticed Miranda's hand.

'Yes, young lady, what do you think is the most important need of these people?'

'A voice?'

'Yes, yes! That's exactly what is needed. Thank you, my dear. You have given me the signpost into the main purpose of my lecture today.'

Miranda found herself blushing at his approval.

He went on to explain a dream of his which was to develop a network of volunteers to undergo appropriate training. Each would then be allocated a disadvantaged participant, or maybe more than one, to support in whatever way was needed.

'I'm thinking of cases where a person with learning difficulties may have ageing parents who are not capable of ensuring their child's welfare.

Chronic mental illness, and even, dementia, are situations that come to mind. I personally believe that many who are institutionalised could live in the community with support, but I think I may be ahead of my time in saying that. I'm afraid that the notion, "out of sight, out of mind" prevails. But if the general public knew what goes on in some of these places ... I could go on, but my main purpose today was to introduce a concept of something which could happen at the grassroots level. I even have a name for it: citizen advocacy.'

Amazingly three-quarters of an hour had passed. Harvey McBride came to the microphone as Adrian Banks took a drink of water.

'I'm sure you all profited from that inspiring glimpse into a possible future,' the co-ordinator said. 'We're nearly at the end of our time, but I'm sure Dr Banks would be happy to answer one or two questions.'

Two or three hands were raised. The questions were mostly related to getting political approval.

'I'm working on it,' was the answer. 'Closing institutions to allow people to live in the community, with assistance, is a two-edged sword. The buildings and land are of immense value, but the current residents would have to be suitably accommodated. Not an easy task. But my idea of using well-trained volunteers has, I think, a lot of merit.'

There was sustained applause as Harvey McBride thanked Dr Banks and reminded the audience that there were monthly evening talks that were publicised in the University bulletin.

On the way home, Miranda felt dazed. Never had she heard a more powerful speaker. Charismatic, she decided, was the best word to describe Dr Adrian Banks. Other words came to mind: visionary, humanitarian, showman, perhaps, leonine. Sex appeal? That was undeniably apparent. *I wonder if he's married*, she thought. *Probably. In fact, very likely. Strange, I haven't had thoughts of desire since, well, since my last night with Michael.*

The diary page for the Adrian Banks lecture recorded her response to the event. One thing that came out of the encounter for her was a new interest in sociology. Any reference to the subject in the past had been fleeting, both at school and nursing training. She looked it up in the dictionary to confirm the definition: 'the study of human society.' She also found out that it was a study area in the Faculty of Arts in most universities.

A little spark had been ignited. *This could be my area of future study.*

The following week brought a concern to her. One home visit she made turned out to be not as routine as others had been. Miranda found the elderly gentleman to be pale and shaky, and his blood pressure was low. She took it twice to make sure of the reading. He didn't understand when she asked if he had changed his medication. Luckily his daughter was there to interpret.

'It might be the new tablets,' Monika suggested.

'What new tablets?' Miranda looked at the medication sheet. The usual drugs were listed, but a new one had been added. It was coded PFZ which meant nothing to her. Mr Zamanski had been taking it for four days according to the doctor's prescription.

'Your father must stay in bed. I'll have to check with Dr Gillies. Maybe he should not be taking the new one.'

Adam Gillies was clearly worried when Miranda reported to him after completing her other listed appointments for the day.

'That's not good news,' he said, frowning.

'Who prescribed it? What – actually – is it?'

'It's, well, it's very new, supposedly an adjunct therapy for severe persistent high blood pressure. I'll have to give you a list of the others we've put on this trial.'

Miranda was startled. 'You mean, it's a drug trial? Is that ethical if the patient isn't aware of it? He looks quite sick to me – should I contact his GP?'

'No, no, don't do that. I'll go over and see him myself. Perhaps the dosage is too high.' He looked troubled. Unlocking his filing cabinet, he rummaged around the bulging files to locate the one he needed. 'There are twelve patients on this list who meet the criteria for additional medication. I'd like you to monitor them more closely, in view of what you found with Mr Zamanski today.' He paused. 'Mind you, it could be due to something he ate, nothing to do with the medication. We just have to see how the others are tolerating the current dosage. They all started four days ago. I'll give you a list of possible side-effects to look out for.'

Miranda was bewildered. 'Has this had official approval? Is it a legitimate drug trial?'

'Yes and no. It's a preliminary study. Yes, we did get signatures from the next of kin or the actual patient. We just said it was for permission to try something new. The data you collected over the first month formed the baseline before this intervention.'

It didn't seem right to Miranda. In her limited experience, the usual procedure involved a double-blind study where no-one knew until the completion of the study whether the substance being given was active or a placebo. What she was being told seemed somewhat random at the very least.

'What drug company is issuing this PFZ?' she asked.

'I'd rather not say at this stage, Miranda. Can you keep all this to yourself? Please?'

'Of course, you're my supervisor, I have to do what you tell me to do. But I'd really like you to call on Mr Zamanski as soon as you can.'

Dr Gillies unlocked a small medicine chest and selected a container.

'I'll go right away. I'll reduce the dosage and get you to check on him first thing tomorrow.' He rang for a taxi, and they went downstairs.

Back home Miranda pondered the situation. Up to now, everything had been straightforward in her work. All the drugs her patients were taking were standard ones, familiar to her. The discovery that an unknown medication was being administered was worrying.

Should she ring Theresa Polkinghorne for advice? Adam Gilllies' words came back to her, 'Keep this to yourself at this stage.' Perhaps it was all above board. It would be more prudent to follow Adam's instructions for the time being until there was more concrete cause for alarm.

'Fancy a walk in the park, Miranda?' came a chirpy voice from down the passage. Lisa Brown was a friendly woman in her thirties who worked at the local library. Miranda loved her quaint Somerset accent and had already accepted the invitation of a weekend away to Bath at some stage.

'Coming,' she yelled. It was just what she needed.

The next day's visit to Mr Zamanski found him more or less back to normal. Monika explained that Dr Gillies had visited and fully examined her father. 'He even looked in his eyes with a torch,' she said. The dosage of the new drug had been reduced and his blood pressure, though still low, was better than yesterday.

It was a good idea to group her home visits so they were all in walking distance, though in different directions. As the days became longer with more sunny breaks, Miranda delighted in the spring blossoms, especially the daffodils and snowdrops in the tiny front gardens.

A letter arrived from Mum in the first week of April. Grace wrote, 'Michael visited us to tell Brian that he couldn't be part of the footy team this season. He looked really down, I felt sorry for him. He's missing you, though I suppose you know that. Brian wasn't here when he came, he's relieving accounts manager at Ararat these days, so we had to pass the message on about the footy. Anyway, when are you going to Scotland? I insist on lots of photos when you do.'

Scotland. Her maternal grandmother's birthplace. She had been told the location of the small village in the Highlands where her grandparents were buried. Yes, a trip up there was a must. Maybe in early summer, sometime when she had a few days off work.

Michael's next letter was short, and, for him, terse. His father was not well and he added, as before, there were financial concerns that were a worry to them both. He said he knew it was her 21st birthday at the end of the month and, because of the way things are, he might not be able to send her a present. So, he said, this was his Happy Birthday greeting ahead of time.

How strange, thought Miranda. What on earth could be happening? In her previous contacts with Major McPherson, all discussion about stock prices and farming in general conveyed a reassurance that all was well. She suspected that somehow Phee was involved. It was a mystery. And with his father being ill, more responsibility would fall on Michael's shoulders.

I wish I could help in some way, she thought. But, realistically, what could she do?

She dashed off another airmail letter thanking him for his good wishes, hoping his father was feeling better and that things had settled.

Some days later, when she arrived home from work, there was a message for her on the notepad next to the communal phone. It was from the Refugee Council asking her to contact Adrian Banks on the number provided.

Momentarily shocked, she felt incapable of action. What was this all about? Should she ring, or perhaps wait until tomorrow. No, she needed to know now, whatever it is. *That's if I have enough coins for the payphone*. She did.

'Sociology Department, London University. How may I help you?'

'I have been asked to ring Dr Adrian Banks. My name is Miranda Shaw.'

'I'll see if he's still in.' There were a few clicks. 'Putting you through now.'

The delightfully modulated voice came through the phone. 'Hello there. Thank you for responding to my call. You're probably wondering what this is about.'

'Well, yes, I am, Dr Banks.'

'I got your number from Ralph Romenski's office, I hope you don't mind. The thing is, I was impressed by your responses at the talk I gave some weeks ago and wondered if you knew anything about the summer school we run on campus. Would you be interested in learning more about it? We have many international students enrol for these, especially as they are often held in the evening or at weekends so it doesn't affect work.'

Miranda's heart skipped a beat, several in fact. She exhaled after realising she'd almost forgotten to breathe.

'Are you still there?'

'Oh, I'm sorry. It's such a surprise. But a very welcome one. I would definitely like to be part of it.' She paused. 'I'd need to know the costs involved, though.'

'Of course. I think you'll find the fees are affordable. And, who knows, the experience may lead you on a different pathway.'

Phew! As she put down the phone having been given a time, date and directions for enrolling in the summer school starting in June, a little thought crept into her mind: *It's as if my dreams could be coming true.*

Chapter 20

Miranda's euphoria suffered a crash at the end of the month. It came from an unlikely source. Among the cards and little parcels from home for her twenty-first birthday was a bulky envelope with a card from Gina Ryan. As well as the warm greeting, she'd written, 'I feel a bit bad sending you this, Miranda, but you would have to know sooner or later.' 'This' turned out to be an article cut out of the *Truth,* the notorious, no-holds-barred Melbourne newspaper noted for digging the dirt.

She spread out the folded page and gasped at the headline: 'Respected Western District Grazier Loses All.' In smaller print, it announced: 'the forced sale of the splendid Stockyard Hill property, Bournagulla, has come about due to the alleged corruption of Leon La Franchi, fiancé of part-owner, Phoebe McPherson. Her father, Major Alexander McPherson, a former Army officer, successfully developed the property in recent years.'

The investigative journalist went on to reveal that much of the initial purchase price of the property came from the daughter's inheritance from her mother's estate. The writer revealed that the former Mrs McPherson had engaged in a clandestine affair with an American millionaire who, on his death, had bequeathed his entire estate to her. Lawsuits filed by his family did not change the outcome. The money was passed down to the daughter after the mother's death only a few months later. While some of the money was invested in Bournagulla, it appears that Miss McPherson recently went guarantor in a speculative get-rich-scheme developed by her fiancé. Mr La Franchi is currently under investigation by the fraud squad after the scheme failed, with investors losing large sums of money. He is a New Zealander and a well-known high-flyer whose lifestyle is noted for its extravagance. To avoid more serious charges, large sums of money have been demanded by the creditors. As guarantor, Phoebe McPherson is liable for this repayment.

Miranda was speechless. Bournagulla sold? It was unthinkable, shocking. How could it happen? But – it has.

She re-read the article. The facts, as printed, certainly helped to fill in the gaps in the story she'd been told over the last few years. Would it have made any difference to her if she had known the background of the McPherson family? Probably not.

No-one could have predicted that Phee would get involved with someone like La Franchi. She almost felt sorry for Michael's socialite sister, but quickly thrust that thought aside as she considered the effect it had on the father and son, two men she admired so much.

What can I say? What can I do?

It was hard to acknowledge that there was nothing she could do to change things, even with the best will in the world.

Write, that's what she could do. First to Gina, to thank her for the card and for the newspaper cutting which contained such dire news, but provided some enlightenment.

Then to her family, telling them she was aware of the situation and asking that they reach out to Michael and his father. 'He may be embarrassed at what's happened, and not want to make contact himself.'

The letter to Michael took more thought. Her shock and sadness at the loss of his property had to be stated. She kept writing as though she was talking to him, 'What's going to happen next? How is your father coping?' She finished by expressing the regret that she wasn't there with him but knew there wasn't any way she could help the situation.

May arrived and with it a touch of warmer weather. Lisa Brown's promised weekend to Bath was a highlight, though thoughts of Michael's predicament preoccupied her to some extent. She explained to her friend that she'd had some news from home that was on her mind, but didn't elaborate. Instead, she took photos of the spectacular scenery and streets around the ancient Roman-built city and bought postcards of the famous baths to send home.

Lisa's parents were hospitable and asked many questions about life in Australia.

'Nearly went there once,' Mr Brown said. 'After the War it was. Couple of Aussies in my regiment suggested it. But with Lisa and the boys still at school, we decided to give it a miss, didn't we, love?' He smiled at his wife.

'Perhaps you could go for a visit now – now they're older.'

'Yes, they're older. But so are we,' was the response.

Miranda told Lisa about the university summer school and how she had signed up for the ten-week course. 'It means I'll be going back later than I had first thought, but it seemed a good opportunity. A little taste of university life.'

Work was progressing well. The twelve participants who were receiving the new medication seemed to be improved by it, and her concerns lessened as the weeks went on. The due date of Adam Gillies' baby loomed. Miranda explored a babywear shop and decided on a pair of lemon-coloured bootees and a matching little bonnet.

'Thank you very much, Miranda. We're happy to have either a boy or a girl, and yellow is okay with either. And by the way, the drug company is very happy with the feedback you've provided on their product. Getting the dosage right has been a challenge. So thanks for all that too.'

Mum's letter was eagerly awaited. Nothing yet from Michael, but she knew the difficulties. Apparently the forced sale of Bournagulla was the talk of the district. A clearing sale was held and a large number of attendees went, some, Mum said, to stickybeak. It was conducted by one of the larger stock and station agents. Little was seen of Michael or his father.

Reading the letter, it occurred to Miranda that she would need to know when the McPhersons were leaving and where they were going. Sure enough a letter arrived two days later.

Michael thanked her for her concern and said it helped. His father had been admitted to the St John of God hospital in Ballarat for medical tests. 'He's not well,' Michael said,' I think his spirit is broken. He was so happy at Bournagulla and now feels betrayed. As I do, too,' he added. 'But there is enough saved from the sale for me to buy a smaller place, so hopefully I'll still be in the area.'

He finished with the usual statement of missing her and counting the days.

Oh dear, thought Miranda. *He's expecting me back in July. But the summer school doesn't finish until August.*

Another complication occurred, though a happy one for Miranda. The monthly meeting of the Refugee Council was scheduled for a morning timeslot. She was asked by Ralph Romenski to stay back for a few minutes. Concerned, she looked across to Theresa Polkinghorne who gave a little nod and smiled. Not bad news then.

'Miranda, Dr Gillies has informed us that the funding body for the research you've been doing, has asked for a six-month extension of the work. So I'm asking whether you can stay on for another six months.'

Miranda's head was spinning. There was much to consider. She wondered fleetingly why Adam had not mentioned this to her before this, though his conversation lately centred on the marvels of his new-born son.

'Do you want some time to think about it?'

'I would have to check it out with – my family,' she said, glancing at Theresa whose expression showed she understood.

Ralph Romenski accepted Miranda's cautious response with, 'Let me know when you can,' before leaving. Theresa stayed behind and Miranda went over to her.

'Have you got a few minutes? I need to tell you what's been happening.'

It was good to be able to put Theresa in the picture. She listened while Miranda told her everything that had happened around the time of her birthday, and the confused feelings she was experiencing. At the end of the lengthy monologue, which included a few tears hastily wiped away, she looked directly at the older woman who had listened so attentively.

'My dear girl, you have so much to consider. I can't make up your mind for you, you know that.' She thought for a moment. 'What time is it in Australia now?'

Surprised, Miranda calculated. 'In Victoria it would be, let's see, it's ten hours ahead, I think. So that would make it nine o'clock at night. Why?'

'I'm prepared to authorise an international call from our office for you to speak to your parents. It would have to be no longer than six minutes. Would you like to do that?'

The smile that lit Miranda's face was all the answer she needed. The smile was still there when she emerged from the office ten minutes later.

'Thank you so much, Theresa. I gave Mum quite a shock. Luckily she was the one to answer the phone, Dad was out. She thought something awful had happened to me. It was so good to talk to her, hear her voice. But she wouldn't tell me what to do, only to be honest with myself. Don't come back because you think you should. It was almost like she was giving me permission to stay.'

'She sounds very understanding.' Miranda nodded emphatically. 'Now – how are you going to handle Michael?'

That was the big question. On the way to complete her afternoon appointments, she mulled over the possibilities, but to no avail. As well, this weekend she was due to go to the first lecture in the summer school. *My life continues to be in turmoil*, she thought. Then the reality of Michael's situation overtook her and guilt crept in.

I'd be giving up a lot if I went back to Australia after only six months.

She put it all out of her mind as she undertook the first of her afternoon visits. It wasn't until she arrived home that she took up the issue again, this time committing it to paper.

Five minutes later she had a new idea. Yes, the McPherson family had suffered a major financial setback. But there was money available for the purchase of a smaller property, he'd said. Could he use a little of that to come over to England for a visit? Yes! Then he would see and understand how her future was developing and why she needed to stay here longer. The letter ran into three pages. In it she suggested that a trip to London would help him deal with the loss of Bournagulla and they would be able to be together. She hoped her enthusiasm would persuade him as she searched for enough stamps and an AIRMAIL sticker.

I can't wait til tomorrow to post it, she thought. She went out into the crisp evening air to the red pillar box halfway down the street to send it on its way. Somehow her spirits lifted and she found herself skipping along the pavement on her way back.

It was fortunate that another of the tenants where she lived had enrolled for the summer school too, though in English, not sociology. Robyn, an Australian from Perth, was into her second year of teaching at one of the local high schools. It had been useful to compare notes when their paths crossed, and especially convenient to be able to make their way together to London University.

'This is exciting – my first time in a uni,' Miranda said. 'Different for you, you spent four years on your education degree, didn't you.'

'Yep. Guess it's been worth it, I wasn't sure at the time. This summer school thing is a bit of an indulgence for me – it's on the Brontës and I just *love* those books,' said Robyn.

They parted at the massive entrance gates where signposts indicated the different faculties. The name tag she'd been issued indicated the number of the room allocated for her study and it was relatively easy to find along the impressive corridor.

There were about fifteen students already in the room when Miranda entered. *Good,* she thought, *not too many names to remember.*

She noticed Harvey McBride on the dais shuffling through some papers. *Of course he'd be here, he is the coordinator of the department,* she remembered.

He opened the session by welcoming them all, introducing himself and giving the name of the lecturer who would deliver the main part of the syllabus as Alud Thomas. 'Sounds Welsh,' whispered the young man next to Miranda. 'As well, Dr Adrian Banks will be part of the teaching team,' Harvey McBride concluded. Miranda's heart skipped a beat.

Later, as the first session ended, she caught a glimpse of the man himself through an open door in conversation with another staff member in the corridor. As she was preparing to leave, he appeared.

'Well, you made it. I'm very pleased.' His luminous eyes looked her up and down. 'We will see more of each other, I imagine.' He turned and went.

Miranda was perplexed. What did he mean? The comments had overtones of – she searched for the right word – flirtation. She shrugged off the thought, it was just his manner, probably greeted everyone like that. But there was no doubt about it. She found him attractive.

Miranda's phone call to the Refugee Council to confirm her acceptance of the extension was taken by Theresa.

'I'm sorry, Ralph isn't in the office but I'll certainly pass on the information, and he'll be glad to hear it. As am I.'

'Thank you, Theresa. I've written to Michael and told him, but I've also suggested that he come over here for a visit, if he can.'

'What a good idea. Let's hope that's what happens.'

Michael's letter arrived a few weeks later. Opening it took some courage. How had he responded to her decision to stay on? Would he be able to fly over as she had suggested?

He'd written:

> 'My dear Miranda,
>
> Your letter was not what I had hoped for. But to be really honest, I cannot say that I was surprised. You have always had an ambition for academic study which is out of my league, as you probably know. Yes, I would love to be able to come over and see you, but unless you were ready to come back with me, I don't think I could handle it. As well, Dad is still in hospital, he's having treatment for depression and some physical problems. I need to be around to support him and to make sure that my sister does not come near him. So, it seems

to me, Miranda, that we're going in different directions. Of
course, if you change your mind it would make me very happy.
I always expected us to be together.
Love, Michael

It cost him a lot to write all that, she knew. *He feels I have abandoned
him.* And, in a way, he's right. *I do want to pursue an academic career.
But I love him. Correction – I loved him.* But enough to turn my back on
what's happening here? The emerald ring was in its box on the dressing
table. *Should I send it back? Or sell it and send him the money?* She
pictured his face, his blond curls, his loving smile.

Oh God, this is hard.

It was Adrian Banks who encouraged her to rethink her future. He had
asked her to stay back after the third week of the summer school. Though
wary, she agreed to meet him. Nevertheless, she was very conscious of
her knees trembling when she entered his office.

'We need to have a little talk, about your future,' he said after inviting
her to sit facing him. 'Theresa Polkinghorne tells me you have a fiancé
back in Australia.'

What? Miranda had never actually described Michael as such to
Theresa. Why would she mislead him in this way? He went on.

'My mission is, in part, to identify promising students and help guide
their progress. I believe you may be underestimating your potential.' He
paused and looked at her warmly. 'Would you like to tell me about your
life and your entire educational journey.' It was more of a command
than a question. 'Start with primary and don't leave anything out. And,
Miranda, if there's one thing I dislike, it is false modesty.'

Hesitantly at first, but encouraged by his thoughtful nods, she
described the events in her life to date. The story of Anne Saunders which
led her to nursing training seemed to especially interest him.

'Now, where does this young farmer, this fiancé, come into it?'

She gave a brief overview of their meeting at her brother's twenty-
first birthday and the relationship that developed over time, mentioning

neither the complexity nor the intimacy. It did not seem appropriate to mention the crisis that had occurred in the last few months either.

'So your plan has been to go back, get married and be the lady of the manor, right?'

'I – I don't know,' she responded. 'It may not be quite like that any more.' He looked at her questioningly. 'I mean – what would you suggest? What is your advice to me?'

That was a bit challenging, but having said it, she felt she had restored a bit of balance to the conversation. He got up from his chair and strolled around the office. *God, he's impressive,* she thought. *And he knows it.*

'Miranda,' he said, resuming his seat, 'I see any number of bright young women, and men, too, clever, enthusiastic and with potential. But every so often one comes along who stands out from the rest. You fall into that category. You have an enquiring mind and a sense of justice that, in my opinion, should be nurtured along the path to, well, let's say, making a difference. I would like to mentor that.'

There was a vague dream crystallising. She was hearing from this dynamic older man the words she had been craving all her life.

It felt as though he was giving her exactly the direction she needed.

It wasn't difficult to say, 'Thank you. No one has said anything like that before, not in such explicit terms. I hope I can repay your encouragement.'

He smiled. 'You can. I'm always right in these things.'

Leaving, Miranda again considered his words, seemingly innocuous. But was there a suggestion of more?

Summer in England was mild in comparison to what is experienced in most parts of Australia. But the days were longer and lighter clothes were needed. Miranda was only too happy to investigate the possibilities of the local charity shops, so tidy and clean in comparison with second-hand shops back home.

Letters from Mum continued to arrive regularly, but nothing from Michael. Gina Ryan wrote a long letter this time, saying she regretted not coming to the UK with Miranda, but still, doing the junior sister year at the Base was very rewarding.

Increasing the time for the research study meant that more patients were added to her case load, but it was still manageable.

'You are entitled to some annual leave, you know,' said Adam Gillies.

'Now that the study won't finish until February next year, you may want to book a trip or something around Christmas. Anyway, bear it in mind.'

Chapter 21

At the final session of the summer school, the assembled group of students listened to Harvey McBride give his summary speech.

'I'm very impressed with the standard of reporting you have all provided. Though there isn't any formal grading system, I can tell you that each of you would be assured of qualifying for university entrance, if you haven't done so already.'

The lavish afternoon tea included the presentation of 'certificates of attendance and completion' to all the participants. There was an atmosphere of triumph, though a bit of poignancy too, as each student was conscious that the series had finished and their paths might not cross again.

University entrance, without matric ... God, if only ...

Adrian Banks was among those whose hand had to be shaken. When it was her turn, he said to her quietly, 'Miranda, I want to see you after all this hoo-ha's finished.'

Hoo-ha? Yes, he'd probably had many of them to endure over the years. It was important for the participants, not so for him.

She stayed behind after the room emptied, ostensibly packing notes into her satchel, taking her time. He came over to her.

'I'd like to take you out for a celebratory drink,' were his first words.

Miranda said, 'Just me?'

'That's right. Something I've wanted to do for some time.'

She felt the same excitement she experienced whenever she was in his presence.

Leaving together by a side door, she was conscious that she still didn't know whether he was married or not. Should she ask? Or would that reveal her feelings of insecurity?

The few drinks led to an invitation to his apartment, within walking distance he assured her. *I shouldn't agree to this*, a cautious little voice niggled. *Why not?* countered the adventurous and inevitably dominant self.

He stopped just before entering an impressive apartment building, placing his hands on her shoulders, and looking into her face.

'Before I seduce you, and we make love, I want you to know that you are already enrolled in the degree course in Sociology starting in September. I know that's what you want to do.'

Stunned, she could not find an answer.

His apartment was on the ground floor. It looked like a bachelor's pad. There were no family photographs around that she could see, just dim lighting, lots of books and a comfortable untidiness.

'Before we start – are you on the Pill?'

'I – I was. But I let it lapse … no need to be protected, I thought.'

'Well, think again. I'm not a fan of condoms, but for now, yes. After that, I hope you will go back on the magic pill.'

He is so sure of himself. *Should I make a break, get out, say 'I'm not like that'?* One look at those mesmerising eyes, and his raw passion made her crumble. *Yes, yes, this is what I want!* The awareness of danger only increased the frisson of excitement. Sex between a staff member and a student was universally frowned on, she knew that. But it could be the most memorable experience of her life.

It was. It was mind-blowingly exquisite. After the tumultuous climax, he said to her 'I can teach you a lot, both in bed and in the classroom. The only stipulation is that this remains absolutely private. Do you understand?'

'Of course.'

He went on to give her the name of a local doctor who would prescribe the contraceptive pill without question. Adrian also said he would investigate the change of her visa from work to student. *Gosh, I hadn't thought of that.* Lastly, he advised her of a number of scholarships she could apply for, though he wasn't sure about the eligibility of international students.

'You look absolutely radiant, Miranda,' said Lisa at breakfast several days later, 'are you in love or something?'

'No, of course not,' Miranda responded,' it's just that I'm going to be a uni student after all. I'm enrolled in Sociology at London University starting in September. It's a real buzz for me.'

'Well, congratulations! How will that affect your work schedule though?'

'I'll have to negotiate that – I can reschedule some of my home visits to weekends if there's a clash.' Adrian had already discussed this with her saying he could always give her personal tuition if she ever had to miss a lecture. He had made it clear that, for a variety of reasons, he could not commit to a regular routine for her visits. She immediately quashed the tiny suspicion that that raised. It was his business, and not her concern.

She was upfront with her mother about her academic plans but made no mention of her clandestine relationship with her senior lecturer. She asked what her father had said about her decision concerning the university enrolment, though in her heart she knew he would not approve. Maybe the next letter from Beaufort would say something about his opinion. But she was determined not to change anything.

Mum's next letter had some interesting news, the main thing being that Brian had told them he was serious about his latest girlfriend and was hoping to get engaged very soon. 'She's very sweet, her name's Jo, and she comes from Perth. They met at a training session in Melbourne, she works in the bank, too. I'll try to send you a photo in my next letter, we took some when she was here last weekend. By the way, Dad's only comment about you and your plans was, "Nothing Miranda does surprises me any more."'

The tone of the letter became more sombre as she told Miranda that Michael had visited them during the week. 'He's so different, really sad looking. He said he knew you had made your decision to stay on overseas, and there was nothing he could do about it. The reason for his visit, he said, was to tell us he's bought the old Ward place over near Lake Goldsmith, and is busy doing up the house, it's very run down. He said if you want to write to him, send it care of us and we can forward it. He's worried about his father too. He had hoped you might have sent him a card or something.'

Miranda felt chastened. Of course she should have done that. Her memories of Alex McPherson were so positive, it was hard to imagine him needing psychiatric treatment, private hospital notwithstanding. *How thoughtless*, she thought. *But what to say? I'll just do it. I have to.*

The start of the first semester at London University coincided with the arrival of autumn. Summer had been pleasant, but nowhere near as hot as in Australia. Now, there was a crispness in the air and leaves were beginning to colour.

Miranda was shocked at the price of the new textbooks she needed, until she was directed to the second-hand bookshop on campus. Even better than the reduced price was the discovery that the previous owner had underlined parts of the text and written little comments in the spaces, adding helpful notes to the printed words. It was just as well she was an avid reader – there was so much material to get through. And so many theories … she jotted important references in her notebook for inclusion in her written submissions.

Busy as she was with her work and the course, there was always time for a visit to Adrian's apartment, arranged by a fleeting contact in the department, or a phone call at home.

'I would very much like to be able to take you out to dinner and a show, believe me. But it isn't possible.'

Miranda didn't need to comment. She knew very well the risk they were both taking and was determined not to spoil the relationship which gave her so much secret pleasure.

Chapter 22

At the final Refugee Council meeting, she had the opportunity to talk privately to Theresa. Starting her university course was the major topic she wanted to share with her friend.

'I have to thank you, Theresa, for giving my details to Dr Banks who introduced me to the summer school which led to this next step.'

'I wasn't sure it was the right thing to do.'

'Is that why you told him I was engaged to be married?'

'It was. I wanted to protect you. I wanted to make sure he knew you were off-limits.' She looked intently at Miranda. 'You may not have known he has quite a bad reputation, especially with attractive young women.'

'Oh. Although it's none of my business if he is or isn't, but surely he's married.'

'Was, I understand. Just keep your feet on the ground and remember Michael.'

The comments hit home. Miranda had not told her of Michael's last letter which indicated that their relationship was over, allowing Theresa to continue to believe that he might be coming over for a visit.

Changing the subject, she told her about her brother's imminent engagement, adding that she would expect to be going over for the wedding.

'That's lovely news, Miranda. Now, take care of yourself, and don't overdo things.'

Good advice, or a warning? thought Miranda, as she made her way home. As she had a free afternoon, she took the route to London University intending to read some reference material in the library.

Adam Gillies looked distracted when she visited his office at the end of the week to hand over her paperwork.

'Is something wrong?'

He didn't look up immediately, eyes intent on the figures in front of him. 'There are some worrying results showing up – half the group have shown progressively lowered white cell counts in their fortnightly blood tests.'

'Are they the ones on the new medication?'

'They are, all of them. Let's see your notes.'

She handed over the pages with graphs attached.

'Hmm – not necessarily a statistical difference, but a variation nonetheless. Yep. Blood pressure better controlled in all of them, but the drop in white cell count is a worry …' His voice trailed off.

'What should be done about it?' Miranda ventured.

'It may mean we have to curtail this experiment. I'll have to get advice on it, Miranda. Perhaps halving the dosage again will do the trick. And weekly rather than fortnightly blood tests for those with the blue dots on their files, the ones on that medication. The others seem all right.'

Miranda opened her diary. Extra appointments would be necessary which would cut across some of her university hours. She'd just have to fit it all in somehow.

She was also concerned for those in her client group who were being affected by the trial medication. They were mostly men, though there were three elderly women on her books. She had managed to establish a rapport with all of them, some more readily than others. Their welcoming smiles, the tantalising smell of goulash and Hungarian spices, food she was often invited to taste, and the warmth of family members caring for their often incapacitated aged parent – would all this come to a halt?

'Do you think the effect of the experimental medication can be reversed?'

'I don't know. I've got to find out from the haematologists. Look, could you come in Tuesday next week, say about three-thirty. Hopefully, I can give you an answer then.'

She had a tutorial at four o'clock the following Tuesday. It was background stuff really – the historical development of social systems – she'd read up on all that. She could miss it, given the importance of Adam's concern. She rang the secretary's number to explain her non-attendance when she heard the familiar voice of Adrian himself.

'Oh, it's Miranda Shaw. I'm just ringing to say I can't make the tutorial next Tuesday because …'

His voice cut across hers. 'Why don't you come over to my place and tell me in person. I'll see you in half an hour.'

The explanation was received and followed up by torrid lovemaking. Both of them were breathing heavily afterwards.

Suddenly the room was flooded with light.

Frantically, Adrian jumped up to switch the overhead light off. Miranda was aware of the presence of another person.

'WHAT do you think you're doing? How did you get in?' he thundered.

A higher-pitched male voice replied, 'The door wasn't locked. I just came in to use the toilet, that's not a crime.'

The bedroom door closed. Miranda pulled the crumpled bedsheet over her as she strained to hear the whispered conversation in the next room.

'No, it's not the Swedish girl,' she heard Adrian say, his voice hissing. 'Now get out Nathan, you've put me in …' She couldn't hear the rest. The front door slammed shut, and she heard the click as it was locked on the inside.

Adrian came back to the bedroom, looking angry

'I'm sorry about that interruption. Unforgivable.'

Miranda slid off the bed and gathered up her clothes as she retreated to the bathroom. A cursory wash before dressing, she steeled herself to face Adrian, 'It's all right. Not your fault,' she managed to say. 'I've got to go anyway.'

Usually, after their lovemaking, Adrian would brew excellent coffee over which they would enjoy a friendly chat.

'Not staying, then?'

She shook her head, hastily gathered her satchel and left the apartment.

I don't know what to think. I have to get home, have a shower, restore my equilibrium.

It didn't happen like that.

Halfway down the street, on the way to the bus stop, she became aware of a young man looking in her direction. He stepped into her path, and she realised that it was the intruder.

'We'd better introduce ourselves,' he said, 'I'm Nathan. And you must be Miranda.'

'How do you know that?' she demanded.

'I've been doing my homework. Keeping an eye on Adrian is one of my pastimes.'

'Are you one of his students?'

'You could say that. Let's say he's taught me quite a lot, as you would no doubt know.'

His face came close to hers. Blonde, smooth skin, pale blue eyes framed by impossibly long eyelashes, a typical – she struggled for the right expression – *pretty boy*. Miranda felt squeamish. This was not a friendly encounter.

'Have you been spying on me?' Her tone was accusing. Miranda hoped it was assertive as well.

Nathan smirked. 'Let's say I know him better than you do. Or ever will.' With that he turned and made off down the street.

Miranda rejected the impulse to look back. Was he going back to Adrian's? Fortunately, she spotted a red bus approaching and broke into a run to catch it.

When she arrived home, there was no time to try to explore her confused feelings. Propped up on the phone was a note with her name on it.

'Please come – help my father – he sick.' It was signed Monika. *Oh God.*

It was not on a bus route, but it was within walking distance, less than four blocks away.

What's happened? All sorts of dire possibilities came to mind as she dashed up to her room to get her equipment bag. Had he had a fall, a heart attack or some other medical calamity? Mentally she rehearsed the CPR procedure as she hurried toward the Zamanski house. It was ages since she'd had to think of resuscitation. She had only been involved twice, once in Casualty, once in the wards on night duty during her training. She couldn't remember the outcome on either occasion.

The ambulance was there when she arrived, clusters of anxious people obscuring her view. As she came nearer, it was clear that the old man was inside, with the ambulance officer treating him, while the daughter Monika was getting into the front passenger seat. Before she could actually speak to her, the door closed and the vehicle was about to move.

The bystanders were nearly all Hungarian, their comments unintelligible to Miranda. To a young onlooker who possibly spoke both languages, she asked, 'What happened?'

'I don't really know. He's got a high temperature and they're giving him oxygen. He looks pretty sick.'

I wonder if Adam knows, Miranda thought. *Probably not. They would take him to Lambeth Hospital, that's the nearest. I should let him know.*

It was easier to go back home and make the phone call from there.

'Shit,' Adam said, 'He's one of those with the really low white cell count. I'll get a taxi to A&E and explain the situation. Will you be home later?'

Miranda considered. 'I've got two appointments this afternoon, I should be home around five.'

'Okay, I'll call you then.'

Miranda made sure she was back before five and waited in the dining room rather than going upstairs to her room. Worried and tired, she sat at the table, stretched out her arms and laid her head down. She heard the front door open. Shortly, another resident, Gwen Lowe, was beside her.

'Are you all right, Miranda? What's wrong?'

Miranda managed a small smile. 'I'm okay. I'm just a bit tired. And I'm worried.'

'About your course?'

'No, not that. It's one of my clients in the research study. He's been taken to hospital. I'm waiting down here 'cos Dr Gillies, my boss, said he'd ring as soon as there's any news.'

'Oh, that's awful for you. Look, I'll make a cup of tea, okay?'

'Thanks.' Her head went down again on her bent arms, her mind spinning from one thing to another: the current crisis, the unplanned but amazing session with Adrian Banks, then the rude interruption and subsequent encounter with Nathan. So puzzling. *I'm confused … and concerned.*

The cup of tea was especially welcome. She managed a grateful 'thanks' to Gwen who sat down opposite her with her own cup.

'Is everything else going all right, Miranda?'

It was an invitation to share a situation that had become murkier with the intrusion of a third party. Miranda was aware she had been handling all this on her own. What a relief it would be to …

Just as she was ready to confide, the phone rang.

'Miranda?' It was Adam.

'Yes, yes. What's happening?'

'Miranda – I'm sorry. They couldn't save him.' There was a pause, 'Are you still there?'

'Yes, I'm here,' she whispered.

'This may, no – will, change everything. There will be an investigation, of course. The medical superintendent has already asked for a full report in view of his depleted white cell count – he died of pneumonia, by the way. I have to go. Can you come into the office first thing on Monday?'

'Adam – how is Monika and the rest of his family?'

'Very upset, as you would imagine. By the way, none of this is your fault, Miranda. See you Monday.'

Two of the other residents had come downstairs. Gwen ushered them into the dining room with a few words of explanation before coming back to invite Miranda to rest in her room. Miranda allowed herself to be guided in and sat down in a comfortable old armchair by the window. She accepted a glass of sherry from the older woman.

'I gather it was not good news. The sherry might help you relax a bit. I'll put on some music.' She bustled around, locating the cassette player and her collection of tapes. 'Is Mantovani all right?'

Miranda nodded. It didn't matter what she put on.

Adam's words came back to her, 'It's not your fault.' It wasn't the first time she'd heard them. Her mind flew back to the scene of Anne's accident when Mr Saunders had blamed her. Dr Santorini had stepped in and told him it was an accident, no one was to blame. When she'd asked her father if Mr Saunders was right and he'd said those same words, 'No Miranda, it's not your fault.' And after Anne's death, Matron had told her the same thing, 'It's not your fault.' She remembered Michael's card on the back seat of the car, just after Anne's funeral. She shuddered. An unexpected wave of longing swept over her, for him, for her parents, especially Mum.

Gwen came back into the room shutting the door behind her. 'Sorry, just went out to check the spaghetti sauce – there's enough for both of us, okay?' Miranda didn't answer. 'Are you all right?'

'Just missing Mum. Wish she was here.'

'Of course you do, love. Do you want to pretend I'm her and say what you want to say to me?'

'It's the hugs I miss most.'

Miranda felt comforted by Gwen's embrace. 'Thanks,' Miranda managed. 'I really need to pull myself together. I'm sorry. It's the shock, I suppose.'

The spaghetti bolognese was delicious. Miranda realised she hadn't eaten anything since breakfast, and so much had happened since then. She reflected that her diary entry for today would probably take up much more space than usual.

'Do you have anyone in your university course, like a tutor or someone, who you could talk to? What about that lecturer you told me about who got you into the summer school? Would he be the sort of father-figure you need?'

Inwardly Miranda smothered a giggle. *Father figure!* If only her friend knew how that man behaved …

'I'll think about it, Gwen. And thanks for all this. I'd better go to my room now. I hope you have a good weekend, and please don't worry about me – I'll be all right.'

Somehow, Miranda got through the weekend by keeping herself busy with everyday chores. She started writing a letter to her mother, but it wouldn't be complete until she knew the outcome of Monday's meeting. She knew there was a possibility that the research could be terminated.

At one stage on Saturday afternoon, she heard someone answer the phone and call out her name.

'Who is it?' she called back.

'Someone from the university.'

If it was Adrian, she didn't want to talk to him, not now anyway

Coming to the top of the stairs, she placed her fingers over her mouth and shook her head. The message was received.

'She's not answering, must be out.'

Whoever it was, she reasoned, it didn't matter. She didn't want to talk to anyone, with the possible exceptions of Adam Gillies or the Zamanski family. She busied herself making sure that all her paperwork was up to date.

By Monday afternoon, Miranda knew the result. It was as she feared. The entire research program was to cease. The data collected was to be handed over to an investigative committee and all participants would be written to, in both English and Hungarian, informing them of the termination of the project and thanking them for their involvement. It was stressed by the chairperson that until a full investigation was completed, no mention was to be made to the media by any person without authority to do so.

Although under pressure himself, Adam Gillies managed to reassure Miranda that her original task of home-visiting, the recording of relevant data, as well as social contact with her study group, would continue for another fortnight.

'But after that, I'm afraid, you'll be paid any leave entitlement owing and that's it.'

There was no reason for her to miss her Tuesday tutorial after all. It would be a distraction from the uncertainty that resulted from the withdrawal of the research. It had been challenging to make the three morning visits without being able to say to her clients that it was all coming to an end. She tried to direct conversations with them to normal events, such as the beauty of the autumn leaves, and the prospect of winter to come after.

Ten minutes early for the class, she crept into the back row of the lecture room and took out the abstract of the article to be discussed in this session.

Head bent, she barely noticed the two young women come in to claim seats in the row in front of her. It was impossible to avoid hearing their conversation

'How about old Banksy! Wasn't he in a foul mood today!'

With a giggle, the other girl agreed. 'Sure was. He gave me seven out of twenty for my work. Snorted, mind you, as he gave it back. He might be a glamour-boy when he's in a good mood ...'

'Doesn't turn me on! ...' interrupted her friend.

'... but he'd be impossible to live with, with that temper. Haven't seen the toyboy around for a while, have you?'

'Nauseating Nathan? Oh, he'll turn up, don't worry.'

The room was filling with a lot of faces unfamiliar to Miranda. Not surprising, as this was a core topic for all the sociology streams. It was a relief to concentrate on the tutor's words. She hoped her heightened colour wasn't obvious to anyone else. Despite Gwen's suggestion, she dismissed any thoughts she had of confiding in the senior lecturer. Still, she had to sort out her next step.

An answer came to her in a flash – Theresa Polkinghorne! She still had her phone number somewhere. *I'll ring her when I get home.*

Later in her bedsit, she considered how much she could divulge to Theresa.

The recent death of a client and the forensic interest in the unofficial drug trial could not be discussed. However, the reality that the research project was to finish in less than two weeks meant she would then be out of a job. Should she see this as an opportunity to open up new horizons?

It was a bit late to make that phone call now, she decided. The days were getting shorter and cooler, too. It was October. *Tomorrow will do.*

The next day's post brought a letter from Mum with exciting news:

> My dear Mirrie,
>
> This letter will come as a surprise to you, I know. Hopefully it will be a good one. It's about Brian and Jo – they're not getting engaged after all, they're getting married instead. There is a reason. Next May, all being well, we'll be grandparents and you'll be an auntie! We were a bit shocked at first, but now we're of course delighted. Anyway, the wedding will be in Perth, and by the time you get this, it will only be three weeks away. I've given Jo's mother your address, so you should get your invitation fairly soon. We all hope you can come.

Miranda was amazed. From her point of view, the timing was brilliant – not only would she have completed her research job, but, not having taken any leave, the money due to her would cover the cost of flying to Western Australia. She smiled to herself when she thought of her big brother becoming a father. Once again she scrutinised the photos Mum had sent earlier. She especially liked the close-up of the pair of them locked in a loving gaze, so happy. A little sigh of regret escaped her lips – *this nearly was mine* – surely she'd heard a song expressing just that sentiment. She searched her memory unsuccessfully

Her spirits rose as she mulled over the contents of the letter, and this helped her to counter the seriousness of the immediate situation.

Because of the need for an autopsy, Mr Zamanski's funeral could not be held for some time. Miranda took a bouquet of white flowers to the grieving family, and with warm hugs and some tears, conveyed her condolences. To the heart-breaking question of 'Why?' she had no answer. One of the relatives said in English, 'It is God's will,' and they were all comforted by the words.

It was a relief to find that all the other participants in the study were doing well. Their blood pressures stayed within normal limits, even without the trial medication.

Friday's mail brought the invitation her mother had predicted. It was a formal invitation with gold lettering.

> *Mr and Mrs Neville Holdsworth request the presence of*
> *Miranda Shaw at the wedding of their daughter Joanne*
> *Amelia to Brian Frederick Shaw at Wesley Church, cnr*
> *William and Hay Streets, Perth on Saturday, 30th October.*
> *RSVP: 4 South Street Claremont W.A. 6010*

Wesley, eh? she thought. They must be Methodists.

Miranda replied immediately. The ordinary blue airmail letter was not very classy, but it would have to do. Along with greetings and best wishes, she mentioned that she had not been to Perth before, so it was a doubly exciting prospect for her. The other thing she needed to do was to reply to Mum's letter, saying it was all going to work out, and she would book her flight within the next few days.

The phone call to Theresa turned out to be something of an anticlimax since the Research Council had already been informed of the curtailment of the project.

'I was just about to ring you. It's very disappointing for you, Miranda. We haven't been told the full story yet, as enquiries are still ongoing, as you know. However, there was a glowing acknowledgment of your work with it. You are very well thought of.'

'Thank you, Theresa. Yes, it is disappointing to have to finish up early, but there's a silver lining for me.'

'Oh, what's that?'

'Remember I told you about my brother?

'Getting engaged? Yes, you told me that.'

'Well, it's now a wedding, in late October. In Perth. And I'll be able to go!'

Theresa noted her excitement. 'I'm really glad for you.' There was a brief pause. 'Are you in a position to make decisions about your future? I mean, you will probably see Michael and ...'

'That, I don't know,' Miranda interrupted, 'Perth's the other side of the country, you know. It's over one and a half thousand miles away from Victoria. I'm not sure even if he's invited, although, of course, I hope so. But to be honest, I do want to continue my uni course. Obviously, I'll need to work, too, but I can look into that when I get back.'

'At the moment we haven't got any vacancies appropriate to your skills and experience. And of course, you might want to return to nursing. Anyway, do keep in touch. I hope the trip back home goes well.'

She stayed sitting by the phone and thought about Theresa's comments. Miranda wondered how she would respond to seeing Michael at the wedding, if he were invited. She knew he and Brian were good friends, it was even possible her brother might have asked him to be best man.

Going up to her room, she selected one of the many postcards she'd collected during her travels around England. She jotted down a question to her mother, Will Michael be coming to the wedding? I'd love to see him! She stamped it, and ran down to the pillar box on the street to send it on its way. Hopefully, it won't be much behind the letter she'd sent her mother yesterday.

Gwen responded enthusiastically when Miranda told her about her forthcoming trip to Australia. 'Isn't that great! After all you've been through lately!' She paused before continuing, 'Hey, remember Robyn – what was her other name? You know – the one who was a teacher, and did the summer school with you. She moved out of here a month or so ago – didn't she come from Perth? Maybe you could get in touch with her and get some info if you haven't been there before.'

'What a good idea. I'll see if I can track her down. Our landlady should have a forwarding address. She'll be coming in on Tuesday to collect the rent. I'll ask her then.'

They settled into a discussion about the possible choices for what to wear as sister of the groom. They giggled. 'I'm the SOG, I suppose that's better than being a SAG.'

'You'll never sag, you're not the type. Not like me,' said Gwen, surveying her more generously built body. 'Too little will power and too many cakes,' she added ruefully.

The airline booking was the first priority. After that, most of the weekend was spent preparing for the trip. She decided her suitcase was too big for the ten days she expected to be away, while the overnight bag she used for short trips was much too small. A visit to a couple of charity shops on Saturday morning rewarded her with an almost new, medium-sized one. *Just right*, she thought. Next week, she'd ask Gwen to join her in a search for the perfect outfit for the celebration.

Miranda was having difficulty getting to sleep. She was unable to get Adrian Banks out of her mind. Was he her lover, her lecturer, or what was he? Was she just a plaything for him with a probable use-by date? And that creepy Nathan – where did he fit in? The fact remained that she needed to tell Adrian of the change in her circumstances, and also her trip back to Australia. Should she seek him out, or not? Sleep, when it finally came, did not solve anything. The questions remained when she woke in the morning.

Monday was the first day of her last week at work. The morning visits were to those she would be seeing again at the end of the week, those she'd been asked to monitor more closely. No explanatory letters from Dr Gillies had arrived yet.

The sociology lecture at four was on Darwin's Theory of Evolution. It was to be delivered by the Professor himself. Miranda always looked forward to hearing this learned academic speak, even though his delivery was not as theatrical as that of Adrian Banks. But the content was so wide-ranging and thought provoking, Miranda often wished she could record every word, instead of trying to get the most important concepts down on paper.

At the end of the session, she moved to the exit with the other students who were chattering, as usual. Adrian Banks appeared at the door, and, on seeing her, gestured toward his office.

'I've tried to contact you a number of times. Now it's time to have a talk,' he said, shutting the door.

'There are things I have to tell you, too,' said Miranda.

'Okay then, you first.' He pulled a chair out for her and took one himself. 'Fire away.'

It was a relief to be able to relate the events of the past two weeks: the sudden death of one of her clients, the investigations going on, and the fact that her position was terminated.

'When you say "investigations", can you be more specific?'

Miranda looked away. Should she confide in him?

'I can see you're reluctant to give more details – I won't insist, if it's a privacy issue.'

Miranda nodded, grateful for the reprieve. 'At this stage, I'm not allowed to say anything to anybody. But the fact remains that the project has been stopped.' Adrian remained silent, just a nod of understanding.

'The other thing I have to tell you is that my brother is getting married in a few weeks. In Perth, Perth Australia, that is,' she added, in case for some reason, he thought she meant Scotland. 'And I can go!'

Her excitement was not lost on him. 'That is good news. Sounds ideal, the timing I mean. So you'll be away for – how long?'

'I've booked a return flight for the ninth of November, which makes it just over two weeks. I'll need to know what study material to take with me so I can try to keep up, even from a distance.'

'Of course.' Adrian sat back in his chair and gazed at her face and then her body with his penetrating eyes. Miranda's senses quickened in response.

It was brief, though. He changed position and cleared his throat.

'The main reason I wanted to talk to you was in regard to our last time together which was so rudely interrupted.'

Miranda made a small gesture of dismissal.

'No', he said, 'it does matter. The person involved is employed by me as a technical assistant. He's responsible for several menial tasks, like copying and distributing lecture notes, mailings, and other things. Sometimes he,' he paused, choosing his words, 'oversteps the mark.'

'Did he tell you he accosted me down the street?'

Adrian looked shocked. 'No, he didn't.' He was silent for a moment. 'All that is unimportant now. Do you remember what I said to you during the summer school? About your potential?'

As if I'd ever forget. 'Yes, I remember. Your words of encouragement really registered.'

'Good. Hang on to that advice. I look forward to seeing you when you come back from your travels.'

That seemed to be it. Miranda murmured thanks as she made to go, but he forestalled her at the door.

'Oh, before I forget. Are you able to retain that third copy of your assessment notes, remember you showed me once when you were telling me about the research?'

Momentarily bemused, she gathered her thoughts. 'I don't know, perhaps I can. Can I ask why?'

'I was thinking there may be some interesting material in that study of an elderly non-English cohort from a sociological point of view. Names obliterated, of course. Just a thought.'

She left his office, her mind buzzing. At the end of the corridor, she saw the pale lean figure of Nathan looking in her direction, then he quickly turned away.

Chapter 23

Midmorning on a sunny late October day and the arrivals terminal of Perth Airport was moderately busy with individuals and family groups waiting for the newly arrived travellers to emerge from the dark-blue double doors. Already, several small clusters had met up and moved on, giving those waiting more room to lean over the rails and gaze eagerly at every movement of the doors.

The overhead display board stated that the BOAC flight from London had landed some thirty-five minutes earlier.

'Are you sure that's the one, Grace?'

She took the telegram from her well-worn handbag and gave it to her husband. 'That's the flight number she gave, so that must be it.'

Brian and his fiancée had been looking out the large front window at the pond with a flotilla of black swans. 'Just like Lake Wendouree,' he said before they rejoined Jack and Grace. 'Takes ages to get through Customs and Immigration, doesn't it.'

'What do you mean 'immigration'? She's Australian, not an immigrant,' Jack retorted.

'I know, Dad. Customs officials still need to check their baggage. She'll probably be through soon.'

Indeed she was. She stopped and looked around uncertainly. Grace saw her and hurried to meet her.

'Mirrie! Oh, darling, you're here!'

Miranda, flushed and smiling, embraced all her family before she found herself looking at the young bride-to-be who would soon also be a Shaw.

'Hello, Jo! It's wonderful to meet you, we must have a long chat so's I can tell you things about my brother you may not know.'

'I've heard so much about you, Miranda. It's so good you could come.' Slightly built, just a bit taller than Miranda, with straight brown hair and a pretty face recognisable from the photographs, Jo Holdsworth was undoubtedly glad to meet her.

They moved to the taxi rank, Brian taking charge of his sister's suitcase. 'We've booked into a hotel not far from the church,' he said, 'Jenny, Jo's mum, recommended it.'

'When did you all get here?'

Her mother answered. 'Yesterday. It seemed a long flight to me. Made me realise how much longer yours would have been. Anyway, we're all together now, aren't we, Jack? Hope we can all fit in the cab.'

The five of them squeezed in and set off for the city.

'Isn't it wonderful – it all looks so new,' exclaimed Miranda as the tall CBD buildings came into view.

'Not like where you've come from, I reckon,' said Dad. Miranda stole a glance at him. She noted more deeply etched lines and weathered skin. She realised she'd become used to the pale smooth complexions of so many English faces.

Michael's name hadn't been mentioned so far.

'Did you get the postcard I sent you after my last letter, Mum?'

'I did. I'll talk to you about it when we get to the hotel.'

So – what does that mean?

After a shower and a change of clothes, Miranda made her way along the hotel corridor to her parents' room. 'Can I come in?' she called at the door.

'We're just getting ready to go out for lunch. Do you want to wait downstairs? Brian and Jo are already there.'

It was a chance to get to know her future sister-in-law. She found them sitting close together having a quiet conversation. Brian saw her first, 'Oh, there you are, Sis. Come and say hello to Jo properly.'

Jo stood up to hug Miranda, who responded, 'I've always wanted a sister. Now I'm getting one.'

'Me, too,' Jo replied. I've got two brothers, one older than me, one younger. Geoff's nearly eight years older than me and he's working in South America. He won't be coming.' To Miranda's questioning look, she added, 'He's, well, he's a missionary. But you'll meet Timothy, he's just nineteen. I'm about the same age as Brian – he's got a birthday coming up next month, mine's in December.'

As soon as Grace and Jack arrived, they walked to a nearby restaurant that Jenny had recommended.

'This is all just wonderful. I can't remember when we stayed in a hotel last, can you, Jack? And to have our daughter here, and a wedding as well!'

Grace's happiness was infectious. They all laughed.

'Don't worry, I've brought my camera,' said Brian. 'It'll be recorded for the family history.'

At the end of the meal, Grace needed to go to the bathroom. 'I'm on stronger water tablets,' she whispered to Miranda.

'I'm coming too,' her daughter responded

At the handbasin afterwards, Miranda opened her mouth to ask …

'I know you want to know about Michael,' Grace forestalled her.

She watched Miranda's face as she explained that Michael wouldn't be coming to the wedding and had declined Brian's invitation to be his best man. He was sorry to have to do that, but he had his reasons. At least that's what Dad said.'

'Dad said what? What did he mean?'

'Your father has been helping him with fencing, stock management, and other jobs he used to do at Taylors ages ago. Brendan does most of the work at the funeral parlour these days, and as you know, Dad always loved farm work so it works out well, especially as Michael's dad can't help these days.'

'What else did he say? Michael, I mean – anything about me?'

'I don't know, you'd have to ask your father about that. But …' She paused, then decided to continue. 'I may as well tell you – he is seeing a young lady who comes from a farming property near Colac. Dad's met her, says she's a really nice girl.' Miranda drew in her breath sharply. Noticing the response, Grace continued. 'You can't blame him, love. He's got to look to his own future.'

Miranda turned away, trying to hide her bitter disappointment. Grace, watching her closely, decided a hug was needed. Very much so …

'We'd better go back, the others will wonder what's happened to us.'

'Mum, thank you. For telling me, I mean. And understanding.' She stopped, looking at her mother intently. 'And you? How are you? You never make any complaints in your letters – are you okay?'

'Oh, Dr Santorini keeps his eye on me, don't worry. He's always glad to hear news of what you're up to, by the way. It's that murmur in my heart that I've always had, just means I can't do as much, or as quickly as before.'

The next two days before the wedding were hectic, but passed pleasantly. It was clear that Jo wanted to get to know her new 'sister'. She confided that, at first, her parents were not happy about her pregnancy, telling her they should have waited until after their marriage.

'They are very conventional, but after they got to know Brian, they realised he was a good, solid man, and accepted the situation. But I'm not allowed to be married in white, so my dress is pale lemon. It's only a small wedding so I didn't need any bridesmaids. Oh, and there won't be any alcohol either,' she chuckled.

Miranda laughed as well. 'The ceremony's only a legal requirement anyway.' She said. ' It's obvious you and Brian are madly in love, and that's what really matters.'

On the afternoon before the big day, the subject of wedding presents was raised. Miranda had brought with her a medieval tapestry, a souvenir from her visit to Canterbury Cathedral. She showed it to her mother.

'Should I get something else as well?'

'No, I don't think so, love. That's a lovely gift, and they know you've had to spend a lot to come over here. Dad and I are giving them a gift certificate from Myers so they can get things that they really need. Brian's been promoted to assistant manager in Hamilton, so they'll be renting for a while. Jenny and Neville will come over and stay with them around the time the baby's due, so they're trying to get a three-bedroom place. Brian's already got some agents looking, I'm sure they'll come up with something.'

After her long explanation of what was going on, Grace was breathless.

'Mum, take it easy. Please. Let me make you a pot of tea. I haven't told you anything yet about what's happening for me, so I'll fill you in over a cuppa.'

Miranda explained about the termination of the research project without giving any details that might make Grace anxious.

'Do you intend to stay in that field?'

'Probably not, Mum. My main goal, as you know, is to finish my degree. 'I'll have to work part-time, though. When I go back, I'll see if there's anything available at St Georges – night duty would be all right, especially with winter coming up.'

Grace smiled, remembering the few weeks when her daughter would come home about nine in the morning, sleep until late afternoon, and go back to the Beaufort hospital about nine-thirty at night. That was nearly a year ago now. The smile turned to a frown.

'Does that leave you any time for, well, socialising? I mean, meeting boys and all that?'

Miranda's laugh was genuine. 'Not high on my agenda at this stage, Mum. I'm heavily involved in my uni course. I'll admit I wasn't sure about Michael, seeing him again, I mean. But that's not going to happen now, and all I can say is I hope he will be happy. By the way – how's his father?'

'Not good, Brian said, he seems to have lost the will to live.'

That was a sobering thought. Miranda resolved to write to him again during her short stay in Australia.

Something else on her agenda was the trip to Scotland to see her grandparents' graves. This time her mother made her promise. 'They actually died in March all those years ago, but you don't have to wait until then.'

Chapter 24

Back in England with its pre-winter gloom, Miranda was disappointed that her trip to Australia was over so quickly. The roads and streets now looked different. Autumn leaves were gone, the tracery of bare branches and tree trunks made the buildings more visible. It was cold, too, noticeable after the delightful warmth of the Perth sun. Miranda stowed her summery travel clothes in a high cupboard and retrieved her winter woollies, including gloves, scarf and warm beret.

Some of her fellow residents offered greetings of, 'welcome back!' and 'how did it all go?' Her closest friend, Gwen, sat on her bed asking questions about the trip.

'Robyn rang just after you left, so she wasn't able to give you any clues on the Perth scene, but I guess you managed all right,' she said.

Miranda had brought back some souvenirs for her friends, such as the little toy quokkas from her visit to Rottnest Island. She also brought out the tourist brochures of trips she'd made with the Holdsworths and her parents after the newlyweds went off to Adelaide for their honeymoon. She had really enjoyed Scarborough Beach with its lovely sand, cliffs and surf.

'Scarborough? That's on the east coast,' someone interrupted.

'Not in Australia – it's on the west coast, with massive waves from the Indian Ocean,' she replied. 'It was just a bit too cool for me to go swimming, unfortunately.'

After a few days, the novelty of her return wore off, and things went back to their normal routine. She dressed warmly for her first lecture back at the university, not sure what weather to expect. Two friends said she could copy their lecture notes. One of them was in the same tutorial group and shared the comments he'd written last week. She was relieved that she had not missed anything especially important. Disappointingly, there was no sign of Dr Adrian Banks.

She called in at the department reception to collect an assignment she'd handed in before leaving the country, and found it to be marked seventeen out of twenty. *Good*, she thought. *What next?*

Her top priority was to find employment. Adam Gillies had promised to write a reference if she needed it. Miranda decided to apply for a position at St Georges since she knew how to get there and was familiar with the layout of the hospital.

'As it happens, we do have a part-time night duty vacancy coming up. But it's for Friday, Saturday and Sunday nights – not a popular roster for younger staff members,' the recruitment officer said, with a smile.

'That would not be a problem for me as I'm also doing a university course. In fact, it would be ideal. In what department would I be working?'

'Again, it's not one young people often choose – it's Oncology, cancer patients, often terminal.'

Miranda absorbed the information and replied, 'My father is an undertaker,' she said, 'I grew up around death and grieving relatives. Yes, somehow, I feel this could be right for me.'

'You had a very favourable report from Dr Gillies, and your references are excellent. If you're sure, I'll get you to fill out the application form now. As a registered nurse you need to provide your own uniform, but we do have a second-hand shop on the premises.'

Miranda nodded gratefully. Formalities completed, Miranda left with a verbal contract which would be confirmed by mail, and the assurance of a pay rate even more generous than what she had received earlier. She was asked to return on Wednesday to become familiar with the ward, with the prospect of starting work on Friday night next week.

How good is that, she thought.

Tucked into her handbag was a little wad of English banknotes. 'Your tax refund came in August,' Mum had said. 'Brian waited until the exchange rate was better to convert it into English currency. We also added a bit extra as a late birthday present.' She had thanked her parents with a kiss, adding that she would write to thank Brian, when he came back from his honeymoon, and when she had his new address. *Into the bank it goes,* she decided. *No lavish spending.*

The eleven o'clock Friday lecture was usually given by Dr Banks. Miranda felt a delicious thrill at the thought of seeing him again, perhaps to be able to tell him about her trip and the new job, and possibly, given the experience of previous occasions, there could be more to expect.

However, a woman walked to the lectern. Tall, thin and dark-skinned, she spoke with an American accent.

'Good morning all. Obviously, I am not Dr Banks, my name is Sarah Young-Johnson. I'm a visiting fellow from Vassar, here in England for two months. Dr Banks is unfortunately not well and I've been asked to take over his sessions. Today the topic I have chosen is philosophical, but a question for us all, "How far is the ideal of universal brotherhood achievable?" Any questions?'

The hand of an assertive young woman, noted for her interjections in previous classes, shot up 'Do we assume when you say "brotherhood" that women, in your opinion, don't count?'

There was the usual titter from the assembled group, as the lecturer patiently clarified her use of the term, but Miranda missed most of it. She was preoccupied with the news that Adrian was ill. *What's wrong with him? Is it serious?*

Afterwards, as she made her way out with the rest of the students, Nathan sidled up to her with an envelope in his hand.

'He told me to give you this,' he said, giving it to her before disappearing into the mass of milling, chattering students. Miranda went to the student lounge, found a chair and opened the letter.

It was handwritten and brief.

'My dear Miranda,
Please do not be alarmed. I have been going downhill in the
last two weeks and am back in hospital on medical advice. Rest
assured I will recover. Continue as you are doing for your sake,
and for mine. With much affection,
Adrian.'

On re-reading the short note, Miranda was struck by the phrase 'back in hospital.' *What does that mean?* To her he'd always seemed in good health, full of life and with amazing energy. It was puzzling. She sat there thinking it over. *What hospital is he in? Is a visit appropriate?*

Miranda decided that the office staff may know. Mrs Lindquist, who seemed to have the most contact with students and staff, would be the person to ask. She went upstairs to the General Office on the first floor.

'Nothing new has come in for you, dear. Were you expecting some more corrected work?' said Mrs Lindquist.

'No, no – it's all up to date. It's, well, I'm sorry to hear about Dr Banks and I thought I'd ask if you know what hospital he's in and whether he's allowed visitors? Or could I send him a Get Well card, perhaps?'

Mrs Lindquist's face became serious as she beckoned Miranda closer.

'I'm afraid I can't tell you, confidentiality and all that. Just a minute, I'll look in his mail slot.' She returned with a piece of paper. 'These are the people who can be informed of his whereabouts when he's ready. The head of the department, the head of the faculty, one of his post-grad students and another student.' She looked at Miranda, 'Oh, it's you, Miranda Shaw. So what he's saying is, when he feels well enough he will release more details. That's what's happened in the past.'

Miranda remained confused. 'But I don't understand. How serious is it? Is he in any danger?'

Her concern was evident. Mrs Lindquist gave a little smile. 'It's not life-threatening, if that's what you mean. As I said, it has happened before, and he always makes a good recovery. I'd say he'd be off until after Christmas.'

'That long!' Miranda gasped.

'We'll just have to wait and see. In the meantime Ms Young-Johnson has taken his place, I hear she's very impressive.'

After agreeing to come to the office again the following Friday after the lecture, Miranda left, her mind whirling with possibilities. She considered, then rejected, the possible diagnoses she could think of, from physical to psychiatric, with no clues coming from her intimate knowledge of him.

It was all too hard. Miranda made her way home, conscious that the days were getting shorter, knowing that nights would be drawing in even earlier as the year progressed.

She suddenly realised that, for weeks to come, she would be arriving at work, and then coming home, in the dark. She decided to see how it went for the first few weeks to see if it was manageable. Otherwise, she might need to find new accommodation closer to both the university and St Georges.

A bulky letter arrived from Mum with wonderful photographs of the wedding. 'Brian had arranged to have them developed quickly before their honeymoon,' she wrote. 'The ones with a red cross on the back are the ones we're having enlarged and framed.'

Miranda wrote back, telling her of her new job starting at the end of the week. She phrased the information about Adrian carefully, saying that one of her favourite lecturers was on sick leave, and had been replaced by an American woman, who happened to be a Negro. She finished by describing the early onset of winter with its gloomy skies, bitter wind and chilling rain. But, to compensate, bright Christmas lights were starting to appear.

Just writing the letter made her feel better. *It's like doing a summary for myself as well as my family*, she thought.

Sarah Young-Johnson delivered the Friday lecture. This time Miranda listened more intently. After the lecture she made her way upstairs to the General Office.

'Nothing to tell you, I'm afraid,' said Mrs Lindquist.

'I hope that means no news is good news. I have to get home and try to get some sleep. I'm starting night duty tonight.'

'Good luck, my dear. I hope it all goes well.'

The Oncology Ward at St Georges was a typical Florence Nightingale design. Rows of iron beds on each side, with curtained screens separating the patients. Miranda would be in charge, with two nursing aides, both older and more experienced, to assist with patient care. There were twenty beds, though some were unoccupied.

The sister who supervised the afternoon shift showed Miranda where all the files were kept.

'You might like to read them during a quiet time. Most of the patients have been here several weeks, their condition remains stable. The man in Bed 8 has a blood transfusion in place. When it finishes, just put up normal saline to flush through – it's all listed here. Come with me and I'll introduce you to the one or two who may need more attention during the night.'

Before leaving, she gave her the keys to the dangerous drugs cupboard. 'We always hand these over last – then we do the count, we sign the book – and then I can go home.' All this was standard procedure Miranda remembered from her training.

The first night passed without incident. Miranda gave her verbal report and handed the DD keys to the day staff. Pleasantly tired, she yawned several times while waiting for the bus. With her woollen beret pulled down over her ears and her scarf covering most of her face, she guessed no one would notice.

Miranda reminisced about how she used to love hopping into a warm bed when everyone else had to get up to face a wintry day. *Hang on, it isn't winter yet. It's a late Autumn cold snap. There's December, January and February to look forward to. Or not.*

By mid-December she had settled into her new routine. There had been only one death on her shift during that time, a patient who lay unconscious for several days before her life slipped away. Her relatives, aware of her decline, had asked not to be informed until morning if she passed away during the night. So Miranda was spared that grim responsibility.

In her most recent letter home, Miranda described the splendour of the Christmas illuminations in the centre of London. 'They're amazing, lots of holly and ivy, coloured lights and Christmas carols coming from the big department stores.'

'Not much of that in Beaufort,' her mother had written in reply. 'By the way, I've sent a little present to you that I hope will arrive before Christmas. Something I made myself.' Miranda immediately thought of her mother's lemon slice – *that's what I'd really like*. Grace also went on to ask which church service Miranda planned to attend.

That was a tricky one. During one of the discussions she'd had with Adrian after their lovemaking, the subject of religious belief came up. He declined to answer her directly when she asked. Instead, he replied 'When you tackle Religions and Belief Systems in second year, you'll find yourself questioning everything you ever believed in.'

She had later looked up some references in the library and was indeed challenged. Maybe it's a cultural thing, she reasoned, you take part, without needing to verify what you claim to be true.

It made her look forward to the subjects to be studied in second year. But the main thing at the moment was to make sure she passed all her first-year subjects. So far, all her grades had been good, which was very encouraging.

On the last Friday before the Christmas break, she went up to the General office as usual. This time Mrs Lindquist had a warm smile and a letter for her.

'Everyone on his list has received one, here's yours.'

Miranda accepted it gratefully and, after wishing her a 'Merry Christmas and Happy New Year', departed hastily to read the message.

Inside was an abstractly designed greeting card with the words, 'I've been in the D phase of M-D. Look it up, and you'll understand better. On the upswing now. See you in the New Year. Love Adrian.'

A flood of relief washed over her. Although she hadn't done the psychiatric nursing course, she knew enough to grasp what his diagnosis was – manic-depressive psychosis, a major mental illness. Yes, it all made sense now. He definitely has a naturally high energy level, the typically manic drive which makes him so attractive. She hadn't seen the reverse, the depression, which she knew was often deeper than the common just being sad or blue. Obviously, it had happened while she was away.

She reread the card, delighting in the use of the word 'love'. There was no way for her to respond, but the promise of seeing him again in a few weeks reassured her. Nothing could have taken the smile from her face as she journeyed home for the pre-night-duty sleep.

'Have you got any Christmas plans?' Gwen asked.

'I'm doing my usual shifts, that's all. What about you?'

'I've asked around and there's only going to be five of us staying here between Christmas and New Year, so we've been planning to have a grand meal here with each of us doing a bit of the preparation. What do you think? Tentatively, we put you down for the pudding, would that be okay?'

Miranda smiled. 'That's perfectly okay, as long as you don't mind it coming from Fortnam and Mason's.' She thought for a moment. 'Hey, it's on a Friday this year, isn't it – that means I need to leave about eight-thirty to get to work. So it'll have to be an afternoon dinner, if that's all right.'

'Course it is, but, gee, it looks as though you'll be on duty for New Year's Eve too.'

Not like last year, Miranda thought. It was like a dream now, being out at Bournagulla with Michael and his father. Hard to believe it was only a year ago.

The Christmas meal went well. Everyone had brought something to add to the occasion, crackers, decorations, and little gifts to be shared. The agreed limit of 30p resulted in some delightfully original gifts. The mulled wine was a bonus, although only one glass for Miranda, which was enough to send her out into the night with a warm glow. In her shoulder bag were little presents for her two workmates, Sheila and Roma, as well as a handful of chocolates from the large box donated to the residents by their generous landlady.

In the week between Christmas and New Year, the parcel from her family arrived with a lovely Australia-themed card and the very welcome gift of hand-knitted bed socks from Mum. *How thoughtful, just what I need at this time of the year.* She looked at the row of cards on her windowsill, each valued for the warm greetings expressed. But nothing from Michael.

She had sent him a card in the small parcel to her family. It was cheerful and friendly, simply wishing him well. *I want him to know I care, always will. I hope he will forgive me one day.*

On the last night of 1970, the ward was quiet as the staff sat together with the radio turned down, listening to Big Ben chime midnight.

'Let's sing Auld Lang Syne softly,' suggested Roma. They started on the traditional favourite, but Miranda's attention wavered.

'Excuse me,' she said, making her way to one of the patients who was stirring.

'Anything the matter, Mrs O'Keefe?' she asked quietly, taking the hand of the frail, ghostly-looking patient.

'Is it the New Year yet?' she asked in a whisper.

'Yes, it is. It's 1971.'

'So I made it after all.' The words were so soft Miranda had to put her ear close to the pallid face to hear.

'Are you in pain? Can I get you anything?'

Again the answer was barely audible. 'No, dear.' After a pause she managed to utter her last words, 'I can die happy. I won my bet.'

Miranda pulled the screens around the bed and sat down on a chair close by her patient. She reached for the dying woman's hand, holding it gently so she could monitor her pulse. Mrs O'Keefe's eyes closed, and her breathing slowed.

Both nurses appeared at the gap in the screen. 'Do you need us?' asked one of them.

Miranda shook her head. 'I'll stay with her now. Can you manage the round without me?' That was not a problem, both nurses worked together as an efficient team

Sometimes, close relatives wanted to be present at the end, but Miranda knew that Mrs O'Keefe was a childless widow. Her nearest relative was an elderly brother in a nursing home. Moreover, she hadn't requested a minister or priest to attend her final hours.

At four-fifteen her breathing ceased. Miranda gently drew the sheet to cover her patient's face, now looking so peaceful.

Sheila peeped between the curtains and, noting that the old lady had died, said, 'First death for 1971. In other hospitals around the country right now they'll be registering the first births of the new year.'

Miranda smiled. *All too true.*

Chapter 25

The students returned to university in the second week of January. The next break would be at Easter in April. It was with a mixture of expectation and apprehension that Miranda made her way to the Friday lecture. *Will he be there?*

To her delight, she saw both Adrian Banks and Sarah Young-Johnson at the dais. Miranda made her way to her usual seat, nodding and smiling to some of the students from her tutorial group.

As Adrian moved to the lectern, becoming the centre of everyone's attention, the visiting lecturer stood to one side. Adrian looked just as imposing as ever. He moved to stand in front of the dais, a smile crinkling his handsome features.

'Happy New Year, and welcome back everybody. It's good to see you all again. I'm perfectly well now since my time out, but I have been advised to limit my workload for the rest of this semester.' He paused theatrically. 'So, I've asked Ms Young-Johnson if she will continue with this unit. I understand she's made an excellent start.' Someone started clapping and the majority joined in, Miranda included. 'Well, that's a satisfying endorsement, isn't it, Sarah?'

Smiling now, Ms Young-Johnson stepped up to stand next to him. 'Thank you so much for your vote of confidence. It's really good to have you back with us, Adrian, and looking so well, too.'

Adrian nodded graciously, and without further ado, strode purposefully from the room. Reassured and relieved, Miranda settled down to concentrate on the lecture. When it ended, she joined the bustle of exiting students, only to become aware of Nathan making his way towards her.

'He wants to see you in his office,' he murmured, before disappearing in the other direction.

'My dear girl – come in. And close the door. Tell me, what has been happening for you?'

'The first thing I must tell you is that I have to leave quite quickly. I'm working night duty and have to have a sleep before I start.'

'Pity,' he said. He sounded subdued.

'I'm so glad you're better. Thank you for the Christmas card and the explanation.' She dropped her gaze. 'I'm sorry, I had no idea ...'

'That I was bi-polar? You weren't to know. It's not something I choose to tell people. This time they've started me on a new treatment, lithium. First discovered by an Australian doctor, I believe. Anyway, I'm doing all right on it, so here's hoping.'

'Was it – was it awful for you?'

'At the time, at its worst, it's like being in quicksand, you can't get out of it. At least this time I didn't get to the stage of wanting to end it all.' Miranda shuddered involuntarily. 'But as you can see, I'm alive, and almost back to my old self.' He said this with such a wide smile that Miranda had to follow suit. 'That's better, you were looking a bit too serious a moment ago. Look, if you have to go now, why not meet up with me next week after your Tuesday class.'

It wasn't a question, more a directive, but Miranda didn't care. She made her way home happy, looking forward to next Tuesday.

On Monday afternoon, having slept for four hours, her usual practice at the end of a three-night stint, she was delighted to find a letter from home. Her mother's words cheered her with New Year's greetings followed by news of Brian and Jo. 'They've found an ideal place to rent, Dad and I are going to visit them next week to take some of Brian's things over to Hamilton.' She went on to mention some local happenings, but it was the last sentence that raised Miranda's concern. 'Dr Santorini wants me to see a specialist, a cardiologist. So I have an appointment in Ballarat next month.'

Putting the letter down, Miranda considered the implication of what she had read. She knew about the rheumatic heart condition that developed as a result of her mother's scarlet fever all those years ago, though it had not appeared to greatly affect her life. She had two healthy children, and she lived a reasonably active life, with few restrictions. But Miranda could not ignore the episodes of breathlessness and limited mobility she had noticed when she was in Perth ten weeks ago. She also knew that the current warm weather in Victoria could exacerbate the symptoms.

She wrote her reply beginning with the comment that it was good to hear she was to see a specialist. 'Tell me exactly (underlined) what he, or she, says after the appointment. That's an order!' She continued with general remarks about her course, with the first year ending in May. 'After that, I'll try to get up to Scotland – it's better to go in summer when the days are longer and it's almost warm.' She ended by saying, 'Please let me know Jo's due date.'

It was the usual communal dinner on Thursday. Those living in the house who were available contributed to provide a meal for everyone. There needed to be enough variety to cater for the two vegetarians and the one on a low-calorie diet, while the wine supply was replenished when necessary out of a small fund to which everyone contributed.

In the discussion during the meal, Kate, one of the newest tenants, said, 'What we need is some guys to socialise with.' At just nineteen and coming from a quiet area near the Medway River in Kent, she was keen for some excitement.

'Anyone got any suggestions?' asked Gwen.

'We could go to a pub somewhere, like Earls Court, or wherever there's some action,' said Marilyn, who, on noticing Miranda, directed a question at her. 'Hey, Miranda, you must know a lot of young men at the university – could you arrange something?'

Miranda smiled. 'You're right, there are quite a few young blokes around, but I can't say I know them.'

'No-one to take your fancy, then?'

'It's not that, it's just that I'm concentrating on my course. Working Friday, Saturday and Sunday nights puts me out of the usual activities you have in mind.'

The other young women decided that Kate's idea was a good one and that they should pursue it.

'Let's make it Thursday evening so you can come.'

Miranda laughingly agreed, though privately had reservations as to whether it would be her scene. She was more preoccupied with meeting Adrian on Tuesday. There was a lot she needed to tell him.

She was about to knock on his door when it opened, and with a theatrical gesture, she was welcomed inside with, *'Entrez mademoiselle!'* He looked animated, though perhaps not quite as larger than life as in the past. She realised, with some surprise, that she actually felt more relaxed this time. Previously, his immediate focus had been on passion, to which she had responded wholeheartedly. *Maybe it's the effect of his medication.*

Almost as though he had read her thoughts, Adrian made the comment that, even though he felt the usual desire, the tablets he was taking affected his ability to make love. 'I was warned about it, but I certainly hope it doesn't stay that way,' he said with a smile. 'Now tell me all that's been going on for you, starting with that trip to Australia.'

Miranda recounted in detail her impressions of the trip.

'And that young farmer – was he there?' His look was intense.

A quick decision. Now was the time to explain the failure of that relationship. She told him of the forced sale of his family property, the public shame, and the outcome. She felt confident enough to mention her confused feelings towards Michael which had been resolved when she knew there was another young woman in his life.

'Good,' Adrian said, 'I'm glad you have told me the full story. I can understand how torn, for want of a better word, you must have felt when his world collapsed.'

Torn? Yes, that probably describes it.

She sat silent for a moment, then raised her eyes to look at him squarely. 'I have to continue the path I'm on now.'

'Absolutely right. Of course you do. In fact, I have a further plan for you if you're agreeable.'

Miranda was instantly alert. 'Yes? What's that?'

He got up and wandered slowly around the room, choosing his words carefully. 'It seems to me that you might benefit from doing another summer school. I'm thinking psychology would be a good choice for you. Concentrating on the individual, the development of normal behaviour, going on to studying dysfunctional presentations. Fascinating stuff. What do you think?'

Miranda was rapt. How right he was, this was exactly what she needed to do. Her vigorous nod conveyed total agreement.

He continued, 'I will not be around in the summer, I'm letting you know before anyone else. I'm going back with Sarah Young-Johnson to take up a short fellowship at Yale. Incidentally, she will be one of the first black American women to join that faculty.

'Oh,' was all Miranda could manage in reply. She looked up to see that Adrian was smiling.

'I shall be away from the beginning of June until the end of August. Last year I had a short three-week break in California, and I let Nathan stay here in my absence. This time I'm taking him with me, and I wonder whether you would like to house-sit for me while I'm away.'

Miranda couldn't believe what she was hearing.

'You're taking Nathan with you?'

'Yes.' He stopped in front of her. 'There are … reasons for that which I won't go into. But I would feel relieved to have someone I trust staying here. Discreetly, of course. Able to answer the phone when I ring from New York,' he added with a smile.

'I would have to leave my current address. I couldn't afford the rent on two places.'

He laughed. 'I agree you should leave where you are now, it is somewhat out of the way for you, anyway. You won't need to pay rent here, Miranda. I own this apartment. It wouldn't cost you anything.'

He made it all sound so easy. *It was almost as though he is in charge of my life. Perhaps he is ...*

Looking at her questioningly, he said 'Do you want time to think about it? Or both, I mean – the summer school and the house sit?'

'No, oh no!' They're both – what can I say? – brilliant. Thank you so much.'

'Well come over here and give me a hug.'

That felt right, too. *I'm so lucky*, she thought.

On the way home, she considered her immediate future. First year sociology would be coming to an end in early May. Adrian said he wanted to leave at the end of May. Perhaps her best chance of making the Scottish trip would be in the second or third week before he left. Not quite summer, but there might be spring blossoms around, who knows? The summer school would probably be organised in a similar way to the one last year which had set her on her current path.

Before she left Adrian, she mentioned that the girls in her house were keen to go out socialising as a group and wanted her to be part of it.

'You should go with them. Definitely. Try to participate in as many activities as you can, it's all part of the life-long learning process.'

He was right, of course, even though it sounded patronising. But the fact that he was encouraging her to meet up with other young people, which would include men, warranted some attention. Clearly, he wasn't possessive of her emotionally. So why this little feeling of disappointment? Not justified, she decided, remembering his earlier observation that 'no-one owns anyone else.' It would be better to continue being grateful for what she had in this clandestine relationship, rather than agonising over what was out of reach. Equilibrium restored, she made her way home in a positive state of mind.

Her next letter home was an exciting one to write, given that there were some good things happening, or about to, all being well. She started by telling her mother she had taken her advice and started to go out socially. 'It was a noisy place with a big group of young people in their twenties or thirties, loud music with a heavy metal beat so you couldn't hear each other speak. But we all agreed it was great. For me, it was a big change from the quiet ward, and the focussed seriousness of university. So, thanks for that, Mum!' She went on to outline her plans for summer, mentioning the proposed trip to Scotland, and the summer school. Without giving specific details, she told of the offer she had received to house-sit, which she thought would be an excellent idea, and promising to send the address when it was all settled. She asked how the trip to Hamilton went, and how Jo's pregnancy was progressing. Finally, she touched on the subject which concerned her most. 'Please let me know what the cardiologist said.'

As she sealed and stamped the bulky letter, she reflected on the journey it was taking from a cold, damp, depressing environment to a hot, dry, vital one. *Wish I could do that so easily.*

When Sister Van Hooten, the Night Sister in Charge, arrived for her customary two o'clock visit to the Oncology Ward, she had an envelope for Miranda. After doing the round by torchlight with her and walking with her as she left the ward, Miranda opened the letter in the Nurses Station.

It was from the Senior Nurse Tutor asking Miranda if she would be agreeable for some third-year students to be on the night duty roster for the next three months. The students had expressed an interest in getting experience in oncological nursing, and all were deemed suitable.

'Is that all right with you two?' she asked Roma and Sheila.

They looked at each other and nodded in agreement. 'We always used to have students on rotation through this area,' Roma paused, 'until that awful incident last year.' Noting Miranda's blank look, she continued. 'No-one told you about it?' She shook her head. 'There was this patient, a really sad case, terminal and in a lot of pain. No pain relief ever worked, unfortunately. He was only about eighteen, too.'

Sheila took over the story. 'This student nurse couldn't stand his cries for help and not being able to do anything for him. What she did was wrong, of course, legally, but understandable. She tried to smother him with a pillow.'

Miranda gasped. The image was grim, awful for everyone concerned. 'What happened?'

'She had to leave, of course. I think she had some mental health treatment, but she wasn't charged with anything. The poor boy died soon after. I believe there was a review of the pain management regime after that. You've noticed they don't order strict four-hourly medication any more, now it's "as necessary".'

Miranda nodded, she had noticed that. Much more humane.

Roma was thoughtful. 'Some student nurses just can't handle the stress at all. Now they're trying to assess who can cope, and who can't before rostering them to this ward. Anyway, it will be good to have a new face or two on night duty.'

Normally, Miranda and the other night staff would leave the hospital building by the back stairs and out the side door, but tonight she thought she had better hand in the letter agreeing to accept third year students to the front office which opened at eight. She glanced over at the display board listing all the medical staff names and noticed a blank where Adam Gillies name was usually found. She asked the office worker whether he had left St Georges to be told that she understood he was under suspension.

'Something to do with a research project, I believe.'

Miranda caught her breath before replying. 'I was on that project. Is there any way I can get in touch with him?'

'We're not allowed to give out private addresses. But if you want to write a note to him, I'll see that it gets sent.'

She handed over a sheet of paper and an envelope. Miranda took a seat and considered what to say. I'll make it personal, she decided, just tell him I've been wondering how he's getting on, hoping that things are working out, and that his wife and baby are okay. She included her address and phone number before sealing the envelope and handing it over with thanks.

'I don't think I've got a stamp on me, could I give you the money to pay for the postage?'

'I'm sure St Georges Board of Directors would not question a free postage now and then. Don't worry about it.'

I wonder if he'll respond, she thought on the way home.

It wasn't the ending she'd expected from her first employment in the UK, but in other ways it had been an enriching experience.

That led her to thinking she should contact Theresa again and update her on her plans for the year. *Yes, when they're all confirmed. But not about the house-sitting. That would be too risky.*

Chapter 26

At home in Speke Street, Beaufort, Grace was in a thoughtful mood. It was not the first time that Dr Santorini had suggested that she be referred to a cardiologist. In the past, Grace had said that she would think about it, without actually agreeing to anything.

This time the genial GP had been more insistent, which had led to her appointment tomorrow. To tell the truth, she wasn't sorry. The trip down to Hamilton had been exhausting for her, although she played it down when anyone asked if she was all right. 'Just the heat, really,' was her standard response. Her daughter-in-law, radiant in mid-term pregnancy, was solicitous, and unfailingly good-natured.

'Wouldn't it be great if our baby came into the world a bit early, in time for Miranda's birthday!'

Jack and Grace had laughed, though Grace had the final word, 'It will come when it's ready to, they always seem to know the right time.'

So, it was time for Grace to have a consultation with the specialist. The trip to Ballarat was much shorter and, of course, familiar. Jack drove along the Western Highway, noting the browned-off paddocks and the water-depleted Lake Burrumbeet. The Arch of Victory came into view, and not long after, the two hospitals, Ballarat Base and St John of God. Jack had checked out the access to the private consulting rooms and the car park.

'Just take a seat, Dr Mainwaring won't be long,' said the receptionist.

Ten minutes later, a grey-suited middle-aged man emerged from the corridor and came over to them.

'Mrs Shaw?' he asked. Grace smiled and nodded. 'Mr Shaw, would you mind waiting here? I'll speak to you both after the consultation.'

Jack settled down to wait. There was an assortment of magazines on a low table by the wall. He selected a *Time* magazine that was only four months out of date, but soon his eyelids drooped. Grace had been restless during the night, so neither of them had had a good sleep.

Three quarters of an hour later he shook himself awake, aware that his wife had returned with the doctor.

'Would you like to come into my office?

Jack looked searchingly at Grace. Her face was serious, but she managed a small smile.

'Come on,' she said.

Not surprisingly, what the doctor had said during the meeting was the topic of conversation on their way home.

'Why didn't you agree to what he suggested right away? It isn't as though he'd be doing the operation himself.'

'Look, Jack, he was thorough and kind and, I think, honest. He went to great lengths to explain the heart valve replacement operation. Jack, it's open-heart surgery, it's scary stuff. I – I couldn't decide anything just yet.'

'You could at least have agreed to make an appointment with the heart surgeon.'

Grace sat silently for a moment. How could she make her husband realise that it just wasn't the right time for her to consider such major surgery, not with a new grandchild coming, not with Miranda overseas.

'Jack, I had no idea he would make this suggestion, I just hoped he'd do something different with my tablets, try something new, perhaps ...'

The hint of timid apology in her words hit home. Slowing down and pulling to a stop on the side of the highway, Jack turned towards his now surprised wife and, somehow avoiding the gearstick, managed to put his arm around her, drawing her close to him.

'I'm sorry, Grace. I shouldn't have spoken so sharply. I'm worried, that's all. You take all the time you need.' Grace was close to tears, but she felt relieved. She squeezed his hand in gratitude.

Later, at home, Jack asked Grace what she intended to say to Miranda about the specialist's appointment. She promised to be truthful, as always, to which he replied, 'Are you going to tell her about Michael and Denise?' That was a hard one. Neither of them had known anything about it until Brian mentioned it during their visit to Hamilton back in January. 'Guess what, I'm not the only one to tie the knot,' he'd said, going on to explain that Michael had asked him to be a witness at a ceremony in the Ballarat Registry Office next month. It was to be a low-key celebration, because his father wasn't well enough to be out of hospital for more than a few hours. His sister had apparently gone to ground and would not have been invited anyway. Denise's parents would make the trip from Colac but had to be back in time for milking. 'No respite in a dairy farmer's life,' Jack had said with grim humour.

'No, Jack, I haven't said anything to Miranda yet. I thought I'd wait until it actually happens. I'd like us to give them a wedding present, though.'

She stretched out on the couch and yawned. Jack pulled the blinds halfway down. 'Do you want the fan on?'

'No, it's warm, but not unbearable. I just feel like a little sleep, if that's all right.'

It was.

Chapter 27

The names of the new student nurses appeared on the ward roster for mid-March. One, Miranda noted, was named Robert. That would be interesting. There had been several male psychiatric nurses doing an abridged course at Ballarat Base during her training. Male nurses were mostly older than the regular intake of trainees and did not usually stay on the Base Hospital staff after graduation.

'Looks like we've got Nurse Maria Lapinski starting with us next week, for one of the three nights anyway. Wonder where she's from?'

Sheila's question was rhetorical. They would have to wait to find out.

The night staff members had a half-hour meal break during the shift. Sometimes there was food left for them in the ward kitchen, but Miranda usually brought a sandwich and a piece of fruit from home. She would move a chair into the spacious linen cupboard, which was more of an alcove, so she could study without distraction. Things were going well at uni and her enthusiasm had not waned at all.

Miranda visited Adrian's office regularly for a brief discussion after her Tuesday lecture. Sometimes, if it was not convenient, Nathan would appear and grudgingly hand her a note from Adrian which might suggest another date or an invitation to meet him at his apartment. 'You, or any student, visiting my office from time to time, is within the guidelines, but more than that could be risky.'

That was all right with Miranda. Going to his apartment was much more pleasurable, especially as she would be actually living there in less than eight weeks.

One thing niggled her though. Where did Nathan fit into the picture? As though he could read her mind, Adrian provided something of an answer.

'I know you're curious about Nathan Kauper.' Not daring to confirm his remark outright, she gave the briefest of nods. 'I will put you in the picture before I go to New York, that's a promise. Now tell me what's been happening at work, and any news from Beaufort?'

Miranda answered the second question first. She told him of her mother's letter with the outcome of her appointment with the specialist.

'Why do you think she's delaying seeing a surgeon?' Miranda found it hard to provide an explanation. 'Is it because you're not there with her?'

'It could be, but she would never say that. All she really said was that she would think about it, but wouldn't do anything before the baby's born. She can be very stubborn when she wants to. If Dad can't make her change her mind, I don't think I could.' End of discussion.

'As to your first question – about work, I guess if you're asking how many patients died in the last week or so, the answer to that is, none. But there is going to be a change, we're getting three student nurses to be part of the night duty team. That'll be good. And one of them is a young man.'

She went on to tell him about the incident which had led to the suspension of a student in the ward a year earlier.

Adrian was thoughtful. 'I've always been in favour of euthanasia, with the appropriate safeguards of course. Maybe one day the law will change, but the Church will need serious convincing in that area. By the way, did you manage to salvage the copies of your individual case notes from the research program?'

'No, I had to give everything back. Sorry about that, I know you were interested in checking them out.'

He waved a hand in dismissal, saying it didn't matter, it was just an idea he'd had. Conversation then centred on some contradictory theories she had encountered in her prescribed reading, and by the time she left, Adrian had helped clarify her thoughts.

Friday night found the first of the student nurses at the ward desk. Maria Lapinski was short, slim and dark-haired. She introduced herself.

'Hello, I'm Maria. I have already worked two nights here.' Her voice had a slight European accent.

'Good, you know the layout then. I'm Miranda, meet Roma and Sheila who also work these nights. Let's do the handover, then we can talk about the routine for the shift.'

Later, during a quieter period, Maria explained that she was born in Poland but, after the war, her family had emigrated to the UK. Her grandfather had recently died of cancer, and this had influenced her to include oncological nursing in her training. *She'll do well*, Miranda thought, noting her patience and caring nature.

'Tell us about the other two students.' The request came from Roma.

'Oh, they are good people. But it is sometimes hard to understand Robert, he is Scottish,' she said with a giggle.

Miranda was immediately alerted. 'Do you know from what part of Scotland?'

Maria shook her head. 'I think he's on next week, or it might be Elaine, I'm not sure.' A check of the roster confirmed that Robert Fraser was listed to work the following Friday, Saturday and Sunday nights. *That's good*, thought Miranda. It would be a chance get some tips for her trip to Scotland. *Not long now. Only Easter and exams to get through.*

Replying to Mum's last letter wasn't easy.

Of course she would have liked to hear that an appointment with the heart surgeon had been made. She agreed with her father on that one. But it was still an option for the future, she wrote.

She pointed out that though March could still be hot, the evenings would be cooler and more tolerable. Over here, she wrote, spring blossoms were cheering everybody up. She hoped to have more to tell in her next letter after talking with a new staff member who was Scottish. Work was going well, study too, and yes, she'd gone out nightclubbing with the girls a couple of times. All good fun.

Miranda anticipated an invitation to Adrian's apartment the following week. So far she had continued taking the Pill, though lately had questioned the need. Adrian had been warm and affectionate towards her, but the old spark of passion was missing.

She had tried to access information about the effects of lithium and asked the pharmacist when she collected her own tablets, saying that one of her patients had been prescribed it. But nothing much had come of the inquiry.

'It's new,' the pharmacist told her. 'It needs to be monitored with a regular blood test, but otherwise it seems to be a relatively safe medication.'

Adrian opened the door, smiling widely. 'Hello,' he said. 'Come on in and let's see that beautiful body of yours.'

Words were unnecessary. Their lovemaking was as passionate as it had been last year. 'That was worth waiting for,' said Miranda breathlessly. 'So the medication hasn't dampened your fire after all!'

'Well, I've reduced the dosage. With permission, in case you're wondering.' Eyebrows raised, she waited for further explanation. 'I took a few double doses before I had the last blood test and of course the readings were too high, so he agreed to a lower level.'

He looked so pleased with himself that Miranda's intended reprimand stayed unvoiced.

'I'm not up for repeat performances, but that can be the next goal.'

They settled back comfortably until Adrian got up to produce the makings of a gin and tonic. 'You're not working tonight, are you?' he asked, before adding the ice and lemon slices. They clicked glasses. After just one sip, Adrian's telephone rang. He excused himself and left the bedroom to take the call while Miranda took the opportunity to freshen up.

'That was the head of the department. Apparently, the Yale people want a synopsis of the course I'll be giving over the summer. Actually, it's been on my mind too. I'd like you to develop some of my ideas.'

Miranda swallowed a surprised gasp. What an honour.

'I'd – I'd love to. What have you been considering?'

That hour-long discussion was a valuable learning experience for Miranda. He referred her to the first lecture she'd attended, back in March last year. Her assured, 'of course I remember it!' delighted Adrian. The concept of citizen advocacy had enormous appeal for him. He'd seen a few published articles, including one from Nebraska where it was proposed to team volunteers and disadvantaged persons. Training and supervision of the volunteers was important, he had ideas on that, as well as on guidelines for the allocation of partnerships.

Hardly pausing for breath, he brought up another topic in which he'd become interested. Again in the US, there has been some progress in establishing day centres for those recovering from mental illness, where equal responsibility and mutual respect between attendees and staff was a major objective.

Miranda tried to make notes of the issues as they arose, realising that, eventually, organisation and a systematic development would deal with all the random ideas that had come tumbling out.

Later, she thought about that evening, worthy of a red circle around the date in her diary, not only because of the resumption of their intimacy, but also the unexpected opportunity to discover what was involved in the development of a new course of study. *Maybe one day that could be part of my own career. Who knows?*

Friday night was her chance to meet the second new student nurse, Robert Fraser. He was at the desk when she arrived. He was tall, sturdily built and had dark red hair. He looked a little older than the average student.

Introductions were made. The shift began with Roma taking Robert around the ward layout while the other two checked the new patients. Sheila noticed an empty bed in the second bay.

'That was where Mr Smythe was, he must have died during the week.'

'I suppose so. He certainly wasn't well,' said Miranda.

It was cup of tea time before the opportunity came for a getting-to-know-you chat with Robert. Miranda had met Scots before, and, like many English people, found the Glaswegian accent hard to understand.

However, Robert spoke quietly with an attractive lilt. He was obviously not Glaswegian.

'No, I'm from up north, Pitlochry.'

Miranda's heart seemed to give a sudden leap. What a stroke of luck!

'That's interesting,' she exclaimed, 'my grandparents are buried near there. As you can probably guess, I'm Australian. My mother insists that I visit their grave.'

'I may be able to help you get there. There's a good rail service, or you could make the trip by coach.'

Miranda couldn't help being thrilled at the melodic accent.

Roma had a question for him. 'What made you come to St Georges to do your training, Robert?'

He laughed. 'This is going to sound a wee bit strange but it's because Mum worked here, an' she had good memories of it. Met Dad here. Before I was born, of course.'

'Is he a Scot, then?'

'Aye, from Pitlochry. He fell ill and was admitted to this hospital when he was studying in London, an' she nursed him, an' they fell in love.'

The three women smiled. Romantic stories didn't often feature in an oncology ward. 'She must be very proud of you,' suggested Sheila.

A shadow crossed the young man's face. 'She would be if she was still alive. She died three years ago. Dad and me did our best, looking after her at home. She told me I was a born nurse, an' I should give up my job at the local library. An' so I did, an' came here.'

Bitter-sweet, thought Miranda. When she went to check a new patient's intravenous drip, Robert went with her. She noticed his skill in rearranging the pillows and making Miss Brownless comfortable. His mum had been right, bless her.

Before the shift ended, Miranda asked Robert if he could bring any books or magazines about Scotland he had. *It would make a change from studying sociology in my lunch break*, she thought with a degree of satisfaction.

Chapter 28

The Shaws always welcomed the phone calls from Hamilton. Sometimes it was Jo who spoke first, always concerned for their wellbeing, Grace's in particular. This time, however, it was Brian on the line.

'Just got back from Ballarat, I would have come through Beaufort, but I didn't want to leave Jo on her own longer than necessary.'

'Are you talking about Michael's wedding?' said Jack. 'Hang on, I'll put your mother on.'

'Hello, darling. How did it go?'

'Okay, Mum. Good really, even though there were only a few people there. They looked both happy and serious, if you know what I mean. Anyway, I thought I'd let you know that if you haven't bought a present already, something for a new baby would be in order.'

That provoked an instant response.

'What? Already? Well, that's – that's lovely. Thanks for telling us. How's Jo?'

'Getting big. Thirty weeks now, and getting lots of kicks, she says.'

'Perhaps you're having a little footballer,' said Grace. Jack was smiling too.

Later, sitting together on the couch, Jack said. 'Seems like Major McPherson and I have something in common.' Grace's expression was questioning. 'We're both about to extend our family tree through our sons. Our daughters don't seem to have that inclination at all.'

Grace agreed, but murmured, 'It's early days yet, at least for Mirrie.'

She had another thought. 'Jack, who's looking after Michael's place while they're away?'

'Bill Lynch, his neighbour at the back. He'll milk the house cow and feed the chooks. They're only going away for a week, anyway.' He smiled fondly, 'Just like us – do you remember?'

By Easter, all three student nurses were familiar with the night duty regime in the oncology ward. Roma had asked to have Easter off to visit her family in Wales. Sheila had called in sick, so the students were rostered on together to cover their absence.

It was obvious that there was a close friendship developing between Robert and Elaine. Miranda smiled to herself as she saw the little looks they exchanged. Actually, they made a good team. Shy by nature, Elaine divulged that she was one of five girls born to an East Anglian couple.

'Mum and Dad said they just wanted us to be happy, and that they'd support us no matter what career we chose. So now there's a teacher, a secretary, a shop assistant, a lawyer and a nurse in the family.

'Do you think you made the right choice?' Miranda asked.

'Oh, I love it,' she replied, her face slightly flushed.

The absence of experienced nursing aides meant more of a supervisory role for Miranda who used every opportunity to share her knowledge with her younger colleagues.

'It's really great working with you, Sister Shaw,' Elaine said at the end of the night shift on Easter Sunday morning, 'I've learned so much from you. Would you agree, Robert?'

'Aye, indeed I would. It's almost as though you're wasted here, except that the patients wouldn't agree.'

On the way home, Miranda thought about Robert's comment. In a way he was right. She remembered the prediction made ages ago that she should aim to be a nurse educator. *Maybe if I wasn't committed to doing this tertiary course, I'd be thinking along those lines*. But at the moment, the combination of work and study felt absolutely right to her.

'Pity you couldn't have managed to get Easter off,' Lisa said when they were preparing the Thursday communal dinner. 'Mum and Dad keep asking me when I'm bringing you back for another visit.'

Miranda thanked her for the invitation, but her hospital work was paramount, especially with co-workers being away.

Her first exam was scheduled for the third week of April. At their last session, the tutor had avoided giving direct answers about what was likely to be on the paper. 'It's based on material you've come across all year,' he said. Sarah Young-Johnson likewise refused to give any hints on her contribution to the three-hour exam.

Miranda was reasonably confident. She'd done well in the assignments during the year which accounted for forty per cent of the overall result. But who knew what would be included in the finals?

All Adrian would say was, 'Trust yourself.'

The venue for the exams was a splendid hall which Miranda hadn't seen before. There were at least a hundred desks regularly spaced, each with an examination paper lying face down. After registering and receiving her number, she made her way to the desk numbered E5. A few familiar faces met her glance of recognition with a nervous smile.

It was all very formal. The supervisor read out the rules, including the procedure for taking a toilet break. 'Raise your hand, wait until an escort reaches you, and try not to disturb the others.' Then, at precisely ten o'clock, the command was given, 'You may turn over your examination paper and commence to write.'

At the end of three hours, the candidates were instructed to, 'Stop writing now'.

Miranda massaged her right hand to relieve the tension. She felt incredibly tired, but, in common with everyone else, there was a huge sense of relief that it was over.

Some of the students were talking quietly as they made their way towards the door, but most, like Miranda, just wanted to return to the real world.

On the whole, it had been a fair paper, some questions had been predicted, others took some thought to interpret. I've done my best, she decided. Only one more to go, now. As luck would have it, that one was on her birthday. *C'est la vie.*

The following week was the last Tuesday session of their academic year with lots of banter and good wishes exchanged between the two tutors and the student body. 'Bring on Year Two of your degree, though most of you have another exam to sit, eh?' That brought groans from the auditorium. 'Good luck.'

'Have you given a final date at your boarding house yet?' was Adrian's opening question when she presented at his office.

'I told the landlady ages ago when I first knew that I would be leaving. She said that would be fine, just let her know a week or so before the actual date. She also said that one of the girls knows someone who might want to take over my room.' She paused, waiting for his response. None was forthcoming, so she continued.

'Did you have any date in mind?'

Adrian looked uncomfortable. 'I'm actually planning to leave a little earlier than I indicated before, perhaps in the third week of May.' Miranda raised her eyebrows, noting his uncharacteristic reluctance. 'Nathan hasn't been to America, so I'd like to take him to a few places over there before my work at Yale begins.' It all came out in a rush, as though he was embarrassed to tell her.

She considered her agenda. So much was due to happen in a short space of time: the last exam and her birthday on the 30th; the expected news from home about a new addition to the family, possibly in early May; her trip to Scotland; and the big move to Adrian's place. There was much to do, she would be busy, and told him so.

'If I leave on the twenty-fifth, would that suit you?' She nodded. 'So, if you're going to be busy, that will keep you out of mischief – unless it's with me.'

She was in high spirits as she headed home.

Chapter 29

Telling Gwen and the other girls in the house that she'd be leaving at the end of May was not easy. Without going into details, Miranda just said that an opportunity had arisen, and it was too good to miss. Their reactions were predictable. They understood but would be sorry to see her go. Gwen reminded Miranda about her birthday and urged her to get the night off. 'And it's your last exam, surely you need to celebrate that, too.'

Initially reluctant, but goaded by the word 'workaholic' from another of the girls, she made the request. It was granted without any problem, and a relieving sister was rostered to take her place on the thirtieth.

Wonder what my housemates have planned?

The day of her last exam was drizzly but not cold. The venue and format were the same as the previous one. Before long, heads were down and writing began. Miranda was delighted to discover all the questions were easy to tackle, and she had no difficulty providing detailed responses. In fact, she had no time to complete her answer to the last question. Since one o'clock was fast approaching, she summarised in point form what would have been her full answer and made a note of this on her paper just before 'Pens down' was announced.

Whew! It was all over. After meeting several of her tutorial group and wishing everyone a good holiday, she made her way home.

There were several envelopes – *cards probably* – and two small parcels, all with overseas stamps, awaiting her return. Making her way upstairs with her collection, she was surprised and delighted to see a handmade poster decorating her door wishing her, 'Happy Birthday Miranda!'

She opened the parcels first. To her delight she found it was a small bottle of boronia-scented perfume and soap from Mum and Dad, with a note on the card hoping it would help her remember the Australian bush. The other parcel was from Brian and Jo. It contained a small diary illustrated with Australian flora and fauna. Brian had written, 'got you this 'cos the year's nearly half over and they reduced the price.' How like Brian, thought Miranda fondly. Actually, the pocket-sized book would be ideal to take on her Scottish trip.

She opened the birthday cards, one of which was from Auntie Lillian and her family. She arranged them on the mantelpiece after reading and admiring each one.

Gwen came into the room.

'Nice,' she said, noting the display, 'Got your outfit ready for tonight?'

'I haven't been told what's happening yet. Can you give me a clue?'

Several hours later, the group of nine emerged with scores of other happily chattering patrons from the Ambassadors Theatre in the West End. 'Wasn't that fun,' Linda exclaimed. 'Such a clever ending!'

What a lovely birthday celebration, Miranda thought. To see '*The Mousetrap*' had been on her must-do-sometime list since she first arrived in London. That choice for tonight's birthday outing was a stroke of genius.

'My mother will be so envious when I tell her.'

The other good news she'd have to tell Mum in her next letter would be about the invitation Robert Fraser had given her on Sunday night. 'My father would like to offer you a room when you come to Pitlochry. It's no' grand but it's homely.'

'Oh, that's very kind of him, Robert. He might be able to direct me to the actual cemetery, which I think is called Moulin.'

'Aye, that's quite near Pitlochry. I'm sure he'll be only too happy to show you around.'

Miranda suspected that Robert had spoken favourably about her to his father, hence the offer of accommodation. She felt a warm flush of gratitude. The next thing she had to do was to settle on a date. She planned to be away for about four days.

'How long does the train trip take?'

'About eight hours. You have to change at Edinburgh to the Highland Line. They'll explain all that when you book your ticket.'

The second week in May seemed to be the best option to make her booking. Fingers crossed there would be news of an addition to the family by then.

It seemed strange not to have lecture notes and textbooks to study in her free time. Her enrolment in the summer school was finalised, and that would occupy her while Adrian was away. She examined her feelings about him. It would be a big change not being able to see him every few days, but different from the time in November when he had been absent because of his illness, and she had been so worried.

It had been a relief, she acknowledged, to be told about his condition, but that brought some concern as well. She wondered whether he was back on the prescribed dose of the mood-stabiliser. *I can't just ask him outright. He would, quite rightly, say it was none of my business.* There were many questions she would like to ask him, but the time was not right. Perhaps the explanation he promised about Nathan would lead to other revelations. She would just have to wait and see.

Chapter 30

At eight-thirty in the morning, the Shaw's phone rang. Jack got to it first and brought the news to Grace that it was Brian calling to tell them Jo had been admitted to hospital. Her labour had begun.

'The fourth of May,' Grace said, 'More or less her due date. I know it could take hours, but I'm not leaving the house at all today. You go to work, Jack, I'll call you if there's any news.'

During the day, Grace thought about the Holdsworths, now over from West Australia, and no doubt as excited and anxious as she was. At last the phone rang just before ten o'clock that night. Jack gestured to Grace that she should take the call.

She gasped and then her face lit up with a brilliant smile as she heard the news. 'Just a minute, Brian.' Then to Jack, 'It's a boy – we have a grandson!' before returning to the new father, asking question after question.

Jack came over and took the phone from her. 'Brian? Well done, great news. Give our love to Jo and to her parents, too.' He hung up and embraced his wife.

It was a moment of elation. But sobering, too. The next generation. Jack acknowledged that he was particularly glad it was a boy, though of course a girl would have been welcomed too.

'I know what you mean, the Shaw name and all that. I'm just glad he's been born, is healthy, and everyone is delighted.' Grace let out a long breath. 'It's a very special day.'

'Wonder if Miranda knows yet?' said Jack later. 'Their time zone's behind us, you know.'

A yell from the front door, 'Miranda, telegram for you!' brought a rapid descent down the stairs. She grabbed the envelope, tore it open and read the message. 'A BOY. ALL WELL. THRILLED. BRIAN'

'Good news, then?' said Kate who had opened the door to the telegram messenger boy.

'The best! I'm an auntie to a little baby boy!'

Sending cards or letters would take too long. She decided to send her own telegram in reply. Words arranged and rearranged themselves in her mind as she made her way to the post office. The Australian address took up most of the allotted twelve words, leaving her with 'CONGRATULATIONS. WELCOME BABY SHAW. LOVE MIRANDA.' That would have to do.

On the way back, she reflected on the truth that, though giving birth is one of the most natural things in the world, it can't be dismissed that things can go wrong. But for Jo and Brian, it was all good. Without feeling the least bit hypocritical, she whispered to herself the words, 'Thank God.'

It took some time to find the right 'Welcome Baby Boy' card. To her delight she also found one expressing congratulations to the new grandparents.

She bought two of them, one for Mum and Dad, the other to send to Jo's parents who were staying in Hamilton. She even bought an EXPRESS DELIVERY sticker for each envelope, hang the expense. 'The fourth of May is a v-e-r-y special day!!', she wrote, with lots of exclamation marks.

Miranda's last visit to see Adrian before her journey north did not follow the usual pattern. When she arrived, Nathan was also there.

Though she greeted the young man cheerfully, his response was surly, reinforcing her impression that he did not like her. He abruptly left the living room to busy himself in the kitchen. Eyebrows raised in question, Miranda looked at Adrian.

'Don't mind him. He turned up unannounced. But it looks as though we have to restrict ourselves to a chat this time.' He went on to say that the examination results would be posted on the departmental noticeboard next week, and would certainly be available by the time she came back from Scotland.

'Guess what – I've got a brand-new little nephew! I'm an auntie!'

Adrian's response was less than enthusiastic. 'I've never been one to encourage procreation. We should provide for those who are already here instead of adding more.'

Noting her frown, he said by way of mild apology, 'Overpopulation may not be an issue in Australia. So, good news, if you're happy about it.'

End of that discussion. Miranda remembered to ask him for the phone number of the apartment, explaining that sending it, and her new mailing address to her family would take a couple of weeks to arrive.

'Of course. But I have to tell you that very few people know either my address or phone number, and I'd like to keep it that way. Just you and your immediate family. Is that all right?' She nodded. He wrote both on a piece of paper for her.

Nathan was making a racket in the kitchen, opening and shutting drawers impatiently. Adrian smiled apologetically. 'He's giving you a message.'

'Oh, is he? Well, I'm going now anyway. I just wanted to confirm dates with you. Thanks for the information – shall I ring you here when I get back?'

'Good idea. I hope you have a good time.'

Miranda decided to document every detail of her trip so her mother could share her experience in Scotland. On her last night on duty, Robert showed her a photograph of his father. Actually, it was a photo of the three of them taken some time before his mother's death.

'Take it,' he said, 'so you'll be able to identify Dad. But I'd like to have it back.' It was a kind gesture. Miranda assured him she would take good care of it.

In her letter home, she said she would try to find something in the Shaw tartan for the new baby. 'Has a name been chosen yet?' Privately she hoped it would be something as special as her own.

Chapter 31

Kings Cross station in north-eastern London was crowded with people moving purposefully in every direction. Miranda made her way through the hubbub to the platform where her train with an impressive number of carriages was already taking on passengers.

Leaving the sprawling metropolis behind, the train made its way smoothly, stopping at several stations before it really settled down for the long trip north. Miranda's view of the countryside was limited due to the speed of the train and the griminess of the carriage windows. The travel magazine she'd bought when she booked her tickets described in depth the regions she was travelling through.

After crossing the border, Miranda was in Scotland. Edinburgh's Waverley Station was the final stop, here she had to change trains. It was a relief to leave the train and stretch her legs. All around her were people talking with delightful Scottish accents and, to cap it all, the mid-afternoon sun was shining brightly.

Miranda had read a little of Edinburgh's history, the monuments, the castle, the Royal Mile and the spectacular Tattoo which had been held every year since 1950. Now she was actually here. There was not time to explore the city now. *I'm definitely going to make a return visit*, she decided.

She checked the second folder of tickets and headed to the platform for the next part of her journey. She had an hour's wait before its departure, time to have a coffee and a sandwich at the station's cafe.

Miranda reached into her satchel for her little Kodak camera. A very kind lady offered to take a picture of her at the entrance to the large station.

'Ye'll want to get one of the Firth of Forth Bridge when ye go across it,' she suggested.

'Thank you, I'll certainly try,' Miranda replied. The distant sound of a piper playing the bagpipes made her feel very welcome. *I'm definitely here*, she thought.

On board again and on the move. She could see they were approaching the famous bridge spanning the wide waterway. Unfortunately, taking photos of the bridge from inside the train wasn't feasible. Miranda decided that she would just buy some postcards of it, some to keep for herself and some to send home to Australia. The train rolled on to Perth, where there was a twenty-minute halt, and finally on to Pitlochry, which was signposted as the 'Gateway to the Highlands'.

As she alighted with her satchel and small suitcase, a man wearing a kilt approached her. Miranda easily recognised him as Robert's father. Solidly built, his once red hair was striped with grey, and, unlike his son, he had a neatly trimmed beard that was almost silver. Miranda guessed that his kilt was of the Fraser tartan. She regretted not wearing her own Shaw tartan skirt.

'How do ye do, Miss Shaw? An' welcome to Pitlochry.' His outstretched hand met hers in a warm clasp before he took hold of her suitcase.

'Thank you, thank you so much. Please call me Miranda. It's good to meet you, Mr Fraser.'

'Duncan, if ye don't mind. Come this way.' He led her to the car park where his dark-green sedan was waiting. Minutes later he pulled up in front of a terrace house, one of a row of stone houses, each with two steps to the front door. It was early spring, the foliage of the trees along the street was a delicate green.

'It looks wonderful – so old, and sort of stately,' she exclaimed.

'Aye, it's auld all right,' he said while opening the heavy wooden door.

Miranda's first evening in Scotland was reassuringly comfortable. Duncan had a cottage pie ready for their evening meal.

'It's from the bakery, I'm afraid. My wife was a great cook. Ah'm not.'

Miranda expressed her regret at the loss of his wife. 'I can assure you she would've been proud of Robert,' she said with sincerity.

An early night was a good decision. 'I had to leave home by seven this morning to catch the train,' Miranda admitted, stifling a yawn.

'Then ye must be really tired. I've put ye in Robert's auld room. Sleep well.'

Over breakfast next morning, Duncan outlined a possible timetable for the next two days. 'Ah know that finding your grandparents' grave is the reason ye've come here, so we should do that first. Then ye must see the salmon leapin', though ah'm not sure they do at this time of the year, an' there are a few special beauty spots to show ye, like Loch Tummel for one.'

The Moulin churchyard cemetery was very old and unkempt. Some of the headstones dated back to the 1700s and 1800s. Miranda knew that her grandparents had been buried in 1946. Would there even be a headstone?

Duncan, who had moved over to the newer part of the graveyard, beckoned her over.

'Ah think this is what ye're lookin' for, lass.'

She moved carefully over the uneven surface to an area where the graves were covered by flat slabs of concrete, each with a small plain plaque, their inscriptions identifying the occupant. Duncan pushed aside the straggly weeds to reveal the wording.

MILLER

FREDERICK THOMAS AND FLORENCE ROSE
TRAGICALLY DIED 10TH MARCH, 1946.
IN GOD'S CARE.

Miranda was overwhelmed. This was it, the purpose of her journey. She was speechless as she stared at the plaque, her mind in a turmoil.

Duncan said gently, 'Ah'll just clean up a few of these weeds so it'll look better in your photographs.' Photographs? Yes, of course. She got out her little camera and took a few pictures. But nothing could disguise the fact that it was a bleak image she was recording. At the same time, it felt as though she had made a connection with part of her family history.

Duncan suggested that he take a picture of her reading the names. Miranda knew her face had a serious look. I can't bring myself to smile.

I wonder how Mum would feel if she were here.

Forcing herself back to the present, she thanked her host for his help, but Duncan brushed it aside.

'Ah think it might be time for a visit to the local pub, an' we can have a wee glass of whatever you fancy.'

The cosy log fire in the Hunters Arms, the glow of the polished wood surrounds and the large pictures of Highland scenes on the dark-red walls all combined to cheer her spirits.

'Would ye like a McEwan ale, or a wee dram of our famous whisky?'

'Gosh, I don't usually drink anything during the day,' she said, 'but maybe a small Scotch since it's such a special day.'

The early train on Friday brought Miranda back to Edinburgh's Waverley station where her connection to London would leave in forty minutes. That gave her just enough time to search the souvenir stalls for gifts for friends and family. In the toy section of one shop there was an assortment of cuddly bears representing different clans. To her delight she found one dressed in a Shaw tartan kilt and a little tam-o'-shanter. It wasn't cheap, but Miranda didn't care. It was exactly the right gift for her new baby nephew.

Tired from the activities of the last two days, Miranda managed to sleep for nearly two hours on the return journey. By late afternoon she was back home with just enough time to get ready for night duty. She knew Robert had been working earlier in the week, so it would be some days before she could give him a report on the trip and return his photo.

The exam results! She'd almost forgotten about them. She made the trip to the university on Saturday afternoon, knowing that the results would be posted along the corridor. Among the numerous notices, she found the First Year Sociology results. Yes! Her name was there, one of the few listed as 'Distinction.' *That's a relief!* That was more good news to put in her letter home, along with an account of her trip north.

The following week would be a busy one. She had to finish her packing and empty the room that had been her home for more than a year. It brought back memories. At some stage she would have to contact Adrian to confirm her actual moving-in date.

On Monday afternoon, after a short sleep, she dialled the number Adrian had given her. It rang out. There was no invitation to leave a message. She tried again the next day, with success. He invited her to come on Wednesday about four o'clock. 'I'll tell you everything you need to know then.'

Chapter 32

Miranda didn't know what to expect when she left for Adrian's apartment on Wednesday afternoon. There would be a lot to discuss: the day she should move in, the responsibilities regarding her occupancy, and, of course, Nathan. *Will it be a passionate encounter?* she wondered.

She knocked on the door, Adrian opened it and, after closing it behind him, gave her a warm hug. 'That's for doing so well. I knew you would, of course.' Releasing her, he held her at arm's length looking at her intently. 'The trip to Scotland was successful, I take it?'

'It was. A great experience, the country is wonderful, and I saw, and took pictures of, my grandparents' grave. The photos aren't developed yet, though.'

He nodded, patting the back of one of the armchairs, inviting her to sit down. He sat close by on the other one. On the small table between them was a pad with hand-written numbered notes.

'I've listed all the instructions you will need, like garbage collection day, what to do with bills when they arrive, local shops I use, and contact numbers for me and my accountant. I think I've covered everything. Anyway, take this with you, and ask any questions on the day you move in.'

Miranda murmured her thanks. She was experiencing familiar little twinges of desire. If Adrian felt the same, he was managing to control himself. Instead, he shuffled a little in the seat, before launching into the next subject.

'Miranda, what I am about to tell you is private, very private, and between you and me only – do you understand?' She nodded. 'You need to realise that I have suffered this bipolar condition for several years. It has shaped my life, you could say. When I was quite a bit younger, I was involved with the theatrical scene here in London, late-night parties, drug experimentation, and, of course, casual sex. All this suited me in the manic phase of my, well, I don't call it an illness, others do, my condition. I was living on the edge. It was highly exciting and somewhat dangerous. Fortunately, I could manage my academic career, just. Anyway, it was an outrageous time of my life.'

He shifted in the chair. Miranda waited for him to continue.

'During that time, I met Nathan Kauper, he would have been about eighteen then. I can see you look surprised. He doesn't look more than that now. I agree. Anyway, he was what is commonly called a rent boy.'

Miranda looked puzzled.

'You haven't heard that expression before? You could say he was a male prostitute. In short, he formed an attachment to me, and his client at the time wasn't happy. It all ended up in a nasty brawl in one of London's more notorious nightclubs.' He paused for a minute, remembering. 'Took a bit of hushing-up, I can tell you. Are you with me so far?'

'Er, yes, I think so.' But there was a question lurking, should she ask about his involvement?

'Anyway, I protected Nathan from the violence and took him under my wing. Yes, I can see by the look on your face, you're wondering about the nature of this involvement. I need to tell you that, as well as being bipolar, I am also bisexual. I say that without any need for apology, it is my nature.'

Miranda leaned back in the chair, unsure of what she made of all this. She remembered Nathan's words when he accosted her the first time, 'I know him better than you do. Or ever will.'

Adrian continued. 'It makes absolutely no difference to our relationship, Miranda, but I have to say that Nathan is possessive, and can be vindictive in his jealousy. He managed to destroy my marriage, but I won't go into that now. However, he is, let's face it, part of my life. Do you remember me telling you he stayed here while I was overseas last year?' Miranda nodded. 'That was a mistake. He thought he'd make himself a bit of money by picking up men and bringing them back here. The one person whom I trust implicitly contacted me when he found out what was going on, and I cut my trip short. You'll meet Simon on the day you move in here, which will be Monday, the twenty-fourth. Is that okay?'

It was an effort for Miranda to reply 'Yes, yes. That will be fine.'

Adrian stood up and stretched. 'That was a lot to get off my chest. I hope you're not too shocked, it's probably well beyond your experience.'

That was an understatement. Miranda was too stunned to know what to think, but, forcing herself to be practical, she said, 'I finish my shift early on Monday morning, so after a couple of hours sleep, I'll make sure everything will be ready for the taxi. I should be here about four. Is that all right?'

'Absolutely. I'll give you the key then and introduce you to Simon. He's my accountant and someone on whom you can rely. Nathan and I will stay at the airport hotel that night, as our flight on the Tuesday is an early one. Here, give me a hug before you go.'

In spite of all she'd heard, and her bewilderment, she felt completely reassured by the warmth of his strong arms around her.

Chapter 33

On Saturday afternoon, she found a letter from home which proved to be a welcome diversion.

She had been preoccupied with Adrian's revelations of two days before, vainly trying to understand same-sex attraction, which she had heard about but had never confronted. Until now.

The three pages from her mother described in detail the arrival of the latest little Shaw. *But has he been given a name?* Apparently, before the birth Jo and Brian had not been able to agree on a choice for either a boy or girl.

'A week or so beforehand,' Grace wrote, 'Jack and I were invited to suggest two names we liked, as were Jo's parents. So, they put all these suggestions in two little boxes. No one was to know what the others had chosen. The day after the baby was born, Brian brought the little boy's name box into the maternity ward for Jo to draw out the winning name. And guess what, Mirrie – she drew out mine! So, our new grandson is called Byron, with James, the second one drawn out, as his middle name. When I named you, I was inspired by literature, and you remember that Byron is one of my favourite poets. Also – it sort of links with Brian. So, what do you think? '

Miranda put the page down and spoke the name 'Byron James Shaw' aloud. Yes, it did sound impressive. She picked up the letter and continued to read. 'When you get this, you will be back from your trip to Scotland. I look forward to your next letter telling me all about it. Also, this will be the last one I'll be sending to this address. I imagine your letter with your new address is on its way.'

News from home always had a positive effect on her. It gave her the impetus to tackle the things she had to do.

There were now only a couple of days before she moved out, and she was working each night. Keeping out basic toiletries and something to wear for these two days, she methodically packed clothes from the wardrobe and the chest of drawers into her suitcases. Everything else, much of it study material, went into cardboard boxes sealed with packing tape and ready for the big move to her new temporary home.

By the time Monday the twenty-fourth arrived, Miranda was almost too excited to sleep. Lying down for two hours, she set the alarm for midday.

Gwen cautiously opened the door. 'Are you up yet?' she asked quietly.

'Just about. I had a catnap really. But there's lots to be done now.'

'Let me help. Not that I want you to leave, though.'

Carrying the boxes between them, they made three trips down to the front door, lining them up in the corridor with her suitcases.

'Hey, have you booked the cab?'

'Yes, for quarter past three. It's good that London taxis have so much floor space in the back.'

At the prearranged time, the driver tooted his arrival. The luggage was quickly stowed, with not much room to spare.

'Will I see you again?' asked Gwen, a plaintive note in her voice.

'Course you will! I'll be back here on Thursday to hand over the keys, remember. Gotta go now. Bye.'

Unloading her luggage at Adrian's address was completed efficiently. Miranda gave the driver a generous tip acknowledging his helpfulness. The front door remained closed.

If he's not home, I'm going to look a bit stupid with all this stuff on his doorstep.

The sound of approaching footsteps made her turn. Adrian was with another man. She realised that it was probably Simon.

'You're a bit earlier than I expected. No matter. Miranda, meet Simon, Simon Forrester. Simon, meet Miranda Shaw.'

Handshakes were exchanged before they then helped Miranda move her belongings inside. The collection of boxes and suitcases took up much of the spare space in the living-room.

'Good, that's all done. I'll make a pot of tea. You two have a chat,' Adrian suggested.

Miranda was conscious that Simon was scrutinising her. *And I'm doing the same thing*, she thought. She noted that he appeared to be of a similar age as Adrian, but the resemblance ended there. He looked very conservative, a city-type, really, with his horn-rimmed glasses, neat casual attire and serious expression. Adrian had described him as an accountant. In Miranda's limited experience, he certainly looked like one.

'I've been looking forward to meeting you, Miranda,' Simon said.

'Thanks,' she replied. How could she admit that she hadn't even heard his name mentioned until a week ago?

Adrian returned with the tea. 'Now, some explanatory remarks for you, Miranda. I have known Simon for, how long would you say?' His friend gave a small shrug. 'Fifteen years at least, through thick and thin, as the saying goes. He has overseen the management of some inheritances that came my way, and my current state of prosperity is due entirely to his excellent financial advice. He's seen me through a few sticky situations. Like my divorce,' he added wryly. Simon remained impassive, obviously not feeling any need to contribute, nor did he seem embarrassed at the generous compliments.

'Anyway, Miranda, what I need to tell you is that I trust Simon implicitly, he is my best friend, pleasantly platonic, I hasten to add.' Miranda nodded, smiling to herself. 'He has my power of attorney if anything untoward happens to me, God forbid, and is executor of my will which is now up to date.'

He paused for a minute, sipped his tea, then got up, went to the drinks cabinet and opened an upper cupboard door to reveal a locked safe.

'In here are my personal documents and valuables. It stays locked. Apart from me, only Simon has a key. Please feel free to look at anything else in the apartment, Miranda, especially my library. In fact, I have selected a couple of books which will be relevant for your summer school.'

He looked across at Simon. 'I may not have told you that Miranda is following up on her introduction to sociology last year with psychology this summer, so that will keep her occupied while I'm away.' Another short pause. 'I plan to keep in touch with both of you, but Simon, I'd really like you to contact Miranda at least once a week, so you can deal with any mail that comes for me, or any problems that might arise. Is that going to be possible?'

'Of course, Adrian, if that's all right with you, Miranda?'

'Of course, I will look forward to seeing you, or at least hearing from you.' Miranda wondered if this arrangement had been in place for Nathan's occupancy. She decided to offer some reassurance. 'I don't expect to be entertaining anyone here, I'm just very grateful for the opportunity Adrian has given me.'

That seemed to bring everything to a close. Adrian checked his watch. 'Time to move, I think. Here's the key, Miranda.' He put the silver Yale key with its London University key ring on the table before going into the bedroom and returning with his briefcase and a medium-sized suitcase.

'Is that all you're taking?' she exclaimed.

'Yep. Fifth Avenue awaits me. I always upgrade my wardrobe on these overseas jaunts.' Simon's eyebrows rose slightly, but he made no comment.

The two men moved to the door. Opening it, Simon turned to say to Miranda, 'It was good to meet you.' Adrian put an arm around her, pulled her close and kissed her on the cheek.

'I'll call you when I arrive in New York.'

'Do have a safe trip. And thank you again.'

They were gone.

Miranda sat back in an armchair thinking deeply. Who would have predicted ten months ago, when she paid her first visit to this place, that she would now call it 'home' for the next four months?

Where to start? Unpack first.

Adrian had emptied some drawers for her use, and there was plenty of hanging space in the wardrobe. Some of the boxes could wait, she didn't need her books yet, not with the splendid choice facing her on his impressive bookshelves.

Next, she needed to explore the apartment and familiarise herself with her new surroundings. She should also become familiar with the area. Russell Square was right across the road – a delightful little park for walking, and maybe some reading. The tube station wasn't far, she'd used it many times going to the university. And she needed to find the post office to arrange for her mail to be redirected, and to buy overseas stamps.

The double bed held special memories for her. She stretched out luxuriously, it felt so welcoming. *I love it here*, she thought. *I'll have a shower first and an early night.* The little waste bin in the bathroom was full. When she emptied it into the larger bin in the kitchen, she was dismayed to find a half-full bottle of Adrian's medication. Maybe he had obtained a new prescription and taken that with him. She would have to ask him about it when he rang.

It was a bonus to have a television for her personal use, and in colour for a change. She turned on the news before making an omelette for her evening meal. The weather report warned of gale-force winds over the Atlantic, the seasonal westerlies. She hoped that wouldn't affect his flight.

A blissful night's sleep restored Miranda's energy. There was plenty to do, starting with an inspection of the small pantry to see what provisions she would need to buy. She checked out the washing machine which fitted snugly under the kitchen bench. But was there a clothesline? She hadn't thought to ask.

The shopping trip took up most of the day. It involved walking around several blocks to discover the locations she needed. By the end, she was glad to be home, and relieved to shed the rucksack, heavy with the fruit and vegetables she'd bought. At least she'd found the post office and the local library. She went to bed early with one of the books Adrian had selected for her to read.

It was an unfamiliar ring-ring that woke her in the middle of the night. Adrian's voice sounded indistinct and far away. His speech was rapid and Miranda could only make out odd words, such as 'I'm here – feeling buggered (mumble) – rough flight – Nathan vomited all over me (more mumbling).'

She tried to stop the flow of words, finally saying firmly, 'Adrian, stop, listen to me.' There was silence. 'Adrian, can you hear me? You left your medication behind. Did you know?'

'What? Oh, that. I'm not taking them anymore – gotta go – ring you next week.'

That was not what Miranda had expected. She'd hoped to hear of a pleasant trip, with information about his hotel and travel plans. Instead, he sounded over-excited, talking incoherently, and had gone off his treatment.

Getting back to sleep wasn't easy. The obvious thing to do was to ring Simon in the morning. He would probably have had a call as well, and she wanted to share her anxiety with someone else. Her concern now was – when was a good time to ring him?

After ten o'clock should be all right, she decided. She dialled Simon's number. After three rings, he answered.

'I hope you don't mind me calling you so soon. Did you by any chance get a call from Adrian during the night?'

Ten minutes later, Miranda put the receiver down. She was glad she had phoned him. In response to her concerns, Simon had told her that travelling across time zones was always problematic for Adrian. 'It's part of his condition,' he said. 'He should settle down in a few days.' Although he didn't actually say that he didn't approve of Nathan's closeness to Adrian, he said it was good that there was someone else with him, 'Even if it's only Nathan Kauper.' As far as non-compliance with medication went, Adrian was notorious for ignoring medical advice, even though he thought the new tablet, lithium, was one that would suit him better.

'The thing is, Miranda, Adrian thrives on the excitement of being full of energy and in total control of his life. He doesn't want that suppressed.'

He went on to say that things did often get out of hand, and, as his accountant and friend, he'd had to bail him out several times over the years.

'Is there anything we can do?'

'Not really,' Simon answered. 'We just have to wait and see. But do your very best in your studies – that matters to him a great deal.'

After their conversation, Miranda reflected on what he'd said. Here was someone who had known Adrian for many years and understood what was driving his behaviour. She found herself wondering about Simon himself. He certainly appeared to be acting in Adrian's best interests, both professionally and as a friend. What was his private life like? One day that might become clearer. It wasn't important now.

The main thing she had to do on Thursday was to make the trip to South London to return the key to her old room. Gwen was there, as well as some of the other residents. All wished her well. She declined the invitation to join them on their weekly outing, but promised to keep in touch.

Her next concern was to find out more about the summer school starting next week, though that could be done by phone. Actually, the material provided on enrolment was comprehensive. It would be much easier to manage than last year's, when she had home visits and meetings to juggle, and she was now familiar with the process.

When she arrived at work on Friday night, Miranda was pleased to see that Robert was also on duty. After settling the patients, she joined him and the two nursing aides in the little kitchen for a cup of coffee.

'Robert, I'm glad to see you. I had a really wonderful time up in Pitlochry. Your father was very hospitable and I'm quite in love with Scotland. I've got your photograph. Thanks for that. I should have one of your father for you. I took it when he wasn't looking, so it will be in profile. It's still being developed.'

During the week, the photos were collected from the camera shop and eagerly examined. She had ordered two copies of each photo, one to be sent home, the other to go in her own album, as well as the one for Robert.

By the end of her first week in the Bloomsbury area, Miranda felt very much at home. She was delighted to get a readdressed letter from her sister-in-law with details of baby Byron's progress. 'Photos to come,' she promised. Mail addressed to Adrian was placed in a cardboard box by the phone. Simon would deal with that.

Would she get a call from New York as she did last Wednesday night? She did, and earlier this time. He sounded better, which was a relief. Maybe jet lag had been part of the problem last time. She told him about the course starting next week.

'Enjoy it,' he said, adding, 'I know you will do well.'

Chapter 34

Miranda found that summer in London now was even more enjoyable than last year when everything was still new to her. She recalled all the significant places she'd explored. She didn't feel like a visitor now, but felt as though she belonged. It was almost unbelievable that everything had turned out so well.

The summer school proved to be as enlightening as Adrian had predicted. She had read up on many of the subjects to be covered, some of which had cropped up in her nursing training. She remembered Piaget as a key figure, also the 'id-ego-superego' definition of the human personality. Now, with experienced lecturers, she was deepening her knowledge. It was all very interesting and satisfying. None of the tutors she'd come across so far was as impressive as Adrian, but that was hardly surprising. She was missing him, of course, but grateful to be in touch every week when he rang.

The students were a mixed lot, but most seemed to be her age, or younger. Some of the older ones considered the summer school to be something of a vacation.

She was surprised to hear a broad Australian accent from one of the younger men. He turned out to be from Sydney and was taking a year off work to experience Europe. He had heard about the summer school and decided to participate, and now he'd decided to do the degree course in Sydney next year. She assumed that it was so he would have a better understanding of people and their reactions to life.

Miranda was attracted to her fellow Aussie. She admired his confidence, which gave the impression that nothing was impossible for him. They exchanged some early chit-chat about what they thought of England, which was pleasant enough, with some shared impressions, and a few disagreements.

His motivation for studying psychology changed her opinion, though. He said it was so he could assess clients' preferences in marketing, giving him an edge over other sales executives. *No, thought Miranda, that's not what it's used for.* To her it seemed exploitative. However, when she checked the career opportunities for psychologists, she found that it did include advertising and marketing.

She realised then that hers were not the only reasons for studying psychology. She wanted to help make changes in people's lives, be a force for good. That was what Adrian was fostering in her. *I miss him.*

Simon rang during the third week of June to confirm that he would drop in on Tuesday afternoon to collect Adrian's mail. He looked just as he had on their first meeting – reserved, courteous and practical. He rifled through the small bundle of mail, mostly in long white envelopes. 'A couple from his doctors, no doubt to remind him of the blood tests which he will have missed. He probably didn't tell them he was going overseas.' He inspected a smaller blue envelope with a handwritten address. 'Some people never give up,' he commented drily, 'this is one very persistent lady.'

Miranda waited for him to say more, and when he didn't, she asked, 'How do you deal with that?'

'A legal letter, implying harassment, usually does the trick.'

'So, you get a solicitor to write it.'

'No, I do it. I did a law degree at LSE a few years ago.' Miranda had heard of the high standard of the London School of Economics. She nodded, impressed. 'I know Adrian refers to me as his accountant, I'm that too. But I also do legal work for him, and I have other clients.' He paused, looking at one of the bills he'd opened. 'I see by this phone bill that you've hardly used it. Adrian should have told you to ring your family in Australia any time you want to, he certainly mentioned it to me.'

It was good to have permission to ring home whenever she wanted to, but she decided the proper thing was to only make calls when necessary.

She was pleased to have a letter bearing her new address arrive during the week. She read it again. Mum started off with, 'Thanks for the photos of Mum and Dad's grave. Your descriptions made me feel like I was there.' She went on, 'talking of graves, sad news to tell you. Bridie wrote a week or so ago to tell us that Phil died in May. He had a stroke and didn't last long. She said she's alright, and so are Joe, Antoinette and their little daughter Alanna. She said it would be lovely if you could visit Ireland some time. Keep it in mind.'

Her letter continued with news of Michael's marriage. She finished by saying, 'Brian, Jo and little Byron are all well, and that he adores his little Scottish bear.'

She explored her feelings about Michael. She decided that his decision to marry was not really a surprise. She had no right to resent it. Her life was taking its own direction, shaped by the decisions she had made. There was no room for regret.

Chapter 35

It was July 26th, two months since Adrian had left for the US, a date she would come to remember as her darkest day ever. Late that night the phone rang. Wakened by the shrill sound, Miranda, expected to hear Adrian's voice. That was unlikely, though, as he had called just two evenings ago, sounding enthusiastic and full of energy, buoyed by the positive response to the course he was giving at Yale. He'd finished by saying how good it was to hear her voice, even though they were so far apart.

It was Simon.

'A shocking thing has happened, Miranda. I'm coming over right now. I don't want to talk over the phone.' He hung up.

My God, what on earth is it? She switched on the table lamp and grabbed her housecoat to put on over her summer nightie.

Within five minutes she opened the door to him, noting his serious expression and sense of urgency.

'Miranda – I'm sorry to have to tell you that Adrian is dead.'

The floor seemed to drop. Time stood still.

'Wh – what did you say?'

'Half an hour ago I was phoned by the New York Police, I am his nominated next of kin. It's – it's hard to take in. Give me a minute and I'll tell you what they said.' He went to the liquor cabinet and took out a bottle of Scotch. 'Do you want one? Of course you do …'

He pulled an armchair close to hers and put her glass on the side table.

'Dead?' she managed to say, 'Tell me it's not true, it can't be.'

A little more composed now, Simon took a long gulp of whisky, shook his head, and turned to face her.

'This is what I was told. It happened in the early hours of this morning in the heart of Manhattan. It was a hot night, crowds of people still on the streets. Adrian and Nathan were on their way back to the hotel when they got separated in the crush. In the crowd, a group of thugs surrounded Nathan and started roughing him up, because of his camp appearance, the police said. When Adrian looked back and saw what was happening, he ran back to try to help him, just as Nathan broke away and, in a panic, ran out onto the busy road. It was Sixth Avenue, always fast-moving traffic. Adrian blindly followed him, oblivious to the traffic. Cars were braking, and swerving to avoid Nathan who was hit by one of them and sustained a minor injury. One car hit Adrian. He was run over, and died instantly. Police and ambulance rushed to the scene, but there wasn't anything anyone could do.'

Then, in a brief instant Simon became overwhelmed with emotion. His hand went over his eyes, and tears glistened on his cheek. Breathing deeply, he regained his composure.

Numbed with shock, Miranda was frozen in her chair.

Several moments passed before Simon managed to speak. 'I always said to Adrian that Nathan would be the death of him. Seems I was right.'

Miranda's eyes were dry, there were no tears coming. She managed to speak almost normally. 'What happens next?'

'I have to deal with all the arrangements. Nathan was taken to hospital to be assessed. I don't know what will happen there. But I have to deal with the funeral, I know Adrian wanted to be cremated, it's in his will. Whether that happens over there or here, I don't know at this stage. Before that there'll be a post-mortem and coroner's report, I imagine …' His voice trailed off. He poured another whisky. Miranda declined his questioning glance with a shake of her head.

'Now, as for you. Can I suggest you make a phone call to your family to tell them? And don't worry about staying on here, that's the least of your worries.' He was at the door, ready to leave.

'Simon,' she said tentatively, 'thank you for coming over to tell me, it's your loss too, he's been your friend for a much longer time.'

'I didn't want you to find out on the television or the newspaper.'

He reached out and took her hand, giving it a firm squeeze before he left.

She calculated that since it was after midnight here, it would be late morning in Australia, a good time to ring.

Across the thousands of miles, her mother's voice sounded as familiar and as warm as always. Miranda poured out the still hard to believe news, accepting the 'three minutes, are you extending?' interruptions several times.

Grace said it was very sad to hear of the death of a valued teacher. When Miranda told her mother that she was living in his apartment while he was away, Grace's response was, 'Are there some things you've not told us, Mirrie?'

'I can stay on here, Mum, his solicitor has told me that.' She finished with 'Are you okay, Mum?' only to be told, 'Much the same as usual, I'm just getting old.'

It had been a relief to make the call, to share the tragic news. Though it still had not sunk in.

Sleep came eventually, but it wasn't peaceful. She changed position restlessly, her subconscious grappled with eerie nightmarish dreams that were confusing, frightening, and without resolution.

The BBC TV morning news reported the accidental death of Dr Adrian Banks, senior lecturer in sociology at London University. There was some footage of the busy one-way street, garishly lit at night with milling crowds on the sidewalk. This came from their worldwide source, the announcer said. There would be more details in later bulletins which would include an interview with the dean of the faculty, and other colleagues.

Miranda realised that there would be widespread shock, he'll be so much missed by the staff and his students. *It's not just me.* But, she considered, they can be open about their involvement with him, they can share anecdotes and memories. *I can't.* Her immense loss, yes, immense is the right word, would have to be private. The only person who has some notion is Simon.

The thought of going to her Wednesday afternoon tutorial caused her more anxiety. Of course, she told herself, Adrian would want her to go. In fact, she would go early and see Ruth Lindquist to find out how the department would respond to the tragedy.

There was a newsagents not far from the university. Would it be reported yet? She bought *The Times* and hastily turned the pages. Yes, it was a late inclusion – 'London University academic, Dr Adrian Banks, was fatally injured in a New York City traffic accident late on Sunday night. Banks, 42, was a visiting fellow at Yale University. His companion, Nathan Kauper, survived and is currently in hospital with minor injuries.'

Seeing it in black and white had the effect of obliterating any hope Miranda may have clung to that it was somehow a mistake. It was something of a shock to discover that he was twenty years older than her. The age difference hadn't been a major issue, at least to Miranda.

Still no tears came. She felt emotionally frozen.

Ruth Lindquist welcomed her with warmth tinged with obvious sadness. 'We were all called in to the main office to be told. Some already knew. It came as a terrible shock, the last thing we expected to hear. Being summer vacation, most of the teaching staff are away on leave. Only those dealing with the summer schools were here. I think the sociology classes have been cancelled for the week, but you're doing psychology, aren't you?'

'I am, though I don't really feel like it.' Mrs Lindquist nodded understandingly. 'I just wondered whether there'll be some sort of, well, ceremony to honour him.'

'I'm sure there will be, but not until everyone's back. It's only just happened, and these things take some time to arrange.'

Back home, Miranda was restless. She wanted to do something, needed to do something. She toyed with the idea of going back to her former home in South London, perhaps to catch up with Gwen and tell her what had happened. But that would involve condolences and commiserations and maybe questions that she didn't really want to answer. The idea of writing a tribute for the obituary page in *The Times* occurred to her and was rejected. For whom would she be doing it?

A phone call from Simon was a welcome reality check. He told her that he would be flying over to America on Friday to deal personally with whatever had to be done. When he suggested that he call in to see her on Thursday, she, on impulse, asked him if he would like to come for a meal.

'That's very kind of you. Yes, I'd like to do that. Adrian used to invite me over sometimes to test some of his experimental dishes. By the way, I'm a vegetarian. He found *that* hard to cope with, I can tell you.'

Miranda was looking forward to his visit. It was good to have something to focus on. Also, she could ask him more about their friend, things that she was reluctant to ask. It was still hot in the evenings, so she decided a cheese salad would be a good choice, followed by the good old Australian standby of fruit salad and ice cream. A bottle each of red and white wine should be enough, she thought.

A small posy of mixed blooms from the florists brightened the dining table as a finishing touch.

'That's a lot more elegant than Adrian used to offer. Well done,' Simon said admiringly. He was complimentary about the meal, too.

'Do you mind if I smoke?' Simon asked as they moved into the living-room. 'Adrian despised the habit, though he used a bit of pot in his day. He could be contradictory at times. He became so obsessive about smoking that he told me he used to deduct two per cent off a student's marks if he knew they were smokers.'

'Go ahead, it doesn't worry me. More wine?'

She poured the rest of the white wine into their almost empty glasses. The dishes could wait until tomorrow. All Miranda wanted to do was to listen to this man who, she now realised, was the only link she had with Adrian. But it was painful even to think about him, so it was better to stick to something more down-to-earth.

'What are your plans, Simon?'

'I've been in touch with the hotel where they were staying. I've registered there for the few days I'll be away.' He took his wallet from an inside pocket of his light jacket and gave her a card. 'This is the address and the room phone number. You can contact me there if you need to. I have appointments lined up with the police, and with Yale, to sort out what's necessary there. I'll also have to see what can be done regarding Nathan.' There was a lack of enthusiasm in his voice. 'No one else will.'

'That sounds like a lot. What about your clients here? What arrangement have you made?'

'That's done already. It's my wife who will be affected most. I'll have to arrange for her carer to live in while I'm away.' Noting Miranda's questioning look, he explained. 'You probably don't know that she has a degenerative muscle-wasting disease and is wheelchair-bound. Don't worry, I'll work things out.' He glanced at his watch. It was time to go. 'Thank you for the meal, Miranda. I won't forget you, but don't expect to hear anything for two or three days.'

'Remember, I work night duty, so if you ring Friday, Saturday or Sunday nights, I won't be here to answer.'

'Right,' he said at the door. 'Well, goodbye for now.'

'Good luck, Simon. And thank you for all that you're doing.'

A few more pieces of the jigsaw were now in place, Miranda thought. What a treasure the accountant-cum-solicitor has turned out to be, stepping in at the deep end to deal with the aftermath of the tragedy. No wonder Adrian had trusted him implicitly.

But how can I live without Adrian? The question was rhetorical. *I have to, that's all there is to it.*

Miranda found herself whispering to herself in the seclusion of the bedroom. It proved to be comforting, in a strange way, to bury her face in one of his shirts. She breathed in the faint smell of him. She fantasised in a whirlpool of swirling memories.

'Adrian – Adrian,' she murmured, 'Come back, come back to me – please' A few tears came as she realised the futility of her entreaty, then more, as she imagined the end of his life. One minute alive, adrenalin-fuelled, the next – the deadly impact, smashing his body, obliterating him. Tears flowed freely at the cursed injustice of it, it wasn't fair, it – just – wasn't – fair.

She vowed to never forget him. The time they had together was out of this world. Nothing could take that away from her. She had something few other people had – physical bliss, yes, but even more priceless, his belief in her potential.

I have to keep on the path he created for me. That is the only thing I can do.

Work on Friday night was busier than usual with two patients needing one-to-one nursing care. Miranda had to put her personal feelings to one side as she checked each patient's intravenous drip, letting the two new students get experience in the technique.

One patient had family members visiting – her son and his wife, apparently. They wanted to stay until midnight.

'Please contact us if she gets worse in the early hours,' the middle-aged son asked as they left, their expressions troubled. Miranda assured them that she would contact, if it were necessary, but pointed out that they needed to get some sleep, as did their mother. She confirmed the contact number before they left.

It was at a late coffee break towards the end of the shift that one of her co-workers asked Miranda whether she knew the sociology lecturer who died in an accident in New York.

'Yes, I was one of his students,' she replied. 'He was a wonderful teacher, and a very special person.'

When Miranda woke on Saturday afternoon, she found a letter for her in the mail box. It was from her friend, Gina Ryan. She started with an apology that she had not been in touch for a while, but had been busy. 'Exciting news, I am engaged to a smashing young man. No-one you know. So, my vague plan of coming over to England has been abandoned, but for the best of reasons!' she wrote. 'By the way, did you know Michael McPherson got married a few months ago? Water under the bridge for you, I guess. I also saw from the birth notices in the *Courier* that you're an auntie now. My brothers haven't got that far yet, but Mum's always hoping.'

The letter got Miranda thinking. It was good news for Gina, of course, so she made a mental note to send her an engagement congratulations card. It made her realise that other people were getting on with their lives. *Good for them*, she thought. *So they should*. She wasn't envious. But she felt so flat, living from day to day at the moment. The anticipated phone call from Simon was foremost in her mind.

After her Wednesday lecture, Miranda visited the university library. She had seen a review of a new book by Elizabeth Kubler-Ross on the subject of grief. Unfortunately, both copies were out on loan, so she put in a reserve request for the book.

During the warmer weather she always walked the half-mile or so home. She knew it was a positive thing to do, but her spirits remained low. High-spirited noisy children playing happily in the park nearby usually delighted her, but not this time. She was grieving, hoping desperately that, as time passed, her pain would lessen.

A sudden thought came to her. *What would I love to do to that revolting Nathan Kauper?* A grim smile crossed her face as she contemplated the extremely vicious torture she would inflict on the rat. But that didn't last long. 'Nauseating Nathan,' as she'd overheard him described once, had also loved Adrian Banks in his own way. He'd have to live with the consequence of his actions for the rest of his life.

Just after ten that night, the phone rang. Simon. 'Is this a good time?' he asked.

'Yes, oh yes! It's good to hear from you. What's happened?'

'It's been really busy, but I've managed to sort some things out. The decision has been made for Adrian to be cremated here. I've organised that for next week, so I can bring his ashes back to the UK. There are no police charges arising from the incident. As for Nathan Kauper, he's gone to ground.'

'What do you mean?'

'I contacted the hospital for an update on his condition and was told that he had discharged himself against medical advice, apparently in the company of an older man. The police are treating Nathan as a missing person. The hotel manager said Nathan, and another man, presumably the same one, demanded access to the room and cleared out his belongings, and, I'm sure, some of Adrian's as well. But he left the briefcase, I'm glad to say. In it I found something special which I'll be bringing back to you.'

'Oh – what's that?'

'It's a large envelope with your name on it. I haven't opened it, of course. I've decided to stay here as long as it takes to have everything sorted out. Luckily, my wife's carer is able to stay on, and my colleague Henry will manage without me for at least another week.'

'Are you all right, Simon?'

'I am. Having all these things to do has helped. What about you?'

Miranda paused briefly, before admitting to him that she was having difficulty in maintaining her normal routine. Thoughts of Adrian and the circumstances of his death would not go away. Simon suggested that she might need to see someone, a doctor, or a counsellor, perhaps, if the situation continued. She agreed that it might be a sensible thing to do.

'I hope to be back by the end of next week, Miranda. There are important matters I have to discuss with you. Until then, try to keep going. For his sake.'

Chapter 36

The next morning, Miranda glanced at the wall calendar and realised that the summer school was due to end in two weeks. Her concentration hadn't been good lately.

There were two assignments, one on Behaviour, the other on Common Mental Disorders, to complete and submit. Both topics were interesting and deserved her full attention. To her consternation, though, her recall of the salient points from lectures was almost non-existent. Fortified by strong coffee, it was time to re-read her lecture notes and the reference books Adrian had selected for her. Early in the course, she'd read them with enthusiasm. Surely some of the material would come back to her.

By concentrating on finishing the two assignments, Miranda managed to submit them on time. Her earlier work had been well-received, and she was optimistic that these were also of a satisfactory standard.

But the outcome this time wouldn't be anything like last year's when she'd been told by Adrian that she was enrolled in the sociology degree. Followed by the start of their affair.

A letter from home arrived on Friday, full of warmth and concern from her mother, and surprisingly, a short note at the end from her father. Jack had written 'Just remember your real home is here, and don't leave it too long to come back.'

Miranda smiled. Typical Dad. Little did she know how significant his words would be …

On Monday, Simon rang again from New York.

'Everything has gone well, I'm glad to say,' he said after the initial greetings. 'I'll be coming back on Wednesday. I will bring Adrian's ashes with me. Will it be all right if I come over to see you on Friday morning?'

'Of course, Simon. Thank you. I'll have something ready for lunch for you. Have a safe trip back.'

Only a few more days to wait now. The envelope addressed to her still intrigued her. *What was that about?*

The next call from Simon was a brief one after he returned to London on Wednesday, confirming his arrival and suggesting eleven in the morning as being a good time for his visit on Friday.

Preparing the lunch gave Miranda an enjoyable sense of purpose.

I bet he's punctual, she thought, as she gave the apartment a thorough clean with vacuum, broom and duster. She made egg and parsley sandwiches for lunch, and there were enough pieces of fruit in the bowl to make a fruit salad. A cheese platter was always good to finish the meal.

As she predicted, the doorbell rang at precisely eleven o'clock. Carrying a large briefcase, he entered, giving her a token kiss on the cheek as he walked past her.

'I've allocated two hours for this, Miranda. I'm wearing my solicitor's hat now.'

That sounded daunting. *This is a first*, she thought. She'd never needed to consult a solicitor before.

Simon spread some documents on the low table. He showed her those which dealt with the accident first: copies of the police report (stamped NYPD), the post-mortem statement and newspaper clippings of the incident with the date heavily underlined. There were also invoices from the hotel, forms relating to the cremation and some other documents which Simon showed her before he gathered them into a bundle and secured them with an elastic band.

'All his accounts have been paid. You can look at them if you want to, but there's nothing to worry about in them. Among his papers and notes were brochures and flyers relating to the travel he must have done with Nathan earlier, including Boston, Niagara Falls, and around New York

City. Do you want these?' Miranda shook her head. 'I returned to Yale all the material relating to the course he was conducting. By the way, did you ever come across an Afro-American lecturer, Sarah Young-Johnson?'

'I certainly did – she took over some of Adrian's classes when he was in hospital last year. Did you get to meet her?'

'Yes. She had asked to be notified if anyone came to Yale in connection with Dr Banks. Lovely woman, we had quite an emotional half-hour together. She was deeply shocked about his death.'

I'm not surprised, thought Miranda. Adrian was very well-respected by his peers. To suppress the sadness which threatened to overwhelm her, Miranda suggested they have lunch.

During the simple meal, he chatted about his reaction to being in the great city. He'd been to New York before, of course, but it seemed to have a different face in different seasons. 'I remember being there in late February and being enthralled by the sight of steam gushing out of basement boilers through grids onto the footpaths, or sidewalks, as they call them.' He paused to take a bite of his sandwich. 'While we're eating, I'll just mention that I didn't get anywhere in the search for Nathan. It seems that he has managed to latch onto the same underworld he had frequented here before Adrian rescued him. So, he is a missing person, but there aren't any charges against him. When his visa expires, if he comes to their notice, he'll probably be deported.'

Lunch over, Simon looked at his watch. 'I've got just under an hour, Miranda, then another appointment.' He took out a small key from his wallet, went over to the liquor cabinet and removed Adrian's will from the safe. 'I have to warn you that this will come as a surprise, a shock even.'

She was bewildered. 'What do you mean?'

'Do you remember Adrian saying his will was up to date when we were here just before he left?' Miranda nodded. 'He had changed it only a few months previously. I admit I was concerned, but he insisted. Of course, he had no idea it would be invoked so soon. Are you ready to see it?'

She nodded and took the document he handed her. The wording was legalistic, but the main points were that he bequeathed ownership and title to the apartment to Miranda Mary Shaw, as well as a yearly sum of five thousand pounds for upkeep and living expenses.

Miranda gasped in disbelief. 'What?'

Wisely, Simon waited before continuing. 'But,' he said, 'there are conditions. This becomes null and void if you sell the property within ten years, is one, the other is if you cohabit here with a male person. I tried to get him to modify it, saying it would limit your freedom significantly, but he was adamant. How do you feel about it?'

Miranda tried to analyse the consequences of the conditions. 'Is it saying that the apartment will be mine, in my name, together with that very generous amount of money, but only if I don't sell it in under ten years, and don't have any male person live with me here?'

'More or less. He's ensuring that you have somewhere to live for the next ten years. Possibly he thought you might still be studying, further degrees perhaps. Anyway, that's the basis of the ownership of this apartment. You would lose the income he's left you if you share it with another man.'

It was hard for her to find words to express her feelings. 'Simon, I'm just so grateful to him, and to you. I think I understand that he wants it to be for my use only.' He nodded. 'And, of course, he could not have known that all this would happen – so soon.'

'No, that's right. But you know, Miranda, Adrian often predicted to me that he wouldn't make old bones. He actually hated the idea of ageing, and any suggestion of one day losing his, um, virility, was anathema to him.'

They both smiled. It was so typical of the Adrian they knew.

Simon picked up the form and looked through it. 'He's left a specific amount to Nathan. I'll have to have that put into a trust. The residue of his estate goes to the university.'

He got to his feet and started replacing the documents in his briefcase. 'Oh, here's that envelope I told you about. I haven't opened it, but if it raises any questions for you, please let me know if I can help.'

As he got ready to leave, he had another thought. 'Miranda, I have already arranged for Adrian's mail to be redirected to my office. That's to protect you from unsolicited mail, especially some who think they may have some entitlement to his estate. In the next few days, I'll apply for probate. I may need your banking details, too, so that when probate is granted, I can arrange for the annual amount to be deposited for you. Is that all right?'

'I can't stop saying thank you. Simon, you have been – how can I say it? – unbelievable. I'll never be able to repay you.'

He laughed at that. 'Not necessary. Like you, I just wish it hadn't turned out this way. Must go now, keep in touch.'

The will, with its coloured tape attached, was on the table. She reread the contents. It was real. A valuable apartment, so ideally located for her, had been gifted to her by inheritance. She was humbled by his generosity.

If only I could thank him …

She re-read the conditions. What effect would these have on her? None, none at all, she decided. The idea of being intimate with anyone else was far from her mind. In fact, she had stopped taking the contraceptive pill two months ago, after Adrian left for New York City. What was the point?

She looked at the envelope Simon had given her. *I bet it's to do with his lecture material.* She decided that she was not in the right mood to look at it now, no matter what it was. It was time to have some sleep before night shift.

Two letters arrived during the week. They were both from the Sociology Department. The first was a reminder to reapply for the coming year in her sociology degree course. *Must do that*, she thought, *and update my mailing address*. The second letter displayed the university crest and, in a formal cursive font, was an invitation to attend the memorial service for the late Dr Adrian Banks to be held in the Great Hall on Thursday, September 9th.

Miranda's first impulse was to contact Simon. *If I go, I want him to come with me.* He was the only one who knew about the relationship between her and the man being honoured. *I'd have to wear dark glasses. I'd cry and I wouldn't want to draw attention.*

She left a message on his phone asking him to contact her.

He did ring back that evening and assured her that he was already involved in the arrangements. 'I saw the Chancellor, top chap. I suggested that Adrian's ashes be interred somewhere on the campus with a shrub or small tree and a commemorative plaque. He thought that would be a fitting tribute to the deceased. Yes, he actually used those words. He asked me what Adrian's favourite plant was. That was impossible to answer, as I've never heard him express any particular preference. I think they've decided on a Japanese maple.'

'Simon, can I come with you? I think it will probably be very emotional. There'll be people giving eulogies, even from those he might have crossed swords with when he was alive. I just – don't know how I will cope.'

'I understand. Of course, we'll go together. After all, we have been privileged to know him as an exceptionally talented and charismatic human being, as have many other people. But we also know he was flawed. And, often, troubled.'

The ceremony of awarding the certificates for completion of the summer school in psychology followed the same procedure as the one Miranda had attended last year. Overall, she felt it had been worthwhile, in spite of the impact of Adrian's death.

Yet another important occasion to describe to Mum, she thought. The big question, though, was – should she tell her family about Adrian's legacy and the very big difference it would make to her future? She was reluctant, given there were still many uncertainties to be finalised. Simon was confident about the outcome, but she decided, at this stage, that it could wait.

Lately, any mail in her letter box was either for her, or unsolicited advertising material. One day a letter arrived for Adrian without a stamp or post-office franking. Hand-delivered was her guess.

Simon answered on her second phone call.

'Should I send it on to you?' she asked, realising that she didn't have his address.

'No, I'm not far away. I'll be over in an hour.'

'Oh, another of his lady friends,' he snorted, opening the letter. 'She obviously hasn't heard what's happened. Inviting him to get in touch, missing him, and all that.' His tone was dismissive.

It seemed to be the right time to ask the question that had been worrying her. 'Are there many – er – girlfriends he's left behind?'

'Well may you ask! He would, to use that old expression, blow hot and cold. His needs would be served for a while but, sooner or later he'd get bored and end the relationship.' He noticed Miranda's puzzled expression. 'But you, you were different. Yes, delightful intimacy, he told me a bit, but it seems to me he was attracted to your mind, your potential. He was genuinely excited about that.'

Reassured, Miranda asked one more question. 'What about his ex-wife?'

'She apparently remarried and lives in Europe. I've sent information about his death to her last known address, but I think she's probably moved on.'

'Thank you for telling me all this. I had wondered …'

'I hope I've settled your concerns. Now it looks as though, the next time we'll meet will be for his memorial service.'

She remained uncertain about whether to go.

Chapter 37

Miranda woke from a deep sleep to the sound of the telephone. Feeling disoriented, she struggled to answer it. Who on earth could be ringing at this ungodly hour?

Her mumbled 'Hello' was answered by her brother. Brian's voice was rapid and urgent. 'Miranda, I'm ringing to tell you that Mum has been taken to hospital. She's very sick, pneumonia and heart failure. You need to get here as quickly as you can.'

Shocked into immediate wakefulness, Miranda blurted out 'When did this happen? What hospital? What are they doing for her?'

'Hang on, one question at a time. Yesterday she was admitted, she's in our local hospital and she's on oxygen and having antibiotics. Just a minute, Dad wants to talk to you.'

Jack came on the line. He came straight to the point. 'Your mother is really seriously ill, Miranda. You've got to come home.'

The line went dead. Her father's words were emphatic. He sounded very worried.

God, this is awful. What on earth is the time? Nearly five o'clock. How can I do this, and quickly, she thought.

A list. As things came to mind, she wrote them down: contact travel agent re flight, ring hospital for compassionate leave, pack suitcase, tell Simon.

The only thing she could do so early in the morning was get her suitcase organised. Take enough clothes for at least two weeks. She decided to put Adrian's will and the still unopened envelope in as well.

Hopefully, she'd be able to show her mother and that would be good, much better than trying to explain by letter.

Her next move was to obtain the earliest possible flight. The travel agent was very helpful, trying various airlines, until she came up with a seat on a Cathay Pacific flight leaving late that night. There would be a four-hour delay in Hong Kong and a change of planes. The arrival time at Tullamarine would be two days later due to the time zones. She would need to be at the airport three hours before departure and to pay for the ticket at the airline desk.

Miranda, grateful, thanked her after confirming the details. She decided to send a telegram home to tell them about the arrival time.

Nursing administration at the hospital also showed understanding when she asked for leave at short notice. 'You have three weeks of annual leave due anyway, if you need more let us know,' she was told.

Oh, Mum, I hope you're better, and responding to treatment.

Simon answered his phone on the second ring. His voice was sympathetic and supportive. 'Miranda, this is such a shock. I do hope you find her on the road to recovery by the time you get there. Please let me know how things are.'

Miranda was glad he hadn't mentioned the memorial service for Adrian, which she would miss. At this stage, all she could think about was her mother. She was aware that he understood that.

Please, please God, please let her be all right.

Brian was at the airport when she landed in Melbourne. Seeing his tall figure among the small number of people at the arrivals gate, Miranda searched his face for any evidence of hope. There was none.

His expression was serious. As they moved closer together, he gave a small shake of the head, conveying to her the worst possible news.

They embraced wordlessly. Into his jacket Miranda murmured, 'When?'

He drew apart from her and said, 'Not long after we got your telegram. She smiled when we read it to her, and, even with the oxygen mask on, we could see that she was so happy to hear you were coming home. Then she closed her eyes and seemed to drift into sleep. We were all there, Dad, Jo, little Byron and me. We left the ward, as she seemed to be resting, and the baby wanted a feed. Dad and I went for a short walk, while Jo fed Byron in the waiting room. When we left, we thought Mum was looking a bit better.' He gulped. 'When we returned, Dr Santorini was there. He came over to Dad and put his arm over his shoulder and said, "I'm sorry, Jack, there wasn't anything more we could do."'

Mum – dead? Her body shuddered and her knees crumpled.

'Sit down, Sis.' Brian steered her towards a seat. 'I'll bring your suitcase, and when you're ready, we'll get the car and go home.'

Go home? His words sounded hollow. *How could it be home – without Mum?*

Miranda only half-heard what Brian was saying as they made their way along the Western Highway, something about Dad ringing Hamilton to say Mum was in hospital, how they packed in a hurry and drove over to Beaufort within hours of the call. She remembered him saying 'Lucky I'm the boss and can take time off when I want to. Did you know I'm the youngest assistant branch manager in the bank so far?'

Only half-listening, she managed a vague reply.

After they had passed through Ballarat, Miranda suddenly asked, 'Brian, where is she now?'

'At the funeral parlour,' he replied, surprised at the question. 'Brendon's in charge for this.'

'Can I see her first, before we go home?'

'Before you see Dad?'

'Yes. Is that all right? I want to talk to her.'

Grace's coffin, on its polished chrome trolley, had pride of place in the viewing room. *Oak*, thought Miranda, *that's good, Mum always liked oak.'*

She approached the coffin and looked down at her mother's body. Her face, so familiar, so much loved, had a calmness that somehow erased the lines of age and worry. Miranda thought she looked at peace.

'Mum, Mum, it's Miranda, your Mirrie. I'm here, Mum. Sorry I was late. I didn't know ...' She went on and on, telling her everything she hadn't told her in life, asking for understanding. 'Please forgive me, Mum, if I haven't done the right thing.' Finally, she burst into tears, quietly sobbing to herself.

Some time later she became aware of Brendon Wilson's presence.

'I'm – I'm all right, I just needed to see her, and say goodbye,' she said, brushing away her tears.

'Your father and brother are here. Would you like them to come in?'

She nodded. Yes, it felt right to share this private family time.

Jack, his face clouded by grief, clasped his daughter in a desperate embrace.

Brian joined in the hug too, before they broke apart and turned towards the coffin. One by one, they leant down to kiss her cold face for the last time, whispering their words of goodbye.

The funeral would be in two days. It was a relief for Miranda that Brian and Jo were staying with them, it was good for Dad, too. And what a joy at this sad time to be able to see, hold and play with her nephew. 'He's a little angel!' she'd exclaim. He would make funny guttural noises in response to any attention, and his cherubic face would crease in a smile.

'He's just adorable!'

Jo, though saddened by the death of her mother-in-law, was clearly glad to see Miranda again. Her friendship helped lighten the heavy load Miranda was carrying in her heart.

Sympathy cards arrived and neighbours called in with offerings of food, along with their condolences. At least two of them tactlessly said to Miranda that it was a pity she didn't make it in time. *Oh God, as if I don't know that.*

The church was packed, which was no surprise. Grace Shaw had lived in Beaufort all her married life, she was loved and remembered fondly by many people. Masses of flowers in wreaths and posies were arranged around the coffin. In the background, the organist played subdued music vaguely familiar to Miranda.

Miranda found it hard to concentrate on the service. The minister himself was overcome by emotion at times. He emphasized that Grace had been a faithful believer and that she was now with God.

After the service, people milled around, offering greetings and sympathy. There were tears, too. Dark glasses on, Miranda made brief responses to the questions she was asked: What was she doing in England? How long was she staying here? Would she be coming back to live with her father? She made non-committal replies before moving to the next well-meaning mourner.

'Hey, don't you remember me?' She looked up to see a pleasantly stout middle-aged lady with an equally overweight man beside her.

The penny dropped. 'Auntie Lillian! Uncle Barry! How good to see you. Thank you for making the trip.'

'Didn't come as far as you did, eh?' Barry said. 'Excuse me, I'll just say hello to Jack.'

He was off. Miranda looked at her mother's sister. There wasn't much of a family likeness. 'I hope you're able to come back for some refreshments, I'm sure Dad and Brian will want to talk to you.'

'We can't stay long, I'm sorry. I said we'd be at Wendy's later this afternoon.' Noting Miranda's puzzled look, she continued. 'I'm sure Grace would have told you our youngest was married two weeks ago, she's living in St Arnaud. A shotgun one, like mine was.' She laughed, but suppressed it straight away. 'This is so sad. Grace going like that. She never was a strong person, though.' She patted Miranda on the shoulder and moved away to talk to someone else, before turning back to say 'Thanks for the photos you took of my parents' grave. Grace sent me a couple.'

Still feeling dazed and confused, Miranda saw in the distance, past the throng of people still talking, the unmistakable figure of Michael McPherson heading towards the car park, holding the hand of a smaller, dark-haired, very pregnant young woman. Miranda experienced a poignant pang of regret. *He would have been with me if things had turned out differently.*

The minister had invited her to come and see him after the funeral.

Nigel Langthorne was well past retirement age. Probably if he'd had a wife and family, he would have retired some time ago, moved into a smaller house, taken the opportunity to enjoy new pursuits. But, it seemed, there was a lack of aspiring younger clergymen eager to take on the parish of Beaufort, so he continued on in the role without complaint.

'It's good to see you, Miranda. Do come in and have a chat.'

He led her into the vicarage sitting room and invited her to sit down. 'Now, how are you feeling?'

His friendly question was an invitation to be honest. She told him how she was filled with guilt and felt that people, without saying it outright, believed she should have come home much earlier to look after her mother when she knew her health was failing. 'I've been selfish, concentrating on pursuing my own career,' she blurted out, on the verge of tears.

'Let me stop you there, my dear. I knew your mother well. I knew her for more than 25 years. She was a very perceptive woman, she knew early on that your path through life would be, well, different. You know, she always thought you should go on to university from school here. That didn't happen, but she was so proud of what you've achieved in England. She was impressed by your dedication and was excited about your future. And, Miranda, she was so grateful that you visited her parents' grave in Scotland, it meant so much to her. There is no justification for you to have feelings of guilt about anything.' He paused. 'And, my dear, your being here would not have changed anything, really.'

Miranda sat silent, trying to absorb the minister's words. It was a revelation to her that her mother had been proud of her, she hadn't actually ever said that, although she had always been supportive. Conscious that the minister was watching her closely, she managed a tentative smile.

'Thank you for telling me, it does make me feel a bit better. Mum always encouraged me, but I never knew what she really thought. Now I do, and it's a comfort.'

The elderly clergyman leaned back in his chair and stretched out his legs before turning to her again.

'So, what are your plans now?'

'I've got two weeks leave. I booked an open ticket for my flight back to England, so I'll need to confirm my departure for the end of the month. I was thinking of seeing if I could do some work at the hospital to show my appreciation for their care of Mum. But I'll need to discuss it with Dad first.'

Dad seemed to be in favour when she broached the subject. He produced a letter addressed to her from the Victorian Nursing Council, saying her mother kept the yearly registration paid, 'in case you ever needed it again.' It was her annual practising certificate.

Did she harbour a secret hope that I would come back and resume nursing here?

'You'd better see if they need an extra pair of hands,' Jack said.

Her phone call resulted in an appointment for an interview tomorrow. There was indeed a vacancy on night duty. That would be ideal, Miranda thought. Jo and Brian approved of it, too.

It was the young couple's last night in Beaufort before returning to Hamilton. Miranda decided to make a generous-sized beef casserole so any leftovers could be reheated for the next day's dinner. It would be much quieter without them, and, of course, little Byron.

Over dinner, the conversation turned to a discussion about her future.

'Are you coming back here after you finish that university course?' Brian asked.

The enquiring looks around the table forced Miranda to disclose her situation. She went to her bedroom and came back with Adrian's will, the contents of which would explain the reasons for her decision to return to the UK.

She showed it to her father first. He beckoned Brian over, 'Take a look at this. What do you make of it?' They took their time reading the document. Jo's raised eyebrows prompted Miranda to explain quietly that she had been left a property and some money in a will.

'I wanted to tell you all, and Mum, in person,' she said. 'The man who died was the university lecturer who has encouraged me from the beginning and was a mentor to me. I didn't have the slightest idea I was included in his will, nor that he would lose his life so soon. He always seemed so alive and – indestructible.' It was hard to keep her voice even.

'Is this for real, I mean, have you had a solicitor look at it?'

'Yes, in fact he asked me to contact him while I'm over here – would that be alright, Dad? I'll pay for the call. You can talk to him yourself.'

Jack was obviously a bit out of his depth. After a minute he said, 'Right. Yes, I'll talk to him. It does seem unusual, I mean, didn't he have any family?'

'You could ask Mr Forrester about that, and anything else you want to know.'

The interview at the hospital turned out to be just a friendly chat. Glenda Henderson, the matron, remembered Miranda from her previous time working there. The older nurse spoke respectfully of Grace Shaw's last few days, saying how profoundly sorry they all were that nothing could be done to save her. They hugged each other warmly before sitting down to discuss the employment arrangements.

Miranda explained her situation, saying she could be available for ten shifts, and was more than happy with night duty, the routine of which was familiar to her.

'My problem is – I didn't bring any uniforms with me. Could I wear a theatre gown instead?'

'That should be all right, no-one would worry too much at night. And it will save you having to wash it. Just get a fresh one each night from the linen cupboard.' Miranda smiled. Matron Henderson was always so practical.

When she got home, Miranda found Brian and Jo had packed the car and were ready to leave. Their four-month-old baby held out his arms to her for a final cuddle, before being put in his carry-basket on the back seat.

'It's been good to see you again, Sis, even though it was for the worst of reasons. Your future looks pretty challenging, I must say. Good luck with everything.' Brian enfolded her in a strong hug, after which Jo kissed her on both cheeks and embraced her warmly too, before getting in the car.

'Keep in touch, now. I'll do my bit in replying, though probably not as well as your mum did,' Jo said in farewell.

Jack and Miranda looked at each other as the Fairlane turned the corner and went out of sight. She spoke first, trying to raise their spirits.

'What a gorgeous little grandson you've got. I imagine Mum really loved him.'

'She certainly did. Her face lit up whenever she saw him, she used to bounce him on her lap and sing little nursery rhymes to him.' They went inside the house, which was now quiet and empty.

'You know, she wasn't even fifty. It's so unfair.'

Miranda voiced her thoughts. 'Dad, do you think it would have made any difference if she'd gone ahead and had the heart surgery?'

'We'll never know. She could be so stubborn about taking risks. I know Dr Santorini tried to persuade her to think about it more carefully. But it was pneumonia that took her in the end.'

That seemed to be the end of the conversation. He moved over to the sink and began stacking the dishes from afternoon tea.

'I can do that, Dad. At least let me be a bit useful while I'm here. By the way, I start at the hospital tomorrow night.'

'Then you'd better ring that solicitor bloke tonight. Brian put the country code you have to use by the phone.'

The left-over casserole served its purpose for the evening meal, though neither of them had much appetite. Miranda calculated the time difference, deciding that if she rang Simon at half past seven, it would be ten-thirty in the morning in England.

She held her breath as the rings sounded before Simon answered.

'Oh, Simon, it's Miranda. Is this a good time to call you?' On hearing his, 'Yes, go ahead,' she told him of the death of her mother before she had landed in Australia.

'I'm so, so sorry, Miranda. It must have been very sudden. How are you coping?'

'It's been hard. The funeral was a wonderful tribute to her, but it's still hard to believe. Oh, how did the memorial service for Adrian go?'

'It was very well handled, very fitting. I'll tell you more about it when you get back.'

'Thank you. Simon, would you be able to speak to Dad? I showed him the will and he was quite stunned. I mean, it was the last thing he expected.'

'Of course I'll speak to him, Miranda. Put him on.'

Jack took the phone and spoke. 'Jack Shaw here, Miranda's father.'

Miranda moved away to avoid overhearing the conversation. She heard her father say, 'Thank you,' which probably meant Simon had expressed his condolences, another time she heard, 'Yes, I'm extending.' In fact, she heard him repeat that several times before the conversation ended.

Coming back to the sitting room, Jack didn't immediately respond to Miranda's questioning look, choosing to rearrange the scattered cushions before sitting down to face her.

'He seems a very responsible person. Answered all my questions appropriately and has convinced me that everything's above board. It seems this Adrian Banks was an only child and has no close relatives to leave his estate to. He took a real interest in your career and made you his beneficiary to make sure your future was secure. Everybody was shocked by his sudden death.' He paused, recollecting the actual conversation. 'Mr Forrester told me he understood my concerns, he has a son about your age, and he'd be asking questions too if he was in my position.'

So, Simon has a son? 'I didn't know that, Dad. I know he has a wife who's disabled. Anyway, I'm glad you have had the chance to ask questions and that you feel better about it all now.'

Returning to nursing at the Beaufort Hospital was like stepping back in time, even though it was not quite two years since she'd worked there. Some of the afternoon staff remembered her, and, of course, the night sister in charge, Nancy Williams, who had been in that role for many years. Welcoming her back, Nancy introduced the nursing aide, Mary O'Reilly, an experienced newcomer on the shift.

'Can you show me which bed was my mother's? Miranda asked later in the shift after the patients had been settled for the night. Although it was now occupied, it was not difficult to imagine Mum being nursed there with an oxygen cylinder by the bed.

One shift down, nine to go, Miranda thought as she walked the short distance home in the morning sunlight. *I'll sleep well – it'll be quiet with Dad at the funeral parlour most of the day.*

Getting ready for her next shift, Miranda picked up the envelope from Adrian. She still hadn't looked at it. Inside were seven handwritten pages, each dated, much like a diary. Adrian had started to slip from her mind over the past week, and this would help her refocus.

The first page was a letter. Her heart raced at the sight of the familiar handwriting.

> 'My dear Miranda,
>
> I'm going to write down all the things I would want to be saying to you. Being so far away from you has helped me crystallise the plans I have for the future. I'll try to put these in order, but cannot guarantee it. We'll discuss it all when I get back.'

Miranda's mind was in turmoil. This was Adrian speaking to her from the grave. She read on, marvelling at the ideas he expressed about shaping her career. Part of her wanted to read all the other sheets later, after she got home, eager to absorb his wisdom, his approval, his vision.

No, that wasn't the way to get the best out of this heaven-sent bequest, this blueprint for her to follow. *One at a time. I'll ration myself.* She decided to take one page per night and read it during her meal break.

'Are you working every night without a break?' Dad asked after her fifth night.

'I am. The person I'm relieving comes back on duty the night after I leave for the UK.'

'I just wondered if you wanted to visit anybody while you're here. Would you like to take a trip out to see Michael's property?'

Ouch. Mum would never have suggested that.

'No, I don't think so, Dad. I saw his wife's name in the maternity booking list though. Denise McPherson. She's due in a couple of weeks, which will be nice for them.'

Dad didn't say anything more on the subject. But he did remark that going back to work was doing her good, she seemed to be more like her old self.

'It's been so hard, Dad, particularly for you. It must feel like a kick in the guts.'

Jack smiled at that. 'At least you've remembered a few Aussie sayings. But you're right.' He paused, gathering his thoughts. 'Are there any things of Mum's that you'd like to have, like jewellery, not that she had much. If there's anything you want, feel free.'

'Thanks, Dad. I gave her an opal ring once, for her forty-fifth, I think. That would be nice to have, not that I need anything to remember her.'

Taking up her father's invitation, Miranda searched through the drawers of the small dressing table in her parent's bedroom. Sure enough, the opal ring was there. She slipped it on her finger. From the door, Jack saw her extend her arm and admire the perfect fit. He nodded.

'She hasn't been able to wear that one for ages, her fingers all swelled up.' He paused. 'Mavis from down the road said she'd come and help me sort out the rest of her things and take them to the op shop. But there's no hurry.'

Miranda took the ring off and put it in a small compartment in her purse, alongside the emerald ring Michael had given her. *Two symbols of cherished memory*, she thought, wistfully. *My first lover and my mother.*

Part of the pleasure of going to work each night was the anticipation of reading the next page of Adrian's letters. It was obvious he was in a different mood each time he sat down to write. In one he disclosed his grievances with Nathan who, it seemed, wanted to go out nightclubbing every night. Almost as if he was on the make, Adrian complained. He went on to say that he was missing her, and couldn't wait to get back.

A particularly exciting entry set out his suggestions for her career.

> 'I see you eventually becoming a leader in the field that's close to
> my heart – advocacy. I'd want you to do some volunteering in
> self-help groups that already exist, with the aim to coordinate
> them, get funding and become an established charity. Public
> speaking, engaging with politicians, all that. But coming from
> a sound academic basis.'

In another, he spoke of the need for her to rent somewhere close to his place, near the university, when he returned.

> 'Much as I'd love to have you live with me, it's neither practical
> nor advisable. A one-bedroom flat suits me, always has. Sharing
> has never worked in the past, and the success of your future,
> and mine, relies on discretion, as I'm sure you realise.'

It was with mixed feelings that Miranda arrived at the hospital for her last shift.

She had already packed everything for her departure the following day. The train left mid-afternoon and would arrive in Melbourne in plenty of time for her to get to the airport. She would be saying goodbye to the evening staff at handover, and to the patients and everyone else in the morning.

The first words from the Night Sister in Charge were disconcerting.

'We've got a patient in early labour. It's her first baby, not due for a few weeks so, hopefully, it will all settle down and the contractions will subside.'

Miranda felt a tinge of alarm. *It couldn't be …*

Nancy Williams turned to her. 'You didn't train as a midwife, did you, Miranda? I thought not. Looks as though I'll be spending most of my time with Mrs McPherson, and you'll be in charge of the rest of the hospital.'

There were only eight patients, so Miranda was confident that, with Nurse O'Reilly, she could manage. She nodded.

'I'll get you to relieve me for my break at twelve-thirty, hopefully there won't be much to do for her.'

So, I will get to meet Mrs McPherson after all, Miranda thought. *But she may well be asleep.* She hoped for her sake that the mother-to-be would settle for a good night's rest.

However, when Sister Williams called her on the internal phone at twelve-twenty, it was not the case. Unfortunately, Mrs McPherson's labour was progressing.

'It was becoming established when I took over, every eight minutes now. All you have to do is record everything on the chart as I've done. If she needs to use the mask, she can. I've shown her how to use it,' she said at the door. 'I'll be back in about forty minutes.'

Miranda turned to the young woman in the bed. She moved over to identify herself, realising the gown, theatre cap and mask she'd put on, coupled with the dim lighting, would make it hard for her to be recognised. On a possibly foolish impulse, she decided not to use her real name.

'I'm Sister Smith, Jane Smith,' she said to the smiling face looking up from the pillow. 'And you're Mrs McPherson, or can I call you Denise?'

'Oh, yes, please do ...' The rest of her comment was lost as another contraction started. Miranda placed a hand on the abdomen and used her watch to time it.

'That lasted almost a minute. Are they getting stronger do you think?' she asked as Denise relaxed back on the pillow.

'They are. Whew, that one was.'

'Okay now? Would you like a drink?'

She accepted gratefully, gulping down the water. 'Do you think I could use the mask? Sister Williams said it has oxygen in it which will help the baby.'

'Sure, good idea,' Miranda answered, handing her the large rubber mask attached to the gas and oxygen cylinder.

Denise took a couple of experimental breaths, then a deep one as another contraction started. At the end of it, she smiled. Such an engaging young woman, Miranda thought.

'They said your husband's away at the moment.'

'Yes, he's in Gippsland on business, something to do with farming diversification. He dropped me off this afternoon when I started to have a few pains. He didn't want me to be out at the farm on my own. They said that probably not much would happen while he's away, but they might be wrong. Oh, here's another!' More concentrated breathing. After it subsided, she giggled.

'This stuff's making me light-headed.'

That's not a bad thing, Miranda thought.

'You know, Sister, Michael was in love with a nurse once.'

Trying to sound as unemotional as possible, Miranda replied 'What happened?'

'She was much cleverer than he is. She wanted to work overseas, so she went to England. He intended to go over there too, but ... Oh, here's another one.' Several deep breaths on the mask and a long sigh as the contraction subsided. 'What was I saying? Oh, yes. His dad got sick, and he couldn't go, even for a visit, so he had to let her get on with her own life. He seemed terribly sad about it.'

Miranda busied herself with the observations. The foetal heart sounded strong and regular, pulse and blood pressure were fine. But the contractions were five minutes apart and lasting a good minute.

After the next contraction, Miranda asked how she and Michael met.

'Through the Young Farmers Club. I was raised on a dairy farm near Colac, and we met at a seminar in Geelong. He's such a lovely person, and he'll be a great father ... Ooh, here we go again.'

Checking her watch, Miranda noted that they were four minutes apart now. 'What are you hoping for, boy or girl?' The standard question for expectant mums.

'We don't mind. A boy would be nice. Every farmer wants a son to take over the property eventually. If it's a boy we're going to call him Alexander, after Michael's father.' She paused, accepting the next contraction, taking huge gulps of the gas and oxygen. 'If we have a daughter, Michael wants to call her Miranda. It's unusual, I don't know where he got it from, but I like it too. Miranda McPherson sounds lovely!'

Luckily for Miranda, her face was hidden behind a surgical mask. That was a complete shock. She was relieved now she hadn't revealed her real name. Aware of Nancy Williams at the door, she reported on her patient's labour. 'They're about every four minutes and strong now.'

'Thank you, Sister, you go back to the general ward now and tell Nurse O'Reilly to come and help me move Mrs McPherson to the delivery room. I'll give her some pain relief.' Miranda was at the door, but Nancy was still talking to her. 'I'll also call Dr Santorini, give him plenty of time. I put the humidicrib on to warm up. You might miss your break tonight.'

Miranda was thankful to be relieved of her post there. She was deeply disturbed by memories of the previous intimate relationship with Michael. His wife, now in labour with his child, had unwittingly brought them to the surface. She was overwhelmed by turbulent emotions. She marvelled at the sweet innocence of this young woman who obviously didn't know who she was, and who had so generously agreed to her husband's choice of name for a baby girl. Probably Michael had never mentioned his former girlfriend by name.

Thank God for the routine of patient care. Miranda was grateful for the occasional ring of a buzzer from a patient wanting assistance. At about three o'clock, she heard a car pull up and someone go in through the maternity entrance. Dr Santorini, no doubt. Denise McPherson was in good hands with him, the experienced Nancy Williams and no-nonsense Nurse O'Reilly all there to help. Michael should have been there, too. It was a shame that he was not around to see his first child born.

To be honest, Miranda was grateful to not have to see him. Sister Williams would have made contact, assuming he'd left a phone number, and he would be on the long drive from Eastern Victoria even now.

She was glad it was her last shift. Only three and a half more hours to work, it would soon be over.

She set out the morning medication in little cardboard cups, normally the senior's job. Nurse O'Reilly hadn't come back, so things must be progressing.

A muffled high-pitched scream came from the maternity ward. It could only have been from Denise. The internal phone shrilled – Nancy Williams shouted, 'Get Matron, tell her to come straight away, tell her it's an obstetric emergency!'

Miranda dialled frantically, Matron answered almost instantly and responded rapidly. Replacing the phone, Miranda was tense with anxiety. What was happening? What had gone wrong?

In less than three minutes, the phone rang again. 'Sister – can you call Father Dwyer, his number's on the red call pad. Tell him we need him urgently.'

'Of course. Matron's on her way. What's happening, Nancy? Has something gone wrong?'

'Yes. The baby's stillborn. There was nothing we could do.'

Miranda couldn't believe it. What a shocking outcome to what was normally such a joyful occasion. She dialled the priest's number and he agreed to come right away. So, Denise was a Catholic, though what difference did that make. Michael was on his way here, unaware of the tragic situation to greet him. It flashed through her mind – *much like me coming home for Mum.*

The day staff came on duty, their faces instantly sobered on hearing the sad news. Nancy Williams, looking exhausted and grim, had come out to tell the story at the end of her shift. Matron Henderson was now in charge in the maternity ward. Nancy said to Miranda, 'The priest's there, I'm not much good with the religious stuff. Could you go and help out.'

It was an order, not a question.

Returning to the delivery room was difficult. It was eerily quiet after the drama of such a short time ago. Matron was checking paperwork at the desk. Dr Santorini was in muted conversation with Father Dwyer. Nurse O'Reilly was busy in the background, she had obviously been weeping.

Miranda looked at the forlorn young woman lying inert on the bed, a baby wrapped in a shawl in her arms.

'Mrs McPherson – Denise – I'm so sorry,' she blurted out. The young mother turned her tear-stained face to say, 'Oh, Sister. Look, isn't she beautiful!' She unwrapped the child to show the tiny lifeless body. She was indeed beautiful, perfectly formed and strangely pale, like alabaster or marble.

Nurse O'Reilly appeared. 'Shall I take her away now?' she offered tentatively.

'No, no. She has to be baptised when Michael gets here.' Denise looked over to the priest who responded immediately, moving over to her bed. After checking her patient, Matron pulled the screens around the bed, and beckoned Miranda into the nursing station. Dr Santorini, obviously distressed, couldn't stop talking.

'I've only ever seen that happen once, years ago, it was during my obstetrical training. It's so rare, usually only found in text-books.'

'Perhaps you could explain it to Sister Shaw, she hasn't done midwifery training. I'll get someone to make us some tea, we need it.'

The doctor explained that the sudden premature detachment of the placenta during labour had resulted in the death of the infant before delivery. It was impossible to predict, and there was nothing at all that could be done. Miranda saw his hands noticeably shaking.

Matron reappeared. 'Tea's coming. Don't blame yourself, Doctor. You did all you possibly could. It's just a terribly sad situation.' She turned to Miranda. 'Perhaps you should go off now, Sister Shaw. I'm sorry your last shift turned out so badly.'

There was no opportunity to say goodbye to Denise, with whom she had shared such a heart-wrenching experience. After the priest left, the screens were removed and one of the day staff comforted the still sobbing patient with the words, just barely heard, 'He'll be here soon, Denise, and Father Dwyer's coming back then.'

Miranda had a sudden inspiration. She went into the change room to discard the theatre gown for the last time and dress in her own clothes.

From her purse she removed the emerald ring secreted in the side pocket.

It took only a minute to go to the ward desk and find a small piece of paper and an envelope, which she addressed simply 'Denise McPherson.' The wording on the letter took more time and thought.

There is so much I want to say. *It was a privilege to be with you, Denise, at this unforgettably sad time, you were so brave. I'm so sorry, Michael, for everything that I couldn't be for you, I want so much for you both to be happy.*

Eventually, she settled for a simple message: 'For you, Denise, in memory of your Miranda.' She placed the ring on the paper, folded it, put it in the envelope and left it at the desk.

One or two of the staff noticed her leaving and called out, 'Good luck, nice to have had you here.' Miranda didn't mind. There was an unusually sombre atmosphere right throughout the hospital, totally understandable. Matron and Dr Santorini would no doubt be nervously waiting for Michael's arrival, and the grief that would follow.

Walking into Speke Street for the last time, towards the place which, until now, she had called home, Miranda found herself crying.

But her tears weren't of sadness – there'd been plenty of those over the last several weeks. It was relief. She realised that, though the worst had happened, she had come through it, she was alive, she had a future.

And, now, she was going home.